INTO THE FIRE

A Flame in the Shadows Trilogy
BOOK ONE

by

STEFANIE MEDREK

Into the Fire

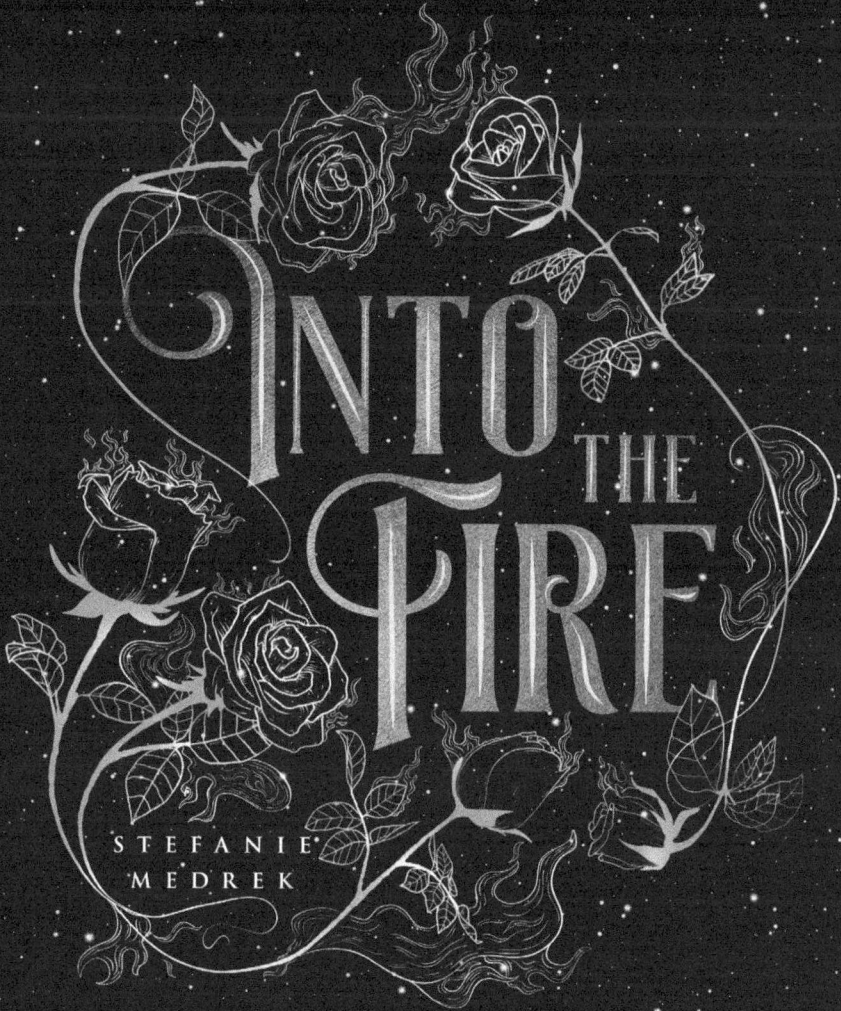

STEFANIE MEDREK

For Dad, who showed me what it is to follow your dreams and who believed in me first.

CONTENT AND TRIGGER WARNINGS

This is a New Adult series and is intended for mature audiences (18+). It contains adult content including but not limited to graphic violence, on-the-page sex, profanity, torture, PTSD, and murder, as well as a brief allusion to the intent for sexual assault. Emergency contraception is used but there are no pregnancies, nor any pregnancy related events in this series.

CHAPTER ONE

MEL

WHO knew a murderer could look so friendly.

The plastic edges of Mara Levett's security badge bite into my fingers as I study her faded picture, fear and anticipation prickling up my neck. She looks more like someone's mom than the CEO of the nation's largest weapons manufacturer.

Honestly, even if the explosion that killed my parents was an accident, she's complicit. The news said she put profits ahead of safety, then dodged the fallout when four people paid with their lives. No consequences for her or anyone in her company, and certainly no remorse.

Fury claws up my throat, my eyes too hot, too wet.

I fling Mara's badge toward my bedroom and return to the mess of colorful tank tops in front of me, unable to stand the sight of her warm smile for another second. I shouldn't have tossed something so important into the box with all my running stuff, even if the movers brought it in last and left it easiest to reach. Careless.

There they are, at the very bottom.

Battered Nikes in hand, I climb to my feet and scan the condo for my new keycard. Early-morning sunshine leaks in through the bare windows, illuminating empty beige walls and pale carpets. A mattress takes up most of the tiny bedroom to the right, and a couple stools sit at the built-in breakfast bar, but that's it. All I have.

Well, that and the boxes. Towers of them hover around me, an intimidating city of brown cardboard skyscrapers that dominate the otherwise barren living room. My eyes skip over the untouched stacks, where half-remembered stories and long-dead laughter lurk like shadows among belongings from another life; too painful to examine, yet too precious to toss away.

The image of Dad, covered in dried purple and blue paint, brows pinched together and brush sweeping over yet another canvas. The sound of Mom's bright voice reminiscing about summers spent working the fields as a farmgirl with Grandma and Grandpa.

To think they grew up here, in tiny Clearwater, New Hampshire, thirty-six hundred miles and a world away from the home we shared. I hoped by living in the town where they were born, I'd feel their presence, but so far all I feel is the distance. Hollow echoes.

Ghosts.

Stop.

I blow out a breath. Force myself to focus. Grab the keycard off the counter, yank on my sneakers, and head for the door. I need to get outside.

Now.

That first step into the newly minted sunshine is a release, the fresh mountain air a thrill in my aching chest. The breeze nips at my damp cheeks and raises goosebumps on my arms, cleaner than I'm used to, but missing the salty tang of the sea. And how is it cold? Early mornings in July are warm back in California. Maybe even hot.

It's uncomfortable, but I don't want to go back inside, where the boxes and memories wait, not even to pull on a hoodie. So, I ignore the chill and hunt along the edge of the trees for the running trail I noted last night on my map of the condo complex. When I find the thin, twisty path, I step into a light jog, warming my stiff muscles. The building is lost as the forest closes around me, still and quiet except for the sound of my breath whooshing in and out.

Too still. Too quiet. It's hard to be sure this isn't a dream, that I'm actually here, on the eve of my first shift as Levett Tech's newest receptionist. Tomorrow is all I've thought about since the police finally released their reports six months ago.

Levett's version of what happened to Mom and Dad had stood. Apparently, I'm supposed to believe they were working late in the R&D lab when the gas lines exploded.

Yeah, right. Dad was a machinist and Mom worked in HR, both at the plant in Coral City, ten minutes from our house. They had nothing to do with R&D and only traveled to New Hampshire for one week each year to attend the annual company-wide conference, always held at Levett's headquarters here in Clearwater.

I used to love when they left because I'd get to stay at Aunt Amy's, where I'd have ice cream for dinner and live it up with no curfew. I never imagined the last time Mom and Dad dropped me off there I wouldn't come home, and they would breathe their last thousands of miles away.

They had no reason to be anywhere near R&D, especially not in New Hampshire.

But Mara Levett didn't answer my questions after the funeral, and the authorities sure as hell didn't address them in their reports. Worse, they refused to release the paperwork for almost five years. The more Aunt Amy badgered them, the snippier they got.

Anger and embarrassment flash over my skin, turning sour in my stomach. Aunt Amy never felt the frustration I did regarding the investigation. She humored me at first, probably because she felt bad for me, or maybe because she thought as my guardian she should. But when the police came down on her, she said it was time to let go.

I lengthen my stride, forcing my attention away from Aunt Amy and the uncooperative cops. Even they couldn't keep the reports locked up forever.

As soon as the case was closed and the paperwork became available, I combed through every word, took a magnifying glass to the photos.

"See?" Aunt Amy said. "It was an accident. I'm sorry, honey, but sometimes these things just happen."

Her words did nothing to stem the rising tide of suspicion that punched a hole through my chest. If Mom and Dad's accident was so straightforward, the investigation wouldn't have dragged on like it did. And, again, why were they in R&D?

Strangest of all were the still photos taken from the CCTV footage of the lab right before the explosion.

Dad was working at a computer. Typing. Then clicking. Then *boom*.

The thing is, Dad was left-handed, everyone knew that. In fact, he joked all the time about how us right-handed people are baffled by left-handed objects, like scissors.

He simply wouldn't have used a right-handed mouse, but he was in those photos.

I begged Aunt Amy to hire a PI. She refused. So, after graduation, I took matters into my own hands.

I've waited so long. Schemed behind Aunt Amy's back, lied to everyone about where I was going this summer and why, but it will all be worth it when I prove I'm right. Something more happened to Mom and Dad.

Levett Tech took them from me. I just have to figure out how.

I slow to a walk and breathe deeply, letting the pounding in my chest calm bit by bit. Sticky sweat coats my skin and drips into my eyes. Where'd the crisp morning air go?

Hang on.

Golden light filters down through the leaves, making bright patterns which dance across the trail around me. The sun's not rising anymore. It's almost overhead.

I've been out here longer than I thought.

Unease blooms in the pit of my stomach as I refocus on my surroundings. I haven't noticed any houses. No roads. No distinguishing landmarks of any kind. Have I even stayed on the same trail?

I swipe a few damp strands of hair off my forehead and pivot. Only one way to find out.

Ten steps back, the path splits.

Shit.

Why didn't I bring my phone with me? I should know better; Dad used to give me trouble all the time for running without it.

Mouth dry, I crouch down to study the compacted dirt. If I'm lucky, maybe my footprints will lead me home.

Well, to the condo any—

"Hey, are you okay?"

I flinch like I've been tasered, falling onto my butt with a loud "Oof!"

There hadn't been any hint of someone approaching. No footsteps, no rustle of leaves or crunch of twigs. At least not that I noticed.

And yet, a guy's leaning over me, hands on his knees. I freeze, breath hitching, and gaze up at the most perfect face I've ever seen.

The stranger's loose curls are warm brown, with gilded undertones that shine in the dappled light. His skin is golden tan, his jaw angular. Eyes of a gorgeous shade of green shot through with gold are framed by thick lashes. He looks older than my nineteen years, but not by much.

Some part of me notes through the shock he's covered in sweat too, clutching a water bottle and wearing a tank top, athletic shorts, and sneakers. He must be a runner. An avid one, by the look of those Asics. They're beat to death.

I blink, stunned by both his beauty and the unexpected arrival. His smile fades as we stare at each other.

I shake myself mentally. "Um, what?"

Concern lights his distinctive eyes. "I asked if you're okay. You're pretty far out here, and you kind of look upset."

"Yeah, I'm lost. I didn't realize how easy it is to get turned around in these woods."

Abruptly, Dad's near constant warnings about runners going missing pop into my head. Abductors are a real threat, especially out here.

The guy nods. "Best to make sure you always have a way to navigate until you know the trails."

Duh. Awesome job, Mel.

"I was overconfident, I guess. I've never been lost on a run before."

The stranger gives me a dazzling smile. "Well, lucky for you, I know these woods inside out. I can help you find your way." He straightens up, holds out a hand.

I chew my lip. Should I tell this guy, however gorgeous, where I live? What if he works at Levett Tech?

Odds are he does. Levett is the only big company in the area, and most of Clearwater's population is employed there.

I stole Mara's badge to access classified intel. I need to keep to myself.

On the other hand, I have no idea how to get home, and circling the woods until an animal eats me will not expose Mom and Dad's killers.

"Thank you," I say, taking his hand. "I appreciate the help."

As I haul myself off the ground, my eyes fall on the bands of lean muscle running up his arm. A quiet gasp slides through my lips, my cheeks warming.

Worried he might catch me looking, I turn my gaze quickly to his face. But I have to wonder, could the rest of his body look as good? No one at my school in California had been muscled up like that, not even the athletes.

My rescuer tugs down his shirt, then fiddles with the thick twine macrame bracelet on his wrist. His eyes sweep the woods around us before settling back on me. "It's going to take a while to get out of here, so we better get moving. Where are we headed?"

"The Golden Valley condo complex in Clearwater. You know it?"

"The new development?"

"Yeah, think so."

He nods, turning and striding away without a word, which is odd considering how chatty he was a second ago.

Heat creeps over my cheeks again as I hurry to catch up. I give him a friendly smile. "I'm Mel."

"Hi, Mel. I'm Tommy."

Tommy doesn't smile back. Doesn't even look my way.

I glance down at my laces, then back at his expressionless face. Did I do something to tick him off?

Or ... Oh no. Did he catch me checking him out?

My face burns. He's probably used to being hit on, but I didn't mean anything by that look. I don't want a relationship, whether he's interested or not.

Even so, it's nice to talk to someone who isn't aware of my history. No awkward, half-sincere pity, no empty words of comfort, and no sidelong glances from people wondering whether I'm still sane, still me. I could use a friend out here, especially one who has no idea I'm an orphan.

As long as he doesn't work at Levett Tech.

I cast around for something to say, to smooth the situation over, and my eyes fall once more on his scruffy Asics. They make my banged-up old Nikes look healthy.

"So, you run?"

"Almost every day." The corner of Tommy's mouth twitches up, but his eyes are cool. Distant. He keeps them fixed ahead.

"You know, I run too. That's how I got so far out here."

He nods once. "I guessed, but I don't want to tire you out trying to run all the way to Clearwater. It's not close."

I bite my tongue against the snarky response that springs to my lips. Why won't he drop the frigid attitude? It's not like my faux pas was a big deal. If anything, he should be flattered.

Fine. I'll show him.

"I bet I can make it," I say with a cheeky grin.

Tommy huffs a reluctant laugh. "I like your confidence, but I don't want to end up carrying you."

I roll my eyes. If only he knew Mom and I always placed first and second in Coral City's annual Turkey Trot Marathon. Every year she let me pull ahead right at the end to claim the gold.

A heavy weight settles in my chest.

Stop. Focus. Breathe.

"You know what? I bet I can make it more easily than you. Want to race?"

I hop from foot to foot, hoping he'll say yes. Okay, so he looks like someone in peak physical condition. Be that as it may, most people can't run as far as I can. It's a talent I've worked on for years, and I'm proud of it.

Tommy snorts. "You don't want to challenge me. Trust me."

"That sounds like an excuse to say no. Worried you'll get beaten by a girl?" My grin turns angelic.

He flashes a real smile then, finally looking my way. His eyes dance. "Yeah, you wish. Okay. You're on."

Without warning, he takes off down the trail. His every movement appears weightless, graceful even as he flies over the bumpy ground. A beat late, I launch myself after him.

I'm forced to lag half a step behind, needing him to show me the way as we dash through the trees. Tommy doesn't falter in his pace, but I don't lose an inch on him either. We run like this for an immeasurable length of time. Maybe an hour, maybe two. Even though we don't speak much, the company is nice.

Eventually, clear yellow light shines through the trees ahead—the woods' edge. I pour on the speed, passing Tommy right before we slip through the last of the branches. Somehow, we're back at my condo complex.

"I win!"

Tommy chuckles, slowing to a walk and taking a long swig from his water bottle. The way he's looking at me … he's impressed. "You weren't lying. Wow."

"That was nothing."

His eyes light up. "How far do you usually run?"

"It depends on the day. On weekends, I log at least fifteen miles, sometimes up to twenty-five. Weekdays, it's more like five. Whatever I can squeeze in before school. Or work, now, I guess."

"Good for you."

"Do you live nearby?" I'd love to have a running partner for a neighbor.

Tommy fidgets, his face falling. Perhaps I'm not the only one with misgivings about handing out my address. Or is he still being weird about before? Does he think I'm coming on to him again?

After a moment, he says, "Uh, yeah, I live in that old manor house. The stone one, down on Route 16. But I'm not home often. I … I work a lot."

"Workaholic, huh? Where do you work?"

Please don't say Levett Tech.

"Um. I'm in … uh, sales."

Does a weapons manufacturer have a sales department? I have no idea.

"Sounds riveting. What do you sell?"

"Parts. Auto. Car parts."

"Ah."

We stand awkwardly facing each other, neither of us speaking. I can't shake the suspicion he's not being honest, but he has no reason to lie to me, a complete stranger, about where he works. Unless…

If Levett Tech can buy their way out of trouble when four people are killed on their watch, they could also send someone to keep tabs on me. Have they figured out who I am? Why I'm here?

Fear creeps up my spine. God knows how far they might go to keep me quiet. I need to find out more, to question Tommy further and look for tells. Liars always have them.

Wringing my hands, I blurt, "Do you want to run with me tomorrow morning? I usually go early, as I said."

He hesitates again, probably trying to figure out how to tell me no, because he's just a normal guy with a normal life and I'm paranoid like everyone back home said. But it's not worth the risk to let this go without making sure I'm safe.

He's still staring at me, a little too intense, like he's fighting some kind of internal battle. Why? A controlling girlfriend? A secret assignment and accompanying guilty conscience?

"Um, yeah. Sure. I'll meet you here. What time?" He gives me a small smile, twisting his bracelet around his wrist.

"Six? It was great to meet you." I hold out my hand.

Tommy takes it, smiling widely now. Sparks skitter over my skin at the casual contact, zapping up my arm and through my chest. The sensation is shocking, and I drop his hand quickly.

"Six. It's nice to meet you too, Mel." His green-and-gold eyes shine.

He waves as he bounds back toward the woods, every motion graceful as a dancer. I watch him go, my hand tingling where he held it.

For the first time in five years, I'm not thinking about my parents.

CHAPTER TWO

TOMMY

SWEAT drips down my temples and slides between my shoulder blades, my damp shirt stuck to my overheated skin. After miles of running followed by hundreds of stairs, I'm beat, but I've finally reached the summit of the mountain I call home. Because of the long climb, this spot's an ideal place to go when I want to be alone with my thoughts.

I stop short when I see Cait, sitting cross-legged in the twilit grass. She pats the ground next to her.

Well, as alone as I ever am.

"I knew I'd find you here," she says. "Where were you? You didn't meet us after guard duty."

I shrug. "I ran a few extra miles instead. Sorry. Should've told you."

Though I try not to think of the girl, her face floats across my mind anyway.

Mel.

"Would've been nice. You missed the big news. Jack and Zara procured intel on the BioAgent shipment. It's due to set out in nine weeks."

"Yeah? That's good. Gives us time to nab the bill of lading."

"Mm-hm. Lisa's pleased."

I sigh as I drop to the ground by Cait's side. Running through the woods with Mel earlier felt amazing. Free. For a short time, it was easy to pretend I was normal.

But I'm not. I have no life, no future aboveground.

"You know what I don't get, though?" Cait fiddles with the end of her long blond braid, a little crease between her brows. Worried. "Why go after this shipment at all? Lisa's top objective has always been to keep the Resistance safe. And yeah, we make it our job to disrupt as many weapons deals as possible, to siphon the Organization's source of profit and power. That I understand. But this mission? Dangerous to us all with a miniscule chance for success."

I frown. Cait rarely questions our assignments. In fact, this might be a first. "Lisa wouldn't risk our safety without good reason. If the BioAgent's important enough to go after, we go after it."

"Oh, I'm not arguing that. Lisa knows best, and it's not like we don't risk our lives regularly. I just want to understand her logic. When I'm responsible for these decisions one day, I need to be sure I'm making good ones. Breaking into Levett Tech is a whole new level of danger. What if someone's caught?"

Cait drops her braid and pins me with her sharp gray stare. "First and foremost, we're meant to protect the hunted. Aka each other. If we were this bold all the time, we'd be dead by now. And maybe that seems like selfish thinking, but if we're dead, we can't save others anymore either."

It's the same thing she told me when I landed on the Resistance's doorstep five years ago with an Organization target on my back. The corrupt, highly dangerous network of homegrown extremists are baked into the fabric of Levett Technologies itself. They thrive there, hidden in plain sight, perfectly placed to funnel Levett weapons to terrorist groups for large sums of money, and to keep plenty for their domestic backers as well.

They're too powerful to make a significant move against. But we chip away at their success by intercepting their smaller arms shipments and stealing their weapons when we can.

"The BioAgent could kill a lot of people," I remind her. "It's higher profile than our usual targets, sure, but it's a weapon of mass destruction. It's worth pursuing. Remember, Lisa has more information than we do. When you're in charge, you will too. You'll make the right calls."

Cait gives me a small smile. "Yeah, I guess that's true. Thanks."

With effort, I grin back, then force myself to study the view, to really see the forest below, swathed in shadow. Here and there, little points of light—towns—twinkle in the dark like clusters of golden stars. Beyond the valley, soaring mountains stand like sentinels, black against a fierce red-and-orange sunset. It's like the land behind them is on fire, a violent sort of splendor.

My fingers twitch, my mind already full of colors, of brushstrokes. This painting might be worth breaking into my watercolors for, but no. I can't. I don't have enough supplies left to do the scene justice.

Cait sighs, and I glance sideways at her again. She's leaning back on her hands, her now-relaxed smile visible in the half-light. She's one of the only people who truly know me, and yet she won't understand my desire—no, my need—to break the rules. To feel free, just one more time.

To Cait, duty and honor are everything.

Turning her gray eyes from the view, she peers into my face. The corners of her mouth tug down into a pout. "Are you all right? You seem kind of weird tonight."

"It's strange a place so wild and open could be a prison, don't you think?"

She tilts her head, confusion touching her exquisite features.

Even after five years, I'm not immune to Cait's beauty. Those silver eyes, the freckles sprinkled over her nose, that long blond hair, those lips. Regardless, she's never been more than a friend to me.

She's still staring, looking worried again. I raise my eyebrows.

"What's wrong?" Her voice is quiet, sympathetic, not at all impatient like it should be.

Where to begin?

Cait knows how the restrictions designed to keep the Resistance safe affect me, how they tighten my chest and steal the air from my lungs. Perhaps I should start by explaining that, for a few short hours today, I was free of the ever-present weight in my gut. For once I felt like any other guy. Maybe she would understand.

Still I delay, my intestines curling into knots.

Cait's eyebrows pull together. "I know you've been struggling lately. Do you want to talk about it?"

I frown. There's no way to justify what I did. I broke the Resistance's most fundamental rule. They saved my life, and I spoke to someone on the outside anyway. Worse, I made plans to do it again tomorrow. Cait will go ballistic.

But I need to tell her. If she doesn't agree to cover for me, there's no way I'll be able to sneak out and meet Mel in the morning.

"Or not," Cait mutters. She leans her head against my shoulder.

"No, you're right." It's easier now I'm not looking at her. "I met someone today. A runner, lost in the woods. I helped her find her way out." Throat dry, I pause.

Cait only sighs. "Sounds like she's lucky you found her. I hope you were careful."

For a moment, her lack of ire surprises me. I expected worse. Of course, it's what I have to say next that'll tick her off.

"I said I'd run with her again tomorrow."

Cait pulls back. "That's not very nice. She'll expect you. Why would you do that?"

She hasn't guessed I intend to follow through. I drop my eyes, ashamed, but knowing I'll run with Mel anyway. It can't be dangerous when she has no idea who I am.

I just have to tell Cait why I need this, to make her understand. She has to understand.

"Because I'm planning on going."

Cait's expression shifts from disapproving to full-on horrified. "What do you mean? You know you can't. It's not safe. Our anonymity is our best protection. Resistance 101."

I take Cait's hands in mine, staring into those stormy eyes. I want her to see the depth of my sincerity. My words blister with it. "I know. Believe me, I know. I'll be careful, and I'll only run with her one more time. Maybe two."

A chilly breeze rustles through the grass around us, blowing tendrils of golden hair across Cait's face. I sweep the strands back as I pause, gathering my thoughts. This is about so much more than me wanting to meet up with some girl.

I belong to the Resistance. I will until I die. Sometimes, late at night, I imagine running away and never looking back. Living a normal life, going out with friends, maybe even selling my paintings.

But I can't run. I can't escape.

That's usually when I run out of air.

"I need this. Today, I felt … free. For the first time in years, I could breathe. I don't want to give that up. Not yet."

Cait looks away for a moment, then scowls at me, eyes hard. But she's not yelling. She's not shooting me down.

Encouraged, I go on. "That's how it felt. Like a breath of fresh air. I know I can't be friends with this girl or see her more than a few times. And I won't tell her anything. It's just nice to be a different person for a short while. While I was with her, I was someone whose future was limitless. Please, Cait. Cover for me."

Cait's eyes blaze. She yanks her hands from mine. "I know you don't love this life, but this is your life. This is your family. That choice will put us all at risk. Who knows who that girl is? She could be anyone. An Organization spy. How can you even consider this?"

The words slice through me like white-hot daggers. She's right.

I'll never be free.

A familiar pressure closes in, setting my heart racing and crushing the breath from my lungs. I launch to my feet, stumble away from Cait. It's not long before I have to drop to my knees. Gasp for air.

Though I try, I can't push the ridiculous weakness away. I can't slow the pounding in my chest. I can't erase the sting behind my eyes.

The world spins around me, shrinking, tightening.

And then Cait is there, kneeling in front of me.

"You really need this, don't you?"

The walls of my invisible prison narrow, and the yearning in my soul to feel free again, one more time, is overpowering. I'm going to do this, and I feel sick. What kind of a person am I?

"Yes," I breathe.

The silence strains tight as the fierce sunset fades beyond the mountains. The purple shadows darken to black.

After what feels like an eternity, she whispers, "I guess I can look the other way, if you promise to be careful."

Shame prickles over my skin. "Thank you," I mumble. "I promise."

Cait pulls me to my feet. "I won't lie for you, though. The most I can do is not rat you out."

I know agreeing to this is costing her. I know she must judge my decision harshly. And yet, here she is.

Cait is a true friend. Selfless. A warm, glowing feeling wells in my chest.

"Thank you," I whisper again. "I won't let you down. Once or twice, and that's it. I'll get this out of my system and never think of it again."

"Just don't get caught."

Cait pulls away, heading toward a nearby jumble of boulders. There's an entrance to the extensive cave system beneath our feet hidden within the rocks. "We should get back."

I follow her, unable to keep a wide smile from breaking across my face. I'm tempting fate, meeting Mel again. But how can I resist shedding my bonds one last time?

As I slip through a gap in the rocks, I take another look at the view. This time, I don't see a prison. I see the endless sky above, dusted with a million glittering stars. Wild, beautiful … free.

CHAPTER THREE

MEL

MY new boss is late.

Perched on the edge of my seat, I watch through the glass office door as he chats with a short, gray-haired woman out in the hall. If I scoot a few inches to the left, I could peek through the files on his desk. As part of Levett's leadership team, odds are he knows something about Mom and Dad, but he'll catch me if I look now.

My palms sweat as I wait. And wait.

Unable to ignore the sickness in my stomach, I tear my eyes from the laughing executives and pull my freshly printed employee badge out of my pocket, careful to leave Mara's hidden. With my pale skin and ice-blue eyes, plus the shape of my face and the way I hold my mouth, I look exactly like Mom in this picture. Except for my jet-black hair—hers had been silver-blond—this photo could be her. This could be the same badge I played with a million times as a child, coloring at her desk while she worked late.

I hope no one notices.

To my horror, my eyes start to sting. I flip the badge over, willing myself to forget, but a well of tears lurks just below the surface. I need something else to think about. Anything.

Even being ditched this morning.

I waited thirty long, chilly minutes by the trailhead, but Tommy didn't show. It's good news, because if he were spying on me for Levett Tech, he'd never have stood me up. Of course, that means I was paranoid. And I lost out on the chance to make a friend.

I miss having friends.

The office door swings open, and finally, my balding, middle-aged boss strolls into the room, coffee in hand. He gives me a polite smile, teeth bright against his dark-brown skin. "I assume you're Melanie O'Hanlon?"

I'm not. O'Hanlon was Mom's maiden name. My real last name is Snow, but I spent a lot of my inheritance on documents to cover that up.

Trying to exude a confidence I don't feel, I jump to my feet and shake his hand firmly. "Yes, I am. Are you Mr. Greene?"

The man nods. "I'm Tony, but most people here call me Mr. Greene. Welcome to the team. Are you ready for your tour?"

He seems friendly enough. I've started to think of Levett employees as bad guys, when really, they're just people. The suspicion I feel regarding Mom and Dad shouldn't automatically apply to them. After all, Mom and Dad worked here too.

I return his smile. "Yes, thank you. I'm excited to be here."

Mr. Greene leads me out of his office and through the back door of the admin building. I had to escape quickly when I signed my new-hire paperwork last week, having spotted Mara's badge unattended on her desk and pocketing it, so I haven't had a chance to see the rest of the campus yet. I'm thankful for an innocent reason to scope it out now.

Oh Mylanta, but it's huge. Way bigger than the one in Coral City.

Several hulking buildings tower around a sweeping, well-manicured quad. Cement paths cut through swaths of lush grass and shade trees. A tall chain-link fence lines the far end of the lawn, the ever-present forest visible just beyond.

As Mr. Greene leads me through the different buildings, he drones on and on about the importance of Levett Tech's mission: to supply the means for our great country's defense. Patriotism is displayed everywhere. Big flags wave on bright posters splashed over every wall, and stars and stripes are embroidered into the shirts and jackets of the workers. During my final interview, I got the sense the company took its mission seriously, but to see it in action is next level.

I keep my eyes peeled for documents or records that could relate to Mom and Dad's accident, and I also look for Tommy, just in case, but we arrive back at the administrative building without my having spotted him or anything helpful. Here, Mr. Greene takes me up a set of stairs, then another, and another. We stop at the top of the staircase, a long industrial hallway stretching out before us. Windows line the left side, doors line the right. The doors are all secured with card readers.

"This whole floor is devoted to recordkeeping," Mr. Greene says. "Due to the sensitive nature of our work, we choose to keep paper records. It avoids cybersecurity vulnerabilities."

Mara's badge is a brand in my pocket.

He indicates the closest card reader. "The first room is accessible with your employee ID card, and houses production schedules, safety plans, nonhazardous material requests, and the like. The others are not accessible, and contain information related to employees, incoming and outgoing shipments, hazardous materials, military contracts, and special projects."

Bingo. This kind of documentation is exactly what I need.

"All records are destroyed after five years, so in addition to filing and auditing, you will be responsible for shredding the oldest on a monthly basis."

Shit. My parents' accident was five years ago this month.

Working to keep my expression courteous, I nod. "Got it. Wow, that's kind of cool. Will I be handling anything classified?" I hope it's not too suspicious a question, given filing is part of my job description.

To my disquiet, Mr. Greene's eyebrows jump up. "Access to sensitive records might seem cool, but they're a big responsibility and far above your pay grade. That's why your security clearance only works on the first room."

My fingers brush Mara's badge and I smile, aiming to appear neutral while I surreptitiously scan the placards posted on the doors over Mr. Greene's shoulder. The first room doesn't contain anything useful, but the next piques my interest. It holds accident reports, shipment and employee records, and hazardous material data sheets.

"Melanie, are you hearing me?"

Heat blooms over my cheeks, and I stare down at my feet. I need to be more careful. "Sorry. Guess I'm getting hungry."

"Don't worry about it, kid. I know this is a lot to take in, especially considering you've not worked in manufacturing before. This is your first real job, right?"

I peek up, relieved to find him smiling. "Yes. I graduated high school last month."

No need to mention how far behind I was, having been useless most of my Freshman year. At least I got my diploma in the end.

"High school? You're younger than I thought. In fact, you're almost the same age as my Zuri. She's a rising sophomore at UNH." He purses his lips. "You didn't want to go to college?"

Uncomfortable, I scuff my foot against the industrial carpet. I did want to go to college, to study creative writing. I was going to find a school on the West Coast and spend my days scribbling stories and poetry in pretty notebooks by the sea. Dad used to beam with pride when I'd talk about it. He'd be disappointed I chose to do this instead, but my inheritance wasn't big enough to do both.

"Not everyone has the means to go to school right away, but yes, that is my eventual plan."

Mr. Greene runs a hand over his shiny pate. "Right. I'm sorry to have … I mean to say … Levett Tech has some excellent scholarship opportunities. I encourage you to check them out. For now, why don't we break for lunch?"

After a quick trip to Mr. Greene's office to grab my bag, I'm left on my own in the cafeteria on the first floor. A few other workers lounge around tables or sit alone in booths. I pick at my homemade sandwich, stomach full of jangling nerves. I've come three thousand miles and uprooted my entire life to get a look at Levett Tech's records of my parents' accident, and they'll be shredded any day—if they haven't been already.

This is why the authorities were so slow to close their investigation. They needed to run out some arbitrary clock.

I shift in my seat. What if I sneak upstairs while I'm unattended and take a quick peek around? Sure, it'll be a fishy thing to do on my first day of work, but those records are my best chance to learn what happened to Mom and Dad.

Chucking my sandwich in the bin, I square my shoulders and march out of the cafeteria. It's quite literally now or never.

My heart thunders as I climb the stairs and slink down the hall, stopping in front of the room that caught my attention earlier. To my immense relief, I don't see a soul.

With a glance over my shoulder, I pull out Mara's badge. Hesitate. Don't be a coward.

I scan the card and the lock beeps. Flashes green.

I slip through the door, pulling it closed with a soft *click*.

Row upon row of shelves tower over me, all loaded with file boxes. The shelves stretch across the center of the room, creating long hallways perpendicular to where I stand by the door. There's space to navigate around the edges, but the walls are filled with still more shelves, more boxes. Thankfully, they seem to be well labeled.

I follow the stickers for employee records and find a lot of subsections: hiring and firing, performance reviews, projected career tracks, and…

My heart stops.

Incident reports.

I waste no time pulling the oldest box from the shelf. Its contents rattle in my shaking hands.

THIRTY-FIVE minutes later, I'm scrambling to clean up the mess I've made. In my fervor to find something useful, I've thrown documents everywhere. The floor is littered with them. Worse, my lunch break is over, and I haven't found anything on my parents. It's like their accident never even happened.

Tears threaten as I shove papers roughly back into boxes. They must've shredded the records. What will I—

Footsteps. Out in the hall.

Fuck.

I drop the documents in my hands and sprint to the back of the room, flinging myself behind the last row of shelves as the steps pause outside the door.

The scan pad beeps, and, through a gap in the boxes, I watch the door swing open. A man in his mid-twenties strolls in and hesitates. Surveys the mess on the floor.

Adrenaline pulses through my system, making me sweat.

Brow furrowed, the man picks up a sheet of paper and starts to read. He picks up another, and another. He checks the dates on the open boxes.

Clearly baffled, he proceeds to clean up my mess, muttering under his breath about being the only one around here who cares about order. When he's done, he files something in the incoming raw materials section and exits the room. His footsteps fade away down the hall.

My limbs tremble as I crawl out of my hiding spot. A glance at my phone tells me I should've been in Mr. Greene's office five minutes ago, but I can't help rifling through the newest raw material receipts to see what the man filed away.

It turns out, Levett Tech is purchasing plenty of interesting materials. Many of the files are stamped with warnings. There are myriad hazardous chemicals, parts of all sorts, dangerous explosives, fuels. There's even a file for something biological in nature that sounds like it was pulled straight out of a spy movie: BioAgent 313.

Cool.

Footsteps tap in the hall again.

What am I doing? Do I want to be caught and fired on my first day?

Carefully, I replace the incoming raw materials box and duck behind the shelves again. This time the footsteps pass without entering. When they're gone, I leave the room and scurry down to Mr. Greene's office.

My palms are slick as I knock.

"Come in."

I push the door open, focusing all my effort on appearing relaxed. I'm not sure I pull it off, but Mr. Greene doesn't seem to suspect anything strange.

"Sorry, I got lost looking for the bathroom."

He gives me a tired smile. "No problem. Are you ready to meet Zuri? She'll be training you on your receptionist duties over the next few weeks."

Profound relief floods my system. "That sounds great. Is this the Zuri you mentioned upstairs?"

"The same." Mr. Greene's smile widens, pride sparkling in his eyes, and suddenly it's not Mr. Greene but Dad standing there. A giant lump forms in my throat.

I spend the afternoon trailing tall, bright-eyed Zuri as she goes about her workday. She's bubbly and enthusiastic, and it doesn't take much on my part to keep her chattering away. Admittedly, I don't learn much about the job, but I do have a pretty good time.

When five o'clock rolls around, I follow her out to the parking lot and climb into my 'new' car. It's got over 150,000 miles on it, but I can't spare more of my inheritance than necessary on transportation. Despite the rust spots, mismatched doors, and crank windows, it's served me well so far.

Turning up the music, I pull out onto the road. Yeah, it's disappointing I didn't find any clues on my parents today, but I've ruled out the accident reports as a source of information. I've avoided suspicion and kept my identity from the others. Mara's badge works. All I have to do is keep trying.

A huge smile curls across my face as I hit the interstate, a heady mix of accomplishment and anticipation glowing in my heart.

Levett Tech, I'm coming for you.

Chapter Four

Tommy

DOING the right thing shouldn't suck so much.

I lie on my bed in the dark, hands behind my head, a defeated sort of numbness dripping through my blood. All last night I tossed and turned as Cait's words burrowed into my brain and seeped under my skin.

This is your life. This is your family. That choice will put us all at risk.

Guilt and shame ate me alive, my selfishness laid bare before the imagined, disgusted faces of my loved ones.

Harmless as it would've been to run with Mel just once more, I couldn't do it. I couldn't put the self-centered impulse above my family's safety.

So I didn't. When morning came, I stayed here. I stood her up.

I'll never be free.

I press my forearm over my eyes, trying to block Mel's image out of my head so I can rest, but she lingers there, behind my lids. Like she did all day while I ran through the forest on guard duty.

It's not only the transient freedom she represents that's stuck on my mind. Not just the way I interacted with her as if I'm your average twenty-year-old looking forward to a life of infinite opportunity. It's … well, it's Mel herself.

She's striking to look at, of course, with long, silk-smooth runner's legs and clear blue eyes that sparkle even in the shade, and she projects a comforting presence, kind and sweet. Like sinking into a warm bed after a day spent on patrol in the cold, or the first bite of Mom's homemade apple pie.

But that's not it either. There's more.

She's strangely familiar. Not enough to have noticed when I was with her, but the more I think about her, the more apparent it is.

Why? Have we met before?

Unlikely. I haven't traveled much, and she's not from Clearwater. I'd remember a face like hers.

The odd familiarity is driving me crazy. I can't get Mel out of my head.

Footsteps sound in the hall beyond my door. I pay them no mind. It's probably whoever's on Fire Duty tonight. Even at this hour, the lanterns need to stay lit.

The tapping slows, and my door bangs open with enough force to bounce off the rocky wall with a thunderous crash.

In one smooth motion, I spin off the bed and raise my fists. As my eyes adjust to the flickering light, I straighten up, surprised.

A woman in her mid-forties stands in the doorway, usual cloud of curly hair hidden under a shiny silk bonnet. A matching black robe is slung over her shoulders, flannel PJs visible underneath.

Lisa, head of the Resistance.

But why is she here, in my room, at one in the morning? Something must be seriously wrong.

Cait's on patrol. With a flash of fear, I picture her surrounded by enemies in the dark woods.

"What is it? What happened?"

Lisa's mouth is a hard line. Her face gives nothing away. "Come with me."

Without waiting for a response, she turns on her heel and glides down the hall.

Wary, I follow her through the network of granite passages that make up our home. Once, I found the labyrinth of burrow-like corridors fascinating. With their floors of smooth stone and craggy irregular walls, the caves felt like something out of a fairy tale, a cross between a medieval castle and a giant rabbit den. Even the lanterns, hung at measured intervals, added to the magic with their dancing yellow light.

Now, after five years, walking through the caves is as normal as strolling the halls of my high school used to be, only instead of football players and classrooms, there are gun-wielding field agents and gyms where we learn to kill our enemies.

As it becomes clear Lisa is heading for her office, my confusion intensifies. She typically brings me here to reprimand me for the various shenanigans I get into with Cait, Hunter, Vik, and Sam. Pulling pranks, starting food fights, making a racket in the halls. But if this were about something like that, Lisa would wait until tomorrow to scold me.

My stomach tightens, worry for Cait buzzing in my mind. She might be our best operative, but even she isn't immune to death. Or worse, capture. Interrogation.

Lisa throws open her door and stands back to let me pass.

Her office resembles the rest of the caves. Cracked granite walls, lanterns, flat stone floor, large fireplace hewn into the rock. A roaring fire is lit in the grate and a candle burns on her simple wooden desk, next to her computer.

Though electricity is available in certain areas, including here, Lisa doesn't waste the precious resource on lighting. Sometimes, I wish she would, that we could splurge a bit for some common comforts. But our water turbine only produces so much energy. Better to power vital things, like the massive air exchange system which keeps the caves livable and disperses our smoke footprint, than to have lights and television and normal toilets.

Lisa sits down behind her desk without a word. It's almost like she's waiting for me to say something.

I stare. After several long moments, she says, "Is there anything you want to tell me?"

Her tone doesn't hint at anger, but her eyes do. Their usual liquid warmth has solidified into a sharp onyx accusation. I think through every dumb or reckless thing I've done in the past week, hoping I'm in trouble for anything other than my time with Mel. But Sam hasn't been around much since Hunter twisted his ankle, and without them, Cait and Vik's good influence is rubbing off on me. There's nothing else.

I grit my teeth. Cait.

She promised not to rat.

A sharp stab of anger fizzes through me. Was I really supposed to leave a scared, lost girl alone so deep in the woods?

Yes.

I shift from foot to foot, fingers brushing over the braided twine on my wrist, the last thing Mom gave me before she died. I reach for it when I need her strength, her love, or her guidance, but no brilliant explanation for my poor behavior pops into my head. When I helped Mel, I broke the rules, plain and simple.

Lisa gestures at the computer in front of her. "I want to show you something."

I make my way around the desk and lean in, hands on the back of her chair. A feed from Levett Tech's internal CCTV is pulled up on her screen. I recognize the spot immediately as the hall outside their record storage rooms.

I've spent countless hours monitoring live footage of Levett's CCTV. Nothing ever happens in this hallway. What could Lisa want to show me here, of all places?

Onscreen, the sun shines through the windows, and the person in the hall doesn't move. This isn't a live feed. It must be a recording of earlier events, a recording Lisa's paused.

I study the frozen image. How could this relate to me? It doesn't make any sense.

That's when I recognize her.

Mel.

Shock locks me in place.

She looks different, dressed for business in a white blouse, a long black skirt, and heels. Dark silky hair flows down her back like an inky waterfall. The way the skirt clings to her curves pulls my attention, and I find myself staring a second too long. A jolt of jittery energy rocks through my core.

It's not like I hadn't known Mel was attractive, but I'd been trying not to notice. Willing myself not to see. Now, with her frozen figure in front of me, looking like that, I can't not see. She's stunning. Radiant.

Clearing my throat, I take a step back, cross my arms, and avert my eyes.

Fuck. She must work at Levett Tech.

"Who is that?" I ask with put-on ignorance.

Lisa swivels in her chair, watching me. "I know what you did yesterday morning. Do you really think I'm not aware of what goes on in my own home?"

My mind flashes to Hunter and Sam. To June.

No, Lisa. You don't know everything.

"And with her, of all people. Watch. This will be an important lesson for you."

Lisa turns back to the computer. I lean in again, eyes trained on Mel. A wave of nausea unfurls in the pit of my stomach.

I put the Resistance in danger by associating with her.

Cait was right.

Lisa presses play, and Mel moves. She glances around, looking nervous, then pulls a card from her pocket and scans it. As she slinks through the door, Lisa's screen switches to a different view, one from within the room.

Mel fidgets just inside, inspecting the shelves. She must see what she's looking for, because she strides along one of the aisles and pulls a box down. She tosses the lid aside, tearing out papers one by one. It's easy to see her frustration mount.

Soon the box is empty, its contents scattered. She doesn't pause, but goes for the next box, and the next. I squint, trying to make out what she's looking at, but I can't see enough detail to learn anything.

Lisa switches off her computer and I stare at the blank screen, my thoughts a snarl. Does Mel know who she's working for, or is she innocent? If she's innocent, why is she digging through Levett's files, looking for all the world like she's trying not to get caught?

"What did I just see?" I manage to choke out.

Lisa glances up, dead serious. "You saw what can happen if you associate with people outside the Resistance. That girl is being tailed by the Organization, thanks to the stunt she pulled today. It's lucky for all of us this didn't happen before you helped her, or she would have led them straight to you. And then, through you, they would have found us. Don't think for a second they've forgotten who you are."

She adjusts her glasses, then goes on. "I don't make these rules up for kicks, you know."

My heart sinks through the soles of my feet, and suddenly I can't breathe. If Mel's become a target of the Organization's, she's as good as dead.

I force my numb lips to move. "Are you sure?"

Lisa nods. "Quite. I hacked Mr. Edwards's communications."

My skin ices over at the mention of the Organization's shadowy, faceless leader. There's no hope for Mel, then. None at all.

Lisa's mouth thins. "Do I have your word you will never do something like this again? I know you thought it was harmless, that you wanted to help her, but—"

"I don't understand. What was Mel—the girl—doing in there?"

Lisa's expression is odd. It almost looks mournful. "You don't recognize her?"

Huh. The inexplicable familiarity driving me insane—Lisa's confirming it. I've met Mel before. Why don't I remember her?

Lisa waits a moment. When I don't answer, she continues, "That's Melanie Snow. Reyna Snow's daughter. They look just alike. I thought…"

Shock slams into me, and I'm wrenched into a memory so sharp and clear I almost believe it's real. I can feel it; I can smell it; I can taste the terror of it, a metallic tang on my tongue.

I'm on my stomach in the narrow gap under my parents' bed, peering out past the airy green bed skirt. I can't see much of the room from here, but I can see enough. Bright crimson pools soak into the beige carpet.

So much blood.

Doesn't matter who's lost the most. The savage intruders don't care. Dad's face presses into the mire on the rug. I know it's him, but I can't recognize him beneath his injuries. No way is he alive.

Mom and Mrs. Snow are still conscious, kneeling among a forest of black-booted feet. I can see their knees. Their fleecy PJ bottoms are stained red.

"We're not getting anywhere," a man complains.

You've got the wrong people! I try to shout, but the words don't pass my frozen lips.

"Let's bring 'em back to base. That'll get 'em talkin'."

No! You're wrong! They don't know anything!

Cold sweat dews on my forehead as the black boots surround Dad and the prone form of Mr. Snow. They're hauled from the room while Mom and Mrs. Snow are yanked to their feet. Mom's marched out on shaky legs, but Mrs. Snow sags. She's too hurt to hold her own weight.

The man supporting her is shouting, his words running together. Mrs. Snow's rough voice hurls insults back.

How is she so brave?

The man yells something about respect. He throws her to the ground; she lands in front of where I lie, sick and trembling, tears burning down my cheeks. Her face is a mask of puffy bruises and raw flesh. Blood runs from her nose and mouth, over her lips and down her chin. I wouldn't recognize her if not for her eyes.

For one eternal moment, they blaze into mine. They burn with an icy fire which shocks me with its brilliance. Nowhere in their depths is there any trace of fear. Her hand twitches to her lips, as if to wipe away blood ... but she's shushing me.

Mom screams from the hall—

With a tremendous effort, I shut the memory down, smother it beneath an iron wall. The world tilts, shrinks, closes in. Panting, I sink to the floor and put my head between my knees. My eyes burn.

Lisa moves closer. "Tommy, honey, it's all right. No harm done. But you can't contact Melanie again. It's too dangerous."

Her words barely touch the surface of my panic.

Come on. Pull it together.

My fingertips skim over my bracelet as I squeeze my eyes shut and breathe deeply. I must block this memory out, or others will follow. The screams. Bones cracking. Metal pounding into flesh. Mom's voice, ragged. Begging.

Slowly, the ringing in my ears dies out, the wobble and shimmer that blurs my sight lifts.

When the world holds steady, I climb to my feet. Lisa gazes at me, dark eyes full of concern. She's the closest thing I have to a mom now. She cares about me. She cares about us all.

I can't believe I came so close to compromising our security—to hurting my adopted family. What must Lisa think of me, of my selfishness and stupidity? What must Cait think? No wonder she turned me in.

In spite of her worry, Lisa's expression hardens a little. "You understand you absolutely cannot contact Melanie again?"

I know I can't. But what about Mel?

A surge of kinship washes through me. Mel and I are the same, alone in the world. She lost everything too. And she's in danger. She probably doesn't even know it.

I gaze at Lisa. How can we leave Mel in this mess? If we do nothing, she'll get hurt, and it will be my fault for keeping her in the dark. But if she's being tailed, there's no way I can safely warn her. I'll lead the Organization straight to our doorstep.

Frowning, I look away.

"Tommy?" Lisa's stern now.

"I won't." Turning back, I glare at her. "What about Mel, though? She's going to get hurt."

Lisa shrugs, eyes lined with guilt. "I doubt it. She's probably looking for clues about her parents, but she has no idea what she's doing. She'll poke around, find nothing, and give up. The Organization knows she's Reyna and Max's daughter, but they won't act unless they believe she's a threat. It wouldn't be worth the trouble for them to cover up another disappearance. Still, they're nothing if not careful. They'll follow her as a precaution for a while."

Something tightens around my heart. I see again the fiery gaze of Reyna Snow, locking eyes with me just before being dragged away to her death, and I blink back tears.

Lisa's expression softens. "We can't guard her needlessly. We don't have the people to spare. But I'll keep an eye out, okay? If I see she's in true danger, we'll do everything in our power to save her. It won't be necessary, though. I'm sure of that."

I nod, but I know in my heart I should do more.

Satisfied with my acquiescence, Lisa looks to the door. A dismissal.

As I leave, a heavy cloud of remorse takes root in my soul. I didn't save Reyna, but I can protect her daughter. I should.

No. The Resistance has to come first. These people took me in, sheltered me, healed me. More than that, they have given up everything, everything, to shield others from the Organization. My parents died for them. I can't compromise their security again.

The trip back to my room takes a lifetime. When I arrive, I slog my way to the bed and collapse on top of the covers.

Lying in the dark, I'm tormented by a specific mental picture.

It's Mel. Her face is a mask of puffy bruises and raw flesh. Blood runs from her nose and mouth, over her lips and down her chin.

I wouldn't recognize her, if not for her eyes.

CHAPTER FIVE

MEL

I HATE running on the street, but there's no way I'm going back into the woods alone.

My muscles bunch and stretch, my footsteps beat out a numbing rhythm against the pavement. *Dum-dum, dum-dum, dum-dum,* over and over. It's not enough to dull the edge of irritation that's gnawed at me all morning.

I miss running in California. Back home, I'd step outside and be bathed in buttery sunshine. I'd run barefoot on the beach, the salty spray an invigorating counterpoint to the dry heat.

Here, it's gray. Cold.

If only I'd made friends with Tommy, at least I could take the trails without getting lost. The forest was a lot more interesting than this endless backcountry road. Plus, it was nice to run with someone, even someone as quiet and awkward as him.

My cheeks heat as I remember waiting at the trailhead for him to show, the mix of relief and disappointment when he didn't. I can't believe I let my suspicions leak out and tarnish a perfectly normal interaction. I must have seemed so weird to him.

I grumble under my breath and push myself faster, heading down Route 16 toward Clearwater proper. Running usually lifts my mood, but today it's only reminding me of all the reasons I'm annoyed. I'll have a problem on my hands if I alienate Zuri with my bad attitude. I need her chatty and unsuspecting.

Maybe if I focus on my surroundings. The shiny pieces in the asphalt winking in the dim light; the cool air moving in and out of my lungs; my heart pumping in my chest; the trees swaying in the summer breeze.

I concentrate on what I hear. That same breeze, whispering through the branches. Those numbing footfalls, gentle against the pavement. The crack of a twig in the woods.

Rustling.

I skid to a stop.

It sounds like some kind of large animal is moving in the forest that lines the road behind me. An image flashes through my mind: a pamphlet I read at a rest stop, just after crossing the border into New Hampshire. It listed some of the wildlife native to this area. Black bears, bobcats, and coyotes, to name a few.

Chills creep up my spine. Slowly, I turn and scour the underbrush, searching for a hint of fur, a flash of teeth, maybe a pair of sinister eyes. I find nothing in the gloom.

The woods must be getting under my skin. The trees here are so tall, the forest so thick, anything could lurk in there unseen.

Frowning, I turn back around and pick up the pace. Twenty feet along, I hear it again. Rustling in the trees.

I spin and raise my fists.

There's still nothing as far as I can see, but the wind didn't make those noises. Something's stalking me. Something big.

A bear?

I think back to the pamphlet. If you encounter a bear, you're supposed to make yourself appear as large as possible. You're supposed to let it know you're there, and you're not supposed to run away.

"Hey!" I shout, waving my arms over my head. "Hey, bear! Get outta here! Go home! Shoo!"

Silence.

I stoop down, grab a rock from the road's edge, and hurl it into the underbrush.

Nothing happens.

An animal would've reacted to the stone, no question.

Could a different kind of predator be following me?

A human predator?

My throat tightens. Once again, I've left my phone at home. Dad would be so upset if he knew.

Deep breaths. You've got this.

I turn around and start walking, listening so hard I think my head might burst. I'm not sure where I should go, what I should do. Young female runners are assaulted all the time. Out here, even on the road, it's empty. There's no one around to hear me scream.

But if I go home, they'll know where I live. Alone.

My breath quickens. Where else? Levett Tech is twenty miles away. If I've got a malicious stalker, I might not make it that far. Town is closer, but still a good distance. I don't know any of my neighbors so I can't ask them for help.

Wait. Not true.

Tommy's manor. That place is so big, he must live with someone. His parents. If he's at work, they'll help me.

I don't have anywhere else to go.

Without thinking it through further, I bolt.

THE charming stone house is enormous. It's intimidating to approach, especially red-faced and sweaty. Though I listen as hard as I can, I don't hear anything behind me as I climb the winding drive.

At the double front doors, I hesitate, a wave of prickling self-consciousness washing over me. So I heard a few sounds in the woods. Big deal. I dawdled in the street long enough, totally alone, and no one hurt me.

I almost turn around and leave, but I can't. I just can't.

Raising my fist, I knock. Footsteps approach, and the door cracks open, revealing a drowsy woman clad in a bathrobe. She's older than me, but nowhere near old enough to be Tommy's mom.

Maybe she's his sister? It's weird, she doesn't look anything like him.

"Can I help you?"

"I'm sorry to bother you, but is Tommy here?"

The woman's expression is blank. "Who?"

"Tommy. Is he here?" I wring my hands, confused by her reaction.

"I'm sorry, you have the wrong address." She closes the door on me, but I throw a hand out, forcing it back open. She stares.

"Is this a joke?" My stomach churns.

"No one named Tommy lives here," the woman says carefully. "This house has been in my family for a long time. No one named Tommy has ever lived here."

She makes to shut the door again, but panic sears through my chest, and I block her. Her eyes widen, her mouth falling open.

"Please. I think I'm being followed. Can I use your phone?"

The woman blinks, then pulls a cell phone from her fluffy pocket. She holds it out. "Be quick, and don't try anything funny. My husband's a lawyer. He'll make you regret it."

I bite my lip. "Um, actually, can you just call me an Uber or something? I can pay you back."

With a roll of her eyes, the woman unlocks her phone and starts typing. "Don't worry about the money. You can wait out here, and I'll wait with you. Okay?"

"Thank you." I wipe my shaking hands on my shorts and step aside to make room for her.

Ten awkward, silent minutes later, the Uber arrives. I climb in, too absorbed in my thoughts to notice who my driver is or what's on the radio. I try to focus on the news report—something about a missing shipment of something from somewhere, and then a commercial for a local music festival—but my mind keeps going back to Tommy. Why did he lie about where he lives? About his job?

I can only think of one reason. I was right after all.

But if I was right, why blow me off yesterday? Why not get close, make friends, to find me out? I haven't seen any trace of him at work.

When I get home, I sprint for the safety of the condo, the creepy feeling of eyes boring into my back the whole way up the walk. Once inside, I lock the door and all the windows. I'm left feeling vulnerable, and more alone than ever.

I briefly consider calling the cops, but what will I tell them?

Hello officer, Melanie Snow—er, O'Hanlon—here. I think I may have been followed, but I'm perfectly fine and have no proof at all. Also, some guy I met in the woods doesn't live where he said he does.

I snort. No, I can't call the police. What a colossal waste of their time.

I'm edgy as I get ready for the day, jumping at every little noise. When I walk to my car, I scan the trees, looking for a stalker. Or for Tommy. No sign.

At work, I relax a bit. No one will be able to bother me in a place this secure, not even Levett Tech themselves, right? I try to focus on Zuri and my training, but my mind is wrapped up in the mystery of Tommy.

What, exactly, is he hiding?

CHAPTER SIX

TOMMY

THE cool glass of the passenger-door window against my temple is uncomfortable enough to keep me from drifting off, even with my head full of fuzz from my sleepless night. The silent game I'm playing helps too. It's something Dad used to do with me on long drives. Find things along the road that start with each letter of the alphabet first, and you win.

I've gone through the whole game twice, but I keep at it. I don't want to let myself think about Mel, about how vibrant she is, about what might be happening to her, even now.

"What's up with you today?"

Cait glances at me, then stares out the windshield at the rain-washed highway, one hand loose on the wheel. Usually when the two of us make a supply run together, we talk for hours.

Not this time. After I ignored her cheerful hello this morning, we spent all day in increasingly prickly silence. Why at five-thirty in the afternoon does she suddenly want to chat?

I'm pissed about what happened last night, about her betrayal, but I'm too ashamed to confront her now. She was right all along. So, I give her a noncommittal shrug.

She tilts her head. "You don't look too good."

"Gee, thanks. That makes me feel much better."

I can tell by her expression she wants to dig into what's bothering me. She's going to dig in, whether I like it or not.

"Tommy—"

"I don't want to talk about it."

"Too bad. You won't feel better 'til you do, so spit it out."

Cait never puts up with my crap. I huff a humorless laugh. "Fine. I know you told Lisa I helped that girl the other day. You promised not to rat."

Rain drums on the roof of the car as Cait's mouth thins, her eyes darting to me and away. "I'm sorry. Really. But I couldn't shake the feeling I was making a huge mistake by keeping it to myself. Lisa needed to know."

Annoyance stabs through me. "You promised."

"I know. But isn't it strange the girl was close enough to the caves to cross your patrol route? Runners and hikers hardly ever get that far out, and the ones who do have enough experience not to get lost. What if … What if she was looking for us?"

I snort. "You worry too much. You'll be gray by twenty-five."

"And you aren't careful enough. Anyway, I know the girl is Reyna and Max Snow's daughter. Is that why you helped her?"

I look out at the storm, torn between aggravation and embarrassment. Lisa must have filled Cait in. I wish she hadn't. Who else knows how badly I screwed up? That I put us all at risk?

"No. I … I felt bad, that's all."

"You *felt bad?*"

My cheeks burn. "You didn't see her. She was scared."

"I know you feel guilty about what happened to her parents, but you can't let that fuck with your judgment. What if she works for the Organization?"

"I didn't know who she was," I snap, the words sour in my mouth. "She doesn't work for the Organization, regardless. They're tailing her. They wouldn't follow their own."

I sigh. "That's another thing. She's in danger and we're supposed to do nothing? Sit on our hands and wait for her to get hurt? We have weapons, knowledge, each other, and she's alone. Lisa won't help. How is that fair?"

"Come on, Tommy. What do you expect us to do? I feel bad for the girl, yeah, but we have rules for a reason."

"You sound exactly like Lisa."

"Well, it's true."

I glare at her. "You really think the Organization will let Mel skip off into the sunset when she's been poking around Levett's confidential files?"

Cait nods, emphatic. "Yes, I do. She won't find anything, and they don't want another death drawing attention. You remember what happened last time. Lots of negative press."

She's referring to the cover story the Organization put out to explain my parents' murder. It was all over the news—four people killed in a tragic accident in Levett's R&D lab, the only culprits being neglected gas line maintenance and outdated safety equipment.

I'm appalled Cait'd bring the subject up, especially to scold me. She's the only person I've confided in about what I saw that night, and she knows how messed up I am over it.

"Oh yes," I say scathingly, "of course. Negative press. That's what I remember about last time."

She has the decency to look abashed. "Tommy, I'm sorry."

"Save it. What if it was you who saw your parents tortured to death? It was savage. How would you like it if I made offhand comments about something so grisly?"

Stricken, she holds up a hand, palm out. "I know. I'm sorry. I shouldn't have said it like that. I just meant—"

The floodgates are open now. I talk over her, not interested in her apology. "And it wasn't only my parents. It was Mel's parents too. Four people pummeled to death while I hid and did nothing. And now I'm supposed to do nothing again. How is that right?"

Cait peeks sideways at me, eyes full of sympathy. "You were fifteen! What could you have done? They'd have killed you too."

I don't try to disguise the regret burning in my expression.

We both fall quiet. Flipping on the turn signal, Cait takes the next exit. It's not ours, but I'm too lost in ugly memories to ask where she's going. Or to care.

She turns down a side street, then another, and pulls over onto the shoulder of a narrow, empty road. She cuts the engine.

I stare at my knees, jaw locked tight, while the downpour thunders around us. After a minute, Cait reaches over to rest her fingers under my chin. She nudges up, and I'm forced to meet her gaze. The muted light of the storm brings out the silver in her eyes. They shimmer, wet with unshed tears.

My heart squeezes, and I cover her small hand with mine. My pain hurts her. It always has. I wish I could make her feel better, make us both feel better, but I don't know how.

She opens her mouth, hesitates, then says, "Your parents wouldn't have wanted you to suffer like this."

"They wouldn't have wanted to be dead, Cait."

A tear slides down Cait's freckled cheek. I drop my eyes. "Mel's parents wouldn't have wanted to be dead either. Maybe a fifteen-year-old couldn't have made a difference, maybe he could have. I'll never know."

Lie. I know all too well.

"What I can do is make a difference now. Mel's on track to meet the same fate." I look back up. "I could stop it this time, but I'm not allowed to act. Do you know what that feels like? The weight of it, of letting it happen again…"

The words get stuck, blazing in my throat. I turn and stare out at the cold drizzle, hands clenched in my lap.

Gentle fingers brush my shoulder. "I know it's sad. I can't imagine how you must feel, but she's one girl. If you see her again, even just to warn her, you'll put twenty-seven other lives at risk, not to mention the people we protect."

She pauses, rubbing circles into my tense shoulder. I lean into her touch, comforted by her care, even as her words prick at my guilt.

"Sacrifice is part of life in the Resistance," she goes on. "Hard choices must be made. Think how many more innocents would be killed every year if we didn't stop what weapons we could from falling into the wrong hands. If her life is the price that must be paid so we're able to continue our mission, well…"

Something Mom used to say pops into my head.

Remember, Tommy. You may not be able to change the world, but if you can touch the life of one person, you have made all the difference.

For a fleeting moment, I see myself acting to save Mel. A wave of exhilaration burns through me as Cait's hand vanishes from my shoulder.

"Tommy?"

"Yeah?"

My voice is thick. I swipe my knuckles under my eyes.

"I know this is a horrible thing to say, but she's one girl among millions." Cait's words are soft. Soothing. "Her life isn't worth endangering who knows how many others."

Revulsion twists my gut. Mel is a human being. How can Cait devalue her like that? How can I?

Suddenly, my decision is easy.

I will not let Mel suffer. Not when I can stop it.

Excitement blazes in my chest, races like adrenaline through my blood. I'm going to save Mel. I'm going to do something good, something to atone for my past, something that will make all these years trapped underground worth it and give this half-life meaning.

Mel will be safe if she runs. The Organization won't take her in, not if she leaves now and never comes back. I'll incapacitate her tail, tell her to skip town, and slip away before they realize I'm there. My family will remain secure. No harm done.

Cait's gentle voice breaks into my scheming. "What are you thinking about?"

There's no way I can tell her. Cait has a good heart, but she's the product of her environment. Raised by an ex-Navy SEAL determined to forge her into a weapon, sharp and efficient and brutal. A blade for the Resistance.

I can't trust her not to go to Lisa.

"It's hard," I say, twisting my bracelet around my wrist. "Letting this unfold. Doing nothing."

When I turn to face her, my expression is blank. It feels strange, deceiving Cait. I've only ever lied to her about one thing.

She gives me a small, sad smile. "I know. But you're making the right choice."

The right choice, indeed. I close my eyes, leaning my seat back and pulling the hood of my sweatshirt up over my head. "Just get us home, okay? It's been a long day. I want to be alone."

CHAPTER SEVEN

MEL

At the end of my shift, I climb into my car, exhausted. If I'm being honest, I didn't pay a lick of attention to Zuri today. Between hunting for clues about Mom and Dad and searching the campus for Tommy, I just couldn't.

I can't fathom why he would lie about where he lives and works unless he's in league with Levett Tech, but if he is, why has he evaporated off the face of the earth? It doesn't make sense, no matter how I analyze it.

When I park at my condo, I cut the engine and stare out the windshield, keys splayed in my fist to use as a weapon. I can't hear anything over the heavy rush of rain, and visibility is terrible. Anyone could sneak up on me in this weather.

With a glance toward the misty woods, I grit my teeth, jump out of the car, and sprint up the path. The light *click* of my front door's single lock does little to calm my nerves. I should install something better. A deadbolt.

I spend ten minutes researching, then order one off Amazon, but I'm still too wound up to relax. So, I whirl through the tiny condo like a hurricane, cleaning surfaces that haven't had time to get dirty yet. When there's nothing left to scrub, I take a scalding shower.

By the time I get out, night's fallen. I pull on my comfiest pajamas, don Mom's fluffy pink slippers, and make a steaming mug of tea.

It's time to get to the bottom of this.

Perched at the miniscule breakfast bar, I fire up my laptop and type *Clearwater NH Tommy* into the search field. Maybe a peek at his social media will give me a clue as to whether he works for Levett. If Tommy's even his real name.

Plenty of results appear, but nothing helpful. Most relate to a local Tommy Hilfiger store.

I delete the search and try *Thomas in Clearwater NH*.

This time, several news articles pop up. The first headline reads: police hunt for suspect in stabbing, burglary

My heart jumps into my mouth. Stabbing? This can't be right.

I click the link anyway. A large photo loads at the head of the article.

It's him.

But also, it's not. This Tommy is younger, and the difference in his demeanor is shocking. He's smiling brightly at the camera, green eyes warm and happy. Carefree.

Scrolling down, I skim through the article. Belinda Stokes, a grandmother living alone, was brutally stabbed to death—*to death*—in her own kitchen.

Bile stings the back of my throat.

Murder.

Thomas Williams was identified by several eyewitnesses running from the scene, after which he vanished without a trace. He's the only potential suspect, and he's still on the run. Wanted.

My stomach turns as I scroll back up, examining Tommy's picture again. That sweet kid killed somebody?

This is why he seemed off. So much darker, moodier than his old picture suggests. He was being evasive.

Murderer.

Abruptly, I'm terrified. Is he an assassin? Am I his mark?

My palms tingle.

Calm down. Check facts. Make sure.

After several deep, steadying breaths, I close the article. It could be outdated. The next one might say the real murderer was caught, proving Tommy's innocence. Mouth full of cotton, I click the second headline.

It's more of the same. So is the next, and the next.

Fifteen-year-old Thomas Williams wanted for murder

Grisly stabbing results in death for Clearwater, NH grandmother

No new leads in Belinda Stokes murder case

Thomas Williams vanishes after horrific slaying

Several sharp taps ring out over the thrum of rain on the roof, and I nearly jump out of my skin. Someone's at the door.

I don't know anyone here.

"Mel! Open up!"

It's Tommy's voice, rough and insistent. Jagged shards of fear wrap around my heart and coil in my stomach.

I stumble off my stool and back into the kitchen, away from the sound. I don't know what to do, how to fight. For the first time in my life, I'm seized by an intense desire for a weapon, something to defend myself with. My hands feel cold, weak, and empty. I think I might be sick.

Tommy pounds on the door. "Come on! I know you're in there. Please. It's very important."

For a brief moment, I consider calling the cops. But before I can do more than scan the room for my phone, there's a series of jiggling noises and that damn cheap lock clicks. I stagger back another step, my gaze hyper-focused as the doorknob, that traitorous doorknob, turns.

The door swings in, and I catch sight of Tommy standing on the stoop, engulfed in sheeting rain. He's wearing a tank top, fatigues, and combat boots, all black. A gun hangs from his hip.

As my eyes fall on the weapon, a bolt of razor-sharp dread lances through my chest.

Without a word, Tommy stalks into my home, closing the door behind him. His hair, darkened by the rain, drips into his eyes and the sodden tank top clings to his damp skin. I can see every hard line of his stomach, every sculpted muscle in his shoulders and arms.

He's built to kill.

With a step toward me, he says, "We need to talk."

"Get away from me!" I rasp, fighting the swell of icy fear rising in my chest. My back hits the fridge, and I raise my fists to my face. "Get out!"

"Shhh, it's okay, I promise," Tommy soothes, palms forward, lovely eyes wary.

My skin prickles. The knives are in their drawer. Too close to him. I can't reach.

"I'm sorry I broke in, but I don't have long, and this is life or death. I need to tell you something important. I need you to pay attention. Can you do that?"

Panic whines in my ears. My limbs lock up.

Tommy's expression softens. He takes another step and I lunge sideways, a scream punching up my throat. He backtracks, hands up by those carved shoulders, as I cower in the farthest corner of the kitchen against the cabinets. With deliberate care, he pulls a second gun from his waistband, sets it on the floor, and kicks it toward me.

"This okay? Now we're even."

He frowns and drops onto one of the stools by the breakfast bar. My computer is right there, a headline accusing him of murder clear to see, but he hasn't noticed it.

I don't take my eyes off him as I scoop the weapon up and weigh it in my hands. It's heavy, the cold metal unforgiving. He must see I wouldn't know how to use it if I tried.

Still, I aim it at his heart. My hands shake. "Get out."

He quirks a brow, his eyes shining, and slides off the stool. Beelines straight for me.

I press back into the counter, the gun slippery in my grip. My stomach pitches and my finger jerks on the trigger as he stops directly in front of me.

The barrel digs into his firm chest. Nothing else happens.

Tommy smirks. Flicks a switch on the side of the handle. "Might work better if you took off the safety."

I stare, mouth dry and heart hammering.

What. The. Fuck.

Is he serious? I just tried to kill him.

I tried to kill a living, breathing person.

"I need you to hear me. Are you listening?"

I could shoot him right now. I have the gun. The safety's off.

But if he wanted to hurt me, he wouldn't help me defend myself. So why is he here? What could he have to say?

I squeeze my eyes shut and swallow. After a moment, I lower the gun and nod.

"You. Are. In. Danger." Tommy enunciates each word. "Someone has been following you since yesterday afternoon. But that's not..." He takes a deep breath, brow furrowed, and glances at his watch. "I need you to get somewhere safe, now, but I can't help you after I leave here."

"You're not making any sense."

"Just listen and you'll understand." Tommy's words are clipped, urgent. He takes another breath. "I'm not who you think I am."

I already know this, but my skin crawls anyway. I'm afraid of what I'm about to hear.

Tommy's hand goes to that twine bracelet on his wrist. A nervous tic?

"My name is Thomas Williams. I belong to a secret society dedicated to protecting others from a dangerous homegrown terrorist organization. That organization infiltrated Levett Tech years ago and now flourishes within the company, undiscovered, except by us. They supply Levett weapons to other terrorist groups across the globe, as well as hoard weapons for themselves. They're doing everything they can to grow strong enough to take down not only our government, but our entire way of life."

Tommy leans toward me. "They're everywhere, could be anyone. Your neighbors, your friends. And now you're on their radar. They're coming for you, Mel. They know who you are, and that you snooped through their files yesterday."

Chills race up my spine, raise the hair on my arms.

"I need you to understand you cannot go to anyone about them. They're too powerful, too well connected. They will crush you if you do. Do you understand?"

I grasp the edge of the counter with sweaty palms.

"They've got a tail on you. I drugged him so I could warn you without them knowing, but he'll wake up soon. You need to get far away before that happens. If you don't, there's still a chance they might leave you alone, but it's not a gamble I'd take. They won't let you live if they think you're a threat to their secrecy."

I blink.

"Do you hear me? Do you believe me?"

I always knew there was something off about Levett Tech, about the way they handled my parents' deaths. I *was* followed this morning. I was tailed…

I have so many questions. In spite of myself, I glance at the computer.

Tommy follows the flicker of my eyes.

"What is that about?" I gesture toward the headline. I can't bring myself to be more specific, to form the accusation. Murderer.

"Listen, I know that looks bad, but I didn't kill that woman. I was framed."

He studies me with sad eyes before going on. "After the Organization murdered my parents, the society I live with, the Resistance, found me hiding in the woods. They took me in, and I disappeared from the outside world. The Organization publicized my parents' murder as a workplace accident, but I was a loose end. They couldn't let my disappearance raise suspicion. So, they staged that woman's death and planted eyewitnesses to pin it on me. That way, the police could bring me in for them. They've got plenty of crooked cops on their payroll, not to mention agents undercover in local governments."

It's like a violent ocean is crashing around in my skull, scouring it from the inside. Tommy's parents, Levett Tech, a workplace accident

... murder and framing and ... this is what happened to Mom and Dad. They were murdered by terrorists.

I'm so dizzy. I suck in deep breath after deep breath, filling my lungs to bursting each time. "Your parents were in the Resistance."

Tommy nods, the corners of his mouth turning down. His eyes drop briefly to his watch.

"My parents." My voice is whisper quiet. "They..."

I can't go on.

Tommy takes my clammy hand in his. "I'm sorry you had to find out like this," he says gently. "Your parents were in the Resistance too. They died the same way mine did. But we're running out of time. I have to go, and so do you."

"How? How did they die?" My words have no volume, but Tommy understands. Something closes down behind his eyes.

"The Organization," is all he says.

I don't know I'm crying until Tommy reaches up, tentatively wiping the wet from my cheek with his thumb. Red-hot sparks shimmer over my skin, trail his soft touch. His beautiful eyes, twin green-and-gold flames, burn into mine.

"I can't see you again." The husky note in Tommy's voice sends a thrill shivering through me. "It's too dangerous, for you and for the Resistance. Don't forget, you can't tell anyone about this. You need to get out of here right away. The tail will wake up soon, within an hour at most."

I open my mouth to reply, but he's already striding away, the powerful muscles in his back shifting as he pulls the door open and disappears outside.

Frost creeps into my heart.

They were murdered.

This is so far beyond what I expected.

When I think of tomorrow's shift at Levett Tech, fear grips me by the throat. I can't go back there. Not now. Not ever. I should leave like Tommy told me to.

But my parents were part of this Resistance. Why? How? Did they know something about the Organization that supposedly wants to take down our way of life? Whatever that means.

I need the truth. The whole truth.

I have to find the Resistance.

If I hurry, I can catch Tommy.

I sprint for my room. Dressing in the warmest clothes I can find, I pull my damp hair into a tight braid. Then I dash through the condo, throwing overnight essentials into my old backpack.

Toothbrush, granola bars, a couple sets of clothes, Mara's badge, my notebook. They all go in the bag.

What else?

I glance around one last time, turning the gun Tommy gave me over and over in my hands. Nerves chew through my insides as I shove it barrel-down into the waistband of my jeans, where it bites into my hip.

Suck it up. There's no time to waste.

Pausing to grab a flashlight, I sling the bag over my shoulder and run out into the stormy night.

CHAPTER EIGHT

TOMMY

I GLIDE through the dark, dripping forest, silent as the reaper himself. By this point I've been soaked through for hours on end, but I don't mind. The discomfort helps ward off the heavy exhaustion that's starting to muddle my senses, not to mention the distraction of my uncooperative emotions.

Against the odds, I managed to warn Mel and get away before her tail woke up. All I have to do now is sneak back into the caves and I'm in the clear.

I thought I'd be thrilled if I managed to get this far. Instead, I'm sad. Unnerved by the feeling that surged through me just before I left Mel's place.

Ever since I laid eyes on her, Mel's pull has hovered at the edges of my awareness. Even now, when I should be concentrating on what I'm doing, her face floats in my mind. Tears glitter like crystals in her thick lashes. And that mouth…

With a sigh, I shove the image away. Yes, she's gorgeous, but her beauty isn't what calls to me so deeply. It's the raw hurt that lies like a wound just under her surface, invisible to most, but not to me. No one has ever understood my grief. Cait tries, but even she can't relate. Her parents are alive.

Mel understands.

I wish I could be allowed to know her.

A sharp *crack* cleaves the night, and I freeze.

Fuck. Did I really step on a twig?

Stupid, dangerous, rookie mistake. It's too dark to see, but I could find my way with no problem if I were paying attention. I'm adept at using other senses to navigate, particularly my hearing. It's a vital skill for those of us who run missions to have, and I've honed it well.

There's no excuse, none at all, for me to exhibit such poor stealth. Stepping on a twig. Seriously?

My face heats when I imagine the ribbing Vik and Hunter would throw at me, the way Sam would smirk and Cait would rake me over the coals if they knew about my carelessness. Good thing I'm alone.

Using my hands, I scale the steep earth toward the main entrance to the caves, concealed within a heap of boulders like our exit at the summit. Each second pulses through me as I get close. If I don't make it back before Bill and Jess take over guard duty at midnight, I'm screwed.

No one else will care I've been out, but Cait's parents will worry. They'll wonder why I'm roaming the forest alone in the middle of the night, especially in this weather. They'll tell Cait, who will know exactly what I was doing. And then Cait will tell Lisa.

I don't have a better way in, though. I could climb the treacherous cliffs that lead to the summit—natural guards that protect our hidden back door. If I made it to the top, I'd be able to slip through undetected, but it's not an ascent I'd want to attempt even in the best conditions. In this weather, I'd fall to my death. And the garage isn't an option either. It's inaccessible from the outside without a remote.

When I reach the right spot, I drop to my knees in the mud. My heart pounds as I pull myself down a short stone tunnel and into a small, irregular cavern, so cramped I can't stand. No matter how many times I've done this, the tiny antechamber never fails to spike my anxiety. There's no room in here. No air.

Eager to escape, I knock on the farthest wall, which isn't rough like the others but cool, slick, and smooth as glass. Three taps, pause, two, pause, and two more. In response, the polished granite glides down, disappearing into the floor with hardly a sound. The domed ceiling of one of the gritty cave tunnels is revealed, flickering with golden light, nothing else visible thanks to the seven-foot drop into the caves. After hours in the black woods, the soft glow dazzles my eyes.

As I swing my legs over the edge, I pray Bill and Jess aren't waiting down there.

The fall is considerable, but it's easy to land lightly on the balls of my feet. My heart sinks.

"Tommy!" Jess's eyebrows pull together over concerned silver eyes. Cait's eyes. "What are you doing out so late?"

Despite my predicament, a drop of warmth slips into my chest, chasing away the chill of the storm. The way the Accettas are looking at me reminds me of my parents.

They care. I just have to lean into my demons and they won't think twice about this.

"Hi, Jess, Bill." My fingers brush the twine on my wrist. "Rough night. Couldn't sleep, needed to clear my head. Getting out of the caves helps." I shrug.

Jess rests a warm palm on my shoulder. "In this weather? Tommy, are you all right? Cait says you've been having a hard time. The nightmares are getting worse."

I run a hand over my face. The way Cait and her mom gossip, it's like they're a couple of mall-obsessed middle schoolers. Is nothing private anymore?

"I'm fine." Cait may have unwittingly helped confirm my cover story, but it's hard to keep the bite out of my tone. "Don't worry. I'm going to clean up. See you later, okay?"

"All right, hon." Jess glances toward her husband.

"Let us know if you need anything," Bill calls as I walk away. I wave in acknowledgment, water dripping from my hair, my clothes, leaving a dark trail on the stone floor behind me.

Once I'm out of the Accettas' sight, my mind goes straight back to Mel. If Bill and Jess are on duty, it must be after midnight, which means her tail has been awake for a while. By now, she either got away or she didn't.

By the time I arrive at my room, my stomach's more knotted than one of Vik's homemade friendship bracelets. I pull the door open and, for the second time in an hour, freeze.

Shit.

Cait. Sitting in the center of my bed.

"Cait," I say warily, closing the door behind me.

She slides off the bed and stalks toward me, expression murderous. "I can't believe you. I just can't believe you. You put all our lives at risk. Again."

I cross my arms and press my lips together. "I don't know what you're talking about."

Cait stops mid-stride, her vicious gaze narrow. Fury rolls off her in toxic waves. "You want to talk about liars, Williams? At least my lie was for the greater good. You lied to me. Then you ran off and risked all our lives."

Nothing I say or do will convince her she's wrong. She knows me too well.

I reach toward her. "I'm sorry. I know I'm a hypocrite, but I did it, Cait. I saved Mel. And I was careful. I surveyed the woods around me the whole way home. I wasn't followed."

My stomach twists as I remember that twig snapping beneath my boot. I made one mistake. What if…

Cait crosses the distance between us, coming close enough for me to feel the heat washing off her skin. For a moment, I think she's going to hit me.

Taking a step back, I put my hands up by my shoulders, palms forward. "I know how to be careful. You know that. Shhh. Calm down."

"Don't you tell me to calm down!"

She throws her hands in the air, then turns and stomps away. "You need to tell Lisa what you did. Right now. Even if you weren't followed, you talked to that girl. What did you tell her? Who does she think you are?"

No one on the outside knows about our existence, save for a couple choice contacts of Lisa's: powerful politicians who help fund our efforts, procure supplies, provide false permits, and the like. I don't think Mel would spill the beans, but I don't really know her. If the Organization questions her… It's a risk I gambled on to keep her safe, for Reyna and Max's sake. God knows I owe them that much.

I squirm, hand going to my bracelet.

Cait tilts her head, studying my reaction. Horror dawns in her gray eyes. "Don't tell me you told her about the Resistance?"

I frown, and she pounces. "Tommy, how could you?"

Burning with the fury of a thousand suns, she strides up to me again and pokes me in the solar plexus. "You tell Lisa what you did, right now, or I will."

I purse my lips, gazing down into Cait's livid face. She's right. But, even knowing I should, I don't want to listen to her now.

Lisa won't feel safe leaving Mel out there with the knowledge I've given her. I know Lisa would never take an innocent life, but she would certainly imprison one.

I'd give almost anything for my freedom. I can't let Mel's be stolen from her, especially because of a choice I made.

Cait can tell what I'm thinking.

"Fine." Mouth hard, she marches around me.

"Wait!" I lunge for her.

She jerks out of my way but pauses.

"Let's think this through. Please."

A scowl crosses her face. I take her cold hand. "Listen. Mel doesn't know enough to be a threat. Even if she were caught and interrogated."

I swallow. The thought of Mel suffering in the hands of the Organization is intolerable.

To my surprise, Cait's fierce eyes soften. "You don't know that. Unless you told her nothing, she holds clues for them. You're not qualified to decide what happens next. Lisa needs to hear about this."

When she puts it like that…

My first duty is to the Resistance. I've done what I can for Mel. With any luck, she's already gone, somewhere neither Lisa nor the Organization will find her.

With a heavy sigh, I nod. Cait gives my hand a reassuring squeeze and leads me from the room.

Half an hour later, I fall into bed. It's been almost thirty-six hours since I last slept, and I can't muster the energy to wash up, to do more than peel off my muddy clothes and pray for a dreamless sleep.

As I drift in the space between awareness and oblivion, Lisa's words run through my mind again. They sting twice as much as they did the first time I heard them, minutes ago.

"You're disobeying orders, sneaking around. If I can't trust you, how can I send you on missions? How can I let you leave the caves?"

"You've created a serious threat to our security. Do you not know what you've done?"

"They'll be aware now something's not right around her; they'll be more suspicious than before. You've put her in greater danger than ever."

I pleaded for Mel's freedom. I begged Lisa to let her run, not to steal her life away. To my astonishment, Lisa agreed.

"I'll do it for Reyna," she said. "Not for you. Reyna didn't want her daughter within a hundred miles of the Resistance. I owe her this much."

Then she sent Cait to check on Mel, to make sure she left town. If she wasn't gone, Cait needed to report back at once.

But why? What will Lisa do if Mel's still there? I groan, tossing and turning. When sleep finally takes me, I'm not lucky enough to rest in peace.

Instead, I stand alone on a rocky precipice, overlooking a violent black sea. The dark waves heave and froth, whipped about by a ferocious storm. Over and over, Mel calls my name from somewhere in the water, desperate. I search for her with increasing urgency but can't find her among the waves. I reach out anyway, hoping to pull her from the wild surf. By the time I realize I've pushed her under, it's too late. There's only silence.

CHAPTER NINE

MEL

SIGH as I walk, my insides gloomier than the chilly mist that swirls over my cheeks and clings to my hair. I've been out here long enough for the rain-washed night to fade into a drizzly gray morning, yet I'm no closer to finding the Resistance than I was back in my warm, dry kitchen.

It's all the same. Trees, trees, and more trees. I don't know why I thought this was a good idea. I'll never find Tommy. I'll probably never find my way home again, either.

I lurch to a halt, wiping my face with the back of my hand. The rain pings loudly on the leaves above.

If I could just get some quiet, a moment to concentrate, to plan my next—

Bang!

I drop into the underbrush, my throat-shredding scream muted, distant in my ringing ears. Terror buzzes like a swarm of bees in my brain.

That was a gunshot.

My tail must be here.

I peer through the shifting mist, heart crashing against my ribs. A flicker of movement catches my attention.

Only yards away, a slender girl about my age is examining

61

something obscured in the underbrush. She's gripping a gun tightly with both hands, arms stiff. A wicked-looking dagger glints at her thigh.

Weapon pointed into the ferns, the girl prods at the thing with her toe. Without warning, she fires again.

The thing on the ground—a *body*, I realize with horror—jerks, and I throw myself back through the brambles.

Someone's dead.

The girl glances my way. She's shorter than I am, small and thin, with long blond hair and a smattering of golden freckles sprinkled over her nose and cheeks. She looks innocent. I almost can't believe she's my tail, that someone my age could be Organization.

But she just killed someone.

No, not someone. Tommy. Who else would be way out here in this weather?

My head throbs and my eyes sting as she chews her lip, her gaze fixed on my face, the gun still pointed at the body. At Tommy.

My fault.

I was being watched. I followed him out here anyway. I led the Organization straight to him.

A hot wave of sickness engulfs me, sharpens into a terror so powerful it hurts. Tommy's dead. If I don't do something now, so am I.

Forcing down the guilt, the impending hysteria, I jump to my feet and rip Tommy's gun from my waistband. "Stop right there!"

The command rings hollow, even to me. The gun wobbles in my slick, shaky hands.

With her weapon trained on my forehead, the girl drops into a lethal-looking crouch. "Put your hands up!"

Her voice is like a frigid stream of water. Smooth and cold as ice. "Drop the gun. Don't move. Don't speak."

I won't win a shootout, so I reach up, Tommy's gun limp in my hand.

Her lip curls. "I said, drop the gun."

It's clear as crystal in those hard eyes. One wrong move and I'm dead. So the question becomes this: which is better, dying now, or letting the Organization have me?

Nausea swirls in my stomach. Death by bullet would be kinder than interrogation by terrorists, but maybe I can still get out of this. Dad always said, if an attacker ever tries to hurt you, fight back. Make noise. Don't let them get you.

I won't let them get me, Dad.

Slow and steady, I toss Tommy's gun into the dripping ferns. Without lowering her weapon, the girl gets to her feet and stalks through the underbrush to retrieve it.

I don't have a prayer of overpowering her, but I'm good with words. They're my best defense now.

"I know who you are."

"Shut up."

I clear my throat, throw some steel into my tone. "I'll run away. I won't tell anyone about this. I won't come back. I swear."

My stomach turns to lead as the words leave my lips. I'm pleading with Tommy's murderer, promising to keep his death quiet to save myself. How gross.

But if it means I can live, I'll do it.

The girl tucks Tommy's gun into her waistband, her own weapon still trained between my eyes. "I thought I told you to shut up."

"I mean it."

Suddenly she's in my face, her silver eyes fierce. The barrel of her gun presses into my temple. "Shut. Up."

A small, terrified whimper breaks through my self-control.

"No talking," the girl snaps.

She twists my arms behind my back and binds my wrists together with a length of scratchy rope. Then she pulls a wad of thick black cloth from her pocket. Pressing it over my eyes, she yanks it tight and secures it behind my head.

I can't see a thing.

Cold fingers grip my elbows. "Walk."

TIME leaps and drags. I trip blindly through the wet forest, my thoughts a riot of guilt and panic, the girl and her gun at my back.

I killed Tommy. I may not have pulled the trigger, but he is dead because of choices I made.

Worse, he died trying to save my life, and look how I repaid him. I'm fodder in the Organization's hands. They must think I know something, or I'd be dead too.

If I pretend to have information, maybe they'll keep me alive long enough for me to escape. Even a few extra hours could make a difference.

Without warning, the girl shoves me down into the muck. I bite back a yelp.

"There's a tunnel in front of you. Crawl in."

I lean back, scraping my boots over what feels like a jumble of boulders. Where are we going? A cave? An underground lair?

When I find the opening, I pause.

This is it. Once I go in, I'll probably never come back out.

The girl jabs me between the shoulders with her gun, and I shimmy forward, feet first. A thin hand pushes my head down as she crams in after me.

Abrasive stone scrapes my exposed skin on all sides. It's tiny in here. My shoes hit a dead end. I'm crunched into a ball, the girl tight against my back.

I start to gasp, fear squeezing my heart, pumping it faster.

Focus. Breathe.

The girl's warm breath hits my cheek as she taps the wall next to my face. It sounds like a pattern. A code?

My boots tug down. The wall. It's moving! Sinking!

As it disappears, my legs spring free of their cramped position. They're left dangling, like I'm a child in an adult-sized chair. Air rasps up and down my throat.

"There will be a drop. Scoot down, or I'll push you."

I perch on the edge, afraid. What's waiting down there? How far is the drop? This must be a secret Organization lair.

"I can't see."

"I don't care. Do it." Hard metal pokes into my back. Trembling, I scoot toward the void.

My stomach jolts when I topple over, my loud scream echoing around me. I crash heavily to my knees. Ow.

Large, calloused hands close around my upper arms, and I'm hauled to my feet, frantic heart a drum in my chest.

"Cait!"

A woman's voice, inches to the left. She's not the one gripping me.

"Mom!" I didn't hear the girl—Cait, I guess—land, but she's here now. "We need to get Lisa. Right away."

"Go." A man this time. He's the one bruising my biceps. His curtness surpasses even that of the girl. Of Cait. "She'll be in her office. Meet us in the cells."

The cells.

My only desperate hope hinges on them believing I have information, but hideous fear clogs my airway.

They're going to torture me.

I can't do this.

Tears start to spill over. My blindfold is drenched in seconds.

I'm guided down a straight path with a flat, even floor. Through my sobs, I try to catalogue my surroundings, in case I get a chance to bolt. The air is cool and still. It smells … earthy.

We bear left, then turn a corner in the same direction. About thirty feet along, my captors halt. A metallic scraping reaches my ears. A key in a lock.

A cell.

I'm marched to the right, presumably through a door, and forced onto a hard wooden chair. I struggle against my restraints, panic searing through my chest.

Gentle fingers tug at the knot on my blindfold. As the wet cloth falls away, I glance around, blinking in the dim light.

What I see is not encouraging.

Chapter Ten

MEL

I'M at the center of a small, empty room, unlike any I've been in before. The walls and ceiling are striated rock. Lanterns hang on iron spikes, washing the cell in warm yellow light. The stone floor is smooth. Unnaturally so. There's only one way out: a heavy metal door, currently closed. There are no windows.

It reminds me of a dungeon.

My middle-aged captors watch in silence from either side of the exit. There are two of them, a man and a woman. The man looks like a soldier, an impression reinforced by the stern twist of his face, not to mention the bulk of his arms.

An enforcer. Someone who knows how to break people.

The woman's face is kinder. Something about her expression, the way she avoids my gaze, makes my breath catch.

She looks guilty.

I try to catch her eye as footsteps approach outside. She meets my stare for a second, then drops her attention to her boots.

The thick door swings forward, revealing Cait and a brown-skinned woman with round, wire-rimmed glasses, soft curves, and a cloud of curly black hair. She looks like a teacher, or possibly a librarian. Not a terrorist.

Strange. These people aren't what I expected from the Organization. Well, except for the enforcer with the bazooka arms.

The new woman's jaw drops. She turns to Cait, dark eyes ablaze. "What have you done?"

"I didn't have a choice."

"There is always a choice."

The woman prods Cait into my cell, pulling the door closed behind them.

"No, Lisa, there isn't." Cait crosses her arms, the picture of defiance.

She looks tough, sure, but I'm impressed she doesn't take a step back. Lisa projects an aura of power that makes her wrath feel especially dangerous.

"Explain."

My thoughts tangle in confusion. The way they're talking doesn't make sense. It's like I'm not supposed to be here.

Bewildered, I watch in silence.

"I went to check on her, like you asked. She was gone by the time I got to her place, so I broke in and looked around. No sign of a struggle, but it was clear she left in a hurry. At first, I thought she skipped town."

Cait throws me a hard glance. "That would've been the smart thing to do. But as I was leaving, I noticed her purse hanging by the door. I went through it. Everything was there: IDs, credit cards, car keys, phone. Obviously she hadn't left town, so I wondered whether the Organization had taken her."

I shift in my chair. Aren't these people from the Organization? I open my mouth to ask, but a glare from the enforcer has me snapping it shut again.

Cait's still talking. "I checked the area around the condo for clues, which wasn't easy in the rain, let me tell you. She'd gone into the woods, alone. I tracked her in. I kept off the trail, and good thing I did, because I found another person following her too. By the time I caught up to them, they were deep in the wilderness. She was hoping to find us, I guess. Why else?"

Lisa's eyes narrow, but Cait keeps going. "I couldn't let the tail go. Mel had given up too much information by trekking out this way. I eliminated him."

She eliminated him. My tail.

Not Tommy.

My chest caves in as she flips her long plait over her shoulder. I'm not responsible for Tommy's death. He's alive.

With a shake of my head, I force myself to focus. I can't afford to miss one second of Cait's story.

"I didn't feel safe reporting back after that. What if the Organization got to Mel while I was gone? Or what if she's a spy? Leaving her, even for a few hours, seemed dangerous."

Cait glances at me again. "On the other hand, she could be innocent. I didn't feel right taking her out. So, here we are."

She shrugs, and my stomach tightens. If these people aren't from the Organization, they must be the Resistance.

A great spark of excitement flares in my chest.

Lisa's dark eyes flash. "Bill. Jess. Please get Tommy."

Tommy! This has to be the Resistance!

The spark explodes, burning away my fear like mist in the sun. I beam through a veil of fresh tears as the guilty woman and the enforcer exit the room.

Lisa and Cait both stare at me.

If this is the Resistance, they won't hurt me. They'll let me go as soon as I convince them I'm not a spy. But before I leave, I need to find out what happened to my parents. They know. They must.

Turning my attention to Lisa, I ask, "Are you with the Resistance?"

Lisa's mouth pulls down on one side. She doesn't answer. Instead, Cait says, "What are we going to do with her now?"

"I won't tell anyone about you," I interject. "I won't ever think of you again. I just wanted—no, needed to find you. I have to know what happened to my parents. Reyna and Max Snow. Did you know them?"

Lisa sighs. She turns to Cait. "I don't know. This is poor repayment for Reyna's sacrifice, no matter what happens now."

A shiver runs through me. "You knew my mother."

I expected as much, but having it confirmed tugs at my heart.

"Yes," Lisa says simply.

"Please. I have to know what happened to her. To them both. I moved here, all the way from California, specifically to find out. I left my friends, my only family, my home… Please."

Lisa shakes her head. "I'm sorry. I can't tell you that."

No way am I giving up so easily.

"I'm not leaving here without answers. If you toss me out, I'll just find you again." I raise my chin, mouth set.

"Oh, you weren't anywhere near us," Cait sneers. "You'll never find us again."

I throw her a frosty glare. "Either way, I don't think you want the Organization watching me search. You're obviously somewhere in the forest, and I know the general direction."

The smirk drops from Cait's face. Her jaw clenches, and she glowers like she wants nothing more than to light me on fire. Turning to Lisa, she says, "How will we get rid of her if she insists on dragging the Organization out here?"

Lisa shakes her head slowly, as if in a daze. "With the death of her tail, they're bound to be suspicious. Even if she leaves town, they'll target her."

I bite my lip. If I want information, I need to offer the Resistance something in exchange. Something they can't refuse. There must be a way I can help them. I've been on-site at Levett Tech, after all.

"I have a solution," I say. "In exchange for information about my parents, I'll help the Resistance. I will do whatever you ask and tell you everything I know about Levett Tech before I sneak out of New Hampshire. Then I'll start over somewhere else and never bother you again."

Lisa's face twists like she swallowed something sour. "That isn't an offer to make lightly. Once you're a part of this, there can be no starting over. You're here for life, or until the Organization falls. You will no longer be able to work. You can't live elsewhere. You can't be seen in public. You must dedicate yourself fully—mind, body, and soul—to our mission. It's the only way to ensure our safety, and yours."

I gape. Either I give up my life on the outside, forever, or I never find out about my parents?

Lisa's expression softens. "It's a lot to lose. Perhaps we can find some way to let you go. I have many connections; we might be able to set you up with a false identity. If you leave now, you can start over somewhere else. Live a normal life."

My gaze wanders. I remember all too clearly the excitement I felt coming to New Hampshire. Starting a real job, getting my own place...

I see myself in a cute little house by the sea with shrubs along the walkway and bright flowers that spill from boxes under the windows. I'm twirling in the whitewashed kitchen with a dark-haired baby on my hip, watched by a handsome man with warm eyes and a kind smile. The man gives me a kiss and scoops the baby into his arms. I laugh as I grab my briefcase and pull on my jacket, ready to head to work, maybe at a literary agency or publisher, or even better, writing my own stories at a cute local coffee shop, my name shooting up the NYT Best Sellers list.

Tears threaten as the vision fades, the colors bleeding away until I'm left in freezing darkness. Empty. Alone, like I have been since my parents died. Even surrounded by people, I'm alone.

This picture is what I wish my life were, not what it is. I have no life, only a barren future to match the past five barren years. I can't move on without knowing the truth.

Mom and Dad wouldn't have died for it unless it was important.

"I will join the Resistance in exchange for information on my parents. I don't care about life on the outside. I want to help."

Lisa's expression darkens. I cringe into my chair.

"You will get no such information unless you earn it. If you prove you're no threat to us, and if you serve us well, maybe then I will consider you a part of this and share some details with you. Maybe."

Chills run over my skin. Lisa doesn't want me here, that much is obvious.

"Cait," Lisa barks, eyes still trained on me. "Please alert the others. I don't want them alarmed to see a new face in the caves."

Cait's staring at Lisa. "But ... you don't mean ... what if..."

"Go."

Without another word, Cait turns on her heel and stomps out. She slams the door behind her.

I'm left pinned in Lisa's livid stare. I want to say something, but my courage has evaporated in the face of her loathing.

"You are not to go outside until you've proven yourself both loyal and capable. You will train on different tasks around the caves until we find what you're best suited to. Here, everyone has a job. You will contribute in whatever way we find most useful."

I want to ask more about the caves, but I bite my tongue. Lisa's revulsion fills me with horror.

This all happened so quickly, and now I'm part of something I know nothing about. A fog of dread descends over me.

What have I gotten myself into?

CHAPTER ELEVEN

TOMMY

I TRAIL Bill and Jess through the caves, my thoughts clouded with exhaustion. Thanks to last night's rescue mission, I slept right through my alarm this morning. Missed my shift on guard duty and was still snoring when Bill shook me awake two minutes ago.

According to him, Lisa needs to see me. Now.

She's going to lose her mind. If only I felt rested, the extra sleep might have been worth it, but I got in so late I only nabbed a few hours. A terrible headache throbs behind my temples.

Bill turns into the lounge, and confusion revives me a bit. If Lisa wanted to eviscerate me for missing my shift, we'd go to her office, not through here. Taking this path, we can only be headed for one of two places: the cells, where we lock anyone who might pose a threat, or the garage, the huge, hidden cavern where we store our vehicles.

Wait.

Mel's tail! Cait must've captured him, and now he's being questioned. Good. We need to know why the Organization has been so active over the last few months. Any small detail could help.

Nervous anticipation hums in my chest, and I step up my pace.

Bill and Jess lead me between the couches and into a long, earthy hall, lit by the standard lanterns. The tunnel is empty, save for three metal doors on our right. The cells.

We stop in front of the third. When Bill pushes it open, shock bolts me to the floor.

Mel.

She's sitting on a simple wooden interrogation chair, arms bound behind her back, leaves and twigs tangled in her disheveled braid. Her muddy clothes are damp, and she's covered in scratches.

Worse than any of that, her eyes are red. Puffy. Tears leak out, cutting clean ivory tracks over her dirty cheeks.

The sight hits me like a blow to the gut.

She's here. Her future is forfeit.

Beside Mel, Lisa glares at me so furiously I stumble back another step. All the usual warmth in her eyes is gone.

"Look what you've done."

Running a hand through my rumpled hair, I force myself to speak. "What … how … but…"

It doesn't make sense. Unless…

Mel must not have run. Cait probably decided she was a security risk. Of course Cait didn't wait, didn't give Mel time to flee before dragging her here and sealing her fate.

Because Mel's life means nothing to Cait. *She's one girl among millions*, after all.

Fury sears through my blood, tingles in my palms.

"Why didn't you leave?" The vicious churning in my stomach edges my tone.

Mel bites her lip, peeking up from under a thick fringe of tear-soaked lashes. Despite the wrath burning my chest, my heart falters. I find I have to look away.

Lisa unfolds her arms, mouth thinner than I've ever seen it.

"Mel's here to stay." Her freezing tone shocks me almost as much as seeing Mel did. I hug my ribs. "She'll need training if she's to be of use. You caused this, you deal with her. I will expect you and Bill in my office at seven tonight to discuss further consequences for your insubordination."

Fuck. If Bill's involved in my punishment, it won't be pleasant.

"And Williams, Mel's not to have access to the outside until I clear it. You better not let her escape."

Without another word, Lisa sweeps from the room, Bill and Jess close behind.

I stare at Mel, battling the overwhelming rage that thrums through me. I can't quite bring myself to believe this is real. I defied orders, risked everything, to give her the chance to run, and here she is, stuck like the rest of us.

Pain stabs behind my eyes. I press the heels of my palms into the ache.

With a deep sigh, I drop my hands and step toward Mel, drawing my knife from my pocket. Carefully, I lean over to slice through the rope that binds her arms and take a step back.

She rubs at her wrists, eyes fixed on the angry welts that mar her light skin. She looks so sad, like a drowned puppy. I crouch in front of her, hoping to put her at ease.

"Where did she find you?" I ask as gently as I can manage. "At home?"

Mel stares at me, the corners of her mouth trembling. Tears slide down her cheeks. "I … I…"

My fury burns hotter, even as my heart twists, and I grind my teeth. Cait will pay for this.

"I tried to follow you," Mel whispers.

My mind goes blank. "What?"

"I went to look for the Resistance. I wanted answers."

My skin turns to ice as her words sink in.

She followed me.

This isn't Cait's fault, not even a little bit. It's all on me.

The awful rage turns inward, and I'm suddenly so disgusted with myself I can't stand it. I launch to my feet, hands fisted by my sides.

"I told you to run. Why didn't you get the hell out?"

Mel flinches, fear stark in her stunning eyes. She tries to speak, her lithe frame shuddering with fresh sobs. "I … I had to find out … what happened to them."

"It's not too late. I'm sure I can convince Lisa to let you go, but you have to get far away from here, immediately. Can you do that?" I shoot her my most withering glare.

Mel's still choking on tears. She jerks her head back and forth.

"You, what? Won't leave?"

"No."

Doesn't she get it? If she stays here, she's as good as a ghost. A phantom doomed to watch life pass her by.

Just like me.

Before I can stop myself, I'm shouting, hurling a mix of dire warnings and furious expletives her way. She has everything I want in her grasp. Freedom and possibilities and life, and she's trashing it all like yesterday's garbage. Why? To reopen old wounds?

The past is gone, as dead as our parents.

She shrinks back in her chair, but the defiance in her eyes only burns brighter.

When I've yelled myself out, Mel stands. She takes a step toward me.

"I will not leave. Lisa said I'm part of the Resistance now. I have just as much of a right to be here as you."

Just as much of a right to be here.

I'd give anything to trade places, to be free. Despair settles like a shadow over my heart. It snuffs out the anger, leaving me rudderless.

"Please?" The word is soft. Fervent.

Mel's eyes tighten. "No."

I sigh.

She's not considering the repercussions of her decision because she doesn't truly understand the cost. Anyone who hasn't lived this life wouldn't get it, not until far too late.

Maybe if I refuse to train her … if she's left alone, isolated, with no opportunity to get the information she seeks and no one to befriend her … maybe then she'll make the right choice. Life here will be so miserable she'll beg Lisa to let her go.

It's a dick move, yeah, but if it saves her…

Mel peers down at her shoes, wringing her filthy hands. This is going to be unbearable. "If you're sure."

She nods.

I want nothing more in this moment than to erase the misery on her face. Instead, I run my eyes critically up and down her ragged form. "I bet you want to clean up."

"Yes, please."

"Okay. I'll get you fresh clothes and take you to the washroom. Be prepared, we don't have hot water here."

Expressionless, I turn and lead Mel out of the cell.

Over the next few hours, I put the beginnings of my plan into action. Once she's clean and dry, I take Mel through the caves, giving only the barest explanation of each room, of each job. I avoid mentioning the library, where we store weapons and classified intel. It's secured anyway, at the end of its own corridor. Locked at all times.

I don't want Mel trying to get in there. If she does, Lisa will never allow her to go free. Not after what happened with June.

Throughout the evening, Mel asks too many questions. I keep my answers short, vague, and cold. I hate to see what I've done, trapping her here, and I channel that revulsion to keep my act believable.

Tour over, I leave Mel in her new room for the night with strict instructions to stay put. Of the twenty-six chambers that line the housing wing, five belong to the dead. There's plenty of space for her.

I make my way across the hall to my own room, mulling over how to move my plan forward from here. Based on Mel's actions during her tour, I know she'll dig for information wherever and whenever she can.

I need to keep her from getting any.

Focused on my thoughts, I hunt up a change of clothes. I'll give Mel so many chores, she won't have time to dig. I'll tell Lisa to assign her a guard, 24/7. And I'll have to continue being cold, distant, no matter how badly I want to make her smile or tell her I'll keep her safe. She needs to choose freedom soon.

If she wasn't Reyna's daughter it'd already be too late. As it stands, there's hope. But the longer she stays, the less likely Lisa will be to let her go.

I frown as I head for the washroom, melancholy dull in my chest.

It doesn't matter that Mel understands me. I have no right to her friendship. My presence in her life has caused nothing but harm, and after I didn't save her parents, I'll do what I must to save her.

Even if I have to sell my soul along the way.

CHAPTER TWELVE

MEL

WHY does everything have to be black?

Midafternoon three weeks after my arrival in the caves, I'm in my room, fishing a pair of shorts and a tank top out of a dresser full of regulation black. I miss having a colorful wardrobe almost as much as I miss the outdoors.

Maybe today I'll get to taste fresh air again. Tommy pulled me from my chores early, his only explanation being I need to train on another set of skills. He told me to change into workout clothes and left it at that.

I have no idea what sort of task might require workout clothes, but I hope if it doesn't involve going outside, it'll at least be something interesting. So far, I've spent my days learning to cook, digging up tubers in the huge cavern that houses the gardens, making sure the many lanterns and fires throughout the caves stay lit, scrubbing the common areas, and washing infinite amounts of dishes and laundry by hand.

I don't mind paying my dues, but I'm more than ready for a change of pace. Living at the headquarters of a secret Resistance is a lot less exciting than I thought it would be, more like a prison than anything else. Except in prison, people have allies, don't they? Here, there's none of that. No opportunity to snoop and no one to answer my questions.

It's why I didn't bother to ask Tommy what new skills I'll be learning today. I already know he won't answer.

I slam the drawer shut.

Tommy has barely spoken to me since the day I got here. At first, I expected him to get over his foul mood and go back to being the person I met last month in the woods. Distant, a little awkward, but nice. Caring enough to go out of his way to help a stranger.

I tried speaking to him, not speaking to him, being angry, appealing to his sympathy. Nothing's worked. He's endlessly frigid.

I yank off my clothes, irritation and hurt stabbing at my heart. When Tommy's not around, I get no reprieve; the others are no better.

They're willing to train me, but every one of them clams up the second I try to talk about anything unrelated to the task at hand. No one speaks to me outside of giving instruction. I have no friends here.

Out of everyone in the Resistance, only five recruits are around my age.

Tommy is one.

Cait is another. On the rare occasion we cross paths, she never fails to shoot me a dirty look before stalking away. More often than not, Tommy's with her. It makes me wonder whether she hates me so much because they're together.

It might explain Tommy's attitude. He must want to show me, and her, that he's not interested in being my friend. Maybe she's mad he went so far out of his way to help me, both that day in the woods and the following night. If so, I wish she'd focus her antagonism on him. It's not like I asked him to intervene.

I've yet to meet the other younger members, but I've heard their names a few times in passing. Sam. Hunter. Vik. If they're Cait and Tommy's friends, I don't have much hope for when we do meet. They'll probably ignore me too.

I pull on a tank top and shorts, angry at myself for caring.

TEN minutes later, I follow Tommy through the craggy halls, my stomach uneasy.

Why is Cait here?

We haven't been this close to each other since the day I joined the Resistance. My back tingles where her gun jabbed into my spine, but I swallow my discomfort. I will not let her see me as weak.

Near the end of a long, empty corridor, Tommy pushes through a plain door I've never noticed before and leads us into a cavernous room. A disbelieving smile spreads across my face.

It's a gym.

The floor is covered in black mats. The walls are made of logs, like a cabin, except the far one, which is mirrored from floor to ceiling. There are real lights in here too, and free weights, and BOSU balls, and treadmills, and a climbing wall, and—*oh*—an obstacle course!

Amazing. They don't have hot water or modern appliances, but they have this. An underground, fully stocked, secret workout club.

To sprint again! To lift! To climb!

A delighted laugh bubbles up my throat, catching me by surprise. It's been a long time since I've felt like laughing. Beaming, I turn to Tommy.

His lips twitch, and I swear I see a spark of amusement flare behind his eyes, but before I can be sure, it's gone.

"How have you not shown me this before? Do you have any idea how much I've missed running?"

His lips quirk up again, just a little, as he runs his fingers through his golden-brown curls. "I'm sorry," he says, but doesn't offer any kind of explanation for having kept me away.

Cait's eyes glint, colder than ice, and her mouth might as well be chiseled from stone. I have no idea what Tommy sees in her. Does she ever smile? I bet she doesn't even know how.

Doing my best to ignore the shudder this thought sends through me, I turn and head for the nearest treadmill. It won't be as good as running outside, but it'll do.

Tommy blocks my path. "Actually, we're here to teach you to fight. The caves could be discovered at any moment, and if they are, you'll need to defend yourself. Organization capture would not only be a death sentence for you, it could also lead to spilled secrets for us. That's dangerous for everyone."

Hang on.

I have to learn to fight? From them?

Anxiety spikes in my chest, not at the idea of Organization capture, but at the prospect of training for combat with Tommy and Cait. I've never fought before, and I'm pretty uncoordinated. I don't want to make a fool of myself, least of all in front of them.

Wringing my hands, I ask, "Isn't there someone, I don't know ... else ... who could teach me?"

"We're two of the best fighters in the Resistance," Cait answers tartly. "You couldn't find more competent instructors. Besides, Lisa said it has to be us, so let's get it done."

I gulp. I'd rather take a swim in the freezing river that runs above the caves than be stuck here for who knows how long with Cait and Tommy. I don't know if my fragile emotional state can bear it.

Two hours and one ultra-embarrassing bloody nose later, I gape at Tommy, all who-knows-how-many pounds of him, sprawled on his back with slim little Cait straddling his hips, her blade at his throat. The way she just spun him over her shoulder like he was nothing. How?

She smirks at him—guess she can smile after all—and hops to her feet, hand extended.

He returns her grin as he pulls himself up. It's annoying how good he looks in gym clothes, those carved muscles working, gleaming with sweat.

"I know it's not in your nature, but how about slowing down so Mel can learn?" he asks her.

Cait rolls her eyes. "Enemies won't go easy." But she turns to me nonetheless, going through the motions again on an invisible opponent. "When you're up against someone bigger than you, you have to be quick, your execution flawless. Use their weight and momentum against them."

I study her movements, the way she coordinates her whole body to channel her strength. I noticed the same sort of graceful flow an hour ago when she and Tommy taught me to punch and kick using sparring pads and a heavyweight bag. But as hard as I tried, I couldn't get my muscles to work together like theirs.

My gaze floats over the other pairs of fighters scattered around us. Their moves are impressive too. Fast, smooth, powerful. Like a violent dance.

"Eyes over here, Mel," Tommy says, and I pull my attention from the woman with spiky brown hair currently pulverizing her opponent across the mat from us. I hope they aren't expecting me to fight like that. I can't even make Tommy's hands move when I punch the sparring pads.

"Sorry. Can you show me that again?"

I do my best to keep my mind on my teachers as the lesson progresses, but it's hard. The later it gets, the more people show up to practice. I've never seen anything like these fighters in my life. They are absolutely lethal.

And when someone tall and tan strolls into the gym, waves toward Tommy and Cait, and heads for the spring that bubbles out of the wall at the end of the room, my eyes follow. He's lean, with dark hair and warm brown eyes; he's also in his early twenties at most.

He must be Sam, Vik, or Hunter.

The stranger peeks at me as he fills his water bottle, curiosity lighting his eyes. Before I can smile, he turns away.

"Excuse me," Cait says, and she's gone, weaving between the other gym-goers with the grace of a prima ballerina. The guy gives her a heart-stopping grin as she leans against the wall by his side to chat. Their laughter carries across the room.

"Mel, eyes over here," Tommy says yet again, and I realize I'm staring.

"Sorry." Not.

"You have the attention span of a butterfly, you know that?" He rolls his shoulders. "And based on these punches you're throwing, you're about as dangerous as one too."

I snort, heat flushing up my neck. He's not exactly wrong, but damn, I can't believe he said that.

"I expected more after watching you run the other week. Where'd all that coordination go?"

"Excuse me?"

"That's what you're missing. Coordination. You're strong, but you lack efficiency. You're working against yourself every time you move."

"I haven't been doing this as long as you."

"I'm not a fan of excuses."

Tommy smirks, and I fume, all the more because of the way my heart skips a beat.

With a toss of her perfect, silky blond hair, Cait claps the stranger on the shoulder and heads back to us. "Maybe we should finish up for today," she says as she arrives, pointedly not looking at me. "She can only do so much right out of the gate. You're going to need dinner before your shift, anyway."

Tommy nods and turns to me. "Let's get some food and get you back to your room."

Ugh. I'd rather starve. The treadmills are beckoning, and the guy is still here, dawdling by the water.

Maybe he's kinder than Tommy and Cait. Maybe he knows something about my parents. If I don't take this chance to introduce myself, I'll never find out.

I cross my arms and pop a hip. "Look, the Resistance can trust me. I haven't put one toe out of line. I want to stay and run. Go have dinner. I'll be fine here."

"You need fuel after all that training."

"I can fuel up after."

Tommy's mouth twists, but footsteps behind us save me from his reply. I turn to see who's approaching, and it's *him*. The stranger. He throws me a cheerful smile.

"I'll stay with her," he says to Tommy. His voice is smooth, friendly.

"I'm responsible for her," Tommy snaps. I'm shocked by his harsh tone, but the guy seems unaffected.

"Calm down." Cait rests a slender hand on Tommy's arm. "You don't have to watch her all the time. Let Sam do it for a while."

So it's Sam.

Tommy glares at him. "Don't you have somewhere to be?"

The words are low. Dangerous. They send chills skittering over my skin.

I thought Tommy and Sam were friends. Why's Tommy being so aggressive?

"Nope," Sam says lightly, popping the *P*. He throws me a conspiratorial smile and winks. "I think I'm right where I need to be."

I can't help but laugh.

Cait rolls her eyes, pulling Tommy toward the exit by the back of his shirt. "Come on. Let's go."

Though Tommy allows himself to be dragged out, he glowers at Sam the whole way.

"That was weird," I note.

"Yeah. Hey, I'm Sam, by the way." He holds out a hand and his lovely brown eyes twinkle.

A grin rises to my lips as we shake. "I'm Mel. Thanks for doing that."

"No problem. You want to spar?"

I don't, to be honest. I miss running. But I'll spar instead if it means I get to hang out with Sam. For the first time in weeks, my foggy sadness has lightened a shade.

"Sure. I've never sparred before, though. Cait and Tommy had me running drills."

Sam grabs the pads Tommy left on the floor and straps them to his hands. "That's fine. Freestyle on these for a bit."

I throw a few jabs, then spin into a sloppy version of a roundhouse kick.

Sam meets me blow for blow. "Not bad. Target behind the pad. It'll help your power."

I throw a punch, incorporating his advice. To my amazement, the hit is much harder. I have to shake out my wrist.

"Thanks!" I beam, then throw several rapid-fire punches his way.

He chuckles. "Having fun?"

I laugh too, savoring the feeling. "Yeah. It's been kind of miserable around here. This is nice."

"I know. I'm sorry. I would've introduced myself earlier, but, well, Tommy asked me not to."

Anger and hurt crash through my chest, ruining the moment of levity. I stop fighting, arms hanging limp while I struggle with a sudden, mortifying urge to cry.

Not only does Tommy not like me, he's also actively keeping the others away. What have I done to deserve that?

"Why? Why does he hate me so much? He wasn't like this at first, you know. He seemed nice."

Sam lowers the pads, eyes full of pity. "He doesn't hate you. He's just an idiot sometimes."

One corner of my mouth lifts in a half-hearted attempt at a smile. Sam's being kind, but his kindness can't change reality. He hasn't seen how coldly Tommy looks at me, or the way Cait glowers every time she's near me.

I push the heels of my palms into my eyes, willing the pressure away. "He does. Cait too."

"Nah. She doesn't." Sam drops the pads and pulls my hands away from my face. "I mean it."

I don't know what to say, so I just look at him and pray the tears don't roll. The sympathy in Sam's gaze intensifies. He purses his lips. "This is all so stupid."

"What?"

"You don't deserve this. You can't leave now, anyway."

"You know you're not making sense, right?"

Sam huffs a laugh. "Yeah, I know." He sighs. "All right. Here's the deal. Tommy's trying to force you out of the Resistance. That's why he's been so cold toward you, and why he's keeping everyone away. Why he told me to keep my distance."

I gape, fury scorching through me again. "What?"

How could he? I might not be his favorite, but he of all people should understand why I need to be here.

"Yeah. So he doesn't hate you, not at all. In fact, I think he quite likes you." Sam waggles his eyebrows, an impish grin playing on his lips.

In spite of myself, I snort. "I think you've got this wrong."

Sam studies his knuckles. "No. Tommy told me about his plan weeks ago. He's going to be so mad I told you." A wicked grin flashes across his face, and he looks up at me.

I start to pace, my throat on fire. "Why would he do that? Doesn't he think I should get a say? And Cait. What's her problem? Is she mad because he got mixed up with me?"

"Hmm. That could be part of it. Her main issue is she doesn't trust you. Cait's whole life is the Resistance. She sees you as a threat to her family, and she's furious you're not rotting away in a cell."

I bark a laugh at that. Imagine Cait seeing me as a threat.

Sam's still talking. "On the other hand, Tommy knows you're no threat. He just wants you to be free. He's got a big problem with being stuck here, and he doesn't want you trapped like he is. He thinks it's his fault you're here."

I trip to a stop, stunned. "His fault? But I wanted to come here."

"I didn't say it makes sense. He can be an idiot, remember?"

Biting my lip, I turn Sam's words over in my mind. Tommy feels guilty. He doesn't want me gone for his sake. He thinks forcing me out is helping me.

Hope curls through my chest. Perhaps life in the Resistance doesn't have to be so miserable. I told Tommy why I want to be here, but he obviously didn't understand. If I explain better, maybe he'll ease up. Being an orphan himself, he'll get it. Right?

"He really doesn't hate me? You're sure?"

Sam shoots me a slight smile. "Didn't I already tell you? He definitely doesn't hate you."

Butterflies flip in my stomach as I consider trying to talk to him.

"I want to confront him about all this, but I don't want to get you in trouble for telling me."

"Confront him. He can't do this to you forever. And don't worry about me. I can handle whatever he throws at me for filling you in."

I smile, tension jittering in my limbs. "Thanks."

"No problem. He's in the CCTV room. Go." Sam's grin widens.

With a wave, I slip out and head down the rocky corridor. My nerves jangle the whole way.

CHAPTER THIRTEEN

TOMMY

CCTV shifts are the bane of my existence. The long hours spent monitoring Levett Tech via screens are dull as mud.

It's important for us to keep an eye on the campus, to make sure the Organization isn't up to anything shady, but it's rare for them to risk overt activity on site. There's nothing happening tonight to hold my attention, to distract me from the guilt that's gnawed at me ever since Mel joined the Resistance.

It hasn't gotten easier to treat her like an outcast. Every day, every hour, it's gotten harder. I hate the gloom in her eyes. I hate knowing it's there because of me.

Feet up on the counter, I lean back in my chair, a sketchpad balanced on my knees, muscles sore from all the extra PT I've been forced to put in over the last three weeks. If my disobedience had resulted in Mel's escape, I'd take Bill's punishment gladly. I'd take it again and again.

As things stand, his demanding early morning training sessions are salt in the wound of my utter failure to protect her.

I angle my pencil tip against the page, shading, then brush a finger over the resultant hue to blend it.

I've been working on this drawing for a few weeks now. It's a landscape. A vast, snowy plain, ringed in pines and firs. A soaring mountain range stands sentry in the distance, and endless stars glitter in the cold, open sky. There's no sign of life, save for a single wolf crossing the frozen valley.

I add another layer of shading, but I'm not paying attention to what my hands are doing. In my head, Sam and Mel spar together.

Anger burns through me, pushing my lips into a line. Sam knows what I'm trying to do. He may not agree with my plan, but he has no right to ruin it, not when Mel's freedom hangs in the balance.

I take a steadying breath. If I'm being honest with myself, Mel's stuck now, anyway. This morning, the Organization put a warrant out for her arrest, alleging she stole trade secrets from Levett Tech. A serious accusation, when you consider stealing from Levett is essentially stealing from the United States military. Mel's face is flooding the news, along with the footage of her pillaging the records room. A video of her tearful aunt begging her to turn herself in has gone viral.

As if we need another thread tying us together. I know what it feels like for the world to believe you're guilty of a heinous crime.

I chew on the end of my pencil, eyes roving over the grid of screens mounted on the wall. Should I tell her? Or maybe someone else would be better, someone who hasn't been an ass for weeks. Sam's good with that kind of thing. Vik too, although they're rougher around the edges.

Behind me, the doorknob turns, and I peek over my shoulder, expecting Cait. With Sam busy and Hunter and Vik on patrol, she'll be bored.

Instead, the door falls open to reveal a fidgety Mel, standing in the hall, alone.

My eyebrows shoot up.

"Hi, Tommy."

She's wary, that much is clear. Stepping into the small room, she closes the door behind her.

I pull my feet off the counter. "Did Sam bring you?"

Mel shakes her head and plunks down in the chair next to mine, drawing her knees up to her chest and wrapping her arms around them. I try not to notice how this makes her shorts ride up her long, sleek legs. "I came on my own. Sam knows I don't need to be babysat 24/7, unlike some people."

Smothering a fresh wave of guilt, I keep my expression cold. I haven't decided how to change tack now that Mel's a fugitive, or how I can possibly explain my terrible behavior so she'll understand. I need time to think. Not much, but I can't tell her right now.

"All right, let's get you back to your room."

"Wait." She throws out a hand and wraps her fingers around my wrist.

Sizzling energy flashes up my arm, like her palm is electrified. A small hiss breaks through my lips, and I jerk away.

"Sorry." Pink creeps into Mel's cheeks.

Working to keep my reaction bland, I get to my feet. "You just surprised me. No big deal. Let's go."

"No. I came to talk to you. Sit down." She pauses, then adds, "Please."

What could she want to talk to me about? Until training tonight, I haven't done anything more than treat her like a prisoner.

Wordlessly, I drop back into my chair.

"Thank you." Mel flashes me a small, nervous smile.

We sit in silence while she struggles to marshal her thoughts, biting that lower lip. Her eyes rove over the CCTV screens, then land on the sketchpad in my hand. Quick as lightning, she lunges forward and snatches it.

By the time I've registered what's happened, she's examining the drawing.

"It's beautiful. So lonely. You drew this?" She glances up at me, and there's wonder in her eyes.

Cheeks hot, I swipe the sketchbook back before she can rifle through the pages. "I might have." I don't show my art to anyone. Well, anyone except Cait.

The admiration's still there on her face, a real smile pulling at her mouth. The way it lights her up is something beyond beautiful. I wish I could sketch it.

"You've got talent, Tommy."

Warmth rises in my chest, mixed with a hearty dose of embarrassment. I turn my face away. "Thanks."

"I love art. I'm not the best at drawing, though. I'm okay with music, but my medium of choice is language."

"Language?" In spite of myself, I look back at her, one eyebrow raised. I'm intrigued.

Mel smiles again. "Yeah. Words are magic. They can be woven together to create something beautiful from nothing, and there are infinite possibilities. You can shape an image, a feeling, even a whole universe, with a few well-chosen lines. Words take a blank page and breathe life into it. There's nothing like them."

I can see the magic she speaks of. It glitters deep in her eyes, drawing me in. The way she feels about her art is exactly how I feel about my own.

I lean toward her. "You write?"

Mel's smile widens. "Yes."

"What do you write?" I find I'm smiling too.

"Whatever happens to be knocking around in my head when my pen hits paper. Poetry, lyrics, stories." She pulls her knees up again, hugging them. "You can't restrain an artist's spirit. Words are how I express mine. Like you with your sketches."

Mel's never looked quite as dazzling as she does right now, glowing with passion for her art. I blink and look away, pretending to watch the screens in front of me, but seeing nothing.

Silence falls, lengthens, until I start to wonder whether she's done talking.

"Sam told me about your plan." Mel's words are soft.

My eyes snap back to her. "What?"

"He told me why you've been so cold."

I seethe. That traitor.

Yeah, my plan has failed. But why wouldn't Sam toss me a heads up before ratting me out? He should've given me a chance to explain myself.

Mel must think I'm such a jerk.

Because I am.

She's still talking. "Ever since my parents died, my life's been empty. One day, things were good. The next, my world shattered. My friends tried to support me, but... Well, we were young, and they didn't understand. I was transferred to my aunt's school district. Eventually they stopped calling."

A frown tugs at Mel's full lips, bringing out a dimple in her chin. The ghost of her pain haunts her voice, shadows her eyes. I find myself leaning toward her again.

"I took the job at Levett Tech because the police reports didn't make sense, and no one took my questions seriously. At first, I was only confused, but after all the evasion I knew something had to be up."

Smart. Most would dismiss their suspicion and buy into whatever BS they'd been fed by the authorities.

"I guessed Mara Levett and her team were negligent in some serious way and used the gas lines as coverup, and I wanted them to pay. People told me to move on, that I was losing my grip on reality, but I couldn't. It didn't get better with time. I only got angrier, more obsessed, especially after reading those damned reports. And now I know there's more to it than a corporation buying their way out of trouble. A life above ground isn't worth missing the chance to learn the truth."

Mel's story hits me with brutal force.

The fury. The isolation. The questions. All of it twisting her up, ripping her apart, turning her into a stranger in her own life.

I could give her what she wants. I know all too well what happened that night.

Mel's eyes flick up to my face, shining with defiance. "You can treat me as awful as you like. I'm not leaving." She pauses, then adds, "I was hoping we could be friends instead, though."

My heart pounds, the breath stuck in my throat. Sharing her pain will only bring us closer. I can't let myself get close to her. I'll fail her, like I failed her parents.

Her gaze softens. "You don't need to rescue me. This is where I want to be. My choice, not yours." Hesitantly, she reaches out to lay a hand over mine. "But thank you. For caring."

I hadn't realized I was making a fist. Her soft touch is soothing, restful. Like moonlight.

Taking another deep breath, I relax the rigid muscles in my hand and turn my palm up for her. She wraps her fingers around mine and squeezes.

In response, my stomach swoops like I missed a step going downstairs.

"I'm sorry." My voice is hoarse. "I hated treating you that way. I just couldn't stand the thought of you caged here like the rest of us, especially because of me."

"Don't put that on yourself. I wanted to find the Resistance, remember?" Mel squeezes my hand again. "You probably saved my life. I wouldn't have given up snooping at work, and the Organization would've gotten me."

I smile, just a little. "So stubborn."

She shrugs and grins back.

Mel won't stop investigating because I've made things difficult. A hundred gruesome pictures flash through my mind. Reyna staring at me, ruined face streaming blood. The flesh ripped clean off Dad's cheek. The sound of Mom's screams as they shattered her bones, one by one.

Every time I close my eyes the memories leak out. Night after night, they rend my mind to pieces, never giving me a moment's rest.

If she finds out what happened, what I did nothing to stop, her eyes will burn with loathing every time she looks at me. But if I don't tell her myself, she'll only despise me more in the end.

Darkness falls over my heart as I lean forward. "If I were you, I'd quit poking around. You don't want to know what happened that night. When they died."

Mel's gaze is suddenly razor-sharp. Her fingers dig into my palm. "You know something?"

I study her hand in mine, tracing her knuckles with my thumb. My heart beats faster. "Yes."

She gasps, one quick intake of breath. "Please, Tommy. Please. You have to tell me."

"Once you know, you can't not know. Are you sure about this?"

Without a moment's hesitation, Mel nods. "Of course. It's been torture, not knowing."

With a huge effort, I fix my eyes on Mel's. The last thing I want to do is tell her, but if this is what she needs, then she deserves to know. I'm only reaping what I've sown.

Calling on all the courage I possess, I face the memories.

I face her judgment.

"They came quickly. The Organization, I mean. I didn't know what was happening. One second, I was talking to our moms in my parents' bedroom. The next, I'd been shoved under the bed, and men in black were pouring in, dragging our dads with them. There were ten of them."

A wall of sorrow presses on my throat. Mel squeezes my hand, and I draw strength from her touch, even as fear rips through me, making my palms sweat.

"You knew them? My parents?"

I swallow. "Sort of. They stayed at my house for a few days every summer, for the annual company-wide meeting at Levett Tech. I was too focused on my own dumb teenaged drama to pay them much attention."

Mel nods, her eyes sad, like she knows what I mean. She doesn't say more, just waits for me to continue.

What should I say, though? I want to give her answers without implicating myself too clearly or passing on my nightmares. I hesitate, the words jammed in my throat.

"Just say it."

I shift in my chair. "All right. The Organization interrogated our parents. I saw everything. It wasn't pretty."

Mel blanches.

Is she wondering what I did while it all went down? Does she know I could have helped, but didn't?

I did nothing but cower under the bed and save myself. Shame pools deep in my gut.

"They were murdered right in front of you?"

Mel's eyes shimmer. Before I know it, her arms surround me in a warm hug. She smells fresh, like cherry blossoms and peaches, even after training all afternoon. Delicious chills run wild through my body.

"I'm sorry," she breathes into my neck. "I can't imagine."

I'm dying to pull her closer. Instead, I pat her back, then gently push her away.

Mel drops into her chair, still bone pale. Revulsion lurks behind her wet eyes.

"How did you get away?"

I don't want to tell. It grates on my heart to imagine the abhorrence in her eyes when she finds out. Of course, I deserve every drop of disgust she's sure to have for me. And even if it costs me her friendship, she deserves the answer to her question.

I can't look. The shame is too suffocating.

So, I study my laces, fighting to speak through the dryness in my mouth. "I hid under the bed until they dragged our parents out. Then I ran into the woods. The Resistance found me a few days later."

No need to reveal the worst of it.

Mel's hearty sniff has me looking up. Her eyes are wide, her cheeks glazed with tears. "It's h-horrible."

Ice cracks down my spine. What form will her hatred take? Will she scream? Hit me?

Mel leans forward. I tense.

She grips my hand. Holding it tight, she bows her head and breaks down completely.

I don't understand. Why is she holding my hand? My inaction cost our parents their lives.

"Oh, Tommy." Mel raises tear-stained eyes to mine. There's no disgust, no blame. It's a plea; a cry for help.

Sympathy and gratitude overwhelm me. She won't have to suffer alone. Not this time.

"Come here." I open my arms.

With a huge sob, Mel climbs into my lap and buries her face in my shoulder. Her body presses against mine, shaking while she cries. Warmth spreads through my blood, even as I'm sick over her pain. Winding my arms around her, I pull her closer.

"I'm so sorry," I whisper into her hair.

I was a fool to keep her away. Mel and I understand each other. We need each other.

Blinking back my own tears, I hold onto Mel like she's an antidote for the poison that stains my soul, a talisman against the demons that lurk in the darkest corners of my mind.

CHAPTER FOURTEEN

TOMMY

FOOTSTEPS thunder out in the hall, shattering the spell that's settled over Mel and me.

Bill's team is stopping an arms deal tonight. Something might have gone wrong.

I'm about to unwind my arms from around Mel when Cait slams her way into the room, Sam on her heels. Her gray eyes spark. "And just what is going on here?"

Mel leaps away from me, palms by her shoulders. "Nothing! I was, um, remembering my parents." She sniffles, wiping her eyes with the back of her hand.

"Get out."

I frown. Cait might not trust Mel, but she doesn't need to be so mean. Mel's had enough of that from me over the last few weeks. "Cool it, Cait. Mel can stay."

Cait gawks at me like I've grown an extra head. "No. We need to talk. Alone."

I want to object, but worry trickles into my chest. Cait must be here about her dad's mission. Why else would she be so worked up?

With an apologetic glance for me, Sam extends a hand toward Mel. "Come on. Let's get dinner."

Eyes cast down, Mel takes Sam's hand, still sniffling as she disappears into the hall. The last of the warmth from our moment goes with her.

A frisson passes over my skin. "The mission?"

"The mission was fine," Cait snaps. "They got back an hour ago."

Good. But then why is she here? And angrier than a bear in winter?

Bewildered, I watch as she stomps my way and falls into the chair Mel vacated. She doesn't look at me. Instead, she scowls at the CCTV screens like they've done her a serious injustice. "Guess I need to make sure the feeds are monitored, since you can't be bothered to do it yourself."

I sigh. "Don't be like that. Mel's hurting. She needed comfort. Why are you so mad, anyway? You and I goof around in here all the time. You don't have a problem with distractions then."

Cait rolls her eyes, still watching the dark campus. "It's not really about that."

I turn my attention to the screens too. Cait'll spit her issue out when she's ready.

She swivels her chair back and forth. After a minute, she spins to face me. Her eyes are hard. "You're such a hypocrite, Williams. I thought you were smarter than this."

I kick my feet up on the counter and cross my arms, glancing at her with an eyebrow raised. "What is that supposed to mean?"

"When Sam met me in the mess hall just now, he told me he left Mel on her own. I ran to find you right away. I thought we could track her down, maybe catch her doing something wrong, finally prove the Organization sent her. Little did I know she was in here, playing you for a fool."

She leans forward, brows pulling together. "Did you learn nothing from what happened with June? Mel is dangerous. What are the chances you randomly found her in the woods that day? She was looking for us, I know it. I thought you knew it too. You've kept her under watch 24/7 since she got here."

Cait's mistrusted Mel from day one. Given Cait's history, I understand why, and it suited my plan not to discourage her suspicion.

Now, though, I'll have to convince her there's no reason to doubt Mel after all.

This is going to be difficult.

Wanting something to keep my hands busy, I grab my sketchbook from the counter and start shading. "I was wrong about Mel. She's Reyna and Max Snow's daughter. You know that, right?"

"So?"

"So why would she help the people who killed her parents?"

"Don't ask me to fathom the way a criminal's mind works." There's no trace of sympathy in Cait's hard tone. "Why the one-eighty? Is it the pretty face? She pouts and has you in the palm of her hand?"

Anger boils through me. Seriously?

"This has nothing to do with her looks. Mel's genuine. You should see the pain in her eyes when she talks about her parents. It's so real, it just about breaks me. It's my pain. In her."

My ravaged soul found its twin in hers. I didn't know such a thing was possible.

I look up at Cait, hoping to get a read on her reaction. "She came here for answers, and I don't blame her one bit. Honestly, I've trusted her all along. The only reason I watched her so closely was to keep her lonely and frustrated. I thought if she were miserable enough, and if she didn't find answers, she'd leave this place while she still could. I was trying to save her."

Cait shakes her head, eyes sad. Pitying, even. It's insulting. "Can't you see? She's using your sympathy against you. You're playing right into her hands."

Tilting her chair back, Cait covers her face. "Ugh. I don't understand why Lisa let her stay. The second Mel finds whatever she's really looking for, she'll expose us. I should've killed her when I had the chance."

My pencil tip snaps. "Cait! We are not cold-blooded murderers."

"No. You're right, and that's why I didn't. It's just, I'm so afraid of what's been unleashed here." Cait drops her hands. "What if my moment of weakness gets us all slaughtered? Or worse?"

Real fear flickers in her suddenly vulnerable eyes.

She doesn't want her family's blood on her conscience. I understand that all too well.

I reach out and pat her knee. "I get how you feel, I really do. But Cait, Mel isn't June. And June wasn't your fault."

"You know that's not true." Cait bites her trembling lip. "I was closer to her than anyone, besides Hunter, and he was too in love with her to catch the signs. I should've seen … I … I don't want you to get hurt. Mel's a spy, Tommy. The first time you met her, she was close enough to the caves to cross our patrol route, and now all her coworkers and guards report her asking lots of probing questions. We need to watch her so we can act on a moment's notice when she steps out of line."

June's betrayal left a deep scar on Cait's heart, but I'm no fool. I thought she trusted my judgment a hell of a lot more than this.

"The Organization's never found us. How would they know where to send Mel?"

"They must've figured out we're in the woods, so they sent her to find out where. You made that job only too easy for her."

I want to roll my eyes, but I ignore the jab. "You're forgetting they had a tail on her. And what about the warrant for her arrest?"

"They've got to make us believe she's not one of them. Obviously, they'll act like it."

"You really think Lisa would let her stay if she were a threat?"

Cait's already shaking her head. "Lisa's only human. She makes mistakes, just like anyone. In this case, I suppose she's blinded by her love for Reyna. I mean, they were best friends. But you have to look at the facts. Mel worked at Levett Tech. She wasn't far from the caves when you met her—looking for us. Ever since she got here, she's been poking around, even under watch. Asking weird questions. Exactly like June did."

Cait rests her elbows on her knees, fixing me with a blazing stare. "She's June all over again. You can't trust her. Even if she is a good person, we don't know what the Organization might have on her. They could be controlling her, making her do things she doesn't want to.

Please, help me keep an eye on her. Hell, if she's being coerced, maybe we can even find a way to help. But first she needs to be exposed."

I drop my eyes to the sketchpad, twirling my ruined pencil in my hand. If Mel were a spy, we would be in grave danger. Could Cait be right?

I've seen my own anguish in the tortured depths of Mel's eyes, in the horror-struck twist of her mouth, in the quiver of her body while she cried on my shoulder. I might not know her well, but I'm sure, all the way to the center of my bones, she wouldn't use something as sacred as her love for her parents to deceive us.

Yes, June fooled us all, but her situation was completely different. Mel deserves a chance to prove herself.

"I understand your concern," I say, glancing up at Cait, "but Mel's trustworthy. You should back off."

Cait's face puckers. "I know you find her attractive. Don't let that blind you."

I huff a laugh. Wow. Who knew Cait thought so little of me.

"You've got me all wrong. Sure, she's hot, but there's nothing more to it. We're going to try to be friends, that's all. Don't give yourself an ulcer. I've got a brain. I can use it."

"Fine!" Cait shoots to her feet. "Don't come crying to me when she stomps on your heart! I've been through this before, Tommy. When I get proof, you'll be eating your words, begging me to forgive you, but I'll remember. I'll remember you chose her over the entire Resistance. Over me."

She whirls and storms from the room, slamming the door behind her. I gape at the shivering wood.

Talk about an overreaction.

Annoyed, I snap my sketchbook shut and toss it on the counter. Cait's fears about Mel are based on Cait's own issues. Nothing else. If she would just trust me, she'd see Mel hasn't done anything wrong. Of course Mel wants to know what happened to her parents. Who wouldn't?

Mel is second-gen Resistance. She earned her place here as soon as Max and Reyna gave their lives for the cause.

Cait will have to deal.

CHAPTER FIFTEEN

MEL

"You've got to eat something."

Sam and I are sitting on my bedroom floor, plates of lukewarm food balanced in our laps. He tried to bring me to the mess hall, but on the way, the sobs I'd been holding back in Cait's presence resurfaced with a vengeance. I was hardly able to put one foot in front of the other, my parents' broken bodies all I could see.

So Sam brought me here. I collapsed on the floor and wept, unaware he left to get us dinner. Tommy's words kept running on repeat through my mind.

The Organization interrogated our parents.

I know what interrogated means. Mom and Dad weren't just murdered; they were tortured for information. Unspeakable things happened before the end.

My heart splintered more with each new horror I imagined, the pictures in my head worse and worse. I barely noticed when Sam returned and sat next to me while I cried, patting my shoulder and handing me tissues every so often.

My tears have finally run dry, but I'm empty. A void.

"Mel?"

"Sorry."

Wow. I sound awful.

I clear my throat, rubbing my swollen eyes with my knuckles.

"Do you want to talk about it?"

Sam's tone is gentle, like he's trying to calm a spooked animal. I blink, lost in horror-stricken numbness.

"Mel?"

With effort, I focus on him.

"What happened in there? Why are you crying?"

A weird little laugh bubbles up my throat. Crying is the understatement of the year for what he just saw. He's known me about three seconds, and he's seen me cry so hard snot ran down my face. But his warm eyes don't judge. They're full of kindness, like he actually cares.

My friends back home 'cared' for a while. Eventually, they got mad, or bored. There came a point when they didn't want to witness my tears or listen to me grieve anymore. To be fair, I didn't want to let them see, either.

Tommy cares, but only because he's an orphan too. He's as damaged as I am.

As far as I'm aware, Sam isn't. He doesn't know me at all, yet he sat with me while I sobbed. He watched me at my worst, and he's still here.

Suddenly, I want nothing more than to share what I learned with him, to connect with another person, a person who isn't tangled up in what happened that night.

So I tell him about opening the door to find state troopers on Aunt Amy's porch back in Coral City. I bring him through the dark years I struggled there, stuck with an aunt who, though well-meaning, didn't really know what to do with me. I tell him how I lost friends until no one was left. I explain my prior suspicion that my parents didn't die because of a gas leak, and how it pushed everyone away—how the anger and the sadness swallowed me up until I graduated and could legally tap into my inheritance to come to New Hampshire and hunt down answers.

Then I tell Sam about meeting Tommy in the woods, about snooping in the records room at Levett Tech, and about Tommy's cryptic nighttime warning in my condo. After all that, I run through what Tommy said in the CCTV room. The truth he revealed.

I tell Sam how empty I feel. Empty and sick and like I'm trapped in a nightmare. Like this isn't even real. I was sure my parents' accident was a lie, but the truth is a thousand times worse than I feared.

As my story comes to an end, I find myself facing Sam, legs crossed.

"Figuring out what happened to them has been my goal for so long. Now I've done it. And yet, I don't feel better. I know what happened, but not why. Why were my parents murdered, especially like that? Why them?"

Sam purses his lips. "You've been through so much, and I understand I can't truly get how you feel, but stop and think. Look at you." He waves a hand in my direction. "Are you glad you know what happened? Wasn't it better not knowing?"

I brace my arms behind me. The truth will haunt me forever. Like Tommy said, now that I know, I can't not. I'll always wonder what they went through. I'll always carry their suffering with me.

Would I wipe my memory clean if I could?

"No. It wasn't better. Even though knowing is horrible, I'm glad I do. My parents deserve to have their suffering be recognized."

"Okay," Sam says slowly, "think about this. You've hurt enough, Mel. Look at Tommy. He carries his past with him every day. He hides his pain, but I know him well, so I see it anyway. He's not happy, not even in his best moments. My point is, you don't want to end up carrying ghosts with you forever. Acknowledge the truth. Honor it. Then let it go."

I look away, twirling a lock of hair around my finger. Sam's right. If I keep digging, who knows what other horrors I'll unearth. Maybe my parents did stuff. Bad stuff. Or maybe I'll learn the specifics of what happened to them. I don't know if I could handle that.

But can I really just … let go?

Tommy's tormented expression hangs in my vision. What sort of violence, exactly, put such agony in his eyes?

Sickness twists my mind, a fervent hatred boiling deep in my marrow. The inferno rises, grows hotter until I'm blazing with it. Drowning in it. Burning alive.

My parents were good. They didn't deserve what happened to them. I'm not letting anything go until I know who did this and why.

Until I hunt them down and make them pay.

It's not easy, but I rein in the fury and turn it into fuel. I will see this through. "I have to know. I have to understand."

Sam sighs. "At least think on it. Give yourself time to process before you decide. You might change your mind."

I give him a tight nod, though my decision's made. "I can do that."

"Good." Sam's smile is brittle. "Hey, will you be okay tonight? It's getting late, but I can stay if you want. We could talk about something else."

The ghost of a grin flits across my face. He might be nice, but I'm not letting a guy I barely know spend the night. "I'll be fine. Thanks, though. For everything. It feels good to get all this out."

"Yeah. You're welcome. I know we only just met, but I'm here for you if you need to talk." Sam gives my knee a squeeze. He climbs to his feet, stifling a yawn with the back of his hand.

After a quick good-night, I'm on my own. I flop down on the bed, revulsion simmering like poison in my blood. Behind my lids, my parents suffer all manner of horrific deaths, over and over.

This is why I'm here. Why I can never let it go.

No matter the cost.

CHAPTER SIXTEEN

MEL

THANK God for coffee.

Last night, I tossed. Turned. Paced. Screamed into my pillow. Did it all again before sitting down at my desk at three in the morning to write out my horror. The short story that emerged was dark and twisted, but it bled some of the toxicity from my soul and allowed me to nab a little sleep.

I take another sip of the scalding, delicious liquid, then return to doodling in my notebook, pen scratching over the lined page. A hooded figure with a scythe and evil eyes emerges, a perfect personification of the knot curdling in my stomach as I wait for Tommy to arrive.

No guard stood outside my door when I went to bathe and grab breakfast earlier. I assumed this was an oversight, that someone would show up looking for me while I was gone, but the hall was still empty when I returned a few minutes ago with a steaming mug cradled in my chilly hands. Hopefully it's proof Tommy meant what he said last night, and he's done icing me out. Life will be so much better around here if we're friends, but more importantly, I need to find out what else he knows about Mom and Dad.

Three sharp taps sound on my door, and as I hurry to wrench it open, anxiety and anticipation hum in my chest.

There he is, leaning against the frame, loose curls falling over his forehead.

Ugh, but he's hot. His simple black tee doesn't hide the sharp cut of his chest and shoulders, and the way those fatigues hang from his hips sends a thrill flaming through my blood. His eyes are gorgeous, especially when he smiles…

Wait.

For once, he's not glaring. He's smiling. At me.

I grin in response, the nerves in my stomach turning to butterflies, but his smile falls a fraction.

"Good morning. You all right?"

I smooth my hair and glance down. No amount of showering or coffee will have erased the bags under my eyes from the sleepless night. "Uh, yeah. Thanks. Does this mean you're actually done being a dick?"

Tommy snorts, but I catch the guilt that touches his expression. "Dick is kind of a strong word, don't you think? I'd say I was more of a dumbass."

"Dumbass is better?"

"It implies stupidity versus intentional assery, even though ass is part of the word. Follow me."

A laugh bursts out of me. "Assery? You are definitely not a writer."

He salutes, a corner of his mouth tugging up. "Why do you think I paint?"

I shake my head and walk with him out of the housing wing and around a few corners, past the mess hall and the kitchen. Neither of us say anything else, and the longer the silence drags on, the more awkward it gets. I need to keep him talking.

"So, what am I doing today? I thought I was with Chef Ari all week." Might as well start out easy.

"We're headed for the shooting range. I'm going to teach you to handle a weapon."

Woah. They're trusting me with a gun.

Satisfaction winds through my chest. He's really, truly dropping the antagonism. Maybe now I'll get my answers. A little bit of freedom.

110

Friends.

I beam, and he does the slightest of double takes before returning my smile.

"Believe I'm done being a dick now?"

"I'll believe you more if you tell me what else you know about our parents."

His face falls, the light in his eyes snuffing out, and guilt bites at the edges of my joy. He's traumatized, and I keep bringing up the cause. Selfish, but I can't ignore the fact he's my best lead.

"I already told you everything that matters."

My fingers brush the back of his wrist, and I pour all the gratitude I feel for what he shared last night into the tentative smile I give him. "I know how hard that was. Thank you. But I have questions."

"You don't want to hear details, I promise."

I swallow back sickness. He's right, but details aren't what I'm after. I need explanations.

"Can I ask other questions?"

Tommy studies me as he opens a door and leads the way into another huge room I've never been in. Fluorescent panels in the ceiling flick on when we enter, illuminating a tunnel approximately twenty feet wide made of compact dirt, with roots twisting through the walls and targets scattered down its length. The industrial lighting is strange in a space that smells of fresh soil and feels more like an animal's burrow than anything else.

I walk to the low wall that cuts the front of the range off from where the targets are located and stroke a hand over the rough wood. Behind me, Tommy clears his throat. "I guess I owe you that much."

"Thank you."

It feels gauche to jump straight into my most burning questions, so I avoid those for now and start with an easy one, something that doesn't even touch on his trauma. "Why does Cait hate me so much?"

I peek back at him in time to catch his eye roll as he pulls two pairs of protective glasses and earmuffs down from a shelf on the wall. "She thinks you're a spy for the Organization."

Sam told me as much, but it's hard to wrap my head around. "Even though they killed my parents?"

"She's not exactly being rational. She has her reasons, but don't worry. She'll come around."

"Will the others talk to me now that you're done with your *assery?*"

He snorts. "I think so. They're not the asses here, but you have to understand, we've been betrayed before. It's hard for them to trust a stranger, even someone whose parents were loyal."

My heart sinks a little as Tommy hands me my safety gear before tugging on his own. I'm right to continue digging if I can't expect the others to open up. Who knows whether I'll ever earn their trust.

"Based on what happened when you tried to murder me in your kitchen, I'm guessing you've never shot a gun before."

Tommy's eyes shine behind his glasses, amusement playing on his lips. I smack his shoulder, then don my own gear. "Who says I didn't spare your sorry life on purpose?"

He laughs as he takes his weapon from its holster and holds it out. "All right. If you're so skilled, show me what you got."

I take it from him gingerly and extend it in front of me, aiming for the nearest target. When I pull the trigger, nothing happens.

"Safety," Tommy says, his voice laced with laughter.

Heat flushes up my neck. I feel for the switch he showed me back in my kitchen and flick it.

"Now widen your stance, one foot in front of the other. Yes, like that. Grip the handle with both hands."

I do as he says, my skin prickling as his eyes travel over my body, checking my form.

"Arms straight. You need to be ready for the kickback. Hold strong through your wrists, arms, and shoulders, and ground through your legs and core. Good, but your grip needs some work. You don't want to lose control on recoil. Like this." Tommy holds up his hands, placing one over the other in front of him, as though aiming his own invisible weapon.

I study his grip and adjust my own, but he shakes his head. "Can I show you?"

"Sure."

He steps behind me, my back against his front, and wraps warm, calloused hands over mine. The heat from his muscled body sinks through my clothes, and I swallow, a buzz building, spreading through my stomach. Every inch he touches tingles. Burns. He might as well be five hundred degrees.

"Like this," he says, helping me cover my dominant hand with the other. I shift, and he freezes for a moment, then lets go and steps back.

"Yep. You got it now. Aim down the sights, line them up with the target. Both eyes open." The words are lower, huskier than before, and heat stings my cheeks.

Nope. No way. Not letting him distract me, no matter how sexy he is. I didn't give up my whole life to indulge in a subterranean fling.

I line the little dots up with the bullseye, shoulders square, and pull the trigger again. This time the gun explodes, wrenching my wrists and jolting my very bones as the barrel flips up toward the ceiling. A new hole rips through the target, third ring from the center, as tears burn in the corners of my eyes and excitement flares in my chest.

"I hit it!"

Tommy stares, a glimmer of pride in his shocked expression. "That ... was really good for a novice. Good job."

I raise my chin and smirk. "You expected less?"

"That was unusually good. *Have* you handled a pistol before?"

The way he's looking at me makes my stomach flip. "Nope."

"For real? Huh. Bet you can't do it again."

The challenge is clear in Tommy's cocky smile, and determination surges as I take careful aim and fire. The kickback is more manageable now I know what to expect, and even better, I hit the target again. Fourth ring this time.

"Hah!"

Tommy's whole face lights up, and my breath catches.

Not going there.

"Damn. We have to hone your technique, but you've got a shit ton of potential."

I bow with flourish.

"Try not to move too early. You're anticipating the shot, moving a fraction of a second before you pull the trigger."

"Got it." I step back into position, line up the sights. "There's something I don't understand. If the Organization killed our parents at your house, then how do the police have footage of them at Levett Tech right before the explosion?"

Tommy sighs. "Those weren't our parents. They were look-alikes."

Shock wipes out the lingering thrill of Tommy's closeness, and of my success with the pistol. That's why Dad was using a right-handed mouse. It wasn't him.

Tommy's still talking. "Did you notice they never faced the cameras?"

I didn't, but it makes sense. I flick on the safety and lower the gun.

"Why were they targeted? Why them?"

Tommy looks down, fidgeting with his bracelet. "I don't know, beyond them working for the Resistance, but the Organization didn't ask a single question about that. They talked a lot about a chip. I have no idea what they meant."

"A chip?"

"I assume a computer chip."

"You never asked Lisa? Or heard any details from the others? They must've mentioned something after it happened."

"No. The information's beyond my clearance."

My face falls, and he glances back up, apologetic.

"Didn't you want to understand?"

"I just wanted to forget."

Guilt nags at my conscience again, but I can't let it stop me.

"What did our parents do for the Resistance?"

The slightest tinge of relief softens Tommy's gaze. "I don't have many specifics, but my parents were spies. They gathered information for Lisa from within Levett Tech itself. Yours did too, from what I've heard. After they died, Lisa pulled back, stopped sending agents out undercover. She's deeply committed to preventing the Organization from harming innocents, but her highest priority is always to protect us."

Everything Tommy's saying makes sense, but he doesn't know as much as I hoped. He's never pushed, never investigated. "Do you think Lisa would share more if we asked?"

Tommy's fidgeting again. "She might have before, but it's not something we should press into now."

"Why not?"

"Because we've seen more arms deals go down over the last few months than we have in the two years before that. The acceleration of Organization activity has leadership worried, and now you're here, asking questions. I'm not sure what will happen if Lisa decides you're a security risk, but it sure as hell won't be pleasant. You need to lie low, show everyone you're trustworthy."

Damn. Why can't it ever be easy?

He's still talking. "The Organization is backed by domestic extremists hell-bent on destroying capitalist society and the rise of advanced technology, which they believe to be a cancer to humankind. The people in the Resistance were all targeted at one point or another—we're victims with little choice in whether or not to stay here. For us, the caves are a sanctuary, the only place we're safe. It's different with you, and that's enough to cast doubt on your motives."

Okay, so openly asking is out. But that's not the only method available to get information.

I bite my lip, unsure whether I should try and convince Tommy to take a more active role in my search. He'd know where sensitive records are kept, would know when and how to sneak access, yet asking him to do something like that could compromise not only my safety, should he feel honor bound to report me, but his. Plus, it would force him to continue to relive his horrific past.

The atmosphere shifts as we lock eyes, my pulse quickening as the air thins.

"Tommy. I need to know why. I just ... I can't move past it. Please, help me piece it together. I promise you can trust me. I'd never hurt the Resistance."

He stares, a frown turning down his perfect mouth.

"Look," he finally says. "I get it, I do. But answers won't make the pain go away. If you don't quit investigating, leadership will come down on you. You'll end up hurt, imprisoned, maybe even killed. Try to drop it, at least for a while."

Anger tightens my chest, my fist clenching around the handle of the gun. He's the second person in twenty-four hours to tell me that.

Mom and Dad deserve better.

"No."

His gaze softens as he reaches out and takes my free hand, a pulse of heat feathering up my arm.

"I promise to answer your questions, and to tell you whatever you need to know, if I have it in my power to do so. I can help you work through this, but please, find another way to heal."

Warmth glows in his eyes, and they soften further. He's looking out for me, like he has since I arrived. Even so, I won't take his advice. He wants to protect my body, but I know what my heart needs.

"I'll think about it."

"Good. Try the shot again."

I lift the gun with steady hands, release the safety, and take aim, my stance solid, rooted to the ground through my boots. Tommy's already told me all he knows. As great as it would be to have his help investigating further, it's clear he wants to leave the horror behind. So, I'll let him. I can do this on my own.

My finger tugs the trigger, and the gun fires. But I hold strong, controlling the kickback as a new hole rips through the center of the bullseye.

CHAPTER SEVENTEEN

MEL

HIGHER *and higher I climb, scrambling over cracked boulders and mossy logs. Golden sunshine filters down through the trees, and the swaying branches make glowing patches of light dance across the forest floor. The sun's warmth kisses my cheeks. My nose. My eyelids.*

Oh, how I've missed being outside.

Hand over hand, I pull myself up the rocky mountain face. There's a brightness ahead which tells me I've almost broken through the tree line. A compulsion to reach the buttery glow overwhelms me, and I pick up the pace, scraping my palms on the jagged stone.

At last, I heave myself over the cliff's edge and the forest falls away behind me. The sunlight here is different than I expected. Harsher. It glares off endless, barren shelves of granite.

A pulse of nervous energy thrums in my chest. It's here, what I'm looking for. So close.

I have to find it.

I run forward, tripping over my own feet, searching frantically but seeing nothing, nothing, nothing except a dark puddle, just ahead.

Wary, I inch closer.

I was wrong. It's not a puddle.

It's a stream.

A stream of thick, red liquid, creeping lazily over the striated stone.

The world jolts, my stomach and my fists clench. Icy spires of fear breathe up my back, lift the hair on my neck.

Slowly, I raise my eyes.

A woman stands before me, feet immersed in the crimson river. She's not of this world. No, she's ethereal, with perfect, moon bright skin and a crown of white gold hair. Her ice-blue eyes are lifeless.

My heart fractures at the sight.

Mom.

With a lurch, I'm tumbling backward over rough granite. The world spins, my own blood-curdling shriek all I can hear.

Belly pressed against freezing stone, I end up under something long, dark, and flat, staring into tormented green-and-gold eyes.

A bed. I'm under a bed.

Tommy stares back, face streaked with blood and tears. The horrible river is coming, inching toward us. It flows under the bed, staining my hands, soaking into my shirt, sliding over my skin.

"Don't look," Tommy whispers.

With an abruptness that leaves me floundering, I'm tangled in a straitjacket of blankets, choking on screams in the dark. Cold sweat coats my face, washed away seconds later by the tears boiling down my cheeks.

I can still feel the blood, its metallic tang sharp in my nose. My skin crawls.

Not real. Not real.

After a few steadying breaths, I extract myself from the blankets to check my deadbolt.

In the four weeks since I learned how my parents died, there have been three occasions when I felt like someone might've trespassed in my room when I wasn't here.

The clues were small. Notebook moved, maybe. Trash spilled. Did I knock it over?

I thought I was imagining things. After the third incident, I wasn't so sure. There are plenty of people in the Resistance who still don't trust me, and I don't know how far they might go to eliminate the threat they think I pose. Locking the door makes me feel better, so I do. Every night.

Yesterday was no exception. I remember sliding the bolt home before going to sleep, but I'm too rattled not to look.

Once I'm satisfied my room is secure, I stoke the fire and drag my comforter to the floor to curl up in front of the hearth. After that nightmare, I don't want to go back to bed.

If only I felt settled enough to write, I could channel this feeling onto the page, get it out of my system. Maybe if I think about something else first. Let my heart slow a bit.

The problem is, there's not much exciting about my daily life to reflect on. Eight hours a day, nearly every day, I work wherever I'm needed. Sam's usually by my side, except on Mondays and Thursdays, when he's off training to be a medic. Our job as members of the maintenance team is to keep the caves livable through completing the wide variety of chores I've been learning since I arrived.

You'd think this would get old, but Sam makes work fun. He's got a sunny aura and a wicked sense of humor, yet he's kind. Restful. It's easy to be around him.

One afternoon a couple weeks ago, I was surprised to learn he, Tommy, Cait, Vik, and Hunter are usually inseparable. Elbow-deep in soapy dishes, I pointed out I've never seen them all together.

"Well, things are weird right now," Sam replied as he took the clean dish I handed him and toweled it dry. "We've been fighting. Cait and Tommy most of all."

"Why?" I asked. Tommy and I train together every day after work, either at the shooting range or on the sparring mat. Cait hasn't attended my lessons since the first one. "Is it because of me?"

Sam frowned a little, stacking the clean dish and taking another. "Yeah. Sorry. She doesn't want you around Tommy. Or me, for that matter."

I knew it.

"Are they … together?" I forced the question through my teeth, trying without success to ignore the envy pricking at my heart.

Sam laughed. "No, little Miss Jealous. They're not. But Cait does care about him."

Heat rose up my neck and spread over my cheeks. "I'm not jealous!"

"Yeah, sure. Save it for someone who believes it." Sam poked me in the ribs.

I snorted, jabbing him right back and leaving a big, soapy mark on his T-shirt. "You're not much of a gentleman, are you?"

Sam's face filled with horror. "What fun would that be?"

I snickered and shook my head. "Seriously, though. Is it tough? The five of you, always together? There must be history. Who's hooked up with who? Tommy and Cait? You and Cait?"

Sam smirked. "Cait's not really my type. As for Tommy and Cait, they've been dancing around something for years. They're incredibly close, but officers aren't allowed to date their subordinates. It's too potentially compromising. Cait's a team lead, she heads up her own special ops mission team, so Tommy's off-limits."

"Woah. That's impressive."

So they're not together, but they're … what? Cait's strong and capable, not to mention unbelievably gorgeous. Head of her own mission team.

I would've thought she was everyone's type.

"I know you're not into Cait, but is there someone else?"

Sam chuckled. "Well … yeah, there's *someone*."

Uh-oh. Sam's preference doesn't run toward pale, impulsive, and clumsy, right?

It's not that he isn't worth having feelings for. He is. It's just someone else has already snared my attention. Much to my chagrin.

I cleared my throat. "Who? If you don't mind me asking."

Sam gave me a once-over, eyes narrowed. "Can you keep a secret?"

My heart started to pound. "Um. Yes."

"I'm seeing Hunter. You know, Hunter Zhang, on Cait's mission team. He's her second in command."

Potent relief swept through me. I don't want feelings to complicate my blossoming friendship with Sam.

"Wow." I only know Hunter by sight, but he's one strapping guy. All bronze skin and dark eyes and lean muscle.

He and Sam. Oh, how cute. I giggled, the mental picture tickling my heart.

Sam snorted. "Yeah. But you can't tell anyone, okay? As Cait's second, he's an officer too. Off-limits for us peons. No one knows besides Tommy and Vik, and Hunter would kill me if he knew I told them."

"Doesn't it bother you, keeping your relationship a secret?"

"Nah. It's not personal. Hunter's title is important to him."

Realizing I'd been scrubbing the same plate for like five minutes, I handed it over, throwing Sam a frown in the process. Something about his face said it did bother him. "How long have you been together?"

Sam took the dish, echoing my frown. "Almost two years."

"And he thinks his title is more important than you?"

"No! It's not like that. Hunter lost someone. He loves me, but he finds a great deal of purpose in going after the people who killed her. You probably understand that better than most." Sam arched a brow, and I bit my lip.

I understand, yes. But it's so unfair to Sam.

A loud *pop* pulls me back to my dark bedroom. I draw the blanket tighter around my shoulders as a shower of orange sparks drift up the shadowy chimney.

Ever since I found out about Sam and Hunter, I've kept a surreptitious eye on them. They don't seem like more than friends, though Sam says they find ways to see each other romantically under the radar.

Mouth tight, I hug my knees to my chest. Hunter better be treating Sam well. No one deserves to be treated well more than Sam.

Except maybe Tommy.

They've been dancing around something for years.

This time, envy doesn't prick at me so much as swallow me whole.

We're friends now, but there's still a certain distance between Tommy and me. I can't put my finger on what it is or why it's there, unless it has to do with my request for help unraveling what happened to Mom and Dad. Either way, considering how he makes me feel, I'm grateful.

It's not the physical attraction that worries me, even though his smile has the power to steal my breath and every touch between us on the mat sends heat streaking through my core and up my spine. As we've gotten to know each other, our relationship has become deeper. He sees me. Accepts my shattered pieces as they are. Not even my best friends back home did that.

And even though Tommy acts like he doesn't reciprocate more than my friendship, sometimes I'm not so sure. I could swear I've caught his eyes dropping to my lips mid-conversation, not to mention his attention definitely lingers a little too long from across the mess hall when he thinks I don't notice.

It's scary. The last thing I need is for a crush to compromise my purpose here.

Agitation jitters through my limbs, making me fidget. Now I think about it, how long has it been since I tried to sneak a peek at Lisa's office? Since I've taken a "bathroom break" and poked around the storage room, looking for clues?

I have let myself become distracted.

Frowning, I glance up at the battery-powered alarm clock on my nightstand. 1:27 a.m.

Well, why not make up for it? Why not right now?

In next to no time, I'm dressed and creeping out of my room.

At this hour, the caves are quiet and still, the guttering lanterns throwing long shadows over the uneven walls. There's always someone manning the CCTV room, as well as guarding the front entrance, but everyone else should be asleep.

As silently as I can, I slip through the empty corridors. My shoes tap against the stone floor, my breath too loud in my ears. Next time we train, I need to ask Tommy to teach me some basic stealth.

The lounge, the storage room, the kitchen, and the mess hall each yawn open, dark inside. The CCTV room is closed, a soft line of brightness visible beneath the door. Excellent.

I take a few careful steps beyond, squinting in the half-light.

That's when I hear them.

Footsteps, echoing in the hall behind me. Coming closer.

I whirl.

A yellow glow illuminates the nearest corner, made brighter

because the lanterns in this hall have sputtered low, burned almost to nothing.

My pulse thunders. I forgot about Fire Duty. Someone's always changing out the lanterns, keeping the fires going day and night.

Without thinking, I dive into the dark kitchen. Whoever is out there is humming to themselves, off-key. Crouching in the shadows, I listen as they move up the hall.

After a minute, a middle-aged woman sashays into view, a cart of oil cans rattling in front of her.

It's Julie Reed, a fellow maintenance team member. She trained me in the gardens, which thrive in a breathtaking greenhouse-like cavern, not long after I arrived. I annoyed her half to death asking questions about the Resistance until she told me off, then made me work in silence for the rest of the day. I haven't spoken to her since, but I'm pretty sure she thinks I'm a mole.

I can't let her find me hiding in here like a criminal. She'll take me straight to Lisa.

Framed in the door, Julie refills the oil in the only lantern I can see before moving on. I wait. She'll have to come back this way when she's done.

It takes forever, but eventually she passes again, cart rattling away.

When her footsteps have faded, I wait sixty seconds, then slip out of the kitchen and slink down the hall. This corridor ends in a split, the main hall branching off to the left. Straight ahead there's nothing but a short walkway ending in what I assume is a simple closet.

I'm mid-turn, heading left, when something about that nondescript closet catches my eye.

It has a keyhole.

Why? None of the other rooms in the caves have locks, save for our bedrooms, the cells, and Lisa's office.

Intrigued, I make my way over to the door. The handle looks normal. Plain.

I grasp the cold metal and twist.

Big surprise, it's locked. Using both hands, I wrench at the knob.

When it doesn't budge, I step back. A keyhole means a key. I'll figure out where it is, swipe it, and try again another night. If only I knew what's in there, though. I don't want to take such a big risk if this *is* just a closet.

Grabbing the closest lantern off the wall, I sit on the floor by the mystery room. Then I lie flat on my stomach, peering through the crack under the door.

I can't make out much, but the lantern does illuminate the first several inches of what looks like another, darker hall.

What could Lisa be keeping back there? Weapons? Information? Something about 'the chip?'

I cup my hands around my eyes and focus on the dark, willing it to resolve into shapes. There's a black shadow to the left, a half-oval, tall … and straight ahead—

Without warning, I'm flipped onto my back and staring up into narrowed gray eyes. Ice floods my system.

Cait.

She's straddling my hips, hatred chiseled into every hard line of her face.

Her hand tangles in my hair. I yell, pain ripping through my scalp as she yanks my head back. Sharp metal bites into my exposed throat.

A knife.

I start to gasp.

"I knew it," she snarls.

"Please, I—"

She leans forward, hissing in my face. "Your days are numbered, Melanie. You might have Tommy and Sam fooled, but not me. I know who you work for. I won't let you hurt the people I love."

"No, you're wrong, I wasn't, I'm not—"

"I can't wait to tell Lisa. You'll finally get what's coming to you."

Cait jumps up and strides away, leaving me a shivering wreck on the floor. She doesn't look back.

Shit.

Lisa might have let me stay, even given me an official place on the maintenance team, but she hasn't decided whether to fully trust me yet. When Cait tells her I was trying to get through this door…

Tommy said bad things would happen if I kept investigating, that leadership would come down on me. That I'd get hurt.

I take several deep breaths, struggling to loosen my rigid muscles. My reason for snooping is innocent. If I go to Lisa now and explain why I was at this door, maybe she'll listen. She already knows I want information on my parents.

But what if Cait doesn't tell her? There's no proof. There are no cameras in the caves. The CCTV Tommy and the others are always watching is from Levett Tech, not here.

Cait probably wants to scare me into confessing. If so, I should forget this ever happened, or I'll risk retribution for nothing.

Fear churns like acid in my stomach. I can't afford to make a wrong move.

I need Tommy and Sam.

No longer bothered about stealth, I sprint for my friends.

My heart hammers out a violent beat as I skid around the corner into the housing wing and crash to a stop outside Tommy's door. I knock.

There's no answer.

With a curse, I stride across the hall and rap on Sam's door instead.

This time, I make out rustling. Soft footsteps pad across the floor, then the door cracks open, one bleary chocolate eye peeking out.

"Mel?" Sam croaks. He's wearing sweatpants and a hoodie, with thick woolen socks.

"Can I come in? It's urgent."

"Of course."

Sam stands aside. I slip past him on wobbly legs.

He eases the door closed and adds a log to his fire. As the flames lick up the dry wood, I sink into his desk chair and drop my head into my hands.

Sam kneels in front of me. "What's going on? You look like hell. Wow, you're shaking. Are you okay?"

"Not really."

Sam's brows pull together. "Why not?"

I throw him a helpless look. "Um. I did something I shouldn't have done, and Cait caught me, and I don't know the best way to handle it."

Looking nauseated, Sam reaches up and strokes a finger over my windpipe, tracing the spot where Cait's knife was. "What did she do?"

I swallow. "She … I didn't hear her coming. I know I shouldn't have, but I was trying to get through a locked door. She pinned me down and held her knife to my throat, which was terrifying, but—"

Sam cuts me off with a low, indiscernible growl.

"Sam, listen. She said she was going to Lisa, and I'm sure that's bad, and I don't know what to do. I swear, I just wanted information on my parents, I'd never hurt you guys. Us! Never!"

My lip quivers, hysteria building in my throat. "What will happen to me now?"

Sam rocks back on his heels. The firelight glitters in his deep eyes. "I don't know. I wish I could help. I'll vouch for you and do whatever I can, but I don't think…"

I tip my head back, willing away tears. Is it hopeless? I should've gone straight to Lisa instead of coming here. I shouldn't have let Cait talk to her without me.

Too late now. I might as well see what Sam thinks of the plan I came up with. He could have some insight I don't.

With an air of grasping at straws, I say, "I have an idea. But I don't really know Lisa, and I wanted to see whether you think it would be smart."

Sam motions for me to go on.

I stare down at my hands. "If I tell Lisa myself—if I own up to what I was doing—I thought maybe she'd give me another chance. Maybe she'd believe my motivations, see my honesty."

I force myself to meet Sam's gaze. "Cait might not tell her. Maybe she's just trying to scare me. If she does say something, there won't be any proof, just her word against mine. So, I could do nothing and hope this goes away. That's another reason why I think telling Lisa myself would be good. It proves I'm trying to be up front and honest, rather than hiding things."

The faintest ray of hope kindles in Sam's grave stare. "You know, I think you're right. Telling Lisa yourself is your best bet, maybe your only chance. You should do it. As soon as possible. Right now. I'll go with you." He holds out a hand.

Tension floods my stomach as I pull myself up. Sam wastes no time dragging me from his room and down the hall.

As we walk, he peeks my way, pensive. "You know what? Maybe you should offer Lisa something beyond the truth about this. To prove the extent of your loyalty."

"I'd give anything. But what can I offer? I don't have any knowledge, no special skills."

"You do have special skills." Sam's eyes are bright, his familiar mischievous grin curling across his face. "I've seen you train with Tommy. You're getting better on the mat, and you're a hell of a good shot. Plus, you've been inside Levett Tech's offices more recently than anyone else."

If hitting the target occasionally means I'm a hell of a good shot, then I'm a ham sandwich, but I nod, frowning.

"There's a mission happening there tomorrow. Maybe you should tell Lisa you want to help with it, as a show of trust. I think she'll love that. I think it's your ticket out of this!"

Hmm. I do know my way around Levett's campus, but Lisa must too. And I'll admit I'm better with guns than I'd have guessed, but I'm nowhere near ready to use one in the field, never mind engage in hand-to-hand combat. Sam's lost his marbles. "Are you yanking my chain?"

His confident smile falters. "I'm dead serious. I think it would go a long way if you offered. Please, please do it. Who will make me look good at work if you're gone?"

"Don't be stupid. If you don't want me to get hurt, don't make asinine suggestions that will get me killed. And if *you* don't want to get hurt, don't joke around right now."

Sam presses his lips together "I'm sorry. I know it's not the time. I wouldn't suggest this if I didn't think it would mean something to Lisa. Why ask for my help if you weren't going to even consider my advice?"

I fix my eyes on the tunnel ahead, chewing over Sam's words.

He thinks I should ask for a mission.

A stream of colorful pictures run through my mind. Tommy taking down the best fighters in the Resistance with lethal grace. Cait pinning him to the floor, rock-solid as she presses her knife to his throat. The way they all move, so silent and steady, like wraiths.

I don't measure up. I'll die if I go on a mission now.

A new image: Sam, wide-eyed and pale in the semi-darkness of his bedroom.

He doesn't think Lisa will believe me. That's why he wants me to do this, because he knows it's my only chance.

A mission may take me out, but if Lisa thinks I'm a traitor, she could kill me herself. Or imprison me for the rest of my life.

My empty stomach rolls. "Okay. I'll do it."

We turn the last corner, heading down the final long hall toward Lisa's office. Sam's smile is gentle. "Good."

Despite the chaos inside, I give Sam a small smile in return, then cock my head, studying him. I've seen him train with the others. He's quick, he's scrappy, he's smart in a fight.

"Why haven't you requested a mission yourself?"

"I'm not really thought of for that kind of thing." A bite of bitterness leaks through in his tone.

"Why not? Don't you want to go on missions?"

Sam studies his fingers. After a moment, he says, "I'd love to, but I'll do whatever helps the Resistance most, and that means serving on the maintenance team and studying to be a medic. They saved my life, you know. When I was an intern at Levett Tech, I figured out what was going on there. The Resistance risked themselves to get me out. I owe them everything."

"I still don't understand. Why not help by going on missions, if that's what you want?"

Color stains Sam's cheeks. He looks away. "I have an aptitude for medicine, and we need more medics. Plus, Lisa thinks I'd be a liability in the field."

My jaw drops. How insulting. "Why?"

Sam glances back at me, lips pursed. "Well, it's kind of my own fault she thinks that way. Remember what I told you about Hunter losing someone?"

"Yeah."

"The person he lost was a sensitive soul. More lover than fighter. She was killed before I arrived here, when she froze up in the middle of a shootout. Couldn't take the violence."

I gasp, hand flying to my mouth, and Sam nods. "Yeah. Originally, I was slated to serve on Cait's mission team with Tommy, Vik, and Hunter. That's why the Resistance saved me in the first place. They needed young blood to fill June's empty spot after she died. But I hated the idea of hurting anyone, even bad guys. The thought of killing a person made me sick."

Sam pauses, eyes far away.

"The night before my first mission, I confessed to Hunter how much it bothered me. He begged me to step down from the team. I didn't want to, but that was when he told me about June. Then he hit me with the most beautiful *I'm falling for you* speech you could imagine."

"Oh, Sam. That's heavy."

"Yep. It was. I was really torn, but I was afraid if I was in the field with Hunter, he'd be distracted. Obviously I couldn't tell Lisa anything that might hint at our relationship, so in order to bail on the team I said I didn't think I could handle the violence of a mission. And yes, I would hate that part, but it's not the real reason I quit. I did it for Hunter, and I've regretted it for a long time, but once that seed of doubt was sown, it was too late. No one wants an unreliable teammate when their life is on the line."

Warmth unfurls in my heart. It means a lot that Sam's confided in me. I wind an arm around his waist as we walk, giving him a small squeeze. "You know, it's possible to be too self-sacrificing. Hiding your love, giving up your spot on the team. What has Hunter done for you? Your relationship seems kind of one-sided."

Sam slings an arm over my shoulders. There's nothing uncomfortable about his proximity, no underlying tension. It's the warm embrace of a dear friend, and it feels like coming home. "I hear you. I'm not trying to make excuses for him, but he's been through hell and back."

Lisa's office swims into view at the end of the hall, and my hands start to shake.

"Anyway, right now isn't about me. It's about you. You've got this, Mel."

With a nod, Sam drops his arm. I hug my ribs.

For a moment, a river of phantom blood soaks my skin and stings my nose. I see Mom, her hair a glistening crown, her eyes dead.

A flush of ferocity pulses in my chest, even as chills prickle over my scalp. The reminder—of why I'm here, of what my parents endured—gives me courage. No matter what happens now, I will be strong.

Chin high, I knock: three sharp taps on Lisa's door.

CHAPTER EIGHTEEN

TOMMY

CAIT's not one to be late. Ever. And yet here I am, waiting on her.

I lean against the newest vehicle in the garage, a sleek black Kia Telluride, and watch the door coming from the caves into the garage. Timeliness is important on missions, even missions as simple as supply runs. If we want to hit all our stops today, we need to leave now. Cait knows this.

So where is she? Is she truly angry enough to disobey orders?

I shift, too restless to stand still. My friendship with Cait has been rocky ever since our fight in the CCTV room four weeks ago. We've been through squabbles before, but we're always speaking again within a few days.

Not this time.

At first, I tried to talk to her, but she slipped away every time she saw me coming. She even went so far as to trade all her shifts so she wouldn't have to go on patrol with me.

I've missed her more every day, but I don't know how to fix the space between us without ditching Mel. Mel doesn't deserve that, and I enjoy our time together too much to want to give it up, anyway.

I glance at my watch. I'll give Cait ten minutes. If she's not here by four a.m., I'll hunt her down and drag her out myself. Lisa was very clear: Cait and I are supposed to use our time together on this supply run to make up, and we're not to set foot back in the caves until we do.

"A team is only as strong as its weakest link," Lisa told us. "We cannot afford vulnerabilities, especially now."

If Cait weren't so concerned about her status as team lead, I'd consider today's undertaking doomed. As it stands, I can only hope her loyalty and ambition win out over her determination to punish me.

Tomorrow we set off on the most dangerous assignment our team's ever been given. We can't let our fight affect the mission.

At long last, Cait appears in the doorway. I push off the SUV and walk forward to meet her.

"Cait," I say with a touch of impatience.

"Tommy."

Sighing, I force my irritation aside. One of us has to play nice first.

"I'm sorry, okay? I know you're having trouble with Mel being here. I should have, I don't know, listened to you better or something." I wave a hand vaguely.

Cait crosses her arms and pops a hip, fixing me with a flat gray stare. Then she rolls her eyes and shoves me aside to climb into the Kia, driver's side. Fresh annoyance frays at my patience, but I bite it back, silently taking my place in the passenger seat.

We pull out into a dark maze of trees, the camouflaged garage door rolling closed behind us. It'll be a while before we find the road, but Cait navigates the thin, winding path with skill.

As we bump along, I struggle to leash the temper that simmers under my skin. Her mouth is set, eyes hard. She's not trying. At all.

Pigheaded, cantankerous, obstinate…

Like she can hear my thoughts, she throws me a scathing glare. "Guess who I saw this morning?"

Her tone instantly puts my back up. "This morning? It's four a.m.! No one's awake but us and the guards."

"Your *girlfriend* is." The word sags with disgust.

"Ugh. I don't have a girlfriend. Mel is my friend, just like you. And she's not a spy. Give it a rest already."

I lean my head back and cover my face with my hands. Yeah, I spend a fair amount of time with Mel, but I'm with Sam and Vik almost as much. Mel and I are just friends. Nothing more.

She's gorgeous, of course. Alluring even. Every time we spar, I light up like a live wire, her touch electric on my skin. And there's a depth to her, a depth that calls to me. She's sweet. Kind, yet a fire burns within, coloring everything she does with vibrant passion. She's fiercely competitive and curious and intelligent. Sometimes, after training, we sit and talk for hours. She understands me in a way no one else ever has, or ever could.

Yes, Mel's … enchanting. But as much as I might want to, I won't let us get anywhere near that invisible line. Mel deserves more in a partner than I could give her. Plus, if she were to commit to me like that, I'd have to tell her everything. And then I'd lose her.

Cait's snort snaps me back to reality. "Oh yeah? Not a spy? How do you know?"

Suddenly, I'm bone-tired. How many times will we go through this? "I know because I know her. If you got to know her too, you might figure it out for yourself."

"I don't have to get to know her. I know what I saw this morning."

Cait's calm. Too calm.

I peek sideways at her. "Well? Spit it out."

"I couldn't sleep, so I was lying in the lounge, in the dark. I heard someone moving out in the hall, and it kind of sounded like they were trying to be quiet, but not doing a good job. I thought it must be Mel, and I was right. I followed her, hoping to figure out what she was doing."

My stomach tightens.

"Turns out, she was trying to break into the library. The library, Tommy! I waited to see whether she'd stolen a key or something, but she hadn't. So, I let her know exactly what will happen to her for crossing us." Cait's voice slips into a low growl.

"What does that mean?" A hundred scenarios chase each other around my mind, each worse than the last. "Tell me what happened. You what, threatened her?"

Cait slams on the brakes. The soft glow from the dash paints her face as she stares at me, incredulous. "Did you even listen to what I just said?"

"What happened, Cait?"

A vicious smile spreads across Cait's face, her eyes sparking like twin storms. "I put my dagger to her throat and told her she'll get what's coming to her. I'm still deciding whether to tell Lisa today, or whether I should find out more first. This is my chance to make up for not catching June, but I need Lisa to believe me. Proof would help."

With a groan, I press back into my seat and close my eyes.

This is bad.

I thought my warning had gotten through to Mel, and she'd given up looking for answers, at least for now. If Cait brings this to Lisa's attention, Mel's finished in the Resistance. What would that mean for her? Will Lisa lock her in a cell? Toss her out, leaving her at the mercy of the Organization?

Unlikely. She knows too much.

What, then? Something worse?

Swallowing my pride, I face Cait and clasp my hands in front of me. "Please. You don't understand. She thinks finding out what happened to our parents will heal her. That's why she wanted to get into the library. I'll talk to her and make sure she knows she can never do something like this again, but don't turn her in. Give her a chance to learn what is and isn't acceptable. Crucifying an innocent person won't make up for shit."

Cait appraises me coolly. "Well, lucky for you, I'm sure Mel won't own up to what I saw, and Lisa's soft on her because of Reyna. I'm worried it'll continue to affect Lisa's judgment."

I wait for her to continue, fiddling with my bracelet. Crickets and frogs sing in the forest around us; the night is alive outside the car.

At length, Cait goes on. "I need you to help uncover Mel's true motive. Use your friendship with her. Ask questions. See if you can find out what else she could be after, whether she's truly as innocent as she seems. If you want me to stay quiet, that's the price. Help me."

It's the tiny note of desperation in her voice that gets to me. Everything she's done has been to protect us, the people she loves.

I could ask Mel a few questions. It wouldn't hurt, especially if I'm honest with her about what I'm doing and why. But I doubt it would put Cait's fears to rest. The animosity between them will only get worse when I fail to uncover an ulterior motive.

"Please, Tommy."

Maybe I can break through Cait's preconceived notions instead, help her understand Mel better. If Cait would give Mel a chance, I bet they'd even end up friends. Win-win.

Using my gentlest tone, I ask, "Will you hear me out before I give you my answer?"

Cait's eyes tighten, but she nods.

"You know what my parents' murder has done to me."

Cait opens her mouth, so I hold up a hand. "You promised."

She snaps it shut.

Holding her gaze, I try again. "You know the scar I bear. You know how bad it is, and it's never really gotten better. Mel's fighting the same battle. My demons are different from hers, but it doesn't mean hers aren't just as real, just as agonizing in their own way. She's fixated on learning the truth about what happened that night and why. I'll admit, I did tell her a little bit, but she wants more. She craves a release from her pain, and she thinks knowledge is the way to find it."

I pause, frowning. "June betrayed us for a reason. She would've done anything to save her dad. Mel has no reason, Cait. She's not a spy. She's just a lost, desperate girl, trying to escape an all-consuming grief."

I search Cait's face, seeking any softness, any trace of mercy. All I find is cold resentment.

"You're wrapped around her little finger."

Fury sears under my skin. "Stop and think. Think. Why would the Organization send some green novice to infiltrate us? Listen to what I'm saying. You'll see I'm right, that it makes sense—"

"I've heard enough." Cait's words whip out, bitter and disdainful. The rest of my argument dies in my throat.

Shifting the car into drive, she hits the gas. I can't tear my eyes from the hate simmering in hers. She's beyond sense.

Maybe if I relent, if I ask Mel the damn questions, Cait will back off long enough for me to figure out how to reach her.

"All right. You win. I'll go along with your plan."

Cait's lip curls. "No, you won't. Not really."

She flashes me a quick, hurt look. "I'm going to Lisa as soon as we get back. It has to be done, before Mel causes more damage than she already has."

I stare at her again, at a total loss. How did this happen? I couldn't have alienated Cait more thoroughly, right before the most dangerous mission we've ever attempted. I don't know how we're going to patch things up before tonight.

And Mel's in danger. Serious danger.

If she'd tried to break in anywhere but the library, I'd have hope. But there are too many parallels between what June did and what Mel's doing now. If I stand with her, if I argue her case, if I refuse to let anyone touch her...

"We can't let this affect the mission," Cait says.

I've never heard her sound so cold.

"No."

"I will work with you until that's over. Then I don't want you near me. You will transfer to another mission team and will not speak to me again. I don't want an apology. You made your choice. Live with it and leave me alone."

Hurt and fury spike in my chest. All the pranks we've pulled together; terrorizing the other Resistance members, laughing until we cry; a hundred adventures in the sun; quiet moments and love and solace and tears. Cait's smile. Her warm hand guiding me through my darkest night.

She's the truest friend I've ever had, and she'd rather throw it all away than listen to me about Mel. She won't even try.

"Fine."

A shadow passes over Cait's face, her furious mask cracking, but the sadness in her eyes is gone so quickly I'm not sure it was ever there.

My anger shifts to dread as darkness consumes my friend.

Chapter Nineteen

MEL

SAM and I sit in rickety wooden chairs in front of Lisa's desk, her bright, cheery fire at odds with the tense atmosphere in the room.

I've spent the last thirty minutes spilling my guts to her. I told her everything, from the moment I learned of my parents' deaths all the way through my encounter with Cait at the mystery door. Sam stayed beside me, holding one of my clammy hands in both of his own. The small reminder of his support has helped me stumble through, even when anxiety threatened to suffocate me.

Lisa hasn't said one word. Hasn't reacted at all. She only stood in front of us, arms crossed, and listened; impossible to read.

I force myself to meet her dark eyes. "I know it was stupid to try and get through that door. But I'm committed to the Resistance, to your cause, and to the people here. In fact, in order to prove it, I'd like to…"

Major gulp. Here goes nothing.

"… volunteer for tomorrow's mission. I've been practicing, and I think I could be an asset to the team."

Lisa's mouth twists, the first hint of emotion I've seen from her since entering her office. The pressure to look away is overwhelming, but I hold her gaze.

After several long seconds, during which the tension in my chest builds almost to a breaking point, Lisa opens her mouth to speak. I brace myself.

"You're so like Reyna." She sighs, liquid eyes full of sorrow.

The words hit me like a punch to the stomach.

"Your mother was my best friend," she goes on quietly. "I knew her very well. The Organization knows this, and so I must be on my guard. A well-trained spy could use my grief against me. You most of all."

A mournful ache fills my heart. Mom's best friend. I never realized, never thought about what the people here meant to my parents. What my parents meant to them.

Tommy and I aren't the only ones who lost family that night.

"I loved my mom and dad. I would never dishonor them by working for their murderers."

Lisa chews her lip as the silence stretches tight.

She thinks I'm lying. She thinks me capable of something so horrendous, so despicable, I can't even stomach the idea of it.

"I believe you."

Relief sweeps through my system, so strong it makes me woozy.

"I probably shouldn't, but my gut says you're genuine. And what you've done, what you're doing... It's what she would have done. Your mother."

I drag in a ragged breath. Sam squeezes my hand, and I peek at him, drawing strength from his warmth.

Lisa's eyes harden. "There are no second chances when it comes to the safety and security of my people. I understand why you are so determined to find answers to your questions, but know this. I will do whatever is necessary to protect the Resistance, no matter whose daughter you are. Do you understand what I'm saying?"

Whatever is necessary. Like putting a bullet in my skull.

Good thing I'm trustworthy.

"Yes," I whisper.

"Good. If you ever do anything like this again, I will be forced to consider you our enemy, and I will react accordingly. That being said, I accept your offer to help on tomorrow's mission."

I sit up straighter, my pulse quickening as she continues.

"We know how Levett's campus is laid out, but it's been years since any of us have set foot in the admin building. You will not join us in the field. However, if you could fill in the gaps in our knowledge and give us more detail regarding records storage, it would help immensely. We will meet with Cait's team tomorrow morning to go over your information, so I suggest you spend today writing down everything you can remember about the fourth floor."

"I would be honored."

Lisa considers me for a moment. "You should know, tomorrow's assignment isn't our standard outing. Missions normally range from routine supply runs and surveillance, to intercepting and destroying weapons shipments. These missions are sometimes quite dangerous, but tomorrow will be even more so. We are breaking into Levett Tech and attempting to secure paperwork related to a material called BioAgent 313. A bill of lading, to be specific."

BioAgent 313. I think I've heard that name before. I quickly run through my brief time at Levett, but I can't place the term.

Lisa's still talking, pacing back and forth with her hands clasped behind her back. "We haven't dared a break-in for years, but this paperwork is worth the risk. With the information held within, we can attempt to intercept the BioAgent shipment and stop the Organization from gaining control of it. If you can remember anything at all that will help us locate the bill of lading, you could mean the difference between life and death, not only for Cait's team, but for many innocent people."

My already worn nerves fray. I know I've heard of BioAgent 313. I rack my brain, trying to think, to remember…

The image of a young man in a filing room fills my mind, and my heart leaps.

I saw it myself, buried in a box of incoming shipment records. There were receipts for chemicals, explosives, fuels … and something biological. Something that sounded like it belonged in a spy movie.

The bill of lading for BioAgent 313. I know exactly where it is.

I swallow the dryness in my throat. "I've seen that bill of lading."

Sam gasps. Lisa's piercing gaze sharpens. "You have? Are you sure?"

I think so. It said *Bill of Lading* at the top.

"I am."

Lisa sizes me up.

"New plan. I need your intimate knowledge on the front lines. With you guiding us, we'll save precious minutes of searching. We can strike with precision, take what we need, and get out."

I stare at the floor, fear razing my confidence to ash. I never expected to play such a vital role in this mission. It's so much more than I bargained for.

"Mel, look at me. You don't have to come to Levett Tech. I will never force you to risk your safety, but your knowledge could turn the tide for us. You can't comprehend the importance of that bill of lading, or how much each second counts on a mission like this."

Lisa adjusts her glasses. Takes a breath. "If the Organization gets their hands on the BioAgent, they will use it to harm others. Children. Help us secure the documents we need, and you will prove to me once and for all you are on our side. You will truly earn your place among us. Know this, though. If you betray us, if you alert the Organization to our presence, the rest of the team will have orders to end you. Immediately."

I shiver.

When I first arrived, Lisa said I might earn the information I seek if I prove myself worthy. This is my chance, but I don't know if I can take it.

I'm such a coward.

Shame wells up in my chest, its bitter sting coats my tongue. Mom and Dad died to help the Resistance, and I can't do this? Families are counting on me. Children.

I will not run away. I will be brave, like my parents, and face this head-on. I will earn Lisa's trust, like a true member of the Resistance.

And I'll be back at Levett Tech, with a team of highly trained operatives to help me investigate. Perhaps while we're there I'll find more than the bill of lading. This is an unexpected opportunity to uncover the truth through a different avenue, if I'm strong, brave, and lucky.

Jerking my chin up, I meet Lisa's eyes. "I accept."

A small, almost wistful smile tugs at her lips. "Good. The team will meet in the lounge tomorrow morning at seven to hear your information and go over the plan. The mission will commence at ten in the evening. You are dismissed."

With that, Lisa turns and strides around her desk, disappearing through a door behind it. I stare after her, the pop and crackle of the fire the only sounds in the room.

"Mel," Sam whispers. "Are you sure?"

Slowly, I turn to him, conviction strong in my heart. "It's the best way forward. And you're right. I can do this."

Though his brows pull together, he simply says, "Okay."

The look on his face makes my insides squirm. Ugh. I don't want to think about the enormity of what I just agreed to. Or what Tommy will say when he finds out.

I need a distraction, something so consuming I won't have time or energy to waste on pointless nerves.

I need to train.

"Well, I'll never get to sleep now." I jump to my feet. "Want to grab an early breakfast? Squeeze in some sparring before our shift?"

Sam yawns as he stands. "Sounds good to me."

After a quick bite of toast, Sam and I spend an hour in the gym, going over how to incapacitate an attacker should I find myself knocked to the ground. I still have much to learn, but Sam's an excellent teacher, and I manage to pick up several new tricks in the short time we have.

Our shift in the kitchen drags. I'm dying to get back onto the mat, but I use my time as best I can. I run through fight sequences in my mind. Walking around the kitchen, I try to emulate the way Tommy moves—with liquid grace, smooth and silent.

After the dinner rush peters out, Chef Ari dismisses me, and I race back to my room to change. Dressed for a workout, I head straight to the gym, ignoring Sam's pleas for me to eat something. I don't have time to eat. I need to use every last second I have to prepare.

When tomorrow comes, I'll be ready.

Chapter Twenty

Tommy

Cait hasn't spoken since before sunrise.

It's clear enough on her face, though; as soon as we get home, she's going to tell Lisa about Mel's break-in attempt. All day I've wracked my brain, looking for ways to get Mel out of this mess. Try as I might, I can't think of any.

And I'm out of time to work.

The SUV glides to a stop in the empty garage as the door creaks down behind us. Cait's out of the car before I can blink, already tearing away toward the caves.

I sprint after her, fear a hard knot in my gut. Whatever fate Lisa decrees for Mel, the Resistance will enforce it. Most don't trust her, and those who do won't undermine Lisa's authority. But if I stand by Mel, if I speak on her behalf...

I won't let them touch her.

Like a whirlwind, I burst from the tunnel into the lounge. Cait's nowhere to be seen. I need to get to Mel before she and Lisa do.

Mel was on kitchen duty today, so she would've had to clean up after dinner before she could eat. It's almost nine, but she's probably still there.

Pushing my body harder, faster, I whip through the corridors. The mouthwatering smell of lasagna reaches me well before I round the last corner into the mess hall.

Empty, and the kitchen's dark. Mel's not here.

Dread flattens my lungs as I race for the housing wing. Cait will have reached Lisa's office by now. If Mel's not in her room, they'll find her first.

I hammer on her door, shouting her name, but it's Sam who answers. His head pops into the hall from the next room over.

"Where is she?"

Sam scans the corridor behind me. "What's going on?"

I don't have time to explain.

"Where's Mel?" I ask again, urgency rolling off me in waves. My hands shake.

"I last saw her heading to the gym, but—"

I'm gone in a flash.

"Wait!"

Sam's footsteps pound after me, but I don't slow. No, I run like Mr. Edwards himself is on my heels, his breath hot on my neck, no more than a death blow away.

Cait and Lisa will get there first. What will they do? Imprison her? Interrogate her? Worse? I don't know how my presence can help, but I can't stand the thought of Mel facing them alone.

Faster, I snarl at myself. My muscles scream. Faster.

I crash into the gym, almost taking the door off its hinges on my way.

There she is.

She's fine. In fact, she's kicking the piss out of one of the punching bags lined up against the far wall. There's no sign of Cait or Lisa.

Mel spins toward me, her stunning eyes wide. A thin scarlet line runs across her windpipe, vivid against that delicate ivory skin.

One small twitch of Cait's hand, and Mel would've drowned in her own blood. Sickness crawls up my throat.

"Tommy! What's wrong? Are you hurt?"

Mel's gaze slides over my body. Checking for injuries.

"No," I wheeze. "But you … Cait … She's telling Lisa, we have to—"

"It's okay, it's okay." Mel gives me a small smile. "I already talked to Lisa myself. I'm off the hook."

I gape as shock buzzes in my ears. Based on conversations I've had with Lisa, even recently, I can't imagine a scenario in which she would let Mel get away with trying to break into the library. "What?"

"Yeah," Mel says, smile widening. "And..."

She falls silent. Footsteps hammer out in the hall.

Mel and I both turn as Sam hurtles into the room and stumbles to a halt. He doubles over, gasping too hard to speak.

In three long strides, Mel's by his side. She rests a gentle hand on his back, and something like petulant annoyance cracks through me, throwing me off balance.

Sam's still breathing too heavily to say anything. I watch, rigid, while Mel slides that hand across his shoulders, her eyes running over him. The maddening vexation grows to form an overwhelming pressure in my chest.

It's jealousy. I'm jealous of the way she's touching him.

How ridiculous. I know beyond the shadow of a doubt they're not more than friends, that Sam isn't interested in women, and yet...

Sam's choking out words now, hands still on his knees. "D-did something more happen?"

Mel answers before I can. "No, no. Tommy just thought I was still in trouble with Lisa, though I don't know how he knew about that?" She turns the statement into a question, cocking her head at me. Her hand still rests on Sam's shoulder.

"Cait," I grind out.

Uncertainty sweeps across Mel's face and a small frown tugs at her full lips. With chagrin, I realize she's not confused by my answer. She's reacting to *me*. I'm stiff as a board, muscles locked and jaw clenched. I don't know what she sees on my face.

Sam's watching too, eyes narrowed.

Deliberately, I uncross my arms and shift my weight. "So, Lisa let you off the hook? How'd you manage that?"

Sam interjects. "It's true Lisa let her off the hook, for now. But..." His eyes flick to the mark on Mel's throat.

Yeah, but. Cait's going to be angrier than ever. Worse, she'll be desperate. Sam meets my gaze, and I know he's thinking the same thing.

Mel glances from him to me. "What am I missing?"

"Cait," Sam says, uncharacteristically serious. "We're worried about how she'll react to Lisa's decision to forgive you."

Mel's hand flies to her neck, fear flashing in her eyes.

I throw her my most reassuring smile. "Don't be afraid. She's not getting through us."

"I should go find her," Sam adds. "I'll figure out what she's thinking, see if I can talk her down. Tommy, stay with Mel."

He turns on his heel and strides out the door. Mel watches him go, a little crease between her brows.

"He'll be okay. Cait would never hurt Sam."

Mel nods slowly. "Will you teach me how to move quietly? You all walk like ghosts. I can't figure out how you do it."

The question is so unexpected it takes a moment to process. "What? You want to learn stealth? Now?"

Mel flashes a brilliant smile. "Yeah, now. You have something better to do?"

Tearing my gaze from her, I glance at the clock on the wall. "Hmm. It's getting late. I have a mission tomorrow, so I need to hit the sack early. But soon. Sure."

"Please? I really, really need to learn. Lisa put me on tomorrow's mission team."

Her words are breathless, but she doesn't look afraid. No, she looks determined.

I stare. Lisa assigned Mel to the Levett mission? What is she playing at?

Mel's not ready. Sure, she's got a fuck ton of potential on the mat and even more at the range, but she's still so green. And what about her utter lack of stealth? When she's not on the mat, she's ... well, a total klutz.

Fury ripples under my skin. This could be Lisa's way of getting rid of Mel without getting her hands dirty.

"She did what?" I ask flatly.

Mel wrings her hands. "Well, I offered. As a way to show her I'm committed to the Resistance. I know where the bill of lading is, so I can lead us exactly where we need to go."

Fuck, but it makes sense. Lisa must think the pros outweigh the cons.

I shake my head. "You're good, but you still have a lot to learn. Is the bill of lading why Lisa let you off the hook?"

"No, it isn't. I was off the hook anyway. But she said if I can prove my loyalty on this mission, I'll earn her trust."

She lifts her chin, a fierce challenge blazing in her beautiful eyes.

There are a million reasons why I should convince Mel to back out, but looking into that fiery gaze, I can't bring myself to try. What right do I have to tell her what to do? My choices have always been wrong, have always hurt her. Mel's free to make her own decisions, and I need to be a good friend and support her, whatever her choices may be.

I nod once. "Okay. We have a lot to go over then. First, you need to be prepared. On a mission like this, sometimes it's necessary to, uh, dispatch the enemy."

Wary, I watch for Mel's reaction. Will she see me differently when she realizes I've killed?

What little color she has drains from her face. "Dispatch the enemy. You mean murder people? I might have to … to kill someone?" Her voice jumps an octave, becoming thin and wobbly.

Still guarded, I nod. "We try to avoid it, but there are times when we can't."

Mel visibly shivers. "Okay."

I step toward her, expression softening. "It's just something to be prepared for. Stick by me tomorrow, okay? I'll watch out for you. Odds are you won't have to make that choice yourself, but you may see it happen. Considering what we're doing, breaking into Levett Tech, there's a high probability."

Mel takes a shuddering breath. "I can handle it."

Nothing can truly prepare her for such a thing, but at least now she won't be caught off guard. "Good."

Silence falls in the empty gym while I consider what sort of training might help in the limited time we have. There's so much she hasn't learned. Stealth would be most useful, but it takes months to get the hang of and years to master. Not to mention, she hasn't even touched on how to handle a weapon in the field versus the range, and she's barely scratched the surface of hand-to-hand combat.

I'm still undecided when Mel's eyes light up. A bright smile spreads across her face.

"Let's make this interesting," she purrs, and she's so unintentionally tempting I have to remind myself to breathe.

I grin. "Let me guess. You think with a short lesson, you'll be able to out-sneak me, and you want to rub it in my face with a bet."

Mel throws her head back and laughs. The sound glitters in the air. "Oh, I'll be able to out-sneak you someday, but I'm not stupid enough to think I can do it yet. Actually, I thought we could play a game, to test all my skills together."

She leans toward me. "What if we played tag? We could use the mats to make a maze of sorts. Your goal is to tap me out. If you do, you win. But if I tap you out, I win."

This sounds like Mel's way of distracting herself from what's coming. We should train, focus on lessons instead, but nothing motivates her like competition. Besides, I want to play, especially if I get to play with her.

I smirk wickedly. "You're on."

Together, Mel and I pull the mats up from the floor and stand them on their sides to create walls scattered throughout the long room. When that's done, we steal several lanterns from the hall, placing them on the floor at various points in the maze. When we turn off the lights, they'll create alternating pools of shivering light and deepest black.

Preparations complete, I do my best to give Mel a crash course in basic stealth, demonstrating how to shift her weight as she moves, how to blend with the shadows and use senses other than sight to find her way in the dark. She's typically a quick study, but she's having trouble grasping this, even more than I expected. I hide my worry. She'll need to be confident to make it through tomorrow.

"Are you ready?" Anticipation thrums through me and my lips curve into a grin.

"I'm ready!" she shouts from the other end of the room. Though I can't see her behind the maze, it's clear she's excited—and overconfident. I'll have to go easy enough to keep her spirits up, while still showing her how much she has yet to learn. Overconfidence on a mission is as deadly as fear.

I flick off the lights. "Go!"

The sudden darkness doesn't faze me. I ghost between the mat walls, not waiting for my eyes to adjust.

Rustling, light footsteps. The softest sounds, but I pick them up immediately. Mel's somewhere ahead and to the right. I take the next turn in that direction, and the next, avoiding routes that will bring me into the revealing light of the lanterns.

Hampered by her attempt at stealth, Mel moves so slowly I catch up to her in seconds. I lurk behind her in the dark, both curious to see what she'll do and not wanting to let her know I caught her already.

She bends forward in a slight crouch, working to shift her weight like I showed her. Her pale skin gleams in the ambient light.

Near the edge of a wall, she pauses. Then she leans out into the open, midnight ponytail swinging behind her shoulder, and creeps around the mat.

Like a shadow, I follow.

I let her go on for several minutes, analyzing how she moves so I can critique her form later. It's an effort of will not to be distracted by the way her tank top clings to her lithe body, highlighting every curve, or by the roll of her hips as she slinks forward.

Mel pauses by a lantern, the space around her flooded with golden light, and glances over her shoulder for the first time. A fierce smile curls across her face as her eyes fall on me, a mere ten feet away.

"Come and get me," she taunts.

Smirking, I stalk toward her. She doesn't shrink away. No, she comes at me with blazing determination.

Instead of taking her down, I hold and let her make the first move. To teach her effectively, I need to see what she'll do.

She feints to the left, then hooks her foot behind my ankle and throws her weight into my shoulder, knocking my feet out from under me. She executes the move well, and I don't have to let her crash me to the floor.

She's quick to take advantage. Dropping down to slide over my abdomen, she locks both legs tightly around my hips. Her ponytail tickles my cheek as she leans forward, wrapping an arm behind my neck and pressing her weight into me. I can feel every line and curve of her body, tight against mine. My eyes drop to her mouth, and a flush of jittery heat flames through me.

Ignore it. Concentrate. She needs to practice.

Trapping her left side, I buck my hips to knock her off balance and roll over, reversing our positions. Quick as a flash, she winds her legs around my waist again, her ankles hooked behind my back. From here, Mel has the upper hand, but she hesitates, unsure.

I use her uncertainty to my advantage, breaking free of her hold and using my right leg to pin hers. Lying across her, I lock one of her arms in a submission hold and apply light pressure, just enough so she'll feel some stress in her joints. Our labored pants are the only sound in the shadowed room.

Aching warmth pools deep in my core. Usually, the light, the noise and activity of the gym help distract me when we're this close, keep me focused. Now, far too aware of Mel's warm body under mine, that peach-and-cherry scent of hers swirling in my head, I make the mistake of meeting her eyes.

Her gaze smolders, dark and intense. Primal. The blood electrifies in my veins.

Slowly, her free hand glides up my arm and across my shoulder. Burning sparks skitter over my skin, trailing her soft touch. My breath hitches.

For one precious second, I let myself wonder what it would be like, not just to feel her skin on mine, but to be hers. To be lucky enough to be the one for her. More than ever before, my damaged soul yearns toward her light.

Dragging in a ragged breath, Mel closes her eyes and tips her head back, perfect lips slightly parted. The heat of her breath washes over my face, muddles my senses. It would be so easy to close the space between us. To kiss her now. To make her mine.

The wildfire searing through me burns hotter at the thought, her pull almost overwhelming.

No! I can't. I can't do this.

It doesn't matter how much I want to. I can't be with Mel. There are so many ways I could fail her. Hurt her.

And I'd have to come clean. I'd have to tell her I could've saved them.

Panic douses the fiery haze in my mind. I spring to my feet.

Mel stares up at me, hurt clear on her beautiful face. Even now, I feel her pull. My very essence is drawn to her.

I have to get out of here.

"I'm sorry, I-I've got to go," I force through my teeth. Regret crashes down on me as I turn and stride away; a thick, depressing weight in my chest.

The dark maze is easy to navigate, and I find my way out quickly. I need to find Sam, to make sure Mel will be safe tonight without me.

I jog through the corridors, heading for the housing wing, where he's likely comforting Cait. Mel will never be mine, and if I'm not careful, I'm going to fall head over heels in love with the damn girl. Sweet, wild, passionate Mel. A force to be reckoned with.

Honestly, I should keep my distance, but I can't. Not with Cait after her, not with the mission tomorrow. Especially not with the debt I owe her parents. Besides, she's become a true friend, not someone I could turn away from.

Soft murmuring floats into the hall as I approach Sam's open door. When I peek in, I find him huddled under a blanket by the fire with Cait. As soon as she sees me, Cait turns her back. A small sniffle hangs in the air behind her.

Sam unfolds himself from the ground and steps out into the hall. I stay only long enough to ensure he'll be by either Cait's or Mel's side until Mel locks herself in for the night, then I head for my room.

In bed, my mind lingers on the blazing look in Mel's eyes; on the way she tipped her face toward mine and the feel of her fingers trembling against my skin.

She wants me too.

Bitterly, I stop that thought in its tracks. Mel isn't meant for me, either way. Dreaming of being with her is like dreaming of dancing among the stars, a captivating impossibility.

I press my arm over my eyes, blocking out the glow of the embers in the hearth, and crush the lovely dream into dust.

Chapter Twenty-One

MEL

IT's uncomfortable, perched on the cupholder between Tommy and Vik Taylor in the back of the black Hyundai Veloster. The full tactical gear we're decked out in makes the space feel even smaller. Try as I might, I can't avoid brushing up against Vik. Or Tommy.

I peek over to find the latter staring out the window, lost in thought. Heat washes up my neck.

Last night. *Oh, last night.*

For a moment I'm back in the dark gym, his fervent gaze locked with mine. My fingertips tingle with the feel of solid muscle beneath silk-smooth skin, and the ghost of his warm breath kisses my lips, makes my blood sing.

I wasn't at all sure Tommy was interested in me like that, not with Cait around, strong and gorgeous and obviously into him. Maybe she's the reason he left me alone on the floor, struggling to find my equilibrium.

He hasn't mentioned it. I'm not sure if he's avoiding the subject on purpose, or if I totally misread his signals. Although I couldn't have misread the hardness pressing into my—

Vik taps my shoulder. "Did you hear me? We're almost there."

My cheeks burn. I need to pull myself together, think of something else.

"Um, yeah, thanks."

They frown, the blue light from the dash illuminating their smooth, dark skin, deep amber eyes, and close-cropped black hair with a zigzag shaved into both sides. "I know it's scary your first time in the field, but we've got you."

I throw them a small smile. "Thanks."

Vik seems nice. No one had been thrilled to learn of my involvement in this mission, but they tolerated me a hell of a lot better than Hunter and Cait. The two of them were openly hostile until Lisa told them off. After that, they became grim and indifferent. As far as I can tell, they're going to act like I'm not even here.

It's probably for the best.

From the corner of my eye, I glance at the driver's seat, at Cait's stone-cold profile. Given the slightest excuse, she'll gut me like a pig. I don't know how I'll focus with that icy gray stare burning holes in my back, especially since I wasn't given a gun to defend myself with.

Lisa made good on her threat. The team was ordered not to harm me unless I put one toe out of line. If I do, they'll take me out immediately, no questions asked.

That instruction was the first thing she said at the meeting this morning. As soon as the words were out of her mouth warmth blossomed over my cheeks and my insides wilted to nothing. Most of my teammates think I'm a spy. I'm safe in my innocence, but to be so mistrusted they'd kill me given the chance is humiliating. It hurts.

I squirmed in my seat as Tommy glowered at each of them in turn, the threat of violence stark on his face. Tough as nails, Cait glared right back, hand tight on the arm of her chair. She more than matched the awful aggression in his eyes. His equal.

Not like me. I don't know how to be fierce, how to be brave like that. I hope I don't freeze, or get lost, or let them down in some other way.

Deep breaths. Breathe.

I lean my head back and close my eyes

The plan feels so disconcertingly easy. Park off one of the many small roads that wind through the thick, never-ending forest. Sneak three miles through the woods. Climb the fence surrounding Levett Tech after Lisa cuts the electricity. Cross the quad.

Then, as the only person who knows where the bill of lading is, I take the lead. If I mess up, I could be killed. Worse, my teammates could.

I squeeze my hands into fists, determined to stop their shaking. Dad always said, if I'm assaulted on a run, I should sprint away, but not in a straight line. Zigzag. Make myself hard to hit in case the assailant has a gun.

I never thought I'd need this advice. Why was Dad always so worried about me being attacked, anyway? Was it because he and Mom went on missions like this, or is irrational fear normal for parents?

Would they be proud of what I'm doing?

In my head I see their reactions, as vivid as if I were back home with them right now. Dad would tell me not to risk my life. After a day spent in the studio, wrapped up in painting another portrait, he'd scratch at the paint smudged on his nose—turquoise, or violet, or sunny yellow—and warn me to be careful, to think of all the days I still have ahead of me. All the things I have left to do, the words I have left to write.

But Mom … she'd stand behind his shoulder, smirking at me. Her brilliant eyes would twinkle, telling me without words to follow my heart, to do what I know is right. She'd tell me to trust my instincts.

Is that what I'm doing?

Before I can think it through further, Cait parks on the shoulder of the thin, night-black lane. It's late, almost eleven, and the darkness is nearly complete.

A flurry of activity surrounds me as the rest of the team pull black masks over their noses and mouths and tug up their hoods. I'm quick to follow suit.

The others slide out of the car without a word. A blast of nerves hits me so powerfully that for a moment, I'm unable to stand.

These could be my last minutes. For all I know, my death waits on the other side of those trees.

By the time I plunge into the dark forest, the team has disappeared ahead of me.

I can't see. I stumble forward, reach out with my other senses, but it's useless. I'm blind as a bat with no super-hearing to guide me, and my teammates are too fast. They expected me to keep up, to follow better than this.

I bounce off trunks, catch my feet on brambles, turn my ankles on rocks and sticks. Already, I have no idea where I am. No idea where they are.

My heart pumps as I spin on the spot, listening as hard as I can. There's nothing. Nothing to see. Nothing to hear. Only silence.

A hand closes around my bicep.

The Organization.

Molten terror shreds through my chest, and I swallow back a scream, jerking away. The grip on my arm only tightens.

"Shhh. It's just me."

Tommy.

I let out a huge gush of air.

Of course it's Tommy. I should've known he'd come back for me. I squint toward his voice, but I can't separate his shape from the darkness. He's completely invisible.

The pressure of Tommy's hand slackens and drops down my sleeve to wrap around my gloved fingers.

"I'll guide you," he breathes.

I follow his pull, tripping as I go. The night is so black my vision still hasn't adjusted. It's like trying to run through the forest with my eyes closed.

We catch up to the team and travel like this for about thirty minutes, no one saying a word, not even Bill, Jess, or Lisa, who are monitoring the Levett CCTV from the caves, connected to us via the small earpieces and mics we're wearing. They won't be able to see us until we reach the campus, but they'll warn us if anything seems off once we get there.

Eventually, enough ambient light filters through the trees ahead for me to make out the rest of the team; dark shadows fanned out in front of me, navigating a forest of thick black stripes. The light grows brighter as we near the tree line, my heart swollen, my windpipe blocked by its thumping beats. Maybe its last.

Too soon, we break through the forest at the edge of the campus.

A tall chain-link fence towers over us, topped with curls of electrified wire. Beyond, orange spotlights illuminate the quad, bordered on three sides by long industrial buildings. It's strange to see them from here.

Tommy looks toward the quad, only his eyes visible above his dark mask. They glint like emeralds in the shadow of his hood.

Twenty-five hours ago, those eyes were burning into mine. I wish he kissed me. I wish I got to taste his lips, just once, before—

Lisa's voice buzzes in my ear. "CCTV looped. Fence disabled. You're good to go."

The others slither up the heavy steel wire. I watch, panic thrumming in my veins.

Tommy's fingers dig into my palm. "Come on. We have to climb."

Don't be a coward.

Mouth tight, I force my numb limbs to move. The combat gloves I'm wearing are light and flexible, helping rather than hindering as I cross over the nullified electric fence and hit the ground on the other side. Tommy drops lightly next to me.

"Patrols are in production and R&D," Lisa crackles.

R&D. Where my parents supposedly died.

At least that building isn't nearby.

The team and I prowl across the grassy quad like panthers, following the plan I helped concoct. All those years, burning with questions, with the need to make things right, have culminated in this night. This moment. This one chance to earn Lisa's trust.

I'm so close.

We approach the administrative building without running into anyone.

"You're clear," Lisa says, and the badge scanner flashes green. The lock clicks.

Cait pulls the door open, and we slip inside. The exit signs at each end of the dark corridor cast an eerie red glow over the scene.

Stomach in knots, I move to the front of the group. We climb four flights of stairs to emerge on the top floor.

It's just as I remember, except for the lighting. A harsh orange glow shines through the windows on the left, cutting through the dark and illuminating the doors on the right. All the scan pads are green.

I take a step forward.

The scan pads flash red, exactly as Lisa swears violently in our ears.

"They've detected the loop. Both patrols are heading your way, fast. Get out of there! Now!"

Fear cracks through my heart. Cait and Hunter spin toward me.

"You," Cait snarls. Her gloved hand twitches toward her gun.

Terrified chills race up my spine. They think it was me.

I'm dead.

I take a step back, slick palms by my shoulders. "I didn't do anything! I swear."

My eyes dart to Tommy, but he doesn't see. He's scowling at Cait, his gaze so vicious I'm shocked she doesn't burst into flame.

"It wasn't her!" Lisa chirps through the comm device. "The guards detected an anomaly on one of their screens. I watched them figure it out myself. Quit wasting time and get out! I'm working to override the lockdown. Should have it sorted before you hit the ground floor."

Vik and Hunter are already gone. With a final, burning glare for me, Cait follows. Tommy's right behind her.

I glance at the security pad. This is my one shot to prove myself, to get the information I need, and the bill of lading is steps away. Patrols were across campus, in production and R&D.

I could grab it in no time ... but the lock is still red...

It flashes green.

"Got it!" Lisa yells.

Tommy hovers at the top of the stairs, no more than a dark shadow. Waiting for me.

"It's right there," I hiss, gesturing toward the room.

"Get over here now."

Terror twists my stomach and coats my tongue. Everything I've given up, everything I've worked for... I will not waste this opportunity.

"Give me thirty seconds," I plead, already shoving through the door.

Lisa's loud in my ear. "Melanie, no! Patrols are crossing the quad. Take the front door instead. A right at the end of the hall, straight past reception. Cross the fence behind the employee lot and hit the woods there."

Most of that instruction is meant for the others. They must be nearly out. Good.

I sprint to the shelves lining the right wall, which holds the incoming shipments section, and yank the first box toward me. As I reach for my flashlight, the door clicks open.

Heart in my throat, I whirl, ready to face death or worse.

But it's just Tommy. His flashlight flares to life, illuminating the box with dazzling light. "Hurry!"

I turn back to the files, adrenaline making me clumsy.

"We're out," Vik buzzes, layered with static.

"Patrols sweeping the ground floor. Tommy, Mel, you can still make it out a second-story window if you move," Lisa barks. "That's an order!"

"Tommy?" Cait squeals through the comm. "Wait. Wait. Tommy's not here. Vik, Hunter! Wait!"

Throat cracked, I reach the last of the papers in the box. No BioAgent 313. I could've sworn it was here.

Cursing, I pitch the whole thing over my shoulder and start on the next.

The earpiece explodes in a riot of noise.

"Patrols moving to the second floor. Cait, what are you doing? Turn around!"

"Catch her!"

"Cait! Stop!"

Is she coming back for us? She was safe outside.

I curse again, her voice shrill in my ear. "Tommy's still in there! We have to get him out."

"Accetta, stand down. There are too many—"

"Get the hell off me!"

I tear through the papers, tossing them aside one by one.

"Cut it out!"

"We can't leave him!"

A grunt of pain, indistinct screaming.

Then Tommy's voice, both in the earpiece and beside me, a blistering command. "Cait, turn your ass around."

"You stupid, arrogant, bleeding idiot!" Cait shrieks. "Hunter, if you don't let go of me, I can't be held responsible for what happens to you."

My hands shake almost too hard to handle the files as I reach the end of the second box. Still nothing.

Face cold, I throw it behind me and start on a third.

Lisa's voice cuts through all the noise, crisp and efficient. "Patrols are hitting the third floor. Cait, stand down."

Crashing, more yelling, then…

The world stands still.

There it is. The bill of lading for BioAgent 313.

"Got it!" I crush the paper into my pocket.

"Patrols are heading for the fourth floor. Tommy, Mel, hide!"

Lisa's shouting, but I can barely make her out over the commotion flooding the line.

Tommy flicks off his flashlight. "Turn off your earpiece."

I do. In the sudden silence, I hear them. Thundering up the stairs.

Ice floods my system.

This is it. The day I die.

What the hell was I thinking?

"Come on," Tommy hisses, yanking me toward the back of the room. He pulls me to the ground behind the last row of shelves.

There's a small click outside as Lisa reengages the locks.

Numerous boots clomp down the hall.

"Don't move," Tommy whispers. Slowly, he shifts away, toward the open space beyond the shelving. "When they enter, I'll draw them off. Sneak around the right side of the room, get out, and run. No matter what, don't stop. Run straight into the woods, and don't look back."

This can't be happening.

I must be dreaming. Having a nightmare. I can't be about to die. And Tommy … if he gets hurt, it'll be my fault, all my fault.

Why did I do this?

It's not worth it.

My limbs shake. My breath turns harsh.

"Shhh," Tommy warns, somewhere to my left.

Before I can respond, the scan pad beeps. The door swings open.

Without hesitation, Tommy throws himself around the shelves, a gun blazing in each hand. My ears explode as the first several guards drop.

I choke on a scream, terror pulsing in my blood.

They're dead. Dead.

I'm next.

Tommy's gone, disappeared like smoke on water. The remaining guards draw back, weapons raised.

The silence vibrates.

Suddenly, a shadow twists in the space between the guards' flashlight beams. Two more fall, throats spilling out onto their uniforms.

I lurch forward, vomit hot in my mouth.

The way their necks *gaped*.

Tommy darts left, drawing a spray of bullets. The scene wobbles, edged in shimmering mist. No one's watching the door.

I could make it out. Tommy told me to. I could escape … live…

My muscles twitch.

I clamp down on them so hard they ache.

I will not run.

Even if it means my own end, I will not abandon Tommy to die. He could've gone with the others. Instead he stayed, risked his life, to help me. I can't desert him.

Gritting my teeth, I force myself to move. To inch closer to the fight.

The guards fire without mercy. Tommy dodges this way and that, keeping their attention on him. Giving me a way out.

My eyes narrow. He must be out of ammo. If I can cause a distraction, just long enough for him to reload…

Tommy jerks.
Tumbles backward into the shelves.
A tower of boxes crashes down on his limp form.

CHAPTER TWENTY-TWO

MEL

HORROR freezes my blood.

They shot him!

The way he's lying there, so still. Our bulletproof vests are far from perfect...

A ferocious, agonized scream claws its way up my throat, hot tears streaking down my cheeks.

I'll tear their limbs from their joints, I'll rip out their throats, I'll gouge their eyes from their sockets!

Yowling madly, I sprint at the guards. I'm on the nearest one before they look my way.

We fly back into the same wrecked shelf Tommy struck. The momentum of my attack carries me too far, and I roll off the murderer as we hit the floor. Adrenaline burns in my veins, bringing everything into sharp focus, including the gun now clattering away across the floor, jolted from the guard's limp hand when we fell.

I lunge for it.

"Don't move."

Stretched out on my belly, I turn my masked face up. The second guard towers over me, his features swathed in shadow.

Is this it?

I wait for fear, but I feel nothing. Because of me, Tommy's ... he's...

My heart shatters into a thousand razor-sharp pieces. The shards scrape. Tear. They rend my soul to bits. They shred my sanity to nothing.

I grab my head, an animalistic, keening wail ripping from my lungs. Through streaming eyes, I watch the disarmed guard retrieve his gun, both attackers studying my grief, their weapons trained on me. Behind them, a shadow crawls on the floor. Struggles to rise.

Dark and dangerous and beautiful beyond imagination.

I can't control the sobs that choke out of me now. The guards glance at each other, then back at me as Tommy inches forward.

I need to keep their attention.

Mustering all my strength, I push up to my knees, spit a vehement "fuck you", and flip them off with both hands.

The beefier one raises the butt of his gun, his lip curling as he steps forward. "You little—"

Tommy's on him, wresting the gun from the man's grip as he simultaneously sweeps the feet out from under the second guard, who crashes to the floor.

I throw myself at the downed guard, making a swipe for his outstretched arm, for the weapon in his hand. Next thing I know, I'm on my back, the guard's heavy weight crushing my hips, his gun pointed straight between my eyes.

My pulse thunders as I stare down the barrel. Death stares back. Thunk.

The man slumps sideways, knocked senseless by the butt of Tommy's pistol. I release a shuddering breath.

"We have to move," Tommy grates out.

Not dead. Not dead.

Uncontrollable tremors roll through my body. I try to speak, but the words are warped, senseless. I can't spit them out past my chattering teeth.

Kneeling next to me, Tommy takes my hands in his. His green eyes are glazed, his breath coming in shallow pants. "Focus."

I drag in a deep breath. Another.

I can't believe he's okay. I can't believe it.

With a sob, I throw my arms around him, burying my face in his neck. "I thought … I thought…"

Tommy rubs my shoulders. "Shh. I'm fine. I promise. But we have to get out of here. We don't have time to waste."

It's hard to pull away, when all I want is to feel Tommy's heartbeat, to breathe in his woodsy scent and reassure myself he's alive.

For now.

We might have survived this fight, but we're still deep within Levett's campus. We need to move.

I'm slowing us down.

"Let's go," I murmur.

"Follow me." Tommy takes my hand, and we thread our way around the bodies on the floor.

Out in the hall, he picks up the pace. Seeing him switch his earpiece back on, I follow suit.

"What's the layout?" he says shortly.

Several relieved voices sing his name.

"Don't ever do something like that again, either of you," Lisa snaps.

I wince. By making the choices I did, I almost cost Tommy his life.

We race down the stairs, Lisa chirping in our ears. "Police will arrive in less than two minutes. No remaining guards on-site."

Hunter curses. "You took out all ten?"

"Beat that," Tommy says dryly.

Hunter barks a laugh.

"Can it, you two. Tommy, Mel, I want you out of there ASAP. The team will wait at the car. One minute."

"We're on our way."

Tommy shoves through the back door, then we're sprinting across the quad, our hoods flopping against our shoulders. Sirens wail from the street.

"Fence still disabled," Lisa reports.

"Don't slow," Tommy tells me. "Up and over, right away."

I scramble up the fence, Tommy hot on my tail. On the other side, he grabs my hand again and drags me into the trees. I stagger behind him, far too loud. I can't help it. My legs are numb.

The sirens blare closer.

As the light from campus fades, I trip along worse than ever. Tommy slows.

"Quieter. And faster."

"I can't see."

"They'll find us."

I stare into the dark. Even though I feel his hand in mine, I can't see him.

"Tommy, I-I can't—"

"Now, Mel."

Without waiting for my reply, Tommy yanks me forward. I sprint after him, clinging on for dear life.

Horrible pictures flash through my head as we run. The guards' throats grinning scarlet as they fall. The mist of blood hanging in the air. Tommy dropping to the floor. The barrel of the loaded gun, inches from my face.

Hideous fear edged with hysteria closes in. I see enemies all around, shifting in the black woods. Everything looks the same, feels the same, and it's like we've been running for hours, maybe forever, without getting anywhere, Levett Tech a ravenous monster at our backs.

Suddenly, we explode onto the moonlit dirt road, about thirty feet from the Veloster. Its door is thrown open as Tommy wrenches me forward and shoves me into the back. He climbs in after, and we're bumping away.

When we hit the freeway, my tears return full force. Shivering, I cringe into Tommy's side. His arms wrap around me, holding me close while I cry.

"How is Cait?" he asks over my head.

Hunter answers from my other side. "She'll be fine. Damn, but she can fight. I had no choice."

Confused, I glance toward the front of the car. Vik's driving, not Cait. Cait's blond head lolls in the passenger seat. She's unconscious.

Time stretches and warps. I cry myself out, then stare numbly at the back of Cait's head. At long last, we pull into the cavernous garage, where a small knot of people waits to welcome us.

Lisa, eyes steely. Bill and Jess Accetta, rushing toward the car. Aaliyah Young, the dark-haired doctor, with a med kit. Sam, drawn and pale, brown hair sticking up in every direction, hovering behind her.

Vik parks and the others climb out of the car. A heavy fog presses down on me like a thick blanket.

Gently, Tommy pushes me away. I grab his wrist.

"Are you okay?" Tommy's gaze is soft.

Brain chugging along too slowly, I can only stare at him.

Hands pull Cait from the front of the car. Bill cradles her in his strong arms while Jess fusses over her and Aaliyah tends to the wound on her head. For a moment, I'm intensely jealous.

Cait is loved. If she doesn't come home, she'll be mourned. Deeply.

Not me. Who would care if I got hurt? Or died?

Only ghosts.

With a jolt, I remember the paper in my pocket. My only tenuous tie to my parents.

"I'm okay," I rasp, releasing Tommy's wrist.

He watches me for another second, beautiful eyes full of sympathy. Then he exits the car without a backward glance.

My excitement mounts as I slide out after him. Everyone's crowded around Cait, everyone but Sam, who's standing on his own, puffy eyes on Hunter. When he sees me, he dashes over and folds me into what is possibly the biggest hug of my life.

Tenderness fills my heart. This. This is who cares. Sam, who's always been there, even in my worst moments. And Tommy, who went so far as to risk his life to save mine. They're my family now.

I hold Sam tight. His warmth radiates out through the tips of my fingers and toes.

"Don't you ever do something like that, ever again." Sam's words are thick. Pulling back, I'm stunned to see fresh tear tracks glittering on his cheeks.

My stomach twists. I'll be forever grateful Tommy didn't pay for my misstep with his life.

"I'm sorry," I say earnestly. Despite the guilt, a smile slowly spreads across my face. "But it was worth it, in the end."

Turning away, I stride toward the knot of people around Cait's family. Lisa's in the middle of reprimanding Tommy.

"…could have compromised the entire Resistance," she barks, eyes blazing like hot coals.

"Um," I interrupt.

Lisa falls silent. Turning, she glares at me with such potent fury I stumble back a step. "I'll deal with you in a minute."

Her words are so frightening I nearly shut up. But I think of all I went through tonight, all Tommy went through, and I square my shoulders instead.

"No. You'll deal with me now."

Both Tommy and Sam gawk, identical expressions of astonishment on their faces. Lisa's nostrils flare. "Excuse me?"

With shaking fingers, I pull out the bill of lading. All eyes follow as I shove it at Lisa.

She takes it, smooths it against her thigh. Her eyes widen.

I can't stop a broad smile from curling across my face as she stares, a glimmer of pride leaking through her shocked expression.

"This changes everything," she whispers, and for the first time, I hear warmth in her voice. Gratitude. "With this information, we have a chance to save many lives. Thank you, Mel. We still have to discuss your actions tonight, but that can wait until tomorrow."

Holding a hand out to me, Lisa grins, her eyes twinkling. The effect it has on her is unbelievable; she's a different woman from the one I've known. Not cool and distant, but warm. Kind.

As I shake her hand, the others gather around, all except Bill and Hunter, who turn away, Cait still senseless in Bill's arms.

They don't matter. I beam at the smiling faces of the others, my heart filling until I think it might burst.

I'm one of them.

I belong.

CHAPTER TWENTY-THREE

TOMMY

MEL'S dead on her feet.

As we head through the passage back to the caves, she stumbles along with the crowd, one arm slung around my neck and the other around Sam's. I have to grit my teeth against the pain that throbs in my ribs, but I don't let her go.

It's a battle of will to keep my eyes on the tunnel ahead. Mel's absolutely radiant right now. A wide smile lights her face; her eyes sparkle with joy. No one can question her loyalty after this.

But at what cost? I hope Lisa doesn't make her a permanent member of the mission team, at least not yet. The number of times she almost bit it tonight… Where would she be now if I was incapacitated?

In an interrogation room.

It takes longer than usual, but eventually we reach the housing wing. Mel, Sam, and I stop in front of Mel's door while the others continue to their rooms, murmuring good night as they pass.

Bitter envy stings in my chest as Mel wraps Sam in a warm embrace. I wish I could let myself get close to her like that. Unguarded, with no secrets and no fears.

Blinking, I tear my eyes from them and look toward Cait's room at the far end of the hall. Hunter must've really thumped her for her to still be out cold, and she is. If she'd woken up, I'd know.

Ugh. I'm not eager for the verbal lashing that's no doubt on the way. If the situation were reversed—if Cait had defied orders and risked her life—I'd do the same. Still, it won't be a fun conversation.

With an angel's smile, Mel releases Sam, who turns and folds his arms around me.

I pat his back, cheeks hot. It's uncomfortable to realize how much it'll hurt my friends if I don't make it home from a mission.

Sam pulls away. "Cait's right. You are an idiot."

Mel covers her mouth and snickers. Sam glares. "You too, Melanie Louisa O'Hanlon Snow. I'm glad you guys got the bill of lading, but please don't scare me like that again. Either of you." He glances between us.

"Don't worry about me," I tell him gruffly. "I'm always fine."

Mel flashes him another warm smile. "Sorry. I won't."

"Good. I should go help Aaliyah with Cait. 'Night, you two." With a wave and a frown, he walks away and disappears into Cait's room.

No one's left in the hall now besides Mel and me. I turn to her, intending to make sure she's all right before heading to bed, but I meet her eyes, and the way she's looking at me, it's … *oh, damn.* An echo of the wildfire from last night flickers to life, low in my gut.

"Tommy," she breathes, stepping closer, so close we're almost touching. "I … when you were shot, I…"

She touches my damaged vest, carefully tracing the spot where the bullet hit. Her eyes squeeze shut. "I thought…"

A tear rolls down her cheek. I want to wipe it away, to hold her like I did in the car, but I don't know how to comfort her without blurring the line between us more than I already have. So I just stand and watch as more tears fall, feeling wretched.

Mel looks up again, those glistening eyes brimming with some kind of profound emotion. The sight cuts straight through my core, stealing my breath and shredding my resolve on its way.

"I don't want to lose you," she whispers through quivering lips.

Lost for words, I hesitantly wipe the wetness from her cheeks. Her skin is so soft. Smooth, like satin. Instead of dropping my hands, I savor the feel of it under my fingers.

I don't want to lose you either.

Mel raises a shaking hand to trace my cheek, my jaw. My eyes drop to the curve of her lips, a slow, fierce burn seeping under my skin. With an intensity I never could have imagined, I crave her.

Before I can get a handle on myself, Mel wraps her arms around my neck. Our breath mingles as she murmurs, "You're important to me, Tommy."

Her eyes shine. Deep, pure, honest. She cares about me. Despite all the mistakes I've made, despite my role in her parents' murder, she cares.

Glittering warmth surges through me, staggering in its potency. It melts my heart; it shimmers in my racing blood; it lights even the darkest corner of my ravaged soul. I stare down at Mel in awe, marveling as the radiant feeling consumes me. Remakes me.

"Mel," I sigh, and her name is a prayer on my tongue.

It's too much. Her call is too strong. Winding my arms around her back, I pull her tight against me and press my lips to hers.

A low moan rises in her throat. Her hands float up, tangling in my hair as her tongue skims my upper lip. Scorching, delicious shivers devour me whole.

I run my hands over her hips, crushing her closer and deepening the kiss despite the pain in my ribs. There's only Mel; the exquisite taste of her, the feel of her body arcing into mine, her scent swirling in my head—cherry blossoms and peaches and wild, wild passion. I'm lost in a blistering haze of desire.

Mel pulls away, her gaze a dark, undiluted flame. My blood sears in my veins as she tugs me toward her room. Struggling to clear my mind, I suck in a shaky breath and hold it.

A kiss is one thing, but what will happen if I let Mel pull me in there? What about all the careful lines I've drawn? The secret I haven't shared?

You're important to me, she said.

Everything I am yearns for her, but I don't move. I only stare, warring with myself, utterly torn.

Mel's perfect mouth lifts in a sweet smile, her eyes warm. She unbuckles her vest, slowly lets it fall from her shoulders. It hits the ground with a dull thud. "I think kissing would be better without these vests in the way, don't you?"

My heart shines, a soft chuckle rising to my lips. What a Mel thing to say at a time like this. She's irresistible. A siren call I can't refuse.

I take a tentative step toward her, then another, then I'm pinning her against the door, my mouth insistent on hers. She kisses me back feverishly, slinging a leg over my hip. The way she's pressing into me … it's … *oh, yes.* I shudder, the heat between us blazing white-hot.

My control wavers and I grind into her, unraveling more with every moan on her lips, every stroke of her tongue, every press of warm pressure right where I want it.

I've never kissed anyone like this. Not even close, and I need her, need that silk-smooth skin under my tongue, need to bury myself inside—

Stop. I need to stop.

Now, while I still can.

It's fucking *hard,* but I take my hands off her and step back.

"Are you sure?" My voice is rough. Intense. "This is what you want?"

The corner of her mouth turns up, her darkened eyes dancing, fanning the flames that lick through my blood. "Yes. So much yes."

And there's something deeper in her expression too. Something that glows, that mirrors the radiance still glimmering through every part of me.

She cares.

I move forward again and angle my mouth toward hers, waiting for that final yes. Mel cups my face in her hands and raises her lips to mine in a soft, gentle brush. The contact zaps through my overheated system like a shock, and I back her into the door as she kisses me again, deeper.

With a turn of the handle, Mel sends us stumbling into her room. I don't let her go as I kick the door closed, trailing kisses across her jaw and down her throat. She unbuckles my vest as we stagger to the bed, pulls my shirt up over my head. I slide hers off too, desperate to free her from it, from the simple black bra underneath. Our clothes leave a path on the floor behind us until we're in nothing but our underwear, Mel's stunning body on full display.

She's luminous, standing there smiling without an ounce of embarrassment. A goddess.

She runs her hands over my chest and gently kisses the ugly purple bruise above my heart. I hiss at the throbbing ache, at the way it spikes the burn in my veins.

I need her. Now.

I grab her around the waist and press her down onto the bed, grazing her earlobe with my teeth, then nipping my way down her neck to kiss the hollow at the base of her throat. Her breathing turns ragged as I skim lower, relishing the way she trembles for me, the soft moan on her lips. She arches off the bed, her fingers dragging down my back, painting my skin with fire.

I'm not in control anymore. Something feral has taken over, driven by Mel's every touch, her every sigh. She is my muse, and my canvas, and my salvation, and I'll worship every inch of her until she's crying out my name, until she loses herself in the half-light of the dying embers.

CHAPTER TWENTY-FOUR

MEL

HEAT floods my core and pools between my legs as Tommy runs his hands down my ribs, trailing feather-light kisses from my collarbone to my sternum, then over my shoulder. My skin pebbles, and I shiver, arching off the comforter again, desperate to have those lips on my aching breasts.

"You're so fucking beautiful," he sighs, nose skimming back up my neck. Chills follow, and I run my fingers over the hard lines of his back, his shoulders, memorizing every dip, every curve, the way the bands of muscle ripple as he moves. He's kissing that spot under my ear now, slow and languid and oh, so hot, the autumn-and-pine scent of his skin wrapping around me like an embrace.

I roll my hips against the hard length of him, and my hands skim up to wind into his hair and pull his lips back to mine. Pleasure streaks through my stomach and down my thighs, pulsing with the pressure. Tommy hisses into my mouth.

He breaks the kiss and leans up on his elbows to stare down at me, beautiful eyes dark. The dim light of the dying fire gilds his skin and lines his sharp features in shadow. His flawless lips part.

"Tommy," I say, and it's half a plea. I flex my hips again.

He closes his eyes, a soft groan low his throat. "Mel." His voice is ragged. Husky. It flames my blood almost as much as his moans.

I drop my hands from his hair, running them over his carved chest, careful not to touch the deep purple stain above his heart. This gorgeous man is here. With me.

I can't believe I almost lost him forever.

My own heart twists, and I pull him to me again, kissing him deeply. Hot shivers wrack my body, the molten knot at my core winding tighter as our tongues slide against each other. Tommy sucks my lower lip into his mouth and gently tugs, his warm hands gliding up to cup my breasts. His thumbs stroke over my nipples, and I moan at the pleasure that radiates out in waves.

"Please."

Tommy breaks our kiss to smirk down at me. "Not yet."

He dips his head, that mouth closing over my left nipple, and flicks with his tongue. I cry out, the pleasure sharp and oh so good.

He keeps going, licking, sucking until he drags another moan from a carnal place deep inside me. My fingers tangle in his hair, and he skims kisses down my center, over my abdomen, kneeling between my legs with his hands splayed on my hips. Trails of sparks singe my skin.

I'm shaking as he traces the line of my panties with his nose, the warmth of his breath soaking through the thin material. Ah, I need him, need that touch … everywhere. He glances up at me, and the pure lust in his darkened eyes scorches my very marrow. I want to push him down on the bed, to give him everything I have. But more than that, I want his mouth *there*, where the ache is pooling, deep and insistent.

Tommy slowly, so slowly, drags my panties off. Tingles follow his touch, spreading up my thighs to buzz between my legs. He tosses the panties on the floor, and I lean up on my elbows to keep him in my sight, fully bare before him. The cool air of the caves stings my flushed skin.

"So. Fucking. Beautiful," he whispers.

I nearly convulse from the words alone. He nips his way up my sensitive inner thigh, and I fall back onto the bed, breath sawing out of me.

The first stroke of his tongue up my slick center sends jagged bliss arcing up my spine. Tommy doesn't let up, hands biting into my thighs as he winds the need in my core tighter, hotter until it's torching me alive.

"Please," I gasp. He drags his tongue over me again and lightning flashes behind my lids. I writhe under him, desperate for release. For him. I need him more than I need air to breathe. "I want you."

Tommy stops his slow torture, sex-hazed eyes meeting mine. The sight of him, between my legs, looking like that…

Holy fuck.

"Now."

I sit up, pushing him back with a hand on his chest so he's sitting in the middle of the bed, with me straddling his lap. His length strains against me through his boxers, and need flares in my stomach, makes my toes curl. His hands run over my hips and up my back as we sit nose to nose, staring into each other's eyes.

"Mel," he sighs, and it's so much more than a word. It's an adoration. He claims my mouth again, our kiss wild, all tongues and teeth and searing need. My fingers drop from his chest, follow the defined lines of his stomach toward his waistband. I stroke him through the cotton.

He moans into my mouth. It's sexy as hell.

"Take these off."

I snap the elastic and he pulls back, pure fire in his darkened eyes. Everything in me tightens.

"You're really sure?"

"Want me to show you how sure I am?" I slip my hand underneath the fabric and he gasps, shuddering as I work him. His eyes close, his breath turns harsh. Suddenly, he pushes me off his lap and loses the boxers.

Then his lips are on mine, urgent as he guides me onto my back and hovers between my legs. I reach down to line him up, and he breaks the kiss to stare into my eyes. The adoration I heard in his voice earlier shines deep in his heated gaze.

Slowly, reverently, he slides in. Electricity crackles up my spine, and an untamed sound breaks from me at the fullness, the exquisite pressure. Holy fucking hell, *yes*.

Tommy gently kisses the corner of my mouth. "Mel … you're important to me too."

Shimmering warmth blooms in my heart and sharp pleasure spirals through my stomach, building, coiling tighter as we find our rhythm. Tommy's hands are in my hair, his lips skimming my neck while he whispers my name over and over like a supplication. Like a prayer. Like I'm all that's ever mattered.

It's the most sublime torment, like nothing I've experienced before. My eyes sting at the unity of it, of being together like this with him. Being cherished like this.

Pleasure sizzles through me, and I scream his name as lightning forks at the edges of my mind and stars burst behind my lids. I shatter around him, again and again, waves of iridescent bliss rocking the very foundation of my world.

"Fuck," Tommy groans, pumping into me twice more, then going still.

We stay like that for a few minutes, joined in silence. When our breathing slows, he lifts onto his elbows to stare down at me, his gaze tender and full of quiet joy. I stroke his hair, my heart glowing with a wholesome warmth that lights everything I am and knocks the breath from my lungs.

I am in so much trouble.

Tommy kisses me once, soft and sweet, then slides to the side and pulls me into his arms. I smile, tracing his beautiful lips, his cheek, the bruise on his chest. The luminous feeling swells, and I close my eyes to hide the pricking behind my lids.

He kisses the top of my head.

I'm not sure how things will change between us after this, but I don't want to think about it now. I only want to live in this moment, to melt into his warmth and listen to his soft breath and count the beats of his heart and know he's alive. We're alive.

And we're together.

CHAPTER TWENTY-FIVE

TOMMY

I'M hidden in the narrow gap under my parents' bed, watching bright crimson pools soak into the light carpet. A lake of blood.

"Where is the chip? Tell us, and it will be over. You don't need to suffer like this."

The she-monster is worse than the others. Her voice reminds me of broken glass, sharp and dangerous.

Mrs. Snow spits out a mouthful of blood. "We'll never tell you anything."

A heavy thud and Mr. Snow's shouting a string of profanities. His wife doesn't yell. No, she's too busy choking on a surge of red-tinged vomit. I see her face for a moment as she curls toward the ground. Her skin streams crimson; puffy and torn.

I retch too, but the monsters don't hear me because the female brute is yelling again.

She hovers over Mom now. Mom, who's already been beaten to a pulp, her fingers snapped, her ribs shattered. Her breathing is shallow.

Two of the fiends push her to the ground, four more pull her arms and legs tight. She doesn't look my way, though she knows I'm here.

I have to do something.

Cold sweat runs down my neck and my eyes dart to Mom's cell phone, five feet away at the head of the bed, half-hidden where it landed under the nightstand.

If I could reach it and call the police … the monsters won't see if I'm careful.

I could save her. All of them.

I try to crawl sideways, but I can't move. My muscles have seized up so tight it hurts.

With a shaky breath, I shove against the terror that locks me in place. I fight viciously to twitch an arm, a leg, to make a sound, to do anything at all, anything but lie here still and silent.

Anything.

Mom's ear-splitting cry of agony spears me to the floor. I heave up more vomit when I spot what they've done.

Her finger.

They cut off her finger.

It's like I'm bound and gagged, a prisoner in my own mind as the monsters slowly fillet my parents and the Snows, breaking them apart piece by piece. Horrible wails of pain persist, worse and worse, until I'm sure I've gone mad.

I pray I'll wake up. I pray I'll pass out. I pray someone will come and save us.

But no one comes.

And the screams continue.

"Tommy! What's wrong? What's happening? Wake up! *Wake up!*"

An angel … an angel's calling my name.

Am I dead?

I jerk into a sitting position, eyes snapping open as a sharp, curling pain hits my gut. The world sways, washing back and forth in my throbbing head. Soft fingers wipe away the wetness that glazes my cheeks.

Mel's room. I'm in Mel's room.

"It's okay, you're okay," Mel soothes, her features only just visible in the dim light cast by what's left of her fire.

"Mel." My voice breaks, and I reach for her like a drowning man, burying my face in her thick hair. She wraps her arms around me, holding me tight while I fight to master myself.

I don't deserve her comfort. If I'd been brave, crawled to that cell phone, her parents might be here now.

Even so, I can't pull away.

Her soft lips brush along my neck, each kiss echoing deep in my ruined soul. The warmth she ignited in my heart earlier swells again, drives out the darkness with its radiance.

When Mel presses her lips gently to my own, a shuddering jolt runs through me, scenes from a few hours ago filling my mind. Mel, head thrown back and cheeks flushed, calling out my name. That ivory skin under my hands, my tongue. The way she shivered for me.

Not a dream. Real.

Mel pulls back, compassion clear in those stunning eyes. She takes my hands. "Were you dreaming about that night? Our parents?"

Heat floods my face. How could she know? What did I do while I was asleep? Was I shouting? Crying?

I don't want to talk about this. Praying she won't ask for details, I nod.

Firelight flickers over Mel, painting her skin in oranges and golds and grays. She rubs little circles into my knuckles with her thumbs. "Do you dream about … that … a lot?"

It takes all my willpower to hold her gaze. "Yes."

Her eyes are full of pity. I don't like being the object of her pity. Of anyone's, but especially hers. I'm the last person she should feel bad for.

I drop my eyes, stare unseeingly at the blanket draped over her lap.

"Tommy," she murmurs. I glance back up.

Even in the semi-darkness, I can see it shining in her eyes: that same profound emotion I recognized earlier. The one that cut down my defenses like they were nothing.

"You're not alone." Mel's words blaze. She squeezes my hands. "You don't have to face the memories alone. Not anymore. I'm here for you."

A shock of glittering tenderness jolts through me, followed immediately by a frisson of icy panic.

I think … I think I love her.

The force of this simple truth knocks the breath out of me. I run my knuckles along the soft curve of her cheek. So beautiful, but much more than that too. Kind. Passionate. Brave. Good.

I love her.

My stomach seizes up as fear slithers through my veins.

"Mel. I … I can't…"

I can't be with her. I'd have to come clean about our parents, and I can't bear to see the betrayal, the hatred, simmering in her eyes. I'll lose her.

The panic intensifies, crushes my lungs until I can't draw breath. It's heavy in my chest. So heavy. Too heavy.

Releasing one of my hands, Mel strokes my cheek. "You don't have to tell me about it. But I'm here if you decide you want someone to talk to."

"No. That's not what I'm talking about. I mean what happened tonight, between us. It shouldn't have happened. I'm sorry, I shouldn't have let it happen." The words are ash on my tongue.

Pain breaks across Mel's face.

I can't look at her, can't handle seeing her hurt, knowing I'm the reason.

"I see," she says, her voice full of an aching sadness that tugs at the deepest part of me. She pulls her hands back, folding them in her lap. "Because of Cait?"

"What does Cait have to do with anything?"

Mel tilts her head, those beautiful eyes shimmering. "Well, you said this"—she waves a hand between us—"shouldn't have happened. I thought you might feel that way because of her."

I suck in a breath as her pain grates against me. Even if I can't be with her, I don't want her to think I don't return her feelings, that tonight meant nothing.

"No, of course not. Cait's a friend. My best friend, but nothing more."

"That girl's crazy about you," Mel sighs.

The idea of Cait having romantic feelings for me is so absurd I huff a laugh, but it's a humorless sound. "You've got her all wrong.

We've been through a lot together, and she's been there for me in more ways than I can count. I love her, and she loves me, but not like that. We're family."

Mel peeks up, her gaze mournful.

"Mel," I whisper, and my anguish is clear in my voice. "I care about you too. I thought it was obvious. I want to be with you, more than you could know. I-I..."

My throat closes, choking the air from my lungs before I can tell her I love her. I fall silent, despair and longing thick in my chest.

"Then be with me." Mel pins me with that fiery look she sometimes gets.

"It's not that simple." The words burn on their way out. "There's something ... I don't..."

I reach over and take her hand. "I wish things were different. I wish I could be good enough for you. But I'm not, and you deserve much, much better than me."

To my horror, tears fill Mel's eyes. "Oh, Tommy. How can you think that? You are good enough. You are more than good enough. You're the best person I know."

Scooting toward me, Mel cups my face in her hands. "I've never felt like this before, the way I feel about you. I think..." She pauses, biting her lip. "I think I might be falling for you."

Everything else fades. A thousand emotions roll through me all at once.

I don't deserve her. But we love each other. By some miracle, she wants me. We have a shot at the kind of happiness I never thought I'd find.

"I think I'm falling for you too," I whisper, half-strangled by the panic mounting in my chest. My hands are cold with it.

A smile brighter than the dawn lights Mel's face. It's so stunning I stop breathing and stare at her in wonder.

She leans up and kisses me, her lips soft. Warm.

With a low groan, I pull her closer, running my hands down the bare skin of her back. Tracing the shape of her.

Mel drops her fingers from my face. They glide down my chest, over my abdomen. Lower.

I lock her wrists in an iron grip. "Wait. I don't want to lose you. Maybe we should stick to being friends."

Even as I say the words, I know it's far too late for that.

As if she can hear my thoughts, Mel says, "How can we be friends when we feel this way about each other?"

I sigh. "Maybe we can't."

"We'll figure this out. Together. We don't have to know what we're doing. As long as I'm what you want, and you're what I want, and we're trying, that's all I need."

She gives me a small, hopeful smile, her eyes soft. And I know, deep in my bones, she's where I want to be. I'll do whatever it takes to be enough for her. To be someone who deserves her, even if it means…

I have to tell her.

My throat is so tight I can hardly breathe. I release her wrists, brushing a strand of dark hair away from her face. "Listen. There's something you still don't know. About that night."

Mel's brows pull together, and my heart pounds like I'm staring down an armed opponent.

Chin up. Spit it out. She needs to know.

"I could've … I could've saved them." I sound like I swallowed a bucket of gravel, but at least the words are out. "My parents. And yours."

Mel blinks, the color draining from her shadowed cheeks.

"When the Organization stormed the room, my mom's phone fell under the nightstand. I tried … to crawl over to it. To call for help. The police. But … I was too afraid. I did nothing instead. And our parents died because of it."

Mel licks her lips, her beautiful eyes wet. "You…"

This is it. The end.

There's no air.

"You think it was your fault."

Yes, I want to say. It was. But the words don't come.

Mel reaches out, covers my hand with hers. My skin prickles, the guilt so sharp in my stomach I think I'll be sick.

"Tommy. Listen to me. If you tried to call someone, the Organization would have seen you or heard you. You would've been killed too. You must realize that."

A tear rolls down her cheek. "It was *not your fault.*"

It would be easy enough to believe her. I want to. But I know how kind she is. She must feel obligated to comfort me despite my revelation.

"Don't do that. Please."

"I mean it."

Her eyes are so clear, so deep, I can see all the way into her soul. There are no shadows within, no doubt, no blame or hatred. Only sadness and love and pain.

She does mean it.

I open my mouth, the words stuck. I was so sure she'd hate me.

I hate me.

Mel presses my knuckles to her cheek. "If our situations were reversed, would you blame me?"

My chest crumbles when I picture it. A young Mel, trapped under the bed, witness to the slaughter. Of course I wouldn't blame her.

"That's different."

"How?"

Mel's room is darker now, the flames almost gone, the embers muted. I stare at their red glow, unable to look at her.

I don't have an answer. Not a good one, anyway.

Overwhelming pressure builds in my chest and stings my eyes. The embers blur as a sob forces its way past my locked jaw, the sharp edge of guilt I've carried for so long softening a fraction.

Her kindness knows no limits.

I suck in a deep breath, press a chaste kiss to her lips. "Thank you."

She only smiles, kisses away my tears. Then she snuggles down into the blankets. Golden warmth glows in my chest.

She knows, and she's still here.

Not just here. *Mine.*

I lie down and pull her close. She nuzzles into me, her soft, contented sigh hanging over us.

As sleep takes me, I dream, but not of horror and pain. Not this time.

A million shimmering stars stretch endlessly in every direction. Shining like the moon, dazzling in her beauty, Mel stands beside me. That sweet smile of hers lights her face as she takes my hand, pulling me into a celestial dance. We twirl together through the night sky, and my love for her burns like a flame in my heart, keeping the darkness at bay.

Chapter Twenty-Six

MEL

I DON'T know if I've ever slept quite so well.

It's like I was aware, even while unconscious, of the sparkling joy that's taken root deep in my soul. Wholesome and powerful, it flows through my veins like a song, lighting me up from the inside out.

Tommy's long legs are tangled up with mine. All the stress around his eyes, his jaw, has melted away. He looks peaceful in sleep. Innocent.

I reach out and trace the shape of his flawless lips, just barely visible in the dark. Heat spawns low in my belly as I trail my fingers down his neck, across his shoulder, and over his bicep. His golden skin is so smooth, the bands of muscle rock-solid underneath.

I breathe in his woodsy scent, like a crisp autumn breeze through the pines, and sigh.

My life is a certifiable disaster. Even discounting last night's near-death experience, my only potential future is here in the caves, scrubbing toilets and sweeping floors, unless I want to risk myself repeatedly on missions.

How can I feel so happy, be this happy, when that is true?

A half-smile softens Tommy's features, and warmth sparks in my heart. I'm tempted to snuggle back into him, to drift away again, but I'm scheduled in the gardens at seven. I don't want to get comfortable just in time for the alarm to wrench me awake.

I squint over my shoulder, searching for the luminous blue digits of my clock. There's only darkness.

Strange. Maybe we knocked it off the table while we were … diverted.

Flipping away from Tommy, I reach over the edge of the bed. As my fingers brush the smooth surface of the clock, Tommy's arms tighten around my ribs.

I glance up to find him watching me with warm eyes and a shy, heart-melting smile. "Good morning."

I beam back. "Good morning yourself."

"How are you?"

I stretch, joints popping, and savor the wellness zinging through my limbs, the all-encompassing joy glowing in my chest.

"Great. You?"

"No regrets?" His smile slips a little.

I snort. "Did you hear what I just said, or not?"

Tommy brushes his knuckles over my cheek. "I'm having a hard time believing this is real."

His words, his expression, tug at my heart. He thinks he's responsible for what happened to our parents, even though he was only fifteen when they died. There was nothing he could have done.

It's survivor's guilt.

With a frown, I capture his hand and press it to my lips. "Why?"

He shakes his head, apprehension stark in his eyes.

It makes me sad he feels so unsure of me, like I'll turn on him instead of helping him through this. I suppose all I can do is show him he isn't at fault for what happened, and I'm not going anywhere.

I kiss him softly, then throw the blankets aside and hop out of bed. As I bend to snatch up my clock, I notice the batteries scattered on the floor.

Whoops.

My cheeks flush as memories, sensations, fill my mind. I didn't even realize we knocked this over.

I pop the batteries back in and the display lights up.

It's 10:47 a.m.

I yelp like I've been zapped. Damn these caves and their utter lack of daylight!

"I was supposed to be in the gardens almost four hours ago!"

"Lisa always gives us the day off after a night mission. Don't sweat it."

I lunge for the small battery-powered lamp on my bedside table. Flipping it on, I find him on his back, studying the craggy ceiling with his hands behind his head and the blankets draped over his muscled abdomen. He's so appealing I briefly consider climbing back under the covers, but Lisa didn't mention anything to me about taking today off. I don't want to make her mad, especially after all the progress I made yesterday.

"She never told me that."

I head for the dresser, pull out fresh clothing, and dress at top speed. Behind me, Tommy sighs. The mattress squeaks as he climbs out of bed.

When I'm decent, I turn to see him dressed and examining the papers scattered on my desk. He's wearing the fatigues and tank top he wore yesterday on the mission, his hoodie and damaged vest folded over an arm.

A smile lifts the corner of my mouth. This amazing man is mine. "I'll see you later, right?"

Tommy doesn't answer. Instead, he plucks a loaded keyring out from under a heap of balled-up sheets—lyrics destined for the trash—and dangles it in front of his face.

"What's that? Are those yours?"

"No." His tone radiates anxiety. "These are Lisa's keys."

Lisa's keys. On my desk?

I glance at the cluttered surface, and my eyes snag on a fat manila envelope, resting on top of my notebook. I've never seen it before.

Huh.

I walk over and pick it up. It's stuffed, practically bursting at the seams. I flip it over. No label.

"I proved myself trustworthy yesterday, didn't I? Lisa must've dropped this off for me last night and forgotten her keys."

My cheeks flame as I consider what she would've seen: Tommy and I asleep together, our clothes all over the floor.

Tommy places the keyring back on the desk. "I don't know about that. It's not like her." He runs a hand through his messy hair. "Well? What's in there?"

Mouth dry, I rip the envelope open and pull out a thick wad of paper. Several photos slip from between the sheets and flutter to the floor. The blood drains from my face when I make out the shapes. The colors.

The bodies.

Pain twists my stomach and holds it tight, like a fist. I dive for the trashcan as the papers tumble from my senseless fingers.

Mom and Dad. It's *Mom and Dad*. Those corpses, warped and brutalized, smashed and shattered. They can't be … they aren't …

Black spots bloom over my vision as I heave over the trash, growing and shrinking and growing again. I can't breathe. I can't stop.

Gentle hands pull the hair away from my face.

I knew they were interrogated. Knew they suffered. But I never imagined the extent of it, couldn't have dreamed what they must've endured for their bodies to have ended up looking like that.

I throw up again, tears mixing with the sticky sheen of sweat that coats my face.

It hits me then. Tommy saw this happen. In person.

My heart bleeds for him, for the depth of his suffering. I peer up at his wan face; it swims in my blurred vision. I try to speak, to confirm what I already know about the identity of the people in those photos, but all that comes out is a strangled whimper.

Tommy doesn't say anything. He only watches me, misery leeching away the life in his eyes.

I shake my head. I don't want to know what else was in the envelope. So many papers, scattered all over the floor.

But I need to look. I hold my breath and pluck a sheet from the ground, heart thundering in my chest.

It's a transcript. Of an interrogation.

The interrogation.

Unable to make sense of it, I check another page, then another, fitting the text together like a ghastly puzzle.

Our parents weren't asked anything about the location of the Resistance, the identity of its members, or the Resistance's plans. Repeatedly, the Organization demanded to know about two things, and two things only: the chip Tommy mentioned at the shooting range, and something else called "the code."

There aren't any clues in the transcript as to what those things are, because not one of our parents cracked. At all. Not even when the interrogators broke their bones and burned their flesh. They denied knowing what the chip and the code were, even as they begged for mercy, then for death.

What they endured was so grisly. My consciousness flags, the room shimmers around me.

"Look at this." Tommy hands me another document.

Not a transcript this time. A contract. Between Lisa Bridger and Mara Levett, dated over twenty years ago.

My mouth falls open.

I didn't know Lisa worked at Levett Tech too. Directly with Mara, no less.

It makes sense, though. This must be how Lisa learned about the Organization in the first place. But according to Tommy and Sam, Lisa believes Mara is unaware of the corruption within her company. If Lisa knew Mara personally, why didn't she warn her about what was happening right under her nose?

Returning my attention to the contract, I learn that Lisa had been head of a top-secret division within Levett Tech. Her department was wholly dedicated to creating a technological weapon for the US government. It's clear from the contract's language no one, besides Mara and Lisa's team, knew about the project.

For Lisa to have held such a secretive, powerful position before going underground … she must have been threatened. That was how she found out about the Organization. They wanted the weapon she was supposed to develop, and they threatened her.

Or, hang on. Lisa's a brilliant programmer. A genius hacker. "The code" from the interrogation is the weapon in this contract.

Lisa created it.

I press my fist to my mouth. I'm right. I can feel it. Mom's best friend created the very thing she was killed over.

How did it come to that? Why did Lisa flee? And why did the Organization think Mom and Dad had anything to do with all this?

Brow furrowed, I read on.

Yes, it's confirmed here: Lisa was to create a computer virus capable of ravaging the hardware and software of any system it came into contact with. Highly transmissible, infecting every system touched by the system harboring it, it was to overcome and destroy all cybersecurity on its way through.

Why on earth would our government want something like this?

Wordlessly, Tommy hands me a packet. Progress reports detailing Lisa's work on the code. There are breakthroughs and setbacks, new ideas, testing. After about a year's worth of notes, a new message appears: Lisa telling Mara she doesn't think this weapon should be developed, explaining what could happen if the code were leaked online.

According to Lisa, it would propagate too quickly to defend against, and not only tear apart the fabric of the Web but fry every physical device connected to it. Because everything is linked online, the virus would spread everywhere. The information lost would not be recoverable.

Bank accounts, security systems, businesses, even governments, all down in a matter of hours. The virus would expand across the world, leaving society as we know it in shambles.

Mara's only response was a clear dismissal of Lisa's concern.

That must be why Lisa never told Mara about the Organization. Or maybe she did, and Mara didn't believe her.

Chest tight, I flip through the rest of the pages, the story of the Resistance's origin unfolding before my eyes. Over the next few years, Lisa's progress on the code slowed and slowed. Her reports became full of unforeseen issues. Real, or was she stalling on purpose?

Then, an incident report. Lisa's lab caught fire. Every computer, every document was burned to a crisp. Not only that, but every electronic record of Lisa's work disappeared too. There was nothing left, no remnant of the code anywhere in Levett's system. In addition, Lisa and her entire team vanished, and neither Mara Levett, nor the Organization, has found any trace of their whereabouts since, at least not as far as these records indicate.

This was when they went underground. Lisa's team from Levett Tech were the original members of the Resistance.

What happened to push them to such an extreme choice? Obviously, Lisa found out about the Organization. How, though? Was she threatened? If so, the Organization must regret that decision now.

The next set of documents are communications between someone named Mr. Edwards and his subordinates in the Organization. After Lisa's disappearance, they went straight for a man named Frank Sullivan. Apparently, Frank was a brilliant coder too, a savant in his field.

Threatening pain and death for Frank's family, they coerced him into redeveloping the virus for them. The dates here indicate he worked on it for years, putting everything he had into creating something perfect. Indestructible, unstoppable, and highly transmissible between systems.

Five years ago, Frank succeeded.

I swallow. The virus is out there somewhere, and the Organization has control of it. Why haven't they used it yet?

Feeling sick, I flip the page. My parents' names leap out at me. It's a set of emails.

Reyna,

I know you and Max are out of the game and want to keep it that way. I understand your motivations for stepping back, truly I do, but the world is quite literally at stake. Sullivan's succeeded.

If the Organization gets their hands on the code, life as we know it is over. While society struggles to deal with the fall of technology, the terrorist cell behind Mr. Edwards will use the ensuing chaos to take action. Despite our best efforts to thwart their shipments, they have plenty of Levett weapons at their disposal. Mara is just as blind to the corruption as ever. Millions will die, Rey. Millions.

You know the address. You know what must be done. Take Sullivan out. We have no choice. Destroy every piece of technology in that house. I've hacked into Sullivan's software and deleted as much as I can from here, but we can't risk missing anything. There's at least one microchip, and we've confirmed he's loaded the code onto it. He means to pass it to the Organization at the annual Levett conference.

Destroy it. If he's made copies, destroy those too.

We cannot get agents across the country in time. You and Max are our only hope. The world's only hope. I'm sorry.

Do not reply. Send word through the Williamses when you come for the conference.

I miss you.

– Lis

And underneath:

Lis,

You already know, but I'll say it anyway. I'll do what must be done.

I've decided not to share your message with Max. He'll be against getting involved, and, well, I want to keep him safe. If things go south for me, at least Mel will have him.

I'll pass you my report through the Williamses, but because Max won't be aware of it, I'll need to do so secretly. You'll know where to find my message when you see it. I'm not going to give the Williamses any details, just in case.

I miss you too, more all the time. I wish you could meet Mel. She's so like Max in some ways, but so like me in others. Oh, you'd laugh if you could see her. Such a rule breaker. My poor mother, I never knew what I put her through all those years until now.

Hugs,

-Rey

And one last message:

Reyna,

Ha, shocker. I'd expect nothing less of your daughter.

DO NOT REPLY. I cannot guarantee the security of incoming messages!

Good luck. Be careful.

-Lis

With trembling fingers, I stroke the text. Mom typed this note. She chose the words, strung them together. It's like a little window into her soul.

Tommy pulls the packet from my hands and wraps his arms around me. I lean into his warmth, icy chills running over my skin, hot tears sliding down my cheeks.

"Shh," he soothes into my hair.

I try to spit out the feeling stuck in my throat, to define the horror surging through me, but I can't. So many things happened over the years to result in the night of their deaths. If just one thing had gone differently, even something unrelated, it wouldn't have happened.

If Aunt Amy hadn't moved to California for school, for example, if Grandma hadn't died soon after and Mom hadn't wanted to be closer to her only sister, we wouldn't have lived near Sullivan. Mom wouldn't have gotten involved.

Why us? Why not somebody else?

Tommy anchors me to the world while dreadful sobs wrack my body and sickness whirls in the pit of my stomach.

Mom. Sweet, loving, bold, fearless. Always laughing. Always smiling.

Dad. Quiet, thoughtful, artistic, kind. One of the kindest people I've ever met. Selfless.

Good people. The best. They didn't deserve the end they met. So much pain, and for what? The Organization is still at large.

Suddenly, I'm aflame with a rage so powerful I can't help the ferocious scream that slices up and out of my throat. I hate the monsters who not only murdered them but destroyed them. Ripped them to shreds. All to find a horrible weapon, to hurt even more people.

I leap to my feet, nails biting into my palms, while the inferno scalds my insides.

Tommy blinks. There's a spark of surprise in his dull eyes, but mostly, they look like desolate wastes.

It wasn't only my parents, or his, who suffered. Could the Organization have more thoroughly destroyed Tommy? Look at the nightmare he had last night. His wild panic, the awful sobs while he slept. His terror, his anguish so clear to see.

The memory fuels my rage further. It blisters in my chest, scorches in my head, washes the room around me scarlet.

"They are going to pay."

"What does that mean?" Tommy frowns, his voice thin.

Striding up and down the room, I seethe. "The Organization. They hurt people. They want to hurt more people, a lot more people. What are we doing to prevent that? Sure, we steal their weapons, disrupt their shipments. Big deal. They already have weapons. We need to stop *them*. To take them down, once and for all."

Tommy's brows pull together. "That's impossible. Too big a job.

The Organization is huge. Well connected, well funded. We do what we can, but in the end we're just twenty-eight people, shackled by our need for secrecy. Our lives depend on it, and if we die, so do the innocents we're able to protect. The Resistance isn't meant to end the Organization."

He pulls himself off the floor, opens his arms to me in a calming gesture. "We can't stop them. We can only delay them, and delay them again, and again. That saves lives. Lisa monitors their comms, and sometimes, we save a person that way too. Like Sam. He used to work at Levett Tech as an accounting intern. He stumbled onto evidence—fudged numbers. He started poking around, figuring things out. Lisa caught Mr. Edwards's order to have him eliminated. We saved his life."

My heart stutters at the thought of Sam in the Organization's hands. Still, it's—

"Not enough," I spit. "Think about what we got for Lisa. What do you suppose BioAgent 313 is? Why would Lisa go to such lengths to steal information on it, when she's usually so cautious? The pattern is repeating. Lisa got desperate, and she sent my mom to get this chip. She's desperate again. Something big is going down."

A cavern yawns open in my chest. "I don't know whether the code still exists, or if Mom destroyed it, but even if the Organization doesn't have it, you said you guys have seen more arms deals go down in the last few months than in the two years before that. There's something important happening. We need to find Lisa. Now."

"Wait!" Tommy grabs my arm as I turn for the door. "Think this through. You're in possession of a file so top secret, even I wasn't allowed to see it. You have Lisa's keys. Something weird is going on."

He pauses, sliding his hand down my arm to lace his fingers with mine. "I don't quite understand what, but it's not going to be good when Lisa finds out you have these documents. You're not just going to be in trouble, you'll be in danger. We have to decide how to deal with the files and the keys. And you can't tell Lisa you know about this."

A beat of doubt pulses through me, but it's incinerated almost immediately by searing, bellowing rage. Tommy's right. Something weird is going on. With the Resistance just starting to trust me, possessing these documents is damning. Someone must've put them here to get rid of me, and it's likely they'll succeed.

But that doesn't matter. Stopping the Organization is more important than my safety.

Mom and Dad proved that.

"I don't care. The Resistance can make a difference. The Resistance should make a difference. If not us, who? If we do nothing, our parents will have died for no reason. We cannot be cowards. We need to finish what they started."

Tommy stumbles back, looking for all the world like I slapped him in the face. Does he think I'm calling him a coward?

I don't have room in me to feel bad. I spin and stride for the door, leaving the documents all over the floor. They can stay there. I have bigger fish to fry.

Like finding Lisa and making her act, consequences be damned.

CHAPTER TWENTY-SEVEN

MEL

RIP the door out of my way and crash into the hall, straight into a solid, muscular body. Cold metal bites into my temple. The click of the gun's hammer is loud in my ear.

I freeze, not daring to breathe as a second person steps close. Small, deft hands twist my arms behind my back and bind my wrists.

Cait.

Of course. She's had it out for me all along.

She put the folder in my room.

She framed me.

"What the hell are you doing?"

I can't see him, but based on the sound of his voice, I can imagine how frightening Tommy must look. Dark and dangerous and beautiful. Has he put the pieces together too?

"We're bringing this traitorous piece of shit to justice." Bill Accetta's words cut through me like shards of ice.

"Drop the gun," Tommy growls.

"Watch yourself, Williams. You're in enough trouble as it is."

Careful not to move too fast, I glance up at the man who holds my life in his hands. Bill glowers over my head, presumably at Tommy.

His expression is so ugly I cringe away without thinking. The gun presses harder into my skin.

From the corner of my eye, I can see Tommy now, arms crossed, shoulders tight. His narrowed eyes burn, his mouth a hard line.

"Check the room," Bill orders, and I catch sight of Cait's long blond ponytail as she shoves past Tommy.

He watches her go, then turns to stare at me, the glow gone from his tan face.

"Yup, they're here," Cait says. "Not just the keys. Wow. Top secret files too, right out in the open. She must think we're complete dolts."

Ugly names spring to the tip of my tongue, but I press my lips together, my stomach tense. Cait knows what she's doing. I won't play into her hands.

"Move," Bill snaps, and shoves me down the hall.

Like a criminal, I'm marched through the stone passages, Bill's gun glued to my head. Rage is still sharp, still hot in my chest, but now it's mixed with a fear so powerful my limbs shake. Will Bill take me to Lisa? To a cell? Or outside to be … dealt with?

I don't dare turn to check Tommy's expression, but I can feel the anxiety rolling off him as he walks beside me. My breaths start to come faster, my heartbeat staccato. We pass the cells. The front door.

Soon, we turn into the mess hall.

I'm flung, stumbling, into the wide room, where the entire Resistance waits around the outer edges, Lisa alone at the center. I scan the crowd, searching for any hint of the acceptance I earned last night. There's none to find.

Almost everyone glares at me with the same hard resentment. There are three exceptions.

Sam, whose bloodless face is a mask of horror; Vik, whose tawny eyes are sad; and Lisa, whose stoic expression gives nothing away.

When my eyes fall on her, my blood boils with a fury so bright I can taste it.

She developed the code. She ordered Mom into Sullivan's house.

She's responsible for what happened after.

Bill hurls me to the ground so violently I don't have a prayer of staying on my feet, but I don't crumple. Tommy's arms, solid around my waist, prevent me from crashing to my knees. I scramble to find my balance, his embrace the only thing keeping me upright.

Once my legs are under me, I meet his gaze. What I find there shocks its way through the wrath throbbing in my head.

Dread. Fear. Despair.

I'm being accused of stealing classified documents. Who does Lisa think told me where to find them? If Tommy defends me now, he'll incriminate himself.

I'll be damned if he goes down with me.

"Go," I whisper through numb lips. "Get out of here."

Eyes hard, he shakes his head. "No way."

"Now."

Tommy flips his knife open, cutting my wrists free and taking my hand. In front of everyone. "No."

With a harsh scowl for Tommy, Bill addresses Lisa. "We've confirmed the keys were in Snow's possession, along with several top-secret files. Cait was right."

Nose in the air, Cait tosses a fat stack of papers on the table in front of Lisa.

Horrible, manipulative bitch.

Lisa is solemn. Unreadable. "Melanie Snow, you have been accused of treason against the Resistance, and have been found in possession of stolen keys and top-secret files, which were taken from the Organization years ago at great cost. If the Organization were to recover the information within, it could help them revive a dangerous plot they had no choice but to abandon when we stole it. What do you have to say for yourself?"

Before I can gather my thoughts, Cait steps forward, her arms open to the crowd. "Why should Snow get to speak? Her actions are loud enough. She's always asking sensitive questions, and I caught her trying to break into the library two days ago, to steal these documents, I'm sure. If that's not bad enough, last night she practically gave Tommy to the Organization. What would've happened then? Would he have held up against their tactics, or would we be drowning in Organization minions right now?"

There are a few scattered grunts of agreement, a few nods.

"I made the choice to stay behind all on my own," Tommy snaps, leveling a venomous glare at Cait. She doesn't see it though, doesn't look at him as she returns to her parents' sides.

I ignore them both. "Lisa, I didn't take your keys, and I didn't steal any files. I don't know how they got into my room." I glance over at Cait, whose expression darkens, pure loathing in her stormy eyes. "I have a guess. Still, I can't prove anything. In the spirit of full disclosure, I did read them. I learned a lot I'm not supposed to know."

Tommy squeezes my hand. A warning. I squeeze back, an acknowledgment, and an apology.

My voice is stronger, harder, rising passionately as I go on. "I know what happened to my parents, and I know why. What I want to know now is, why have you allowed the Organization to continue to exist, to hurt and maim and kill? You can stop them. All of you."

I sweep my gaze over the faces in the room. "You know what the Organization is doing, and you let it go on. They are taking innocent lives."

I train my focus back on Lisa, and my words burn with recrimination. "It's your fault the code exists."

"That is top secret."

"It's your fault Mom and Dad died. Now it is your duty, our duty, not only to stop the Organization from passing weapons to terrorists, but to *raze them to the ground.*"

A few whoops from the crowd, a smatter of applause, but also hisses and boos. I hold Lisa's sharp, suddenly pain-filled gaze.

"There is much you don't know or understand about that time. You are right. I am responsible. But to bring down the Organization … it is not so simple. I have done my best to make amends and save lives."

She clears her throat, cuts a glance toward Cait before looking back at me. "I know you did not steal the files."

She knows! She knows it was Cait—

"Accetta."

Cait stiffens.

"Your father might be blind to your deceit, but I am aware it was you who put those documents in Mel's room."

A matching wave of fury crashes over both Cait's and Bill's faces. The crowd shifts, restless as Lisa goes on.

"I never imagined you would stoop to something so treacherous, so dangerous to our family. You are hereby stripped of your position as team lead."

The proclamation clangs through the room.

"Excuse me?" Bill's hands rest on his daughter's slender shoulders, his expression murderous.

My attention drops to Cait's face. She's gaping at Lisa, anger sparking in her eyes, but her skin is milk-white under the golden freckles. Bet she didn't expect her plan to end up like this.

"Cait's judgment is currently compromised." Lisa's tone is pure steel.

Bill's cheeks redden. "And how do you presume to accuse her of such a blatant act of treason? She's proven herself time and time again, while Snow was caught in possession of the keys and files. I saw her myself."

"Lisa," Cait starts, but Lisa holds up a hand to silence her.

"Cait has fought against Mel's presence here from the beginning. As a team lead, she is one of the only people who had access to both the library to steal the documents and to my bedroom to steal my personal keys. Not to mention she's the best among a select few skilled enough to do so unnoticed while I slept. Or do you mean to tell me you think Mel was able to sneak in without waking me up? There was a tiny window of opportunity between when I placed them on my bedside table last night and when I woke to find them gone."

Bill's jaw works as I fidget, embarrassed by the insinuation I wouldn't be stealthy enough to do so, even if Lisa's one hundred percent correct in her assumption.

Silent tears begin to streak down Cait's cheeks. "Lisa, please hear me—"

"You may not speak."

For the second time, Cait's mouth snaps shut. After a moment, Bill says, "Williams obviously helped Snow. Cait's worked damn hard, and—"

"Enough," Jess barks, so much colder than I've heard her before. "I went to check on Cait last night and found her room empty. I assumed she had gone to the bathroom, or to get more painkillers from Aaliyah, but if she has let her judgment become so clouded she would do something like this, then she should not retain her position. We cannot let her get away with it."

"You are letting your bias interfere with your sense, Bill," Lisa adds with a touch of regret. "Have you not paid attention to Cait over the last few weeks? To her reactions during this trial alone? Mel's and Tommy's too."

I glance up at Tommy. The shock and betrayal emanating from him are palpable, second only to the hatred lining his sharp features as he glares at Cait. The crowd rustles, ill at ease. Bill's only response is an ugly grimace for his daughter.

Poor Cait. I never thought I'd feel sorry for her, but the day has come.

Lisa appears unmoved. She holds a hand out. "Keys."

Head held high, Cait pulls a pair of keys from her pocket and walks forward on shaky legs to drop them in Lisa's palm.

With a nod, Lisa says, "I must impress upon all present how serious this security breach could have been. Cait will be reassigned to the maintenance team as she can no longer be trusted in the field, and she should be damn glad her punishment is not worse. Her team will meet with leadership tomorrow to restructure roles. Dismissed."

"Wait." I frown at Lisa, ignoring Cait's silent return to her parents' side. "What about the Organization?"

"What about them?"

"What do you mean, what about them?" The horrific ire that plagued me minutes ago rises again, burns hotter. I want the monsters who murdered my parents to suffer. I'm thirsty for it. "They need to be exposed."

Lisa's dark eyes narrow. "You're right. The Organization must be stopped, now more than ever. They are mere weeks away from launching an assault on the American people that will kill thousands. Maybe millions."

Horror prickles over my skin.

"If we could reveal them, if we could deliver the justice they deserve, we could save those lives and prevent not only this assault, but all future Organization attacks. However, they have too many moles in important places. If we try to go to the police, to the feds, to anyone, all we'll do is bring their wrath down on us. That is why the Resistance must take a different tack. That is why we oppose them as we do, and not more boldly."

The Organization can't control everyone though. We need to show the truth to the right people.

"What about social media?" I dare to ask. "We could make a video that will expose the Organization to the public. Let's go over their heads, over law enforcement. If we show the masses the truth, the government and Mara Levett won't be able to ignore the evidence anymore. We should gather footage, proof of the Organization's crimes. You can hack all the major social platforms. Make sure our video floods them all."

Wicked satisfaction curls through me, and I smile fiercely. Beside me, Tommy twitches, his palm slick in mine.

Lisa tilts her head. "It's a good idea, and one I have considered, but it would be an exceedingly dangerous mission with a very slim chance of success. I cannot gamble on a crapshoot with my people's lives as the price."

A faint glimmer of regret shines in her eyes.

I get it. Truly. The Resistance are more than undercover agents. They're a family. Especially knowing her role in her best friend's death, I can see how Lisa would be unable to stomach the risk.

But the Organization is weeks away from launching a major attack that will kill thousands. We need to stop them.

I need to stop them.

I don't have anything left to live for besides my parents' legacy.

What better way to honor their sacrifice, to make them proud, than to finish their work and protect the people they cared about at the same time.

"I'll take on the risk. You have families, lives, reasons to stay safe. I have nothing. If I'm the one to lead the mission and speak in the video, you can continue your work in the event I fail. None of you will be exposed."

Tommy leans in close, his warm breath tickling my ear. "What are you doing? That assignment is a death sentence. We'll find another way."

"I have nothing left," I murmur, still caught in Lisa's gaze. "I want this."

The room watches in silence as Tommy takes my other hand and pulls me around to face him. His eyes glisten. "What about me? Us? You said it yourself. The pattern is repeating. What happened last time? Don't sacrifice yourself like an animal for slaughter. Please."

He swallows. Squeezes my hands. "We're worth living for. Don't do this."

My heart fractures at the pain, the fear in his voice. "I have to."

"No, you don't. Revenge isn't worth it."

Thousands will die if the Organization goes through with their plan. They're why Mom did what she did, and why I must too.

"It's not only about revenge. This is the right thing to do."

Guilt floods my chest as grief ripples across Tommy's face. He drops my hands, backing away toward the door.

"Wait." I jolt forward, my fingers extended.

He shakes his head, then turns and shoves through the crowd. He's gone before I can move.

I take another step, but I can't deal with him now. We have only weeks until the Organization's attack. There's no time.

The fissures in my heart weep and throb, but I turn to face Lisa, who frowns and crosses her arms.

"I admire your commitment to doing the right thing, I really do, but I don't think I can allow you to take on such a dangerous task. Even if you live, once you expose the Organization so publicly, they'll hunt you for the rest of your days. It won't be like it is now, with them satisfied to have you quiet and out of the way. They will not rest until you are made an example of."

"With all due respect, that isn't your choice to make. I'm doing this with or without your help." Never mind that my plan hinges on her hacking prowess. Or that she could toss me in a cell and throw away the key with one word.

The seconds trickle by. Lisa chews her lip. No one so much as twitches a finger.

Finally, she blows out a breath, gives a curt nod. "Then I will assist you."

Something deep inside me unclenches. "Thank you."

"Lisa," Bill growls, Cait pale and hollow at his side. "I am honor bound to register my opposition to this course of action."

"Opposition noted and overridden," Lisa says. "I have warred with myself over attempting this sort of attack on the Organization for too long, and with the BioAgent delivery on the horizon, it's time."

"Then assign someone else."

"I refuse to order anyone to publicly out the Organization. Mel has volunteered. If another would like to take her place, they are free to do so."

Nervous energy buzzes through the room like a swarm of bees. It sets my teeth on edge.

Lisa ignores the unsettled atmosphere and returns her attention to me. "You will need information."

"Let's start with this plan of the Organization's," I say, determined to ignore it too. "What are they trying to do? How much time do we have?"

"You are aware I needed the bill of lading for something called BioAgent 313, which is a biological weapon the Organization, or rather the extremists they serve, plan to unleash on the public. It is taking an indirect route across the country now and is slated to arrive at Levett Tech in one week's time."

One week? My heart buckles.

Lisa's still talking. "We will have to expose them soon, with enough time for the public to put pressure on the government to investigate before they deploy it. That leaves us a very small window in which to produce this video."

"Can you elaborate more on BioAgent 313? What will happen when it reaches Levett Tech?"

Lisa hesitates.

I narrow my eyes. "No more secrets. I'm taking an awfully big risk. I deserve to know. We all deserve to know."

With a sigh, Lisa says, "It is a genetically engineered pathogen. A highly communicable, deadly bacterium the terrorists plan to leak into the water supply of several major US cities. If they are successful, it will infect thousands and spread quickly from there."

Shit. This is worse than I expected.

"I thought the terrorists wanted a microchip. A computer virus, not a real one."

Lisa scowls, a hand on her hip. "That sort of detail is classified and is neither here nor there."

My only reply is a tilt of my head, a twitch of my lips.

"Lisa," Bill warns.

Lisa huffs another sigh. I don't miss the twinge of sadness that flashes behind her gaze, quickly stifled. "If we do this, Bill, everything will come out anyway. There is no longer any reason to hide the extent of the truth from our own."

Training her attention back on me, she says, "They put many years and countless dollars into that computer virus, and in the end, they've got nothing to show for it. They gave up on it, for now, anyway, and pursued a different route to achieve their end goal."

"And what is their end goal?"

"They believe society has gone sideways, that the First World, and the technology that fuels it, is inherently evil. They will stop at nothing to cleanse humanity of it."

Lisa adjusts her glasses before going on. "They grew slowly, over the span of many years, born of our own American people. As consumerism and high tech have grown, so have they. The spread of their diseased ideas was gradual. Quiet and insidious, on the fringes and in the echo chambers of the internet. Still they're growing, turning greater numbers to their cause, increasing their power."

I shift my weight.

"Their ultimate goal is to find a way to cripple our civilization, and to use the resultant chaos to their advantage, swiftly and violently staging a coup. Then they plan to use the might of the US military, in addition to their own homegrown armies, to lead a bloody crusade against the rest of the modern world. They want to establish a dictatorship with themselves at the helm, to eradicate what they perceive as a blight large enough to ruin not only everything good we humans can be, but our ability to survive long-term on this planet. The code, and now the pathogen, are different means to this end."

Holy shit.

"They want to fight for the good of mankind by killing untold numbers of innocent people?"

"The most ravenous are convinced our consumerism and self-absorption will be the literal end of the world and feel any means to avoid it are worth the cost. The less enthusiastic often find themselves pulled in too far, unable to escape."

Oof. We need to act fast. "I'll get started today."

Lisa scans the room. "You will need a team to help gather evidence, but again, I will not order anyone to take on such a perilous assignment. I wouldn't even consider condoning it at all if the stakes weren't so high, but as things are, if any are willing to pay the price…"

Her eyes linger on the faces of her family. "I can only say to those who have given so much already: do what you feel is right. Melanie's mission could save many lives, but more than likely, it will end hers, and yours."

I turn toward the others, prepared to beg, to get down on my knees if I have to. "I can't do this alone. I know my plan is risky, but what if it works? Please. Help me."

Another wave of agitation shivers through the room. No one steps forward. No one says anything. Until…

"I'm in." Sam's pale as a sheet, but his brown eyes blaze.

I smile, even as part of me shrivels. I don't want to lead Sam into danger, but this is his decision. He knows what he can handle.

"I would recommend limiting volunteers to experienced field

agents," Lisa says flatly to me. "You need skilled teammates."

"Sam is skilled."

"Yes. But he has a gentle heart and no on-the-ground experience."

"Neither do I, and I survived last night. Sam has worked so hard, yet you've always passed him over. A kind heart is not a weakness."

Sam throws me a grateful glance.

Lisa's mouth twitches, her eyes unhappy. "So be it. I will not take away his choice in this."

My stomach flips, but I give Sam a nod. He's up to the challenge.

Vik steps to his side. "I'm in too."

I tamp down my surprise before it can show on my face. Vik's an experienced field agent, unlike Sam and me. Their help will be invaluable.

With an expression like he's chewing sour dirt, Hunter appears at Sam's other shoulder. "And me."

My heart stutters, and this time I'm not fast enough to hide my confusion. Hunter hates me. He must be doing this for Sam.

I wait, tense. No one else volunteers.

"Thank you." I give my new teammates a small, shaky smile.

"Melanie," Lisa says tightly, "be in my office in one hour to strategize. You can coordinate with your team after. I would join you, but I need to concentrate, to make sure I'm ready for the hack when you are. Vik and Hunter are used to working together, and they are both experienced and intelligent. Use them." She pauses, then adds, "Perhaps you should check in with Tommy too. He's one of our best."

My sore heart throbs. I won't pressure him to take part in something that hurts him so much, but I can at least ask for his support. He just needs to remember what's at stake.

I nod. "I'll talk to him."

"Good." There's a beat of silence. Lisa looks past me, to the crowd. "Show's over. Clear out. Sam, Vik, Hunter, you are excused from daily tasks until further notice."

"Meet me in the lounge in two hours," I add, working to inject a note of authority into my voice. I've never been in charge of anyone before.

They nod and file out with the crowd. The terrible rage in my heart has cooled. In its wake, prickles of doubt needle at me. So many lives hang on my ability to lead this mission.

Including my best friend's.

"Thanks for sticking up for me," Sam says, and I start. I thought he left with Hunter and Vik, but he's right here. We're alone in the empty mess hall.

Despite the barrage of emotions treating my heart like a sparring mat, I grin. "Of course. There's no one I'd rather have by my side."

"This mission is going to be very dangerous, especially for you. I'm glad I get to have your back through it."

The tightness in my chest eases a little. I can breathe better, knowing I'll have Sam with me. I give his hand a squeeze. "I appreciate you, Sam."

He ruffles my hair affectionately. "Same."

"I'll always have your back."

"We're officially a team. Can't get rid of me now."

I snort, then frown. "I need to find Tommy. I didn't explain myself very well before."

Sam's smile falters. "Yeah. Not gonna lie, that scene between you two was bad. Check the summit. Tommy likes to go there when he's having a hard time."

I nod, the fissures in my heart smarting. There must be some way I can fix things between us, make him see my plan is the best way forward.

And I only have an hour to figure out how.

Chapter Twenty-Eight

MEL

DASH through the caves, my heart pounding with each tick of the clock.

All those lives. Tommy will understand. He'll want to help.

I thunder around the last corner leading to the gym, losing my footing when I try to take the turn too quickly. A strong hand seizes my shoulder and steadies me. Warmth fills my chest, and I look up with a wide smile, but…

My stomach drops.

The face that's staring down at me is twisted in anger. The dark eyes burn.

Not Tommy.

Hunter's fingers dig into my shoulder, and I balk. Teammates or not, it's obvious he hates me as much as ever. Maybe he was in on Cait's little scheme to get me in trouble. My jaw works, but no words rise to my lips.

"I'll get right to the point." The hand on my shoulder flexes again. "Kick Sam off your team."

As if I'm going to take orders from him. "Excuse me?"

"You heard me." Hunter releases my shoulder, crosses his powerful arms.

I cross mine too. "No."

"Yes."

My eyes narrow, anger building like a firestorm in my heart. Hunter has no right to make such a demand. Lisa doesn't believe in Sam thanks to him, but as the person Sam cares about most, Hunter should. Especially knowing why Sam dropped out of his original mission team assignment.

The flame in my chest burns brighter. "Why would I want someone so talented off my team?"

"Don't play cute. You know Sam has never been in the field. Vik and I can provide more than enough support. Do you want him to get hurt? Or are you hoping his inexperience will get us all caught?"

"The 'Mel is a traitor' act is getting tired. Why don't you go find Cait and complain to her instead of bothering me? I wouldn't be surprised if you helped her set me up."

Hunter scoffs, rolls his eyes, but doesn't deny it.

My blood sizzles. "Sam is just as capable as any of you. What gives you the right to decide he can't go on missions?"

"What gives you the right to decide he can? Who are you to lead us, anyway? Who are you?"

Heat creeps over my cheeks. Hunter might be a prick, but he's right about this. I'm no one. "I'm the only person willing to step up. You want to lead this mission? Have at it."

Hunter cocks his head. "There are reasons we stay in the shadows, you know. Why should we trust your decisions? What have you ever done in your life that makes you worth following?"

"I got the bill of lading."

"Dumb luck. You didn't know what you were doing, and if Williams hadn't helped, you would've been worm food. That is, if you're really on our side. Something I'm not at all convinced of."

I shift. Hunter's right. I didn't know what I was doing then, and I don't know what I'm doing now.

Still, I have to try. If not me, who?

"That's fine. I won't waste my breath trying to convince you, and I'm not taking Sam off the team," I say, feigning cool indifference. "You don't think I have what it takes to lead us. Fine. I'm team lead regardless of your opinion. You're free to remove yourself if you so choose."

Hunter's mouth flattens. "I'll ask again. Why do you think you're qualified to make that decision with Sam's life on the line?"

The darkness in his narrowed gaze sends a beat of fear thrumming through me, but I ignore it. "I'm not, but Sam is. I trust him. He knows what he can do."

"You actually care about him, don't you?"

"Of course I do!" I throw my hands into the air. "He is strong, and smart, and talented. Have you ever watched him in the sparring ring? Seen the courage behind his kindness? He deserves a shot to prove himself. If none of you will give him that, I will. You'll all see."

"Mel," Hunter says fervently. He runs both hands through his hair. "Please. If you truly care about Sam, leave him out of this."

"Why?" I snap.

"Because he isn't the sort of person who could hurt someone, even if he needed to. Because he will get hurt."

I frown, a flush of dread dousing my fury.

The violence of last night's mission is seared into my brain. The guards' heads as they exploded. Their throats spilling out. I can't imagine Sam in the middle of that.

But I know what it feels like to be underestimated, to be constantly doubted and questioned. If I kick Sam off my team, he'll never get his shot in the field.

Empathy is not a weakness. I know Sam can do this. I believe in him.

Conviction rises like molten steel in my chest.

Sam can do this. And so can I.

Voice soft, I say, "Sam is kind and gentle, but that doesn't mean he's not qualified, and it doesn't mean he needs your protection."

Loathing sharpens Hunter's features. "You have no idea what you're talking about."

My blood boils anew, my own eyes pricking at the injustice of it. How dare Hunter go behind Sam's back and try to ruin this for him? How dare he beg for Sam's choice to be taken away? Even Lisa respected his right to choose.

How dare he?

Before I think better of it, I'm in Hunter's face.

"Of all people, you should support Sam in this. How do you think he feels, knowing you don't believe in him? He has to hear Lisa and everyone else tell him he's not good enough over and over again. You should be the one backing him up, telling him he is good enough and he can do this."

I stop short, throat stuck. I might be yelling at Hunter, and with good reason. But still, as the words roll off my tongue, the hurt behind them, the anger and fire … I can't help but feel they're aimed at someone else.

Someone who bailed the second I volunteered to lead this mission.

Hunter stares at me, his expression appropriate to being walloped with a battering ram. I don't give him a chance to recover.

"You should be in Sam's corner no matter what. Yet here you are, going behind his back, trying to get him kicked off the team. Honestly, Sam is too good for you. Far too good. He deserves better."

With a simmering glare, I turn on my heel and march toward the gym and the stairway to the summit. My palms tingle, but it won't help anything to turn around and smack Hunter, even if it'd make me feel better.

"What did you say?"

I freeze, taken aback by the accusatory tone in his voice.

Shit.

I'm not supposed to know about Hunter and Sam.

Heart in my throat, I turn around.

Hunter's bronze skin is wan. "Did you say Sam's too good for me? What the fuck is that supposed to mean? He's my best friend."

I gulp. "Um. He deserves better friends."

Hunter's eyes harden, his jaw flexed. Without another word, he turns his back and stalks away toward the main body of the caves.

"Wait!" I lurch forward, stomach churning as he disappears around the corner.

Shiiiiit.

I practically told him I know about him and Sam. I should

find Sam, to warn him, but my meeting with Lisa is ticking closer, and I need to hash things out with Tommy before I speak with her. Otherwise, he won't be there for my team's initial planning session, and I need his knowledge, his steady support behind me.

Throat dry, I turn for the gym. I'll hurry with Tommy, then find Sam and make things right before I meet Lisa.

There'll be time. There has to be.

CHAPTER TWENTY-NINE

MEL

I STAND alone at the mountain's highest point, staring out over the sun-drenched valley, cold wind whipping strands of hair into my face. Down in the forest, splashes of vibrant red, brilliant orange, and sunny yellow leaves wink up at me, waving in the breeze.

The sight should be magnificent, but the anxiety gnawing at my stomach is so strong I can't take it in. I was sure Tommy would be here.

My next guess is he's in his room, a sketchpad balanced on his knees, headphones on and music blaring. Good thing the housing wing is only about as far from here as possible.

With a curse, I turn and sprint back down the stairs. It's already been almost thirty minutes, and if I'm wrong again, there won't be time to find him before my meeting with Lisa. Either way, I won't be able to warn Sam about my slip with Hunter until afterward.

Sweat drips down my neck as I hit the bottom of the staircase and race through the corridors, dodging around bystanders too quickly to clock their reactions. Sam flashes by, deep in conversation with a blotchy-faced Cait. There's Vik in the mess hall, laughing with a couple of older mechanics. No sign of Hunter. No Lisa.

I crash to a stop outside Tommy's door, my breath sharp in my heaving chest, and knock.

No answer.

I try again. "Tommy? Please let me in. We need to talk."

Nothing.

It feels wrong to barge into his room, but this is important and there's no time to waste. My hands shake as I grip the handle and turn.

To my relief, the door falls open. To my crushing disappointment, Tommy's not inside.

I glance at the clock on his bedside table, the room an exact replica of my own, only neater.

Dammit. Fifteen minutes left. I'll have to track him down later, and I was counting on his insight and support. He's the only experienced field agent who's one hundred percent behind me.

My shoulders sag as I cross the hall to my room, the sweat from my sprint cooling on my skin. If I'm lucky, maybe Lisa won't take an entire hour, and I can find Tommy before my team expects me. Or maybe he'll surprise me and show up.

I slip through the door and head toward the dresser to grab a hoodie, but halfway there a square of dark color on my pillow catches my eye.

After this morning, I've had enough of surprises in my room. Still, I step over to the bed and pick up what turns out to be a small painting.

Two silhouettes dance among a cloud of stars, holding each other close. The lovers are mostly hidden in the purple-blue night, but enough detail shines through for their identities to be clear, and for the warmth of their mutual adoration to send a lump into my throat.

I run my finger over the image, absorbing the magic. Strange Tommy would leave this here instead of giving it to me in person.

Hoping for a clue as to why, I flip the canvas over. Scrawled on the back is a note.

Mel,

You mean more to me than I can say, but hopefully this painting gives you an idea. I can't lose another loved one, especially not to the monsters in the Organization. I'll do anything to keep you safe, and that includes making sure your plan is unnecessary. Wait for me, and we can decide our next move after I've taken care of the threat. I will not fail you.

I love you.

-T

My mind hums, my heart pounding like I'm sprinting through the caves again. Hinges squeak behind me, and I jump and spin.

Sam's peeking in the doorway. "You all right? Looked like someone was trying to do you in when you blew by me just now."

I blink.

We can decide our next move after I've taken care of the threat.

It could mean so many different things, none of them good.

Sam comes closer. His eyes dart from the canvas clutched to my chest back up to my face. "What's that?"

"Tommy." The word trembles in time with my hands as I turn the note toward Sam. His brow furrows as he reads.

"He wouldn't."

My heart shatters. "He's going after the pathogen, isn't he?"

I don't want to believe it, but it's the only conclusion that makes sense.

Sam's already pulling me into the hall by the hand. "We need to stop him."

"The garage."

I pick up the pace, dragging Sam now, desperate to reach Tommy before it's too late. There's no way he's thought this through. Instead of supporting my mission, sanctioned and aided by Lisa and the Resistance, he dipped out to 'take care of the threat' on his own. Without a plan. Without backup or any kind of help. Without telling me first.

Hurt and anger sear through my chest as fear spikes into my throat.

"He couldn't take a car," Sam wheezes behind me, "without Lisa's keys, and it's the middle of the day. The mechanics would think it was weird if he left through the garage on foot. But he does know a back way out. When June deserted, she rappelled down from the summit."

"June. Hunter's ex. She deserted?" The words spin in my mind, not adding up. I thought June froze on a mission and got shot.

We flash past the mess hall again. Vik's suspicious stare bores into my back.

"The day she died, she was taking information to the Organization. She escaped from the summit to avoid detection. It's so hard to scale hikers never attempt the climb, and because of all the stairs it's rare for anyone in the Resistance to bother accessing it from the caves. Except for Tommy."

I skid to a stop, sneakers rooted to the floor. June took information to the Organization.

"She didn't die in a shootout?"

"Well, yeah, she did. It happened when Cait, Tommy, and Hunter went to bring her back. She had already reached Levett's perimeter."

June betrayed them. Her friends. The person she claimed to love.

No wonder Cait doesn't trust me. No wonder *Hunter* doesn't trust me.

But Tommy is a traitor now too. He's going to die.

Because of me.

"Sam," I rasp. "Please." What am I begging for?

"The summit," he says decisively, and we take off in a new direction like bats out of hell, the same startled people blurring in my peripherals as we retrace my earlier sprint in reverse. We pass Cait, sitting on the floor this time, face pressed to her knees. She lifts her head, her red-rimmed eyes widening as we thunder by.

"Stop!"

Her clear voice cuts through my panic like glass, and for the second time, I lurch to a halt, tugging Sam with me. Cait avoids my eyes, instead peering at the canvas still gripped in my sweaty hand, then looks up at Sam. "What's going on?"

"Tommy's idiocy has reached new heights."

Sam's moving again, slower than before. I follow, and to my dismay, so does Cait. Even puffy, her gaze is fierce. Angry.

And frightened.

"Explain," she growls.

I shove the canvas at her and pick up the pace, ignoring the sound of her faltering steps behind us, her sharp intake of breath.

"Stop," she spits again, and this time it's Sam who obeys.

"I know, Cait, but there's no time—"

She cuts him off.

"Go to Lisa." Her burning gaze flicks to me and away, back to Sam. "We went after June on our own, and we failed. We cannot fail Tommy."

"Every second counts," Sam argues back. "Going to Lisa will give him too much of a head start."

"No!" Cait advances on us like a wild animal. "You weren't there! That's what we said when we followed June, and she died. We can't!"

My heart cracks, and the seconds slip by as we all stare at each other. She's right. We don't know where Tommy went, what his plan is. We can't save him.

Lisa can. She'll bring him home.

Sam shakes his head, breaks Cait's frenzied stare, and hauls me back into a sprint.

"Wait!" She tears after us again.

"Lisa's office," I huff at Sam.

He doesn't slow. "But—"

"It's not our responsibility." The words are bitter on my tongue. But if we go after Tommy, that's it. My mission is shot. People die.

"Mel—"

"I'm your team lead." My eyes sting at the betrayal of not doing anything to help Tommy. But he betrayed me first by putting me in this situation. He should've talked to me.

"What about Tommy?" Sam asks.

"Lisa will find him. We have to focus on our mission."

The gym flashes by, and with it the stairway to the summit. Everything I am pulls toward it, but I keep going.

The three of us clatter to a halt at the end of the hall. Cait and I both hammer on Lisa's door.

She pulls it wide, alarmed as Cait, Sam, and I all rush to explain at the same time.

"Whoa, whoa, slow down," she says, her startled gaze roving over our panicked expressions. Cait hands her the canvas, and Lisa's eyes narrow. A filthy string of curses slips through her clenched teeth. "Fucking young people," she says, seething, then turns and strides to her desk. We follow.

"Bill," she snaps into a walkie-talkie, shuffling through the papers scattered in front of her computer. "Come to my office immediately."

"Copy."

She glares at us as she lowers the radio. "Do you three know where he's going?"

"No," I reply.

She riffles through the papers again. "One of the copies I made last night of the bill of lading is missing. There were four. I left them right here."

"Fuck," Cait groans.

"You did the right thing coming to me. I will take care of this. Mel, you and Sam focus on your mission. Cait, you will help your father track Tommy down. You know him better than anyone, and time is of the essence. But you best believe I will not hesitate to throw you in a cell when you return if you deviate from your father's orders at all." Lisa runs a hand over her face, then pushes her glasses up. "If we're lucky, we'll intercept Tommy before he draws unwanted attention. Or worse."

Or worse. My mind spins with possibilities, the pictures of our parents' bodies stuck at the forefront.

Stop. Breathe.

I close my eyes and pull in a deep breath. Lisa will find him. She will.

When I release the air, I release the fear and pain as best I can. If I let myself panic or succumb to despair, and if Tommy can't 'take care of the threat' by himself, then people will die.

And what happens if he's discovered? He could push the Organization to launch their plan early, before I'm able to produce the video.

We need to act fast.

"Sam," I say, glancing at the clock on the wall, "Vik and Hunter are expecting us in an hour. Obviously Lisa has other things to worry about now, so can you please find them and bring them to the lounge early? I still want to touch base with Lisa real quick, then I'll meet you guys there. Oh, and don't tell them about the situation with Tommy yet. I don't want their focus divided."

"All right. Don't worry, I've got your back." With a slightly forced smile and a pat on my shoulder, Sam leaves.

He thinks we made the wrong choice, coming here. Dread threatens to suffocate me, but I shove it down, bury it under a wave of focus aimed solely at our objective.

I can't let myself go there, or we'll fail.

CHAPTER THIRTY

MEL

$\mathcal{G}$ ROLL my shoulders and lean back into one of the squashy armchairs in the lounge. Vik and Hunter are sitting on an adjacent sofa, Sam perched on the cushioned arm.

Lisa and I didn't have time to truly strategize like we were supposed to, but while we waited for Bill, we mapped out exactly what we'd include in the video, Cait a silent and awkward third wheel at my side. Lisa told me to let her know when we need her technical help to break into Levett Tech, but said she has to focus on Tommy and how to hack the social media platforms until then.

In other words, keeping Tommy's knowledge of the Resistance and our plans out of the Organization's clutches is the priority. She won't be available to help us strategize, though she agreed we need to work as quickly as possible in light of Tommy's desertion.

"As you can see, it's not clear how we should proceed," I say, wrapping up the short summary I've just given the team. "Lisa already has some digital evidence. For example, she has footage of the Organization's attack on me and Tommy in the records room, thanks to the CCTV. But it doesn't prove anything except that we trespassed at Levett Tech. I told her I want to break in again and find concrete evidence of their illegal weapons trade. There must be some way to prove their inventory numbers don't line up. Math doesn't lie, right?"

I smile at Sam, ignoring the pang of guilt in my chest when he grins back as if Tommy's life isn't currently in danger. Either his acting is superb, or he's able to compartmentalize his worry. Like I'm desperately trying to.

"I can help with that," he says lightly. "Just get me into the admin building."

"Great. Thank you. And then we'll need to find out where and when Levett employees might meet to engage in something illegal, so we can capture damning footage of them. I'm not sure the best way to go about that."

I peek at Vik and Hunter. Vik's mouth quirks to the side. Hunter visibly seethes.

"Any ideas?"

"Yeah," Hunter spits. "You and Sam go scrub a toilet and get Accetta and Williams back in here."

My heart falters at Tommy's name. I glance at Sam, who looks both guilty and hurt, then I scowl at Hunter. Jerk. "If you don't have anything constructive to say, shut it."

"Or what?"

"Hunter," Sam chides softly. He quails under Hunter's withering glare.

"Vik?" I ask. "Any ideas?"

They shrug. "You're team lead. You tell us what to do, not the other way around."

Apprehension swirls in my stomach, but I square my shoulders. "Yes, well, I'm not experienced like you are. We should brainstorm together."

"We take our orders from Cait, not you," Hunter snaps. "She always has a plan. You're blowing it."

Too bad she's banned from missions, not to mention she's got her hands full hunting down an arrogant dumbass.

"Cait is no longer your team lead," I remind him.

"She may have gone too far, yeah, but I understand why," he retorts. "She was trying to protect us. I follow her."

"Hunter," Sam says, stronger this time. "Stop. Give Mel a chance."

The glower Hunter levels at Sam could incinerate hot coals. I throw my hands up, palms forward. "Enough. I know I'm not your first choice as team lead, or even on your list, but I'm the only one willing to put myself on the line for this. You're here, which tells me you care about the people the Organization will kill if we don't succeed. So let's cooperate, okay?"

Silence falls, buzzing with tension. I swallow.

Vik tilts their head, lips pursed. "Well, we know a few key things. We know Mara Levett will be in Texas inspecting the Austin plant this week, and we know on the second Tuesday of every month Mr. Edwards meets with his top buyers. That's tomorrow."

"It's useless, Taylor," Hunter snipes. "Can't you see she doesn't understand a word?"

I bristle. "I'm not an idiot, Zhang. The only thing I'm not sure about is who Mr. Edwards is. I saw his name in those classified documents, but..."

Vik gapes, sending embarrassment prickling over my skin. "You don't know who he is?"

They glance at Hunter, who rolls his eyes.

I bite back my reaction. Hunter's trying to undermine me. I won't let him.

"I know he's important, just not who he actually is. I want to make sure I have the pertinent facts, that's all."

"Mr. Edwards is the leader of the Organization," Sam cuts in, and I throw him a grateful smile. "I'm not surprised you don't know that. We don't have much reason to discuss him on the maintenance team. And to be fair, no one knows who he really is. His identity is well hidden."

"So he's top of the food chain. Got it." I chew my lip. "Why do we care if he's meeting with his buyers tomorrow? Do you think we could get footage of that?"

Sam shrugs. Beside him, Hunter snorts.

"You know, I really think we ought to get Cait involved," Vik says. "She can help from the caves, at least in the planning stage. No offense, Mel, but you just don't understand how this stuff works."

Sam's mouth tilts down. "Why don't you help her understand? Come on, Vik. Give her a chance."

Vik eyes me for a long moment. "All right. We can't get footage of that meeting because we don't know where or when it will take place, and we don't know who Mr. Edwards really is, so we can't tail him. What we do know is Mara will be in Austin tomorrow, and Mr. Edwards will be somewhere off-site, which means tomorrow would be the perfect time to break into Levett's campus. No high-ranking authority figures connected to either the Organization or Levett Tech will be around."

I wring my hands. Something feels off about this. It's too convenient.

"Isn't it weird Mara and Mr. Edwards will both be gone exactly when we need them to be? Wouldn't you expect Mr. Edwards to make sure he's around when Mara's not?"

Sam's eyebrows pull together, but Hunter heaves a long-suffering sigh and says, "Accetta never overanalyzes irrelevant details. You're wasting our time."

"It's not unusual," Vik says, fiddling with the end of their sleeve. "Mara is running a huge conglomerate with multiple locations across the country. She visits each one. They're away at the same time plenty. Plus, both have lots of lower-level executives who will still be here."

I push down a pang of unease. "Okay. So we break in tomorrow night, using the same plan as last night."

Hunter shifts in his seat. "What about patrol patterns? You don't think they've changed those up? Added security? We need to do some recon first. Tomorrow's too soon."

"We don't have time to waste," I counter. Not with Tommy out there doing God knows what. Sam nods emphatically.

"Oh yeah," Hunter sneers. "I'm sure a couple novices know what's best. Or maybe Mel's hoping to lure us into a trap. They found us right away yesterday. I wonder why that was?"

Vik blinks, their full lips tugging down as they study me. My insides wilt under their scrutiny.

"All right, I think we've had enough for now," I say, ignoring the heat washing up my neck. "It's one thirty. Lunch break. Meet me in an hour, and please, let's be ready to play nice and actually get something done."

"I'm going to Lisa," Hunter growls. "This is ridiculous."

Without giving Sam so much as a glance, he stalks from the room. Vik avoids my eyes as they follow on his heels.

I slump back into my chair. "Well, that went great."

Sam grimaces. "It could've gone worse. Vik will work with us, even if they're unsure about you. It's Hunter who'll be a problem." He pauses, his frown deepening. "I know he doesn't trust you, but that was weird. He doesn't normally act that way."

My stomach turns as Sam goes on. "I mean, with me, he's usually a little standoffish in public. I might not like it, but I'm used to it. I understand. This was different. He's never been so mean."

He sighs. "I wish you could know the Hunter I know. You must think I'm a total pushover to be with him after what you just saw."

"Sam…"

"Yeah?"

"I know why Hunter's being weird. I did something, uh, bad. By accident, but still."

Sam's gaze sharpens. "What?"

Here goes nothing.

"I sort of let it slip I know you two are together." I wring my hands. "He was upset. I'm so sorry."

Sam's face drains of color, his eyes wide. "You what?"

Everything in me shrinks. "It was an accident. He was trying to get me to boot you off the team, and I—"

"How could you do that? I told you no one could know. I trusted you!" Sam leaps to his feet. "Hunter is going to kill me."

The warmth is gone from Sam's eyes. I never imagined he could look so cold.

I put a hand on his arm, but he shakes it off. "I feel awful."

"Whatever. I need to find Hunter."

Without looking back, Sam storms out of the lounge.

A small whimper escapes my lips. I've lost Tommy, and now I've lost Sam too. After betraying his trust, I deserve his anger, I know. That doesn't make it easier to deal with.

I drop my face into my hands. This team is one snide remark away from imploding.

Hunter's right. I'm going to fail.

And innocent people will pay the price.

CHAPTER THIRTY-ONE

MEL

FIVE hours, ten minutes, and fifteen seconds from now, we'll be crossing the fence behind Levett Tech.

It's not enough time. We're not ready.

But Tommy remains at large, his knowledge of our goal at risk of falling into the wrong hands. We need to strike while we still can.

My stomach crawls and I hug my ribs. My team and I have been in the lounge all day, just like we were yesterday.

Despite Hunter's lack of civility, Sam's dour silence, and Vik's wariness, we've managed to cobble together a plan for tonight. The problem will be getting them to work as a cohesive unit. If we can't even look at each other, how will we ever get through a freaking mission?

The fact that Cait and her dad haven't returned with Tommy yet is the whipped cream on top of the shit sundae that is my life.

"I think we're good to go," I say, voice thin. "Can you guys think of anything we've missed?"

Would they tell me if they spotted a hole in the plan? Sam would. Vik too, I think.

The seconds drip by.

Only when I've counted to thirty-three does Vik say, "I think we're covered."

My breath escapes in a whoosh. "Great."

The others stare off in different directions, not looking at me. Not looking at each other. They know how many lives depend on us. Don't they care?

This will be the most important thing I ever do. The last thing, probably. They better not ruin it.

I clear my throat. "Look, we need to be able to work together."

Hunter huffs a scornful laugh. "Teaching us about teamwork? How very grade school of you."

Heat stains my cheeks, but I will not let him get to me. "I'm serious."

"Oh, I know."

Grief sinks into my bones, into my very soul. I've failed before I've even gotten started, and now Mom and Dad's murderers will get away with what they did. They'll kill again. Countless lives will end, all because I couldn't get this team to work together.

Pressure rises in my chest, pushing against my throat. I gave everything for this mission. My freedom, my future, Sam, Tommy. I have nothing left, yet I'm the only one making an effort now.

My teammates are spitting on my sacrifices. They're willing to damn who knows how many others to death, all so they can wallow in their petty dramas.

I clench my jaw against the rage that sears under my skin. This team doesn't respect me. I don't think yelling at them will make it any better.

On the other hand, I've tried reasoning. I've tried being kind. If I sit back and let this play out, the mission will fail. Our lives will be forfeit, along with all those the video could save.

Cold resolve settles over me.

"You should be ashamed of yourselves."

Every eye lands on me.

"Have you forgotten why we're here? Have you forgotten about the people we're trying to save?" My voice rises, strong and furious. "Cut the bull. It doesn't matter. What matters are the moms and dads, the grandparents and children we're trying to save. Or do you think your hatred of me is more important than their lives?"

I meet each of their stares in turn. Sam's brows contract, Vik's amber eyes are wide. Hunter's steely gaze remains hard.

"You don't have to like me or this team," I growl, hot wrath tingling through me, "but we have to work together to get this done. There is no other option. If you can't do that, the coming bloodshed is on you."

Stricken, Sam frowns. "You're right."

Vik nods, their brown cheeks darkening a shade. Hunter doesn't move.

I lock him in a blazing stare. "Can we count on you, Hunter?"

His jaw tightens. But then he says, "Yes."

I give him a curt nod. "And you, Vik?"

"Of course," they whisper. "Teamwork makes the dream work, after all."

My heart skips a beat, and Dad's gentle smile flashes behind my eyes. He used to love to say that. He'd sing it to me any time I had the nerve to complain about group work at school, drama on my soccer team, or fights with my friends.

"Teamwork makes the dream work, Mel-bear," he'd say, a twinkle in his eye. "Sounds like you better hop off the wambulence and find a way to work together."

Step up, Dad's voice seems to echo through the years. Under the teasing and silly catchphrases, that's what he was telling me. *No excuses. Get off your butt and make it happen.*

I will, Dad.

"Sam?"

Sam's chin dips. "I'm not going to let anyone hurt innocent citizens."

Exhilaration swells through the anger in my chest. I took charge, and it worked.

Mouth hard, I meet each pair of eyes again. "Good. We have a solid plan. Take a few hours to rest and eat. We'll meet in the garage at seven."

Vik and Hunter get to their feet, but I grab Sam's sleeve before he can rise.

"A word?"

His mouth slants down, his tired eyes fixed on his laces. I don't speak until Hunter pulls the door closed behind him.

"Sam…"

Only when his eyes meet mine do I notice the slight rim of red around them.

"What?"

His voice is flat. Not mean, just empty. I reach toward him, but he shrinks away. "Are you okay?"

"I'm fine."

If Sam's fighting with Hunter, it's my fault. "What happened?"

Sam's brows pinch together.

"Please."

"Hunter ended things."

Oh no. I was afraid I caused trouble between them, but I didn't anticipate this. And right before tonight's mission.

"Why?" My voice is small.

"He said he couldn't risk losing his position, especially now that Cait's gone. He said he can't ever trust me again." A small sob breaks through Sam's control, and he squeezes his lips together.

My insides twist, his pain pulsing in my own heart. I move from my armchair to plunk down on the couch next to him. "Oh, Sam," I say, a catch in my voice. I wrap an arm around his shoulders. "I'm sorry."

He shakes his head, silent tears streaming.

"You deserve better than this."

"No. It's m-my fault. I sh-shouldn't have told anyone."

For Sam to feel that way, for Hunter to choose his job over this wonderful person … it's inexcusable.

"Look at me."

Sam's teeth sink into his lip as he focuses on my face.

"This is not your fault. You should never have been made to hide like that in the first place." I squeeze his shoulders.

"It's not … you just … it's not personal. Hunter has his priorities, and he has them for a reason."

I nod slowly. "Maybe. But it's been years. Can you really tell me you're happy burying your love in the shadows? Are you fulfilled living that way?"

The corners of Sam's mouth turn down, and I know my comment hit its mark.

"I understand Hunter's need for revenge, trust me. I'm sad for him. But you're an amazing human being. You deserve to love someone who will make you their priority, no matter what. You deserve to have someone shouting from the rooftops over you and believing in your capabilities. Someone who will support your wants and needs as much as their own."

A ripple of sorrow runs through me. I wish I could say the same to Tommy. If he would quit trying to save me and treat me like a partner instead, he'd be here now. We'd storm Levett Tech together.

Sam leans into my shoulder, and I hold onto him tighter.

"I'm sorry," I say again. "I didn't mean for this to happen. I didn't want to break you guys up."

"I know. It's just hard. I love him. I want him to be happy."

I rest my cheek on the top of Sam's head. That's something I can relate to. I'd give the world to see Tommy smile.

The seconds tick by. Sam's warmth seeps into me, thawing the icy numbness that's encased my heart since finding that canvas on my pillow.

"So," he says, "fill me in on you and Tommy."

My stomach flips. "What do you mean?"

"Oh, come on. I read his note."

I pull my knees up to my chest. I don't necessarily want to reveal everything. That one night was too intimate. I want to take it with me to my grave.

"You saw Tommy get shot, right? On the CCTV?"

Sam shudders. "Yeah."

"After, when everyone else was in bed, we had a moment."

Sam shifts away to study my expression, and heat washes over my cheeks. "I told him I was falling for him."

A grin breaks across Sam's face.

"He said the same back. We were going to try to be together."

Sam tilts his head. "Were?"

"He left." I drop my face to my knees. "I don't know whether he's even alive."

I'm pulled sideways, Sam's arm coming around me. He heaves a sigh. "Tommy's an idiot."

I snort, but the sound is thin. It doesn't mask the pain underneath.

"I'm serious."

"He had his reasons." My heart throbs thinking of them, of Tommy's enduring suffering.

Sam plays with my hair, his arm still slung over my shoulder. After a minute, he says, "You told me I deserve to be with someone who will prioritize me, no matter what. Well, you deserve to be with someone who will support you no matter what too. Who will treat you like an equal."

An uncomfortable shiver runs up my spine.

"Tommy's past is horrible," Sam goes on, "but it shouldn't keep him from doing that. He should have your back, not run away behind it, even if he *is* trying to protect you."

"I know. I think this is more about him than me, though."

"Didn't he say he can't lose another loved one?"

I shrug. "I think he's convinced this is a suicide mission."

"And what about you?"

I close my eyes, relaxing automatically as Sam's fingers comb through my long hair. "I know it's risky, but I think we have a shot."

"He should do more than not run away. He should see your strengths, believe in you even more than you believe in yourself."

A stab of bruised resentment pulses through me. Sam's telling me the same thing I told Hunter when Hunter tried to get Sam booted off the team.

Tommy's afraid, but that doesn't excuse his behavior. He's suffered, but so have I. I deserve someone who will stand by me as a partner, not treat me like a helpless dependent. Plus, this isn't only about me and him. It's about stopping the Organization before they can hurt anyone else. Working together would've given us the best chance for success.

"I'm exhausted," I tell Sam. "I'm going to try and nap before tonight." I could use a few hours to get my head straight.

"Good idea. I might too."

I push off the couch, then whirl toward him, sudden worry constricting my lungs. Sam's never been in the field. Considering what he's just gone through, his focus could be shattered.

"Will you be okay tonight? Working with Hunter, I mean."

Sam's eyes darken, but his head bobs.

"Are you sure?"

"You can count on me." Conviction simmers in every word.

I blow out a breath. If Sam says he can do this, then he can. He's aware of his capabilities and limitations. "I know that. I trust you with my life."

Sam gives me a small smile. "Go rest. I'll see you in a few hours."

With a wave, I'm out the door. The summit calls me, but I ignore the urge to head there, even though the drive to go after Tommy grows stronger with every hour.

I can't afford the distraction.

Chapter Thirty-Two

MEL

I HOLD the flashlight high, peering over Sam's shoulder as he deftly combs through the top drawer of his old boss's filing cabinet. It's almost eleven, and we're on the third floor of the admin building at Levett Tech.

Unease percolates in my stomach. This has been too easy.

My suspicions seem confirmed by how jumpy Vik and Hunter are, and by the filthy looks Hunter keeps shooting my way.

Not only that, but our earpieces have remained silent ever since we crossed the fence behind the quad. I'm not sure it's a coincidence they've stopped working exactly when we need them most.

Tommy's words from the other day chase each other through my mind.

That assignment is a death sentence.

Hunter's are equally loud in my head.

You're blowing it. Who are you to lead us, anyway?

And Cait's.

She practically gave Tommy to the Organization.

I have a bad feeling they were right about me.

I turn and sweep the room behind me. Vik and Hunter are digging through the desk drawers, murmuring to one another. Nothing appears out of sorts.

At least we've found useful information tonight. We discovered the dates and times some of the Levett higher-ups plan to meet off-campus, and although this doesn't mean they're Organization lackeys, it's a strong indication they are. Now we'll be able to spy on those meetings, maybe even get video evidence from them. Additionally, we located and stole encoded shipment records. I can't be sure they'll prove anything nefarious, but my gut says they will. Why encode them if there's nothing to hide?

The final thing we need is evidence of doctored financials—things like the Organization laundering their profits through Levett Tech, disguising suspicious spending, et cetera. I wouldn't have the faintest idea how to uncover this kind of evidence, but Sam, bless him, knows exactly what to look for and remembers where to find it.

Just a little longer and we can slip out of here.

"The desk is clear," Vik reports, straightening from where they were crouched behind it. Hunter stands too. Though most of his face is hidden under his mask and hood, I can see the hatred festering in his eyes.

Suddenly, he throws his palms up. "Quiet!"

"What—" Sam starts, but he falls silent, and we all know why. A plethora of voices are echoing up the stairwell.

My whole body tenses.

Fuck.

We're too high up to go out a window. Those stairs are our only escape.

"I have enough, I think," Sam says softly. "Maybe we can sneak away before they find us."

I gulp, eyes roving over the masked faces of my teammates. Vik and Hunter glare in dire accusation. Sam's arms are full of financial records. He nods once and shoves the records into the bag slung over his shoulder. Determination blazes in his brown eyes even as sweat glistens on his brow. "We'll fight our way out. It'll be okay."

"At this point, we have no choice," Hunter growls. "Sam, get behind this desk with Vik and me." His hard gaze drags up and down Sam's trembling form. "I hope you're prepared to use your pistol."

Mouth dry, I slink to the door and crack it, cocking my ear toward the end of the hall and the stairwell beyond. Footsteps thunder up. A lot of footsteps. At least as many as I heard the other time I was trapped here. Tommy said there were ten guards that night.

I peek over my shoulder at the others. They're behind the desk, their eyes glittering under their hoods. Their guns are out, pointing at the door; therefore, at me.

"There are a lot of them," I say quietly. "More than the other night, I think. I don't know whether we would all make it through if we fight."

I fall silent, listening again. There are sounds of movement under our feet now. They're sweeping the second floor. Maybe we can sneak down the stairs while they're occupied.

That is, if Sam and I don't draw attention with our untrained attempt at stealth. I can't believe I led him into this.

But we have to try. There's no other option.

Just as I'm about to say so, a single voice floats up the stairwell.

"Mr. Edwards was right. How did he know they'd break in again?"

"Edwards is privy to a lot of information we are not," another man answers dryly. After a pause, he says, "The real question is, why did he post so many of us tonight? There were only a few rebels here before, and they barely escaped. We don't need twenty guards to deal with a few rebels. We could take them alive with half as many."

A wave of dizziness passes over me, the air thick in my lungs. Twenty guards.

Glancing over my shoulder, I whisper, "Did you hear that?"

Hunter and Vik don't grace me with an answer. It's Sam, gun shaking in his white-knuckled hand, who says, "We can't make out what they're saying from back here."

"Twenty guards," I report. "They're blocking the stairwell, sweeping the second floor."

If we try to fight, we will die. I meet Sam's frightened gaze, my pulse thundering in my ears.

Come on. Think.

I've let them down, led them to the worst kind of end.

My heart races and my palms sweat as the bone-crushing terror of a memory slices through me. Again I see Tommy darting in front of the guards who trapped us in the records room, one floor up. Creating a diversion so I could slip away. So I could live.

This is my answer. I need to lead the guards away, to distract them while my teammates sneak out unnoticed.

I see Tommy taking that bullet, collapsing on the floor. It was pure luck he survived such a thing. Afterward, he had me there to pull the guards' attention away from him. I gave him the chance to get up. Capable as he is, he wouldn't have been able to take them down without my help.

I will be alone. I will be facing twenty, not two or three. And I am untrained.

I will not walk away from this alive.

Dread whips up my spine, tingles in my limbs, but I smother it before it can paralyze me. I will not let the others suffer.

Unexpectedly, grief swells under the fear. Its icy fingers wind into my lungs, into my bones, freezing them until they're too cold, too heavy to move.

In the days since Tommy disappeared, I've done my best to block him from my thoughts, to numb the pain of his absence, the fear for his safety, the ache of his betrayal. Now, though, his name fills my soul with a sorrow so bitter I can hardly breathe. No matter how hurt I am, how angry, I've seen the depth of his pain. I know what my death will do to him, if he comes home at all.

For a moment, I let myself drown in that knowledge. Then I lock it away with my fear. Swallowing the sandy feeling in my mouth, I turn to face my team.

"Stay here." I'm proud when the words don't tremble. "I'm going to create a diversion. You will slip out at the first opportunity. Run like hell away from here. Leave as soon as you reach the car. Do not wait for me."

Sam's eyes are wide, the little bit of skin visible under his hood and mask ashen.

"Like we're going to listen to you," Hunter hisses from beside him.

"You will do as I say," I snap, focusing on Hunter, trying to ignore the way Sam's staring at me. "I am team lead. You have no other option, anyway."

Hunter curses, low and filthy. I'm not listening though, because Sam's standing up and hurrying around the desk.

He holsters his gun and takes my hands in his. "What are you thinking? We can fight. We'll fight together. Teammates, right?"

Warmth and pain roil in my chest.

"We won't win," I tell him gently. "This is the only way."

My own eyes fill when Sam's tears run over. His hands shake in mine.

"I won't let you do this."

Voices float through the open door again. The sounds from the floor below are moving back to the stairwell.

There's no time.

"You have to." My voice cracks. I squeeze his hands.

Resolve sparks in his liquid eyes. "Okay. But you won't be alone."

My heart glows, thumping erratically. At least I found Sam before the end. I hadn't known such a true friend could exist in the real world.

But I won't let him die with me.

"I won't be the reason you don't make it out of here."

Sam's eyes narrow. "Yeah? Well, I say it's not up to you."

The glow in my heart pulses, warms me against the frigid terror that looms at the edge of my consciousness. "You have to go. Think of Tommy. Think of Cait and Hunter and Vik. What will they do without you? Tommy's going to need you after this. Even Cait needs you." I pause, staring into Sam's eyes. "They need you, Sam. You're a ray of sunshine in this dark life."

"I won't abandon you."

"We don't both have to die. Stay here for your family. Let me have your back."

There's a heavy pause.

"I love you," Sam sobs. He pulls me into a rib-cracking hug.

I squeeze back fiercely. "I love you. Take care of Tommy for me. Tell him I'm sorry."

As I slip out the door, I look back, just once. Vik and Hunter peek over the desk, Vik's eyes huge and watery, Hunter's confused. Sam stands in the middle of the room, his shoulders slumped. His eyes—the depth of grief in them, the depth of friendship … I lock the image in my mind, the feeling in my heart.

It's what I will carry with me as I face the horror ahead.

CHAPTER THIRTY-THREE

MEL

I DON'T turn left, toward the stairs and the echoing footsteps of the guards. Instead, I spin to the right, sprinting for the large office at the end of the hall. Thankfully, Lisa's maintained control of the security system. The scan pad outside the office door is green. Unlocked.

I hurtle into the dark room. A large mahogany desk faces me, a laptop and a binder stacked on the surface, along with several loose papers. Behind the desk, a glass wall reaches from floor to ceiling, with the orange glow of the quad visible far below. A couple chairs squat in the far corners, a wide bookshelf covers the right-hand wall, and several filing cabinets line the left.

The guards are in the hall now. I make for the bookshelf, heart hammering against my ribs. With an almighty crash, I send the heavy structure tumbling to the floor. Books sail in every direction as I dive behind the desk and yank the gun from my hip. I listen with bated breath, praying the guards will investigate the noise and leave the rest of the team alone.

Come on. Come this way. Come get me.

They do. The air scrapes up and down my windpipe as they spill into the room.

But getting them here isn't enough. I need to hold their attention, or my team won't have time to escape. With no time left to plan, I do the first stupid, reckless thing that comes to mind.

Leaping to my feet, I fire my weapon indiscriminately above the crowd of guards, hurling myself backward with as much force as I can muster. My legs buckle when I crack my head against the smooth glass behind me.

Stars explode in my vision, blinding pain lancing through my skull. I stumble sideways, the room unstable around me. I thought I could go through, that plunging out the window would be distracting enough to hold the guards' attention. But life isn't like the movies.

A shimmering mirage of shadowy faces swim behind the forest of guns around me. My stomach rolls and the room sways as I slide down the glass wall. I try to focus, to count the guards.

Eighteen, I think.

Two are missing. Securing the stairwell?

"Get up," a man's rough voice commands.

The words spear through my rattled brain. I swing my face toward him, vision blurred.

Buy them time.

"No," I slur, sending him an insolent grin. Not that he can see it beneath my mask.

The man grips the front of my vest with both hands and yanks me to my feet. My head spins.

"You don't want to start off so disrespectfully," he snarls in my face. His breath reeks of coffee. "Things will be worse if you do."

Fear electrifies my blood, my parents' broken bodies too bright in my mind. My breath comes in short gasps.

The others are closing in now. They pat me down and take my weapons. All eyes are on me.

My team can make it out.

Now! I yell at them in my head. Go!

The man still clutching my vest is in my face again. "Where are the others?"

Disarmed and vulnerable though I am, defiance rises like a storm in my soul. I will not betray my fear.

Chin up, I glare malevolently at my questioner. "What others? You must be quite an idiot to think so many could infiltrate a place like this. Obviously, we could only send one or two. Today, it was one."

I hope the lie isn't obvious.

"Don't play with me, girl." He runs a thick finger along my cheek, peeling my mask down as he does, so it hangs around my neck. His putrid breath washes over my face, lust clear in his dim blue eyes.

My skin crawls, acid stinging the back of my throat.

Please, no. I hadn't counted on this.

"Edwards wants them unscathed," someone barks from the back of the room. "Get her in the van. The rest of us will finish the sweep and find her team."

Wide-eyed, I stare past the thug in front of me toward that voice. So familiar.

A balding, middle-aged man stares back, the gun twitching in his hands. Mr. Greene, my old supervisor. I suck in a startled breath.

The revolting guard gives me an expectant look that curdles my blood. "Soon enough."

"No," Mr. Greene says sharply. "Now. I'm not taking the flak for your inability to follow orders. I'll take her to the van. Brad, you're with me. The rest of you, get out. We've been here too long already."

Baring yellowed teeth, the gross thug drops his hand from my vest and strides from the room. My knees wobble as most of the others prowl out in his wake.

Mr. Greene.

For the short time we worked together, I thought he was a nice guy, but here he is. An Organization thug. Does he remember me?

A brown-haired man with ruddy cheeks and a paunch—Brad, I guess—is quick to twist my arms behind my back and cuff my wrists. Mr. Greene grips my shoulder, his gun poking into my side below the protection of my vest. Brad grips my other arm hard enough to bruise.

They march me down the hall in silence. Guards are moving through the offices, but there's no indication they've found my team.

No gunfire. No fighting. No shouting.

We emerge into the stairwell, where two sentries lie limp on the ground, their throats pouring out in a lake of gore. Even as my stomach pitches, my chest loosens.

They made it.

Brad and Mr. Greene don't stop, though Brad radios the other guards to report the bodies. They rush from all over the third floor to congregate at the scene behind us as I'm dragged down the stairs and out through reception into the employee lot. My heart pounds so fiercely I feel it in my fingers and toes, and my mind scatters as fear surges, obliterating every thought.

I glance back, desperate for confirmation my team is safe, but the quad is completely hidden from here.

Halfway across the lot, four loud pops echo behind us. Three more. Five.

Shouting. More gunfire.

My stomach clenches, Sam's face hanging in my mind.

"Go help," Mr. Greene snaps at Brad. "You're not needed here."

Straight-faced, Brad nods and takes off, running full tilt for the barrage of shots. Mr. Greene watches him go, then leads me toward a windowless white van. Levett Tech's logo is splashed across the side. Professional. Clean.

Hideous fear claws in my lungs and drags up my back. You'd never know the van's purpose is to carry victims.

Mr. Greene drops his grip and leans against its side. He crosses his arms, gun loose in his hand.

There's no point in trying to run, so I lean against the van too, doing my best to ignore the sickening, gnawing panic.

After a tense minute, I whisper, "Thank you. For stopping that man, I mean."

Mr. Greene glances at me sidelong. I'm surprised to see sorrow in his eyes. "Melanie, right? The nosy receptionist."

So he does remember. I nod, wary.

Mr. Greene's mouth tilts down. "So young," he sighs.

He pities me, I realize with a shock. Mr. Greene feels bad for me.

My muddled brain stutters, whirring into action. I think back to the time I spent with him on the campus tour, combing through the memories for anything I can use to my advantage now. Mostly, I remember his pride in Levett Tech's mission. But there was more. It was in the way he spoke to me, how he treated me.

Kid, he called me.

"Why?" he asks. "Why are you mixed up in this? You've got to be about my daughter's age. She has no idea what goes on in the world, couldn't give a shit. But here you are, facing … facing…"

He falls silent, his lips going pale. Turns his face away.

Like a pair of curtains have opened before me, I see what I must do, my ticket out of this. The problem is, I'll have to tell the truth about who I am, and Mr. Greene is a member of the Organization.

My heart pounds faster. Honestly, I can't see how the information could hurt the Resistance. The Organization already knows who Reyna and Max Snow were. My being their daughter won't affect anything, all this time later. I'm no one of consequence.

I chew my lip, cuffed hands squeezing into fists. I could escape the horror that hangs in my path, sure as death.

And I picture Tommy's tormented face, the agony in his lovely eyes.

I could make it back to him. I don't have to add to his nightmares. Not today.

Taking a deep breath, I go for the jugular. "My parents were tortured and killed five years ago by the Organization."

Mr. Greene's mouth tightens. "I'm sorry."

"Why are you mixed up in all this? What about your daughter? Zuri, right?" I let the smallest trace of sorrow leak into my tone.

Mr. Greene licks his lips, shifting his weight uncomfortably. "Sometimes, a person has to choose between two evils." His words sag with revulsion, and sympathy stirs in my heart.

Maybe I was right, all those weeks ago. Maybe Mr. Greene is a nice guy.

Only one way to find out.

I tilt my head, pinning him with an intense stare. "And if you were killed? What would she do? Would she go after your killers, do you think? Would you want her to?"

The questions are part of the act, but I find myself eager to hear his answer. Would Mom and Dad be happy with my choices? Would they be proud?

"No, I wouldn't want her to," he snaps, and the words are a fist to my stomach. "Your parents wouldn't want you to, either. Trust me."

My eyes sting. I try to push the disappointment back, to hold his bitter gaze, but I can't. My control slips, and I know he can see the awful fear writhing below the surface.

The hate in Mr. Greene's eyes sinks slowly into horror. Color leeches from his face.

I drop my eyes, and the tears and gasps that start to escape are no act. "What are you going to do to me?"

Mr. Greene's head wags from side to side, his posture rigid. His attention darts over the parking lot, then lands back on me. He looks like he's going to be sick.

"I don't want to die." A full sob strangles in my throat.

Beads of perspiration pop out on Mr. Greene's shiny forehead. His hands tremble.

I curl in on myself, the cuffs biting into my wrists.

"Let's go. Time to get in the van."

My stomach plummets, and I start to hyperventilate. I'm not going to make it out.

Grabbing my forearm, Mr. Greene drags me around the back of the van. He throws the rear door open and shoves me roughly behind it. I cringe away as he reaches for his back pocket.

When his hand comes back into view, there's nothing in it save for a small silver key. He stretches around me, unlocks the cuffs, and presses his gun into my limp hand.

Still leaning into me, he breathes in my ear, "The cameras can't see us back here. The van's in the way. Shoot me and run straight into the woods, understand? Get across the highway. You won't have long, so disappear fast. Then, do your parents a favor and get the hell out of New Hampshire. For good."

I gape, torn between running now and trying to convince Mr. Greene to come with me. "I won't shoot you."

"You must! If it looks like I let you go, my daughter …" He gulps. "They'll kill her."

With a frown, I tuck his gun away in my holster. "I've got an idea. Turn around."

Confusion flashes across Mr. Greene's face, but he complies. Leaning up on my toes, I wrap an arm around his neck and grab my opposite bicep, placing his windpipe in the crook of my elbow. With my free hand, I gently apply pressure to the back of his head. "This will stop the flow of blood to your brain and knock you out. Not for long, but it'll be enough."

That is, if I remember Tommy's training right.

"You have to squeeze harder," Mr. Greene chokes out.

I apply more pressure, flexing my biceps to tighten the chokehold. Within seconds, Mr. Greene's shoulders tighten. His muscles twitch. He goes limp.

He's too heavy for me to slow his fall much, and I wince at the sound his head makes when it smacks the pavement. I hope he's okay, but I don't have time to check.

I scan the empty lot around me, then I'm running as I've never run before, straight into the woods behind the van.

CHAPTER THIRTY-FOUR

TOMMY

IT wasn't supposed to go down like this.

Trees loom like monsters outside the windshield, stark in the headlights, the rest of the forest black. The purr of the engine and the scratch of branches against the car's body are too loud, the only sounds inside the dark SUV. Neither Bill nor Cait, silhouetted in the front seat, have spoken a word since we left the safehouse yesterday.

I wish they'd scream at me. Berate me for fucking up so badly. Anything but this never-ending silence.

I squeeze my eyes shut, the tang of failure sharp in my throat.

Everything went wrong the second I arrived at the pathogen's stopping point in Michigan, using the navigation system in the minivan I stole in Clearwater to find the address listed on the bill of lading. I've crashed enough of the Organization's weapon shipments for those missions to be second nature. Lurk in the shadows. Distract or take out the lackeys. Steal the weapons.

Based on the bill of lading, the pathogen is being transported in sealed vials which are secured in a box about the size of a loaf of bread, hidden in a cargo truck among crates of legitimately shipped materials. Without a team to help, I knew improvisation would be necessary to locate and nab it, especially considering the number of sentries I found traveling alongside the truck. What I never could have planned for was making it halfway through the Organization's camp, only to find Jack and Zara undercover among the guards.

Jack and Zara, who had been with Lisa from the very start. Who helped train me to run missions. Who laughed with Cait and me instead of turning us in when they caught us sneaking caterpillars into Bill's pillowcase.

I tripped up, unsure what to do next. Let the distraction get me caught.

Then came a shootout I couldn't avoid. It forced Jack and Zara to choose between revealing themselves to protect me, or preserving their covert mission.

I tried to help as the Organization turned on them. Even as Jack shouted at me to run, Zara's pain-laced shriek drowning out half his words, I fought to reach them. Next thing I knew, Bill was staring down at me in our Michigan safehouse, a bump throbbing on the back of my head from where he knocked me out amid the fray. His shadowy, twisted expression said enough about Jack and Zara's fate. It burned a new hole through my damaged heart.

More death on my hands. More family used as shields to save my sorry ass. I was so desperate to protect Mel I was blind to everything else, and now Jack and Zara are dead.

It should've been me.

The car lurches to a halt, and I open my stinging eyes to see the rock facade of the garage rolling upward, the lights flicking on within. Empty.

Good. The last thing I want is to face Mel, to tell her how badly I failed and that the Organization's hold on the pathogen survived while Jack and Zara did not.

When the door clears the top of the Telluride, Bill maneuvers us smoothly into its usual parking spot. The Veloster and the Civic are both missing, which means another team are out on a mission right now. The Civic is stuck wherever Jack and Zara abandoned it, or else it's lost to the Organization. I'm glad they didn't take the Veloster. I've always loved that car.

It's strange, though. When I left, no other missions were planned. We usually have at least a couple weeks' notice before a non-routine job, and yeah, there are four separate mission teams in the Resistance, but we're all privy to each other's assignments. I should've been aware if there was a mission planned for tonight.

Although Jack and Zara's task was kept secret. Lisa must've sent more operatives out without telling the rest of us.

Or ... but no. Even if Mel ignored my note, she wouldn't be in the field yet. I've only been gone two days.

Bill cuts the engine, and the three of us slide out of our seats in silence, dread weighting my every movement, making me slow. I've only taken one step toward the caves when Bill blocks my path, arms crossed, every bit the ex-Navy SEAL.

"You are suspended from the mission team effective immediately. You are not permitted to leave the caves. If it weren't for what your death would do to my daughter, you'd be carrion. I would've taken you out and helped Jack and Zara instead."

The only thing icier than Bill's tone is the chill that freezes the air in my lungs.

"Cait, do not let him out of your sight. Leadership will decide his fate."

Cait nods curtly, avoiding my eyes.

"I need to find Lisa. I suggest you both move out."

"Yes, sir."

Usually, hearing Cait address her dad that way stirs my pity, but not today.

As much as I fucked up by going after the pathogen, I can't forget what she did to Mel.

"Good." With one more glare for me, Bill turns and disappears quickly into the tunnel heading to the caves.

Cait doesn't move. I search her gray stare, anticipating more of the hard resentment she's thrown my way for the past few weeks. Instead I find weariness. Sadness. There's not one flicker of her usual fight left.

"So you're my guard now?"

"Guess so."

Great.

I move to step around her, but she halts me with a hand on my chest. I jerk away. "Don't touch me."

Her eyes flash, a bit of the anger I expected leaking through. "How could you do that to me?" She steps forward, hurt swimming underneath her furious expression.

Unwanted guilt squirms in my stomach. She's comparing me to June, but it's not a fair assessment. June intended to give the Organization information. I hoped to wreck their plans.

"This has nothing to do with you," I growl, sidestepping her, but she blocks my path again.

"Traitor!" she half-screams, her voice cracking.

Fury burns its way through the emptiness that's frozen my insides since Jack and Zara died.

"I'm a traitor? What about you, huh? All I did was try to protect the person I love."

Cait's lip curls. "Ditto."

Just then, light floods the garage and the Veloster pulls through the open door and slides into its spot, driving a little too fast. Seconds later, Lisa, Aaliyah, and Jess rush from the tunnel and surround the car. No one notices us.

Their worried expressions and absolute focus kick up my heartrate.

Something went wrong on the other mission.

The Veloster's front doors open and shock bolts me in place as Vik and Hunter climb out, unharmed. They belong to Cait's former mission team, just like me, which means they should never have been sent out lacking their leader.

I can only think of one reason why they would.

My breath sticks in my throat as they move to the back of the car, fully concentrating on whoever's in there. Lisa, Aaliyah, and Jess make room as a door opens.

Sam climbs out, and my blood runs cold. That's Mel, cradled in his arms, dark-red streaks crusted down the side of her face.

She ignored my note. Didn't wait. And now—

"She's mostly okay. A little confused," Sam's saying to Aaliyah. "It could be a bad one."

Concussion.

Mel's arms tighten around his neck. "Mr. Greene," she tells Lisa, who frowns as Aaliyah shines a flashlight into Mel's unfocused pupils.

"Hey!" She turns her face into Sam's neck, then whimpers; Aaliyah's running nimble fingers over her scalp.

"She'll need Advil, ice, and bed rest, but she'll be all right. Can you carry her all the way to her room?"

"Sure."

Sam shifts Mel in his arms, and despite the distance, I reach out, wanting to help. Five pairs of eyes swing my way.

"What…" I clear my throat. "What happened?"

"Take her," Lisa says to Sam, attention fixed on me. It's like standing blind in a spotlight. "I need a private word with Williams."

Cait twitches at my side.

"I need to talk with him too," Aaliyah cuts in. "You guys go on. I'll meet you in Mel's room. Lisa, Cait—a moment of privacy, please."

I blink. I have no idea why Aaliyah would need to see me, especially in private. As our doctor, she's patched me up plenty of times, but beyond that we don't have much to do with each other.

"Be quick," Lisa snaps. "Come with me, Cait."

Aaliyah watches everyone move into the tunnel. Mel never looks up, her face still pressed into Sam's neck, but the glares of my teammates linger even after they've disappeared. When we're alone, Aaliyah turns to me, her dark ponytail bouncing.

"A few days ago, Mel came to see me. For emergency contraception." Her tan cheeks go slightly pink, but she holds my gaze.

All my insides evaporate like steam in the wind. Totally wrong-footed, I stare in horror as she goes on. "Luckily, I happened to have some on hand, but that won't always be the case. I might not have been able to help. You both need to be more careful in the future. This is no life to bring a child into."

She pauses, and I'm left floundering. Babies. As if I could ever.

"I saw Cait grow up in these caves, you know," Aaliyah goes on softly. "She had a childhood without other kids around. She didn't get to play sports or go to school. She was given a lot of love from us grown-ups, but our love could never replace a real friendship with someone her own age. When she was fourteen, you got here. Imagine. At fourteen, you were the first friend she ever had. No child deserves to grow up like that. Be smart, Tommy."

Pity wells up through the swirl of other, sharper emotions churning in me. Of course, I already know all about Cait's past, but I never considered what growing up here must have been like. I never thought about what my friendship might mean to her as a result.

I frown, picturing a young Cait, sitting alone in the caves while the adults busy themselves with running the Resistance.

With a shake of my head, I block out the image. I can't think about Cait right now.

"I will."

"Good. I need to go treat Mel."

Without another word, Aaliyah turns and heads to the tunnel. Cait and Lisa reappear as soon as she's gone, the expression on Lisa's face something past anger, past disappointment. Cold and hard, it twists my numb insides and holds them tight.

"I am beyond words." Her furious gaze darts between us. "What the two of you have done over the last few days is frankly appalling. Accetta."

A fresh wave of fury cuts through my dread as Cait shifts her weight, ill at ease.

"You should not require explanations from your superiors. However, I would like you to know Mel is the only reason for her team's safe and successful return from Levett Tech tonight."

Cait's eyebrows contract as Lisa's words hit me like a blow.

"I monitored the mission myself. Our comms went down as soon as the team crossed the fence behind Levett's campus, and when I hacked their security system to unlock the admin building, it tripped a silent alarm. I maintained control of the locks and the CCTV, but the guards were immediately notified of intruders, and we couldn't reach the team to warn them about it. Worse, there didn't seem to be any normal patrol officers on duty. They were all Organization. So much easier for them, not having to hide or involve the police. They knew we were coming."

Even though I'm aware the team will make it out, my throat tightens.

"Mel led the others up to the third floor, to the offices there, where they were quickly boxed in. There was no escape. We were sure they were dead, sure the Organization would interrogate and kill them. We planned to evacuate the caves, but we continued to watch the screens to try and gauge how long we'd have to get everyone out."

I shift my weight, hardly able to breathe. The thought of Mel and my friends surrounded…

"Sam, Hunter, and Vik took cover. Mel didn't."

Immediately, I see where this is going. I squeeze my eyes shut.

"She went out the door. Sam tried to go after her, but Hunter and Vik dragged him back. Meanwhile, she caused a diversion and drew the guards away in the nick of time. She held their attention while the others snuck down the stairs, disposing of the sentries posted there."

Of course Mel sacrificed herself. Of course she did.

There had to have been a better way. If I'd been there, I would have stopped her.

"Two guards brought her outside and discovered the bodies in the stairwell. They called the rest, who rushed out to the quad in time to see Vik, Sam, and Hunter going over the fence. Gunfire was exchanged, but ultimately the three of them disappeared into the trees. Even Sam. You'd never guess this was his first mission. I should've promoted him before now. Mel was right about that."

I'm too wrapped up in Mel's fate to spare much emotion for Sam's triumph, though I'm not surprised by his success. I've known for a while he'd be an excellent addition to the mission team.

I'll catch up with him later. There's only one thing I want to know right now.

"How did Mel get away?"

Lisa glances at me. "She was ultimately left with a single guard, cuffed and disarmed. We couldn't see what went down, but somehow, she overpowered him and escaped."

I frown. It seems too simple. Too lucky.

Lisa's focus is back on Cait, who stares listlessly at the floor. "She gave herself up to save the rest of them. She was willing to die for them. She is not a spy, and I have no more patience for your arguments to the contrary."

"And you," Lisa snaps, turning flinty eyes back on me. "Because of you, two wonderful, selfless people are dead."

I hold her accusatory gaze as my ears rush and the room spins, emptying of air. It takes all my strength not to sag under the weight of my guilt.

"Not only that, but their mission failed, and now the Organization is aware we know about the pathogen and seek to destroy it."

Pressure builds in my chest until I have to drop my eyes.

"The only reason you will not rot in the cells for the foreseeable future is because I know your heart remains loyal. Both of you acted out of stupidity, not betrayal. However, you are both confined to the caves until you can learn some sense. Until then, you have no place in the field. I cannot express the depth of my disappointment."

With one last burning stare, Lisa turns and strides back into the tunnel, tapping the button to lower the garage door on her way by. It clatters down and bangs into the ground, leaving a ringing silence in its wake.

Cait and I don't move.

It doesn't even look like she's breathing. She's still staring at the floor, shoulders slumped, fingers knotted in front of her. I clench my jaw, determined not to feel bad, not to imagine what Bill has said since Mel's trial or how many ways it has broken her.

She brought this on herself.

We both did.

With a heavy sigh, I force my feet to move, even though my boots feel like they've sunk into quicksand. I need to make sure Mel's okay.

"Wait," Cait whispers.

I freeze, fury immediately rising, warring with the unwelcome pity in my chest.

"I want to talk to you."

"Trust me, you don't." I start to walk, anxious to find Mel, even though I'll have to admit my failure to her. Again.

Cait comes up behind me, ignoring my warning as completely as if I didn't speak at all. It grates on my nerves. "I'm sorry. I was wrong. Please, wait!"

I jolt to a stop, and she narrowly avoids crashing into my back. She never admits to being wrong.

Muscles tight, I take a deep breath, working to get a handle on the rage that blazes under my skin, threatening to burn through my tenuous grip on control.

Cait's fast to take advantage of my silence.

"I don't like Mel," she states baldly.

No shit. My blood boils hotter, my jaw flexing against the furious accusations I want to hurl at her like knives. None of us would be in the positions we're in if Cait hadn't tried to sabotage Mel in the first place.

"But she's no spy. I know that now, and I'm sorry for how I've acted. I'll do better, be better, if you give me the chance."

"You planted those files in her room." My words bleed, dark with condemnation. "You hoped she'd be exiled, in which case the Organization would have gotten to her. Or you hoped Lisa would order her execution. Either way, you wanted her dead."

To her credit, Cait doesn't deny it. "I thought we'd be safer with her gone. I was wrong. Please. Forgive me. I did what I thought was necessary at the time to protect our family. Kind of like you, going after the pathogen. We both fucked up."

She's got me there. Still... "You showed her pictures of her parents in pieces, Cait. What kind of a monster does that?"

Cait's lips go white. "There were pictures?"

"For fuck's sake, you didn't check what you were handing over to the supposed enemy?"

"I knew she wouldn't escape. We guarded her room, and regardless of the outcome of the trial, Lisa would never risk letting her go now. She knows too much. But Tommy, I promise I had no idea those were in there. I just wanted to protect everyone, and I thought those files were the best way, given her excuse ... her reason for being here."

Her eyes glisten, and she clasps her hands in front of her. "You're my best friend in the whole world. I just lost everything I've worked my whole life for. I can't imagine losing you too. Please, please, give me another chance."

Guilt eats at my gut, Aaliyah's words coming back to haunt me. *You were the first friend she ever had.*

We've been a team for so long. Cait's saved my life countless times. More than that, those first hellish months after I arrived, she walked with me through the darkness of my grief. She led me out the other side, damaged, but breathing. Somewhat myself again. I shouldn't turn my back on her, regardless of the circumstances.

But after what she did to Mel, after realizing her utter lack of faith in my intelligence, my judgment, I don't know if I can forgive her.

I frown, watching warily as she steps forward and takes my hand.

Once, Cait's hand in mine felt nice. Safe and wholesome, like sinking into a warm bed after a long day on patrol in the cold. Now, though, I have to stop myself from pulling away.

She can tell. The sorrow in her eyes deepens.

"I'll work on it," I say roughly. "I'm ... mad isn't a strong enough word. Horrified might be closer. But you're my best friend too. We've both made mistakes. I'm not going anywhere."

I squeeze her hand, then drop it, sort of feeling like I swallowed a lemon.

"What can I do? How can I fix this?"

"I don't know. Space, I guess. Give me time."

Cait throws me a sad smile. "I can do that." She tilts her head at the tunnel. "Do you want to see her?"

My shattered heart aches, the shadows in me yearning, as always, toward Mel's light. "Yes."

"Well, let's go then." Cait holds her hand out again, waiting, this time, to see if I'll take it.

"Space," I remind her. "That kind of thing isn't right. Not anymore. I'm with Mel now."

Cait nods, her eyes emptying. "Sorry."

"It's fine."

My stomach twists with guilt, but I force myself to walk beside her. Forgiving Cait feels like a betrayal. Even so, I can't deny I'm less lonely with her here. At least now she knows how wrong she was. Hopefully she learned something from all this.

In my future darkness looms, so close at hand, swallowing the path ahead like a bottomless pit. It's a path I know too well. My broken heart throbs, the pain leaving no part of me unscathed. I don't know how I will make it if Mel dies too.

Alone, I have no chance. None at all. But maybe … maybe with Cait's help, I'll survive. Maybe I'll come out the other side.

Chapter Thirty-Five

MEL

ALIYAH pulls my bedroom door closed, leaving me to stare at the shadows that shiver across the striated ceiling. The movement makes my pounding head spin, and I squeeze my eyes shut as nausea rolls through me again.

A concussion is exactly what I don't need.

I grit my teeth against the unfairness of it. I'm the one who stood up and said enough was enough, the one who made this mission happen, then ensured we came home even after we were surrounded. Yet here I am, stuck in bed alone while the rest of the team celebrate our success in the mess hall.

With caution, I crack my lids. The soft light from the small fire Sam left burning in the grate sends jagged shards of agony spearing through my brain, but I don't close my eyes this time. I ball my fists and ride it out.

Breathe in. Breathe out. Look around the room, will it to hold steady. Breathe. Sit up, slide back against the pillows. Let the pain wash through, have its moment. Then let it go.

After a few minutes, the Advil kicks in, and the sharp ache numbs to a constant but easily ignored throb in the back of my head. I'm not sure how much say Aaliyah has in what I'm allowed to do now, but I will not relinquish control of my mission. Odds are, Lisa won't support that anyway. This is not a Resistance mission. It's mine.

I hug my knees to my chest and study the stitching on my comforter, already itching to get back to work. I'll be fine. And if I'm not, who cares? If my health is the cost of bringing down Mom and Dad's killers and saving lives, I'll gladly pay it.

Three soft knocks stab into my head.

Sam. I knew he wouldn't leave me to rot alone in the dark.

"Come in," I call, then wince when agony flashes behind my eyeballs. Stupid concussed brain.

The door hinges squeak, and before I really register what I'm seeing, my heart's jammed in my airway.

Tommy.

A strangled cry breaks through my lips as I lurch to my feet, ignoring the renewed spinning in my head, and stagger toward him. It's hard to check for injuries with the dim light, but I frantically scan his shadowy form anyway. Relief and a deep, glowing warmth unfurl in the pit of my stomach when I find none, and I throw myself into his open arms and breathe in his woodsy scent, like an October wind through the pines. It's a balm to my soul.

My eyes burn.

He holds me tight, pressing his face into my hair and rocking us gently side to side.

He's alive. He's okay. He made it back.

He made it home.

I hold him tighter, all the fear I've carried for him crashing down on me at once. But as the reality of his safety sinks in, threads of resentment start to sting at the edges of my joy.

He left without even the courtesy of a conversation first.

He could've died. Could've ruined everything.

Fury brighter than a supernova blooms like an explosion in my heart. I place my palms on his firm chest and *shove*.

He stumbles back, surprise clear on his shadowed, beautiful face.

"How could you do that?" I half-growl, half-scream. "You said you were falling for me, then disappeared the next day. Didn't wait to talk, or even say goodbye. Didn't lend an ounce of support when I volunteered to lead a dangerous mission, just left me to wonder whether you were even *alive*. Left me distracted and worried sick while I tried to fumble my way through as a team lead with no experience and teammates who were mostly waiting for me to fail!"

I shove again, and this time he doesn't falter. He's like a rock, solid and immovable under my tingling palms. Another wave of white-hot rage scorches through me.

"Mel, please," he whispers.

"I don't want to hear it. Get out."

I'm not prepared for any of this, but especially not for the heartbreak that's so clear on his face. Not even the shadows can hide it.

Deep sadness seeps under the surface of my anger, but I hug my ribs to hold it at bay. Tommy betrayed me. Instead of treating me like an equal, he left me here to twiddle my thumbs and wait for the hero to save the day, like I was a damsel in distress.

I'm no damsel.

"I'm sorry," he says, the words a hair too thick. "I was wrong."

I purse my lips. Yeah, you sure as hell were.

"You don't know what you mean to me."

"I don't care."

"Please. Hear me out."

I grit my teeth, unable to ignore the grief in his eyes or the way my heart aches in response. I might be furious, but I love him too much to shut him down without a thought. "Fine. Say what you need to say."

"Thank you." Tommy fidgets with his bracelet. "It's just … I can't describe what it's like. I see their deaths over and over again. I have for years. Now it's you in their place, ripped apart every time I close my eyes. I can't bear it, Mel. I *can't*."

His voice breaks, and I suppress the urge to reach for him, to wrap my arms around his middle and lay my head on his chest and soothe away his pain.

He's still talking, the words intense and dripping with fear. "I stole the bill of lading from Lisa's office while everyone was at your trial and went after the pathogen. I didn't know she'd already sent Jack and Zara. I thought they were stationed at our California safehouse, like they have been for weeks, but they were there, undercover, when the shooting started. They didn't make it out."

He swallows as his eyes glitter in the firelight. "Everything I touch turns to ash."

My chest aches, the echo of his remorse so strong I can't help but step toward him.

"You're next," he whispers.

I close the distance between us, cradling his cheek. He leans into my palm and shuts his eyes, as if in defeat.

"I know you're afraid, and the last thing I want to do is hurt you. But you can't keep me in a cage, Tommy. We're in this together."

His eyes crack open, hollow and etched with despair. "I never should have interfered in your life."

"I'm glad you did."

"I can't lose you. Not like this. Please don't make the video. We'll find another way."

I bite my lip. His fear cuts deep, but this is my life to spend as I choose. I won't shy away from the responsibility of completing Mom and Dad's mission. "Those lives are worth the price."

"I know. What if you posted an anonymous exposé instead? You could keep your face hidden."

"It wouldn't hit the same. The public are much more likely to trust someone they can see and relate to." My voice lowers, every word limned with hatred. "And I want Mr. Edwards to look into my eyes and know I'm coming. I want Reyna and Max Snow's daughter to haunt his dreams."

Tommy stares, anguished. "I can't watch you do this. It will destroy me."

I take a deep breath as disappointment trickles under my skin and turns my heart to stone. "I understand, and I'd never ask that of you. But if you aren't going to support me, then please leave."

"No! I support you, just not … I can't … they'll break you, Mel."

My chest tightens as I push at him again, the disappointment burning its way up my throat. "Leave!"

He steps back, eyes wide. His fear and pain slice through my heart, but I won't let them stop me. "You can't watch. I understand. You need to go."

"I can still help."

"Go!"

With one final, agonized look, Tommy does as I ask, leaving me in the dark, alone. His absence sends a fresh wave of hurt stabbing through me, worse than anything the concussion could dish out.

I don't know why I expected him to stay.

CHAPTER THIRTY-SIX

MEL

RECOVERING from my concussion has been beyond frustrating.

Four days confined to my bed, four days stuck on the sidelines. I've been symptom-free for two, but Aaliyah's insistent: no physical activity until she allows it. And she won't clear me until at least seven days have passed from the date of the injury, no matter how well I feel.

I'm lucky to be alive, I know, but three more days...

I yank on a pair of fatigues and a tank top, hair wet from the subzero shower I've just taken. Shower's not really the right word; it's more like a freezing waterfall, siphoned from the ice-cold river that runs above the washroom. The water spills through a hole in the ceiling and splatters on the stone floor below. There's no drain. Instead, the runoff flows into a deep trough around the perimeter of the room, which carries it under the wall and into the bathroom next door. The primitive toilets in there are only seats situated above the overflow from the washroom. From there, the stream carries everything out of the caves to rejoin the river downhill.

It's genius. Still, as I pull on a soft hoodie over my tank top, I dream of hot showers and steaming, bubbly baths.

Aaliyah would be happy. According to her, dreaming is about as far as I should push my brain right now. She was pissed when I went against her orders and took charge of coordinating my team's efforts to collect the rest of the evidence for our video, but we couldn't wait, not with the BioAgent delivery looming closer every day.

I was an integral part of the planning process. Even so, I hated being stuck here while Sam, Hunter, and Vik surveyed an off-site meeting of Organization agents, using the information we found at Levett Tech to locate the gathering. Thankfully they got out unseen and brought back some excellent footage of those agents—faces identifiable—planning a handoff of weapons to their criminal backers.

The next night, they recorded the delivery itself, again without my help. They weren't able to catch faces this time, but video evidence of the drop should be enough, together with everything else we've assembled.

Lying in bed waiting for them to come home was infuriating. I wanted to be on the front lines, to actively tear the Organization down with my bare hands. Instead, I'm almost like a mascot or a cheerleader, yelling "Go team!" while the others make the winning play.

At least I still got to be in the video. Yesterday, I worked with Sam and Lisa to record my part and edit it all together.

The final product is powerful. It shows overwhelming evidence of the Organization's wicked actions, along with dire warnings about what they hope to accomplish.

We're launching it today. This morning. As soon as I get down to the mess hall.

I stare at my pale face in the long mirror, something stronger than nerves running around the pit of my stomach. My eyes are bright. Alive. Even with the concussion, even aching from Tommy's choice, I've got more life in me right now than I've had in a long, long time.

With a deep breath, I twist my dripping hair into a knot atop my head and secure it with an elastic.

When we launch the video, my future will be irrevocably changed. The Organization is already after me, but once this hits the Web, I'll be their number one target.

I shudder, imagining what they'll do if they get the chance.

All those people will die if I don't do this. Moms and dads and kids and grandparents.

I have to get it done now, before I chicken out.

I suck in another breath, nod at my reflection, and stalk out the door.

THE mess hall is crowded by the time I arrive. Even Tommy's here, lurking in the back of the room like a phantom with his arms crossed, Cait a constant shadow at his side.

Pain and guilt spiral through me at the sight of his drawn face. Though I've tried my best to lock him out of my thoughts, I haven't been able to curb the ache in my empty chest, nor my worry at his absence from normal life around the caves. He tried to come by a couple times over the last few days, but I didn't let him in. I have enough on my plate without extra helpings of relationship drama.

Memories of our last encounter—the agony in his eyes, the way he pleaded—haunt me late into the night, where they lash my heart to bits.

Seeing him now, he looks worse than I feared. His eyes are desolate, shadowed purple like he hasn't slept in days. There's no life, no spark in them.

I bite my lip and turn away. I can't let myself give in to the pain. Not my own. Not his. Not even if his hurts worse than mine ever could.

Sisters and brothers. Aunts and uncles. Cousins and neighbors and lovers.

Lisa's set up a large flatscreen on a table at the end of the room, her laptop already hooked up to it. I make my way toward her, insides squirming.

She smiles at me. "Are you ready?"

I swallow against the dryness in my throat. "Yes."

"This will work."

Her intensity only fuels my nervous energy.

She turns toward the noisy crowd. An excited buzz runs through the room, but when Lisa raises her arms, silence descends.

"This is a pivotal moment for the Resistance," she calls, loud and confident. "Never before have we openly attacked the Organization, nor have we tried to reveal them to the public. Yes, it is a bold and dangerous move, but desperate times call. You are all aware, after the information was divulged at Melanie's trial last week, that their newest strategy involves the release of a deadly pathogen. This attempt to expose them is our last chance to prevent that disaster."

Lisa pauses, eyes roving the group. "The pathogen is being shipped across the country as we speak, moving in a zigzag pattern during daylight hours and halting, heavily guarded, at night. Most of you don't know I sent Jack and Zara to pose as low-level lackeys in order to intercept and destroy the shipment after we procured the bill of lading last week. The pathogen cannot survive extreme heat, and so we'd hoped to plant bombs and detonate the truck carrying it from afar, neutralizing the threat. Unfortunately, the Organization was alerted to our interference before Jack and Zara could complete their mission. They did not make it out alive."

A horrified shock vibrates through the crowd as Lisa pauses again, bowing her head. I glance at Tommy, who's staring at his boots.

My nails bite into my palms.

Too much pain. Too much death.

The crowd rustles and whispers. A few people weep, Vik among them, a shaking hand held over their mouth.

When Lisa looks up, there are tears gleaming in her dark eyes too. "Now that the Organization is aware we are after the pathogen, they have tripled the number of guards traveling with it, making it impossible for a team to reach with any hope of survival. They will be on high alert for additional imposters among their ranks, and the shipment is due to arrive at Levett Tech tomorrow."

She sighs. "I will not send another family member to their death. And so, this video is our one and only shot at saving lives. Melanie and her team have risked everything to create it, and for that, I honor them. Mel, Hunter, Vik, Sam. Thank you."

Lisa gives us each a small smile and a salute. I'm too stunned to react.

Part of me hoped, even if the video failed, Lisa could find another way to stop the Organization. But this is truly our one and only shot.

"Melanie, I'd love nothing more than to give you the honor of launching the video. All you need to do is click here, where it says initiate."

Lisa leans forward and touches a button on the screen of her laptop. "When you do, the video will be pushed onto all the major social media platforms, where it will be forcibly played on each device currently connected to them. It will then remain embedded in every account's social feeds, able to be replayed and shared. Assuming I've done this correctly, that is."

Lisa's smile is brittle. She's nervous too.

Heart hammering, I search the shadows behind the crowd. I find Tommy in the same spot as before, watching me. His eyes are carefully blank, his expression empty save for a slight tightness around his mouth.

His voice echoes in my head, begging me not to do this.

But if I don't, Jack and Zara died for nothing. Our parents died for nothing. Millions more will die. What is my life worth in the face of that truth?

Sons and daughters. Students and teachers. Friends. Good people. Beloved people.

I tear my eyes from Tommy's, a piece of myself breaking away as I do. With trembling, numb fingers, I move the cursor over the initiate button and click.

The video pops up on the big screen.

I'm standing in a dark room, dressed head to toe in Resistance black, weapons strapped to my hips, my thighs. My eyes burn like icy fire.

Chills race up my spine. I look tough. Dangerous, even.

I didn't know I could look like that.

"We are invisible," I say on the screen. "You don't see us. You don't know we exist. We are forgotten. But we do not forget you."

Images flash across—photos from the interrogation of my parents, of Tommy's parents; the footage my team captured of the weapons drop; of the secret meeting of Organization higher-ups; the suspicious financial sheets Sam procured at Levett Tech; the encoded shipment records; recordings Lisa captured of the Levett CCTV showing the Organization's attack on me and Tommy in the records room, then their attack on me four nights ago.

All the while, I'm talking.

"We protect you. Every day, we shield you from dangers you can't begin to imagine. Hunted, tortured, framed, and murdered, we endure. We act. For you.

"There is a terrorist group hidden in plain sight in Clearwater, New Hampshire. They have infiltrated the government-contracted weapons manufacturer called Levett Technologies so effectively, the government and even most workers at the facility don't know they are there. This group of murderous criminals not only pass military-grade weapons to terrorists, they also develop dangerous tech to be used against the American people. They do all this under the nose of the government, undiscovered.

"Now they have developed a new threat, a bioweapon they plan to unleash on you only days from now. They have too much control, too many powerful people in high places. The government will not discover this threat until it is far, far too late."

The screen cuts back to me.

"The magnitude of this attack is beyond what we, your forgotten protectors, can defend against. We cannot save you this time.

"You must save yourselves. Demand an investigation into Levett Technologies, into BioAgent 313. Put so much pressure on the government they have no choice but to uncover what lies hidden within Levett Tech. Do not delay. Time is short."

The screen goes black.

There is a beat of total silence.

Then … whooping, cheering, yelling, clapping. People screaming in celebration, people shouting my name.

Sam's arms are around me, and bodies are pressing in on me, and hands are raining down on my back, and voices are declaring me a hero. A huge, beaming smile breaks across my face.

We did it. We really did it!

"Look, Mel!" Lisa calls, pointing over the crowd at the screen, which now shows a summary of what is trending on the major social platforms.

Our video is climbing on every one of them. It's been attached to the hashtag *#bringdownlevetttech*.

A thrill zaps through my chest.

It's working! And that hashtag. They believe us!

I laugh, astonished as the number of likes and shares surge. We're going viral. Already.

#bringdownlevetttech, they say. And now, *#freetheforgotten*.

That strangers would care, that they would choose to fixate on that part of my message ... I dab at my eyes.

This is for you, Mom and Dad.

Looking for the one person I want to share my success with above all others, I search the blur of smiling faces around me, but Tommy isn't here. My eyes skip to the back of the room. There's only Cait, standing alone. Her oddly sad gaze locks with mine.

Worry pricks at me, but I push it aside. He'll be okay. This is going to work, and when it does, he'll see. The Organization will fall. He'll finally be free.

And then, maybe, we can be together.

I turn my attention back to the screen, to the numbers shooting higher still, and I smile.

Get ready, Mr. Edwards. Here I come.

CHAPTER THIRTY-SEVEN

MEL

MY team and I sprawl over the three mismatched couches surrounding the fireplace in Lisa's office, our attention fixed on the large screen now parked on the mantel over her crackling fire. The ten p.m. news broadcast has just started, the jingle finishing up. Predictably, my face appears over a headline which, no matter how many times I see it, doesn't fail to turn my stomach.

A New Generation of Domestic Terrorism: Extremist Melanie Snow Utilizes Social Media to Sow Unrest, Incite Fear

The story's all over the national news. Everyone back home in California will have seen it. My old friends, Aunt Amy. What do they think of me? When they look at my face on the screen, do they remember who I am? Or do they see someone hateful? Someone violent?

A terrorist.

I curl over my ribs, fighting another roll of nausea. I knew I was taking an awful risk when I released the video into cyberspace, but to be painted in such an ugly light is horrifying.

With a vapid smile that doesn't reach her eyes, the news anchor starts to talk. Her voice is lilting, cheerful even as she discusses terrorism and doom.

"In reaction to a shocking video released via social media early this morning, Homeland Security officials are warning the public not to fall prey to the destabilizing tactics of nineteen-year-old Melanie

Snow, figurehead for the elusive and dangerous terrorist group known as 'the Forgotten.'"

I hug my knees tighter to my chest, my stomach full of lead. To the American public, I'm not a hero. I'm a symbol of fear.

"The video, which started to go viral before authorities could remove it from circulation, warned the public of an impending assault on their safety, alleging our military's largest and most reliable weapons supplier, Levett Technologies, is behind the threat. We've got Alyssa MacDonald, head of the Department of Homeland Security, with us tonight. Welcome, Alyssa."

The screen splits to show the anchor on the left and a dark-haired woman wearing a navy blazer and deep red lipstick on the right. Underneath the new woman's shoulders is a gold banner with 'Alyssa MacDonald, Department of Homeland Security' on it.

"Happy to be here," she says.

"Can you shed some light on the situation for us?"

Alyssa folds her hands in front of her. "What we're seeing is propaganda, plain and simple. A brash and transparent attempt to intimidate the American people, and to create civilian mistrust toward not only our military, but our government. That the Forgotten have grown bold enough to launch an attack of this magnitude is worrisome, to say the least."

The anchor nods, still smiling. "Snow, who was indicted in July for attempting to steal top-secret information from Levett Technologies, has since vanished without a trace. How has she been able to evade the authorities so successfully?"

"We've been struggling to locate and dissolve the terrorist cell known as the Forgotten for years," says Alyssa. "They're a slippery group, to be sure. It comes as no surprise, given our difficulty in tracking her down, that Snow is now revealed to be in league with them."

I snort. In league with them indeed. If only Alyssa understood what she was saying.

"And what of the method the group made use of to distribute their misinformation?" the anchor asks.

"Social media is a powerful weapon for those who would seek to wield it. Its reach is incredible. The public needs to remember people can say anything they want online. A video created by known terrorists is not a reliable source of information. You must look to reputable outlets, and consider all the facts, before you make up your mind about what to believe. In this case, there is overwhelming evidence to support Levett Technologies and to condemn Snow."

The reporter gives another curt nod. "Is there anything the public can do to help as law enforcement deals with this new-age threat?"

Alyssa leans forward. "Yes. If anyone has information as to the whereabouts of Snow, please inform the authorities immediately. This was an act of domestic terrorism, and we will treat it as such. The American people can rest assured justice will be served, and it will be swift and thorough."

"Thank you for those reassuring words, Alyssa. We here at KLY News are glad to hear it."

I bury my face in my knees. Sam, who's sitting beside me, wraps a comforting arm around my shoulders.

I failed. We may have swayed the masses at first, but in the end, we had no impact on Levett Tech whatsoever. They censored our video and destroyed our credibility.

We knew they probably would—but to fail so quickly, without anything to show for our efforts, stings.

And now, so many innocents will die.

"All those people," I moan, leaning into Sam.

"This mission was always a long shot. We did everything we could."

Did we, though? I gave all I had to stop the Organization. Jack and Zara gave their lives. Where has it gotten us? What was made better by their sacrifice?

Nothing, that's what. Nothing's changed at all. The pathogen is still on its way here, the Organization barely inconvenienced by our actions. Jack and Zara are my parents all over again. Tortured and killed for nothing.

Anger and frustration rise, for them, for my parents and the Williamses, and for the others here who have dedicated their lives to ending the corruption.

How long will we fight and die before we have any kind of effect? Will any of it matter, ever?

We need to push harder. If we want to stop the coming devastation, we have to fully commit, to see this through all the way to its bitter end. Lisa said no one would be able to destroy the pathogen and make it out alive, but what if we destroy the pathogen, knowing we won't make it out?

I've seen the BioAgent bill of lading a thousand times when planning with my team, and so I know right now, the pathogen is parked for the night, concealed in the vast wilderness outside Burlington, Vermont. If we don't destroy it, it will arrive at Levett Tech by mid-morning tomorrow. The Organization could launch their first assault less than twenty-four hours from now.

We still have a chance to achieve something. We could save thousands, no, millions of lives.

I look up at the reporter on the screen, now extolling the many long-enduring virtues of Levett Tech. My picture's fixed in the top right-hand corner, along with a hotline number to call should I be spotted.

I'm the perfect person to lead a doomed mission. My future's already ruined. In any case, there's no way I'm not finishing what I started.

I won't order Sam, Vik, and Hunter to follow me to their deaths, but they should be given the choice. We're the ones who will otherwise have to live with the consequence of our failure; of watching so many suffer and die knowing we could have done more to save them. It would be as good as having their blood on our own hands.

Adrenaline zings through my veins, jittering in my tense limbs. I jump to my feet.

"Stay here," I say to Sam. "I want to ask Lisa something."

Concern colors his features. "Um, okay. Hey, don't forget, we're all here for you. I know this seems really, really bad, but you'll make it through. I promise."

I smile as Sam's warmth wraps around my heart. "What would I do without you?"

Despite the hopeless air in the room, his brown eyes sparkle. "You'd be lost. Obviously."

Even with everything that's happened over the last few days, even with Hunter sitting across the room, so cold and distant, Sam's innate light can't help but shine through. He's stronger than anyone I know.

"No doubt." I punch his shoulder affectionately. "I'll be back in a minute."

"Kay," he calls as I wend my way around the couches.

Lisa's sitting by herself behind her desk, chin in her palm and misted eyes far away. She doesn't seem to notice my approach.

I know what her answer will be. I have to try anyway.

I brace a hand by her hip, leaning down to whisper in her ear. "Can I have a word, please? In private?"

As if she's peering through a thick veil, Lisa blinks up at me. It takes her a moment to focus. "Of course. We can go to my room, through the door behind my desk."

Sliding my hands into my pockets, I straighten up. "All right."

The others pay us little heed as we pass. They're still staring morosely at the news.

Ensconced in Lisa's room, I turn on her, ready to explain how we could still save everyone. Before I can, though, Lisa speaks, arms locked over her ribs. "I know what you want, and the answer is no."

"What? How could you possibly know?"

"You are forgetting I grew up with your mother." Lisa sighs. "You've got her fire in you, Mel. I know what Reyna would want to do now, and I can see it, there in your eyes. What kind of a friend would I be if I let you run off and get yourself killed for nothing? Reyna would never forgive me."

Pride swells in my chest. To be compared to my mother, the bravest woman I've ever known, means the world. "Thank you."

Lisa gives me a tiny, sad smile. "It's no more than the truth. But you must listen to me now. We've done what we can. The answer is no."

"Lisa…"

She sizes me up. "This isn't up for discussion, so you might as well save your breath."

When I open my mouth to respond, Lisa rolls her eyes, and an unexpected pang of grief stabs through my chest. Though their features aren't remotely similar, she looks just like Mom right now.

Pressing my lips together, I force the ache down. "I'm sorry you're in this position, but we must do everything in our power to save those people. We're the only ones who can stop the Organization. You know it's the right thing to do."

"I certainly do not know that," Lisa snaps, her gaze suddenly crackling. "How many of our own have I sent to their deaths? To worse—torment and ruin? We are innocent too. I will not be responsible for the death of another friend."

My stomach drops, my heart twisting as I consider how Lisa must feel right now. I never thought about the weight of responsibility she bears. Jack and Zara just died. My parents and Tommy's suffered a terrible fate. Lisa blames herself. I can see it in the depth of pain flickering behind her bright eyes.

How many others have there been? How many ghosts does she carry with her?

Her severe expression softens a little as I stare, lost for words. "I appreciate why you feel the way you do, but it is far too dangerous to attempt another mission. Although it's sad we have failed to protect the public, our first responsibility is always to each other, to our family here in the Resistance. They trust me to take care of them. I will not gamble their lives again. Not even if they volunteer."

I snap my mouth shut, Lisa having answered the question I'd been about to ask. The woman knows me, and this will be a hindrance should I—

I stop that thought in its tracks. I must not think about my options right now, or I'll risk Lisa catching on.

Numbing my mind, I slump my shoulders. "I don't agree with

you, but I can see arguing won't get me anywhere. You win."

Lisa arches a brow. "That's it? You're giving up?"

I shrug. "You won't be convinced, and I don't have access to weapons or a vehicle. There's nothing more I can do. What choice do I have? Listen, I'm tired and upset. I want to go to bed."

Lisa tilts her head, eyes narrowed. "I'm watching you. I'm going to post a guard outside your room."

"Do what you want, but I don't appreciate being treated like a prisoner again after everything I've done."

Pinching her nose, Lisa murmurs something under her breath. "Fine, Melanie. But if you so much as look in the wrong direction—"

I roll my eyes. "I know, I know, you'll chuck me in the cells and throw away the key, or something equally harsh. Now please, leave me alone. I'll talk to you tomorrow."

With a grimace, Lisa watches me turn and stride out. Sam's worried gaze tracks me as I cross her office, but I give him a tiny shake of my head, trying to communicate without words.

I need to be alone.

Something about my expression must get the message across. His mouth tightens, but he nods in acknowledgment.

I head straight for the seldom-used corridor which leads to the locked mystery door Cait busted me at a few weeks ago. Only when I reach the solitude of the shadowy hall do I allow myself to think freely.

I can expect no help from the Resistance. If I do this—if I run this mission solo—it will mean my end, plain and simple. I will not make it back.

Cold and shivery, I sink to the floor against the door I've since learned guards not only the Resistance's classified information, but their staggering assortment of deadly arms.

This feels so different from the other time I chose to give my life, back at Levett Tech with my team. There hadn't been time to doubt my actions, and there hadn't been any possibility of safety, no matter what I did. I was already in the thick of it, for better or worse. It was easy to be brave, then.

Now, though … I imagine slipping out into the chilly night alone, leaving the safety of the caves and the warmth of friends behind. There won't be any goodbyes. Sam would try to come with me, and even if Tommy didn't stop me, I could never put him through such a thing.

I've already seen the people I've come to love for the last time. Because, petrified as I am, I'm going to stop the Organization. I will not let innocent people die, not when I have it in my power to save them. I will not run away. Until my last breath, I will stand and fight.

I reach into the pocket of my fatigues, fingering the keys I lifted off Lisa when I leaned over to whisper in her ear. I have to be quick, and stealthier than I've ever been in my life, but I can do this.

Terror floods my stomach, freezes my blood; warring with a grief so sharp, so potent, it's physical pain. I allow them both to consume me for one minute, and one minute only, while I agonize over the goodbyes I won't get to give, the words I'll never say.

Tommy and Sam's anguished faces float behind my lids.

I love you both. I love you, and I'm sorry.

With everything I have, I imagine somehow they will hear me. Tears coat my cheeks as my heart ices over. I cannot carry the warmth of friendship, of love, with me tonight.

There's no time for this. If I'm not gone by the time Lisa notices her keys are missing, she will stop me.

Climbing to my feet, I crush my quivering lips together and scrub the wet from my eyes. I bury the pain and fear deep within me, build an impenetrable iron box around them, and lock it up tight.

Cold purpose floods my aching soul and breathes strength into my wobbly limbs. Using Lisa's keys, I slip quietly through the mystery door and into the weapons storage room.

I am Reyna Snow's daughter. I will do what must be done.

CHAPTER THIRTY-EIGHT

TOMMY

I'M slumped on the floor, leaning listlessly against the rough granite wall in a far corner of the night-black lounge. The barest flicker of yellow light from the hallway illuminates the crack under the closed door, and a matching dim glow limns the opening of tunnel to the garage, but it's not enough to see by. In fact, it's so dark I can barely make out Cait's shape, even though she's sitting so close we're almost touching.

I wish she weren't.

All week, I've been forced to abandon my favorite spot at the summit specifically to avoid her. Each night I get more creative, haunt new and weirder places, but it doesn't matter. She always finds me.

Right now, it's harder than usual to have her here. With Mel's video twisting me into knots, I have no room left to tolerate her company.

I could've predicted this outcome. Mel's plan wasn't so much a failure as a catastrophic train wreck. She's the most wanted person in the country.

The Organization won't forget, even if it takes them fifty years to find her. And with her identity as Reyna's daughter revealed, they've got her whole life history at their disposal.

Jagged peaks of stone bite into my back. I embrace the discomfort. The last thing I want to do is fall asleep. Even the horror that is my reality is better than facing my latest nightmares, than seeing Mel flayed and tortured and begging for mercy at the hands of some bulked-up brute.

I turn and punch the wall, a hiss breaking through my lips as pain bursts across my knuckles. I can't escape the pictures. I can't avoid the agony. I can't bear it for another second.

"Hey." Gentle fingers brush my arm, and I stiffen, the urge to pull away nearly overwhelming.

I'm trying. Truly, with everything I have. But as much as I owe Cait, all I see when I look at her is betrayal. I look into Cait's eyes, the same eyes that flared with loathing as she condemned Mel, and I see my own failures too. Every mistake I've made, all the ways I've harmed the people I love, stacked up nice and neat in that gray stare.

I did everything wrong. My intentions were always good, but what does that matter when I couldn't have hurt them worse if I tried.

"Shh," Cait soothes, and I twist out from under her touch.

"Don't."

"Right. Sorry." The word's tinged with regret.

"Don't be."

She sucks in a breath—getting ready to speak, it sounds like. Instead, she pauses, shifts slightly. "Someone's coming, out in the hall. Sorry, I know you don't want to hear this, but … it kind of sounds like Mel did when she tried to break into the library. I think she's sneaking this way."

I send Cait a frown she can't see. Mel has no reason to sneak around anymore. Despite the media's response today, she's a local hero. I've never seen everyone so jazzed about one person's 'accomplishment.'

The thing is, Cait's never wrong. Not when it comes to her flawless senses.

Raising my head, I tilt my ear toward the door. At first, I don't hear much, but then yes, of course Cait's right. Mel's coming this way, and she's trying to be stealthy, as only Mel would.

I've always found her inability to grasp stealth endearing. Now it draws my grief out, twisting it into new, excruciating shapes.

Cait and I listen to Mel's approach, the only sound in the deep silence of the caves. Late as it is, no one else is wandering the hall. Most are asleep, the rest either on duty or still watching the news in Lisa's office.

Mel's careful steps halt outside the lounge, and I suck in a breath. The door creaks open.

Her silhouette is stark against the dancing glow of the lanterns. There's no missing the bulky M320 grenade launcher strapped to her hip. Before I can get a better look, she's through the door and easing it closed, the darkness swallowing her whole.

What the fuck?

She's got to be torn up about the video. Not so much for herself, but for everyone she wasn't able to save.

She wouldn't try and blow the pathogen on her own though, right? Not with so little experience. Not after the Organization tripled the number of guards watching over the BioAgent. And not after my total and utter failure to reach it resulted in Jack and Zara's deaths.

The air is suddenly dense in my lungs.

Cait doesn't react to Mel's presence as she creeps across the room and disappears into the passage to the garage. In fact, Cait's so still, I'm sure she isn't breathing either.

The seconds tick by.

"Go to bed, Cait."

She shifts in the dark, pulling her knees under her and facing me. "Tommy…"

I clench my jaw. "Go to bed."

Cait fidgets for a moment. Then she says, soft and halting, "It-it's her choice."

Rage sizzles through me. "Like you give a shit."

Cait doesn't answer, and every second that passes flays my nerves more. Fighting with her will only slow me down.

I need to get her out of here. Quickly.

Gripping the rocky wall, I drag myself off the floor. "I just want to see what she's doing, all right? And I don't want you to come with me."

Cait's voice is stronger, if flat. "You know what she's doing."

"Then you know why I need to catch her. So, get out." I jerk a thumb toward the door, my tone sharper than I intend. "Please," I add, with a touch more tact. "She won't listen to me if you're there."

Cait climbs to her feet. To my astonishment, she doesn't react at all to my rude tone. "You're just going to stop her, right? You're not going with her? You swear?"

She sounds fragile, like she's made of glass. It's so jarring I gape in the direction of her soft breath.

"Yeah," I finally rasp. "I swear."

Cait doesn't move. "What if she won't listen?"

"Then she won't listen. But I have to try. Go."

The quiet between us swells, festers, and still she doesn't move.

"Go!" I bark.

With a gasp, Cait races for the door. She wrenches it open and pauses on the threshold, her breath catching, faltering. I stare. I've hardly ever seen Cait truly cry, but she is now—she's *crying*. My gut twists as she disappears, but I shove the guilt aside.

Seized by a rush of reckless abandon, I sprint into the dimly lit tunnel after Mel. I don't know what I plan to do when I catch her. All I know is I can't stand to let her slip away like this, to meet her death alone.

By the time I come up on her, we're most of the way to the garage.

I take a moment to study her, a thrill humming through me. Her dark hair is pulled back in a thick, shining braid that runs from the crown of her head down her back. A tight-fitting, long-sleeved black shirt hugs her lithe body like a second skin, highlighting every curve. She's wearing tactical gloves but no vest, mask, or hood. She's got a pistol strapped to her thigh, and the grenade launcher I noted earlier hangs from a wide belt slung across her hips, along with several pouches of rounds.

She's death walking.

And she's beautiful.

"Mel." My voice wraps around her name.

She whirls, a small gasp on her lips, and that brilliant gaze spears me to the floor as she takes several quick steps back.

I clear my throat. "What are you doing?"

It's a stupid question. Still, I wait for her answer.

She just bites that perfect lower lip, wringing her hands.

"Go on, spit it out."

"Don't make me say it. Please. I don't like hurting you."

Ice chills my blood, the now-familiar grief a dagger in my chest.

"Please," she begs again, barely more than a whisper. "Please go back. I have to hurry."

I can't leave her like this. I can't.

The Organization stole so much from me: my family, my freedom, my future. Yet I've done nothing to strike back. Instead, I've allowed the Resistance to keep me safe. I've allowed my fear to destroy everything I care about.

Tonight, I will not stay safe.

Consequences be damned.

I step right up to Mel, cupping her face in my hands and leaning in, questions in my eyes. Though I half expect her to, she doesn't pull away.

No, she sighs into the kiss, her body melting, molding to mine. Her fingers dig into my shoulders and her tongue traces my upper lip. Scorching heat washes through me, mingling oddly with the frost that still lingers in my veins.

It's intoxicating. Fire and ice, existing together, burning me up from the inside out.

"You don't have to do this alone," I growl against her mouth.

I feel her smile. Pulling back, she strokes my cheek, her eyes aglow. "Really? You aren't going to stop me?"

"I'm done letting fear rule my life. All along, you've shown me who you are—a far braver and better person than I am. I've done nothing but hold you back and drag you down. Not tonight. Tonight, I rise to your level. We'll save those people, and we'll do it together."

Her smile softens, tender and so beautiful it hurts. "Thank you."

"I'm sorry. Fuck, Mel, I'm so sorry." The words reflect a depth of emotion I hadn't known could exist until she came roaring into my life, tearing me down and building me up again. A better man. "I'll never try to force my will on you again."

I kiss her gently once, relishing the feel of her soft lips on mine. "So, what's your plan? How did you expect to steal a car? I can hotwire one, but ... hang on. How did you arm yourself?"

Mel grins up at me deviously. "I might have stolen Lisa's keys. Might've lifted them right off her hip."

I chuckle, both at her attitude and her sheer brass.

Her smile fades. "Are you sure about this?"

I press a finger to her lips. "If you're going to throw yourself to the wolves, I get to come along for the ride. You're not the only one with a score to settle." I smirk. "Honestly, you don't stand a chance of reaching the pathogen by yourself, anyway."

I refrain from mentioning that together, our odds aren't much better.

She rolls her eyes, an answering grin tugging at her lips. "Okay then. But we have to hurry."

Hand in hand, we walk the last several feet into the garage. Mel explains she knows where the pathogen is parked, about three hours from here.

"Mind if I drive?" I ask.

A spark of excitement ignites in my gut. Lisa taught me how when I turned sixteen, but I haven't driven much since. Cait's my partner on missions, and she always drives. I'm happy to let her—she loves driving. It's some of the only freedom she's had in her life.

My solo race to Michigan last week doesn't count. It was tainted, drenched in desperation. Fear had me in a chokehold, chained tighter than ever before.

Tonight is different. I want to experience that sense of freedom before the end. I want to feel the rush of speed, see the forest whipping by.

"Sure," Mel says easily, tossing me the keys. A huge smile curls across my face as I make for the Veloster.

Once inside, I wait for Mel to enter the address she memorized from the bill of lading into the car's GPS. My gaze roves around the garage. I'll never see this place again. If only I'd taken the time to appreciate the caves more, to—

My eyes fall on a slim figure, hugging herself just inside the mouth of the tunnel. Cait's trembling shoulders are curled inward.

My heart stutters as our eyes meet. We might have our issues, but we've been so close for so long. She's part of me, and I'm part of her. Now I'm abandoning her, leaving her to face life in the Resistance alone.

She has Sam and Vik and Hunter. She's strong. She'll be okay.

Still, as I dip my chin in farewell, as I watch her crumple to the floor, I feel her anguish as acutely as if it were my own.

There's nothing I can do. With a deep breath, I leave her behind, reversing into the dark woods.

Mel takes my hand, gives it a light squeeze. "I'm sorry."

"I'm not." Though I regret Cait's pain more than I could ever express, I mean it. This is where I'm supposed to be.

When we hit the highway, I open up the throttle, a feral grin spreading across my face. The speed, the recklessness, the feel of Mel's steady hand in mine all light my heart with a wild sort of exhilaration, even as we race toward our doom.

For the first time in five years, I'm free.

CHAPTER THIRTY-NINE

MEL

I'M not sure whether it was an angel or a demon who brought Tommy following after me back in the caves, but either way, I'm grateful.

As much as I hate to admit it, he was right. I wouldn't have lasted two seconds out here on my own. Because of his expertise, we might stand a chance at destroying the pathogen.

On the other hand, my life won't be the only price paid. Now we'll both die tonight.

Hidden among the trees at the edge of the forest, we have an excellent view of the field where the Organization has camped. Guards are everywhere, patrolling between rows of one-man tents, stoking fires, wending around cars, standing outside a tiny, ramshackle cabin on the far side of the clearing. An unmarked eighteen-wheeler cargo truck is parked in the center of it all, surrounded by grim-faced sentries.

Tommy is half-hidden in shadow beside me, so close I can smell his autumn-and-pine scent on the breeze. There's enough light emanating from the fires below to see the determination in his narrowed green eyes. The intensity of his focus sharpens his features, turning his beautiful face into something fierce.

The sight leaves me breathless. Even now, on the brink of death.

With a small shake of his head, he whispers, "There are so many."

"They're not playing around."

"No. The pathogen could be anywhere in the truck, by the way."

"Thank you, Captain Obvious."

The corner of his mouth lifts, but he otherwise ignores my teasing. "It's going to be almost impossible to get close enough to fire on it."

"Well, it'd be ideal to get closer, sure, but why can't we just blow it from here?"

He gives me a wry smile. "You know we're not in an action movie, right?"

I tilt my head, waiting for him to explain.

"Even if we ignore the fact that we're way out of range, a grenade can't blow up a whole truck on its own, not even these high-explosive rounds. At best, we might destroy some of the pathogen, if we're lucky. We'd probably just give away our position though, and possibly leak BioAgent into the clearing."

He pauses, pursing his lips as he takes another long look at our target. "We'll fire at the gas tank. That explosion will kill the pathogen for sure, but to get an accurate shot, we'll need to move quite a bit closer. We'll only get one try before they're on us."

I glance at the clearing. Guards are everywhere. "But how will we do that without getting caught?"

Tommy takes my icy hands in his. "It's the only way. If we're … *stealthy* enough"—he stumbles over the word, probably because he knows I'm not up to the task—"we might stand a chance."

I bite my lip, cheeks hot. How awful. The fate of thousands rests on my ability to sneak.

"You can do this." Tommy gives my hands a squeeze. "Remember the day we met, when we raced through the woods? This is like that. Focus on your breathing, let your body take over. Don't overthink. Trust yourself."

Tommy's eyes burn, twin emerald flames in the night. There's an air to him I've never sensed before: a vitality, an openness, some kind of profound release. It's like a shadow's lifted off him, and for the first time, I can see his full, vibrant color, the shining kaleidoscope that is his magnificent soul.

In a few minutes, that soul will cease to exist. What a sad, beautiful thing to have escaped his pain just in time to die.

Throat tight, I nod.

"Follow me. Move how I move, when I move. You'll have to trust me. We can't blow our cover to check the guards' positions, but I'll be listening for them." He taps his ear.

With a reluctant smile, I say, "Trust you? Ugh. We're doomed."

He rolls his eyes, humor tugging at his flawless lips. "Ha-ha. Are you ready? We shouldn't wait. Every second counts."

I throw my arms around his neck, leaning up on my toes to give him a quick, soft kiss. One last embrace to carry with me as I meet my end. I breathe in his woodsy scent as I whisper, "I'm ready."

Tommy winds his arms around my waist, gorgeous eyes glowing. His sweet, shy smile knocks me senseless.

I love him so. Deep in my bones, and with everything I am. I don't know how I haven't disintegrated from the force of it.

"Okay then. Let's get this done," he growls, dark and intense. The way he looks right now…

Heat floods my system. Tommy's smile turns a bit smug as I hesitate, aching to pull him closer, knowing I shouldn't.

Not here, not now.

"There's no time," he murmurs, and I'm thrilled by the rough edge that's crept into his voice, by the way his eyes smolder as they flick to my mouth. "Later. When we make it out alive."

With a steadying breath, I drop my arms and step back. "When we make it out."

Tommy brushes his fingers lightly down my cheek, eyes brimming with emotion. Then he's gone, pacing away toward the clearing.

Absolutely silent, he slinks from the trees with me hot on his heels. Somehow, he finds the darkest, emptiest route through the city of tents. His every movement flows like water in a stream. Graceful, mesmerizing. I try to copy the way he rolls into his movements, almost melting into each step, each turn.

On several occasions, Tommy throws out an arm, signaling me to stop. We freeze, listening together to the soft steps of the guards, to their muted conversations. When the coast is clear, Tommy motions and we creep forward again. Slowly, painfully slowly, the truck looms closer.

Just when I think we can't possibly go farther thanks to the guards surrounding every inch of the semi, Tommy halts behind one of the dark tents.

"We're plenty close enough." He's barely audible over the chilly wind whipping around us. Tendrils of hair pull free of my braid and lash across my face as panic sears through my chest.

This is it. Our last chance to turn back. Every fiber of my being pulls toward the dark forest, toward safety, but I can't give in. I'm all that stands between life and death for thousands of innocent people. I will not fail them.

Tommy indicates the grenade launcher at my hip. "Do you know how to use that thing?"

"Sam taught me the theory."

Although Tommy has helped hone my skill with handguns over the last few months, Sam took it upon himself to teach me about as many other types of weapons as possible, from daggers to machine guns to this. We've practiced nearly every day since I volunteered to lead the video mission, but I didn't spend long with the M320. I never expected to need it.

"Will you do it?" I ask, my breaths starting to come faster. "I might miss, I might screw it up, I might—"

"Shh." Tommy cuts me off, a gentle smile playing on his lips. "You've earned the right to take this shot. I know you can do it. I'm right here with you, whatever happens."

With shaking hands, I pull the grenade launcher free of its holster. The arctic breeze stings my exposed skin as I snap the handle out and flick the sights into place. I have to pause and swallow the dryness in my mouth before I pop the launcher open and slide a grenade in. My heart thunders as I click off the safety.

"Mel," Tommy murmurs, just loud enough for me to hear over the howling wind. I turn toward him, the air rasping too quickly up and down my desiccated throat.

His eyes are warm and glazed with grief. It's not the same sadness I've seen there before. This grief isn't painful; it isn't tortured. This grief is sweet. Full of support. Of love.

The unconditional kind.

I'm right here with you.

My heart shimmers. Stings. When I fire this shot, I will give away our position. The guards will be on us before we can move.

These are our last … our last moments…

"I love you, Mel."

Tommy's words whisper through the wind, stretching across the space between us to wrap around my heart. Glittering warmth blooms in my chest, swelling until it blocks my throat.

I stare at him, at the wet now swimming in his stunning eyes, and it hits me again, harder this time, more painful than a deathblow. When I pull the trigger, I will not be the only one to die.

Anguish rips through me as a hundred beautiful pictures flash in my mind. Tommy, flushed and roaring with laughter; the way his green-and-gold eyes dance when he teases me; that heart-melting, shy smile; pages and pages of sketches, haunting in their beauty; the grace with which he moves. Tommy diving in front of a bullet to save me. His hands gliding over my skin; those tempting lips—everywhere; the fire in his eyes when he gave in to my pleas; the way he breathed my name, like a prayer.

Am I strong enough? Can I give, not only my life, but his life, his infinitely precious life, to save nameless and faceless people?

Could I live with myself if I let them die, knowing I could have prevented it?

Tears well up and spill over, dripping down my cheeks. "I love you too, Tommy."

Tommy smiles through his own tears, glowing with quiet joy. He doesn't speak. He just nods once.

It's time, he seems to say.

Dragging in a breath, I tear my eyes from his and raise the launcher. My arms tremble so hard I can barely keep my grip on it.

"Range is about fifty meters," Tommy breathes in my ear. "See the silver cylinder, there, under the semi's cabin? You want to aim for that.

Don't forget to account for the wind."

I peer through the sight, lining up the shot according to Tommy's information.

"Easy," he cautions. "Wait until you're sure you've got a line on it."

I gulp down the icy air, working to still the shaking in my hands. My finger twitches on the trigger.

Snap.

A twig. Someone's behind us.

Abruptly, a thick, hairy arm is around my neck and my feet dangle off the ground. The launcher's muzzle swings out as the trigger slides home, sending the grenade rocketing over the truck and into the forest behind the tents. I drop the launcher and yelp, thrashing against the man now pinning me to his doughy abdomen while the grenade explodes harmlessly in the woods. I can't see Tommy, but I hear him struggling too. The man squeezes tighter ... tighter...

Black oblivion descends. I fight viciously against the chokehold, my vision flagging. I can't ... I can't ... see...

Chapter Forty

Tommy

Jagged rocks bite into my cheek, my chest, my abdomen. Thick fabric is tied over my eyes and stuffed into my mouth, but I can hear. Five guards stand in a semicircle around us. A length of scratchy rope binds my arms tightly behind my back.

Shit.

I was too focused on Mel, on our last moments together, to notice them coming.

Is she alive?

I reach out with my ears, chest tight to the point of pain.

Yes. Her rough breath isn't far away, but she's down too. Unmoving.

Fear slices through me, hard and fast.

Breathe. Think.

I need to stay calm. If they assume I'm still out, I might have time to figure out a plan before they move us.

Panic whines in my head, makes it hard to focus. Mel must be bound and gagged too. Even if I come up with an idea, I can't communicate with her.

"This one's awake." The barrel of a gun jabs into my back, right between my shoulder blades.

Damn it all.

"Edwards wants to question them himself. Where should we take them?"

"The cabin," a female guard says.

My stomach pitches, fear hot at the back of my throat. There's no way out. No way to fight. The best we can hope for is a quick death. Maybe if we piss them off...

The man digging his weapon into my spine grunts. "This one can walk. I'll carry the girl."

Two pairs of rough hands grip me under my arms and haul me to my feet. My terror surges, a metallic tang on my tongue.

"Forward," the woman barks.

I stumble ahead, my usual sure gait eluding me. The thunder of my pulse gets in the way as I try to listen and figure out what's happening to Mel. If I could just brush her hand, let her know she's not alone ... but I can't. I can't hear her, can't concentrate on anything besides the vicious panic that grows and grows, scouring away my insides until I'm nothing but fear.

Fresh tears soak into the fabric covering my eyes.

Chin up, I scold myself, scrabbling for some deeply hidden reserve of courage. You chose this path. Walk it well.

A door creaks, and I'm guided across what sounds and feels like a soft wooden floor and forced into a metal chair. The smell of wood rot fills my nose.

"Struggle and you die." The woman's voice is flat. Someone reaches around my ankles and lashes them to the legs of the chair with more rope.

I'm sorely tempted to kick out, to see if the woman will make good on her threat. Better to go now than suffer through what's coming.

But what about Mel? I have no way to tell her what I'm doing or why. She'd be left to face this interrogation alone.

I can't abandon her.

Once my ankles and waist are bound, the blindfold and gag are removed. Mel's being carried in through the open door, slung over the shoulder of a huge, hulking man with thinning blond hair and a scrubby beard. Her wrists are bound behind her back like mine, but they've tied her ankles too. Her blindfold and gag hang around her neck, likely knocked out of place thanks to the tremendous fight she's putting up. She writhes like she's being electrocuted, a string of filthy curses sliding through her bared teeth.

The hulking man is visibly struggling. "A little help?"

"Be still," the woman beside me snaps, some color bleeding into her voice. "If you fight, I will kill him."

She cocks her gun and rests the barrel against my temple.

I stare at Mel through streaming eyes, my gut snarled up. She twists around, her hard gaze falling on me. Immediately, she goes limp.

The hulking man tosses her roughly into another chair. He rebinds her ankles and ties down her waist, ensuring she's firmly strapped in place.

Once Mel's secure, the woman guard orders all the others to leave, except the beast of a man who dealt with Mel. The thud of the door closing echoes ominously through the room.

Nausea overwhelms me as I catalogue our surroundings. We're in a tiny, half-rotted, one-room cabin. There's nothing here besides a long oval table, a few metal chairs scattered around it, and four lamps standing in the corners of the room. These cast everything in harsh white light.

About six feet separate me from Mel. The monotone woman and the hulking man stand to my right—Mel's left—and watch us. The man spins a knife around and around in his large, meaty hand. The woman's arms are crossed, her face blank.

A sudden shock runs me through, so powerful I stop breathing.

That's Mara Levett.

I didn't recognize her at first, decked out in a common guard's uniform, but that fair skin, those dark, almond-shaped eyes, the shoulder-length chocolate-brown hair. I know that face.

"Well, hello there, little terrorist," Mara says coolly to Mel.

The way she's taken charge, the way the guards immediately follow her commands, the air of control surrounding her, even now … the pieces fall into place, one by one.

This is why Mara and Mr. Edwards are never in the same place at the same time, why Mara's always been oblivious to the corruption flourishing under her nose. It's how the Organization has hidden so effectively within Levett Tech for so long.

"You're Mr. Edwards."

Mara throws me a cold, empty smile, then turns back to Mel. "I know exactly who you are, Melanie Snow."

I hate the way Mel glares at Mara, no trace of fear visible in the hard lines of her face. I might as well be fifteen again, hidden under the bed while Reyna aims the same fiery stare at her tormentors. Blood runs into Reyna's eyes, flows from her crooked nose, dribbles over her ruined lips…

"And you, Thomas Williams." Mara gives me another wintry look.

It's in my best interest to stay quiet, but the way the beefy man sneers at Mel leaves me wanting to pull their attention my way. Anything to get their focus off her. "What do you want?"

"You know how this ends," Mara says softly. "It can be easy, or it can be difficult. The choice is yours."

Sickness roils in my stomach, the blood draining from my face as I glance desperately at Mel. I can already see her, bleeding and broken. I can already hear her screams.

If I don't answer Mara's questions, Mel's worse than dead.

I can't quite swallow the sob that escapes my locked jaw.

Mara tilts her head, observing me like I'm a science experiment. "You want to spare the girl, yeah? Talk, Williams."

Too late, I realize I've given Mara valuable information. Namely, how much I care for Mel. I lick my dry lips and will strength into my words. "What do you want to know?"

Mel's eyes cut into me, burning with censure. Her head jerks from side to side.

I don't acknowledge her. I focus solely on Mara, who says silkily, "You know what I want."

Before I can respond, Mel taunts, "We don't know anything about the chip."

My heart sinks, and I hang my head. Mara was fishing for information with that open-ended statement, trying to find out what we expect her to ask without revealing anything in the process.

Unless Mel has a plan I don't know about, she just played right into Mara's tactic. And now Mara thinks we do know about the chip.

I hope Mel knows what she's doing.

"I knew it," Mara murmurs, the words alight with a frenzied sort of euphoria. "You!" She snaps at Mel, clicking her fingers. "Your mother had it last, yes? We weren't able to recover it from her. You know where it is. Tell me. Now."

"I said, we don't know anything about it."

Everything in me tightens as the bulky man strides up to Mel and yanks her braid back, pulling her chin up to expose the pale skin of her throat. The almost-healed cut Cait left there stands out, a faint pink line.

The man presses his own knife lightly to the mark. Beads of red appear along the blade. "You would do well to show some respect, sweetheart."

Before I can stop myself, I'm shouting. "Take your *fucking* hands off her, or I'll use that dagger to saw your fingers off, one at a time."

At a nod from Mara, the thug lowers the knife and releases Mel's hair. Blood dribbles from the new cut, vibrant against her fair skin.

"Language, Williams," Mara chides. "Do you have something you want to tell me?"

"*Don't touch her,*" I growl, tone laced with dark violence.

"If you don't want her touched, you know the solution." Mara's not even looking at us. She's examining her nails.

I lock my jaw, despair rising up to smother me. There's nothing to be done. Even if I wanted to, I couldn't give Mara the information she seeks. I don't have it.

Mara's mouth twists. She strolls sedately to stand behind Mel's chair. "Have it your way. Jeff."

Terror explodes in the pit of my stomach as the thug—Jeff—leers at Mel, twirling his dagger between his thick fingers. He tilts his head, considering her, then drags the point of the knife over her cheek, lightly enough that it doesn't draw blood. That unbelievable bravery of hers is starting to crack. She's white as a ghost, her breath coming in harsh, jagged gasps.

Jeff glances my way, blade now tracing Mel's jaw. "It'd be a shame to carve up such pretty skin, don't you think?"

The room spins, waves of razor-sharp dread breaking over me.

With blinding speed, Jeff pulls back his fist and smashes Mel in the eye. Her head snaps back and her cry of pain reverberates in the air between us.

Before she can gather herself, Jeff's other fist comes around in a brutal hook, slamming her face sideways.

Awful sickness swirls in my gut as a terrible, burning chasm opens in my chest. All fear, all sense evaporates, burned away by pure agony. Her jaw. Her cheekbone. And it's going to get a lot worse.

Screaming incoherently, I wrench on my restraints.

"Shut up shut up shut UP!" Jeff explodes, stalking across the room toward me. In the split second before his blow lands, I see the savage light in his eyes, the total absence of any sort of scruples.

This is a man with no limits.

The hit connects over my left temple. My head explodes in blistering pain, slamming to the right with such force the muscles in my neck strain. Ringing fills my ears, everything around me suddenly shrouded in bright, shining mist. I slowly raise my eyes and my head swims with a sick, stabbing sort of pressure.

"Cut that out," Mara barks. The sharp sound ratchets up the ache in my skull. "If you knock him out, he can't talk. Focus on the girl and keep them awake, you absolute imbecile."

Mel holds my gaze. The area around her right eye is pink, swelling fast. Bright crimson blood trickles from the corner of her mouth, slides over her chin. It runs in rivulets from the cut on her throat, soaking into the neck of her shirt.

This can't be real. It must be another nightmare.

Wake up. Wake up, wake up, wake up, please wake up...

"Ahh," Mara says, detached as ever. "That's not a nice look for either of you."

My attention cuts to her as her words set my head throbbing.

"This is nothing," she continues, waving a hand at Mel. "We have hours. Hours and hours. Oh, yes, you'll tell me what I want to know before the end. Why not make it easy on yourself? On her?"

Turning dead eyes to Mel, she says, "You don't have to go through this. I can make it quick. Tell me where the chip is, and I'll end it, nice and clean."

For a moment, I'm under a bed, listening to a cold female voice promise my parents the same thing.

The same voice.

A flood of molten anger burns through the fog in my head. "You were there. You interrogated my parents. You murdered them! You... you..."

There aren't words evil enough to name what she is.

Mara's lips twitch. "Indeed. As were you, so it seems. Interesting."

Mel spits a mouthful of blood onto the floor. "You're a monster. We'll never tell you anything."

A sense of unreality washes over me as I hear Reyna in my mind.

Mara jerks her chin at Mel, and Jeff rains blows down on her. Her face, her ribs, her gut. Mel stares at me when she can, dragging her eyes back to mine again and again. She's intensely focused, her jaw locked against the screams she's battling to keep in.

I hold her searing gaze, suffering with her through the vicious beating. With my eyes, I tell her she's strong and fierce and brave. I tell her she's not alone.

"Stop," Mara commands.

Jeff falls back, revealing the full impact of what he's done. Mel's whole face is puffy, mottled red and purple. It shines with blood that weeps from the many cuts, runs from her nose over her lips, drips down her chin. She's panting, sagging in her restraints as she holds onto my gaze like it's a lifeline.

"Mel," I moan, my cheeks slick.

Mara almost looks bored. She's examining her nails again. "Are either of you ready to talk yet?"

"Never," Mel rasps, at the same time as I say, "We truly don't know anything."

Jeff's hand twitches, but Mara holds hers up, halting him. She glances at me. "You don't? Nothing at all?"

"No. All we know is a chip existed at some point. That's it. I swear."

Mara chews her cheek, head tilted as she contemplates me. "Why were the Snows at your house that night?"

"I don't know. They came every summer for a few days. I didn't know the Resistance even existed. Neither did Mel."

Mara gives me a cold smile. "Perhaps you didn't. Still, I'm sure there's something useful you could give me. Information you've learned since."

"I knew nothing about the chip until recently, and now, I only know it existed."

"Liar. I think it's time to start breaking bones, don't you, Jeff?"

"Please," I beg, and the word is acrid in my mouth. "I'm telling the truth!"

Jeff kneels next to Mel, gently untying one of her legs while Mara presses a dagger to her throat.

"I'm gonna get a hammer," he grunts as he stands up.

When he leaves, Mara shakes her head. "Are you sure about this?" She looks between Mel and me.

"We don't know anything," Mel spits, but the tremor in her voice ruins the effect she's going for.

"I'm sure you can think of something to tell me. Williams, you say you saw me at your parents' interrogation. If that's so, you were there with the Snows immediately before we arrived. You must have been."

"So? I was fifteen. Barely more than a child."

"You're telling me a fifteen-year-old can't be observant? Give me details. Any details you can. What did the Snows say? How did they act? Were they carrying anything with them? Did they hide anything as we stormed the house?"

My stomach jolts, Mom's twine bracelet suddenly white-hot on my wrist. I try not to glance at it as I see her, moments before the monsters arrived, shoving it in my face.

Keep it safe.

"Ah." Mara's arctic smile broadens, more a grimace than anything. "You do know something, don't you?"

I always thought Mom's last request was strange. Why would she care so much about a simple twine bracelet she would give it to me for safekeeping? I assumed it must've been sentimental, though I never saw her wear it.

A piece of Reyna's last email to Lisa flashes through my mind.

I'll pass you my report through the Williamses, but because Max won't be aware of it, I'll need to do so secretly ... You'll know where to find my message when you see it.

I swallow, mouth exceptionally dry. Could there be a note from Reyna concealed within my bracelet? It's a thick weave. Bulky enough to hide something, for sure.

Vomit rises in my throat as Jeff reenters the room, a hammer swinging from his fleshy fist. Mel's lips go white.

Mara waits to speak until Jeff has Mel's leg stretched out before him, her foot resting on an empty chair. "Last chance, Williams."

I stare at Mel, at her mangled face. The remnants of my soul scream at the sight. And I know, *I know*, they've only just gotten started.

They will beat her senseless. They will keep going, until, brave as she is, even she begs for death. And then they will torture her more.

Unless I give them the bracelet.

I didn't save my parents. I didn't save hers. But I have it in my power to stop this.

Mel's eyes are leaking tears, her mouth and limbs quivering. Even so, the glare she shoots me is more than clear: say nothing.

My heart hammers, the blood throbbing in my ears. What Mel's going through now—what my parents went through—has all been to thwart the Organization. If I give Mara what she wants, I render their sacrifices null and void. It would be like spitting on their suffering. It would be the most selfish, cowardly thing I could ever do.

Some things are more important than pain, even hers.

I will not allow the Organization to find Reyna's message.

Mara can see the resolve form in my eyes.

"Jeff," she says, practically oozing apathy.

Jeff rests the hammer on Mel's trembling shin. It swings up, then flashes down, and the sharp crack of Mel's bones rips through me like a serrated blade. Her blood-curdling scream twists the knife, drags it back and forth. The rolling sickness in my stomach peaks, and I retch.

Mel's sobbing now; huge, quaking sobs. Bill nudges the misshapen purple lump on Mel's shin. Her answering howl frays at my sanity.

I watch, lost in a fog of horror, as he slides the hammer up, rests it on her knee. He's going to shatter every piece of her. My stomach turns again, the words bubbling up my throat like more vomit.

Before Jeff can raise the hammer, an almighty *BOOM* rocks the floorboards under our feet. Another, then another, and another; each one powerful enough to shake the cabin's foundation.

All four of us look toward the door.

Shouting, gunfire, running, more shouting, more gunfire.

Mara's lip curls. "What in the—"

Just then, the door bursts open. A sweaty guard stands panting on the threshold.

"Rebels in the woods, firing on us. The camp's burning. Don't know how many."

Mara curses.

"Come," she hisses at Jeff, then races with the guard into the night. Looking sour, Jeff removes the hammer from above Mel's knee and lumbers after them.

The door bangs shut behind him, sealing our tomb around us.

CHAPTER FORTY-ONE

ᴹEL

DEEP, excruciating waves of agony ripple up and down my leg, emanating from my ruined shin as if it were a pulsar. Every breath hurts. Every sob sends splinters of glass stabbing through my chest, my head, my jaw.

Only one thing holds steady in the shifting mist of pain. Tommy's bright gaze, so intent on mine, keeps me tethered to reality. It reminds me who I am, and why I'm here, and why I must be strong.

I peer blearily across the space between us, determined not to let go of my lifeline. I thought I heard explosions, and now people are screaming and running outside. Is that gunfire too? The truck must've blown up.

But no, that can't be right. I missed my shot. They captured us.

I'm so ... so confused...

"Mel," Tommy moans, my name mangled on his tongue. I twitch, wanting to reach for him, but my bound wrists burn, drenched in hot, sticky wetness. Proof of how hard I struggled. Proof it wasn't enough.

"I'm sorry," he cries, again and again.

Forcing myself to focus, I give him a quick once-over. He looks terrible. He's bound too, his tan skin chalky and shining with sweat. His lips are bloodless, his eyes puffy, his cheeks glazed with tears.

There's a huge red welt beside his eye that stretches from his hairline down to graze his cheekbone.

Worse than any of that is his expression. It's like he's being continuously scalded. His tortured eyes burn into mine, half-mad with anguish.

"D-d-don't be," I rasp between the harsh gasps hissing through my teeth.

Tommy stares, looking like he's been lit on fire.

"Th-th-th-they're g-g-gone?" I can barely spit the question out through the pain in my jaw.

"For now." Tommy's words are no more than a breath.

This is the chance I hoped against hope for. Tipping my face up, I lower my braid as far down between my shoulders and the chair's back as I can, reaching for it clumsily with my burning, tied hands. My fingers brush the tuft of hair at the end and I desperately pinch at it, sliding my grip up until I find the hair tie.

Please, please let this work.

The aches and awkward angle make it difficult, but I manage to slip the tie from my hair, keeping hold of the braid as I do. Carefully, I start to unwind the thick plait.

"What are you doing?" Tommy whispers.

"Y-you'll see," I pant through the pain. "If it w-works."

The tresses loosen and I tip my head farther, arching my back to ensure I don't lose contact with the entwined locks. My ribs scream, but it's got to be close … somewhere around… here.

My fingers slip against something long, thin, and razor-sharp, woven into the center of the braid. Hissing at the sting, I squeeze the smooth, jagged shard of glass with everything I have and yank it free, along with several broken strands of hair.

Yes.

Tommy gasps as I awkwardly saw at the rope binding my wrists, sliding the shard back and forth with as much force as I can muster. Fresh, sticky warmth runs down my hand, but I don't loosen my grip. The rope starts to fray.

"You hid that? In your braid?"

I glance up. Tommy's even paler than before. How much blood has he lost?

"Yes. After I raided weapons storage, I broke a baking dish. Thought maybe … if they took my weapons… it'd come in handy."

"You're amazing."

After another few seconds, the binding snaps and my arms are free. Immediately, I get to work on the rope securing my waist. My hands shake so badly I can hardly use them.

To calm myself, I keep talking. "I got the idea from a project my mom did with me when I was a little girl. Weaving macrame bracelets. She said she and her … her best fr-friend"—I stutter, realizing who that best friend must have been—"used to pass messages that way. You know, by weaving them into…"

I freeze.

Tommy's bracelet. Twin to the one I wove with my mom all those years ago.

I've seen it every day for the past two months. It's as much a part of Tommy as his ethereal grace, or his pensive nature. He's never without it.

How did I not make the connection?

My mind hums, blank with shock.

Tommy gives me a knowing nod. "Mel? We don't have long."

Now isn't the time to think about this. I shove the matter from my mind and get back to work.

Soon the binding around my waist falls away too. I reach down for the knot holding my good ankle to the chair. Yes, there it is, and yes, I'm sure I can undo it.

Huffing in relief, I slip the glass shard into my pocket and fumble with the knot instead.

By the time I pull my ankle free, the sounds of chaos outside have dimmed. I gulp down several shaky breaths, ignoring the stabbing in my chest. This is really going to hurt, but we're out of time.

Without letting myself consider what's to come, I wrench my injured leg off the chair supporting it. White-hot pain cracks up my shin, a scream sharp in my throat. I lock my jaw desperately against it and swallow the noise. It's never been so important to keep quiet.

Tears blur my vision, but I don't pause. I crawl toward Tommy as fast as I can. He watches over his shoulder as I reach for his bindings.

It doesn't take more than a minute to untie them all. Quick as a flash, he's out of his chair and hauling me to my feet.

I sway on the spot, leaning heavily on his forearms. My injured leg dangles under me.

Tommy frowns. "We won't get far like this. I'll have to carry you, okay?"

I don't want to hold him back, but if I try to send him away without me, he'll argue. We'll waste precious time, and neither of us will make it out. "Okay."

His every movement gentler than I'd have thought possible, Tommy sweeps me up into his arms and cradles me against his chest. It hurts, of course it does, but I sigh, almost happy in a weird way. Even though we're in extreme danger, I feel safe.

Tommy steps to the cabin's door and pauses just behind it, his ear tilted toward the camp beyond. He gives his head a tiny shake, then listens again.

"I can't hear properly."

I lift a wobbling hand, tracing the brutal swelling over his temple. "We have to go for it anyway, or we'll die."

We're probably dead either way, but still.

With a grimace, Tommy uses the doorframe to help support my weight as he turns the knob. Inch by inch, he nudges the door open. There are no guards immediately beyond.

Tommy slips out into the freezing night and glides around the corner of the cabin. Immersed in shadow, he pauses to survey the scene in the camp.

There's no evidence of the explosions we heard, no fires burning besides those tended by the Organization. The camp itself is mostly empty, except for the guards who still circle the truck, but the apparent lack of watchmen doesn't make me feel better.

"Where are they?"

Tommy draws us deeper into the gloom cast by the cabin. His breath tickles my cheek as he answers. "Look at the forest."

I scan the dense ring of trees around the clearing. The darkness underneath moves, crawling with guards.

Alarmed, I peek over Tommy's shoulder to search the woods that brush up against the back of the cabin. Sure enough, there are people moving there too, not far from us. Thankfully they're heading deeper into the forest, away from the camp.

"Back there."

A tremor runs through him. "Yeah, I know."

Fighting a crescendo of panic, I gulp down several mouthfuls of chilly air. "We have to sneak through the camp while their focus is elsewhere."

"Too exposed."

"Well, what do you suggest then?"

He drags his gaze from the woods, peering down into my aching face. My chest tightens at the desperate hopelessness in his eyes. "I don't know."

I bite my lip, examining the camp, searching for…

My heart stands still. Our weapons, including the extra grenades, are scattered near the cabin's door. The guards must've dropped them when the explosions went off in the camp.

If Tommy were armed, it would make all the difference. Gunfire would reveal his position, but I've seen him with a dagger. He's lethal. No more than shadow given substance. He could fight his way through the swarm of guards, silent as a wraith. They wouldn't even know he passed by until he was already gone.

Of course, I'd have to make him leave without me because I'm not going anywhere. I can't walk, let alone run. I'd weigh him down, make it impossible for him to fight.

Also, the M320 is *right there.*

We're not far from the truck. By my estimation, we're about one hundred meters out. Well within the weapon's range.

I stare into Tommy's lovely, anxious face. If I can convince him to sneak away without me, the explosion I'll cause will draw the guards out of the forest and back into the camp. It'll be only too easy for him to escape once the woods are clear.

Tommy stares back, eyes lined with despair. He must know he could make it out alone, and yet, he only holds me tighter.

I'm right here with you.

My eyes fill. I'm terrified out of my wits at the prospect of being hauled back into that ghastly cabin. Tommy was the only thing that kept me sane in there. Even so, I'd go to the ends of the earth to spare him from enduring such agony again. I'd suffer the Organization's wrath a thousand times over if it kept him out of their hands.

I'll have to lie. It's the only way.

My heart burns with regret, knowing the last words he'll hear from me will be a betrayal.

"Put me down," I rasp.

Tommy raises a brow. "Your leg…"

"It hurts, but I can walk on it. It'll be easier for us to escape if I do."

Tommy's mouth presses into a line.

"Come on," I push, a hard edge creeping into my tone. "You don't need to save me. We can save each other."

Doubt fills Tommy's face, but he lowers me to the ground. I bite back a hiss of pain, digging my fingers into his shoulder to support myself.

"Just give me … a minute."

Tommy's misgivings visibly mount with every passing second.

Standing here isn't helping either of us. I have to act now, before my strength gives out, before I fall, before I drown in the prickling, insidious fear.

A surge of adrenaline punches through me. It takes all my willpower to clamp down on the overwhelming energy and moderate my voice into a thin whisper.

"This is what we're going to do. You're going to scout the woods behind the cabin. You're going to take this." I pull out the jagged shard of bloodstained glass and press it into his palm. "I'll wait here. When the coast is clear—as clear as we can hope for—you come for me, and we run."

Tommy's mouth twitches down, his eyes bleak. "That will never work. You're not running anywhere on that leg."

"Carry me, then," I snap, the rush of adrenaline-fueled strength pushing me over the edge. "We need to know the layout first, either way. Go!"

"But—"

"Go!" Using the cabin's outer wall to support myself, I shove at him. "You're wasting time. I do not want to die here."

Stricken, Tommy backs away. He stumbles a little as he melts into the shadows.

It's now or never.

Energy flows through my limbs as I fling myself around the corner of the cabin. My shin barks, twisting under me, and I collapse. Fire sears in my bones, but I grit my teeth and crawl, my useless leg dragging behind me.

With a final, monumental effort, I dive for the grenade launcher. The guards by the truck start to shout and run toward the cabin. A hail of bullets peppers the rotten logs behind me as I scramble to load a grenade, the round slipping and sliding in my slick, bloody hands.

Forcing myself to my feet, I concentrate with every fiber of my being on holding the launcher steady while I line up the sights. The soft wood of the cabin digs into my back, supporting me.

Right before I squeeze the trigger, something small and hard slams into my stomach, and I jerk against the wall behind me.

Numbness steals through my belly, reaching out with long, creeping fingers to ice my blood.

I've been shot.

Focus. Just ten more seconds. Focus.

I raise the M320 once more, sighting the gas tank. My arms are rock-steady, even as my side begins to warm. Begins to burn.

I don't let myself think. Baring my teeth against the pain, I fire.

Yes!

A huge, flaming cloud splits the night, and the boom rattles the earth. Bodies and shrapnel fly everywhere as a hot wind slams into me. I slide down the wall of the cabin, the launcher slipping out of my numb fingers.

I did it. I really did it. Innocent people will live. Tommy will live.

My lips twitch up as my side blazes hotter.

"I love you," I whisper through the burn. "I'm sorry."

It hurts so much. And still, it gets hotter … hotter … *hotter…*

I'm drowning in scorching agony. The intensity of it dulls every other sensation, every other thought, until I don't know where I am. I don't remember my own name.

All I know is the searing, blistering blaze that eats me alive from the inside out. Make it stop, please make it stop…

CHAPTER FORTY-TWO

TOMMY

ECHOES of the unexpected blast pulse through my aching skull as the forest ahead erupts with movement. Flashlight beams swing through the trees; guards yell and curse in the dark. Safe in the deep shadow of a sycamore, I thank my lucky stars I hadn't caught up with them yet. If they were closer, I'd be screwed.

But what was that? Was it back at the camp? Is Mel okay?

Screams shatter the night, high-pitched, agonized screams, coming from where I left her.

Mel's screams.

To hell with stealth.

I dart out of my hiding spot and sprint for the cabin. Her raw screams drag over my scalp, pushing me faster.

Faster.

As I barrel through the last of the trees, I search the shadows by the cabin where she should be.

She's not there.

Stomach full of needles, I skid around the corner, almost losing my balance thanks to the spinning in my head.

There.

Writhing on the ground by the door, her mottled skin sallow and shining with sweat. Her hands are clamped around her gut, which is soaked in blood.

"Mel!"

I stumble forward and fall to my knees by her side. She's still thrashing when I yank her messy hands away, her yells hoarse, horrific wails starting to rise in the camp behind us. Thick, dark blood seeps from a small but nasty hole in her abdomen.

She groans. Her body shudders. Then the tension bleeds out of her, leaving her still, white, and cold.

Dead.

Mel is … dead.

"No!" Tears scald my cheeks. "No, Mel! Please, no!"

Voices approach from behind the cabin, getting louder. The guards. We have to move.

I haul her limp body over my shoulders and bolt through the cabin door, hiding behind it just in time. Sentries melt out of the woods from every direction, running toward the chaos in the center of the camp.

Mel's blood paints my skin as I watch them dash by, relief nearly sending me to my knees when I note her labored breath in my ear. The guards don't look for us, don't give the blood in the dirt a second glance, utterly focused on the scene of destruction before them. Their own noise, coupled with the cries of the injured in the camp, must've disguised ours.

Raising my eyes, I take in the charred semi. The trailer's engulfed in a ball of flame, sending huge, billowing clouds of orange fire leaping for the stars. The smell of burning metal stings my nose. The pathogen couldn't have survived a blast like that.

I swallow back the sob that presses in on me.

Headstrong, brave, incredible Mel. She did it.

She gave up her own life to save everyone else, but she's not dead. She won't die.

I won't let her.

The guards disappear into the commotion around the truck, and I dart out the door with Mel slung over my shoulders, slipping into the shadow of the forest that tickles the cabin's rear wall. The Veloster is parked on an empty dirt road, about a mile's trek through the woods directly across camp from where we are now.

The guards are distracted. If I'm quick, I might be able to skirt the clearing before they pull together a coordinated search. Then I'll sprint through the woods, straight for the car.

I'm fast. Even with Mel's weight, I will outpace them. I will get her home.

The earth seems to shift under my feet as I run, keeping to the dark edge of the forest. The night presses in, my ears full of an incessant ringing. Without my impeccable sense of hearing I'm half-blind, relying on my eyes alone to navigate the murky woods.

Mel's dead weight doesn't help. Her labored pants spike the panic that stabs like daggers in my chest. I need to get her to a doctor.

The Resistance must be here somewhere. No one else would've attacked the camp while Mel and I were being interrogated.

They can save her.

I stumble over my boots as I pick up the pace, staring into the dark for any sign of my adopted family. I'm most of the way around the clearing, on a ridge overlooking the camp below, when I see her.

Cait.

Curled on the ground just outside the tree line, about fifteen feet ahead and to the right of where I am now. Four surly guards stand around her, pistols drawn.

I pause, shocked into stillness. Cait's wrists and ankles are bound. Her thin shoulders are hunched, her forehead pressed to her knees. Her long blond hair is a mess. As I hesitate, she raises her head, revealing a fat black eye and a swollen, bleeding lip.

My heart shivers.

Oh, Cait. Why?

If she were here with the Resistance, she'd be in full tactical gear, no question. But all she's wearing are her normal fatigues and a hoodie. If she brought weapons, they are no longer in her possession.

She followed us. Went rogue.

Mel's harsh breath stutters as I glance down at the camp, at the bottom of the ridge beyond Cait.

Squads of sentries have spread in an organized wave through the rows of tents. The nearest group moves straight for the woods ahead, almost directly at the spot where Mel and I stood earlier tonight.

They're going to cut off my route to the Veloster.

Once they get ahead of me, they'll find the car. There'll be no escaping. We'll be stranded, dodging through the woods until they find us.

And they will find us.

If I run now, if I put my head down and sprint, I could still beat them to the car. I could still get Mel out.

But Cait.

I stare at her as she buries her face back in her knees. If I leave her, she will die at the hands of those evil interrogators. She won't have anyone to save her.

My throat burns. The guards sweep closer, the opportunity for escape narrowing, and still I can't bring myself to act.

My boots twitch toward the deeper woods, toward the Veloster waiting beyond, but I can't leave Cait. I can't.

As gently as possible, I lay Mel down at the base of a sprawling pine. Her blood is everywhere, saturating her clothes and smeared over my neck and shoulders, causing the fabric of my shirt to cling to my back.

I rest my ear on her chest and hold a palm in front of her mouth. Yes, she's alive. The relief is so powerful I can hardly see straight.

"Keep breathing," I whisper, brushing a loose strand of hair from her swollen face. "Keep fighting. Stay with me."

With a soft kiss on her forehead, I leave her huddled beneath the sweeping boughs of the tree.

Dizziness slows me as I creep toward Cait, Mel's glass shard clenched in my hand. Cait raises her head again, her uninjured eye wide. Her lip curls, and she jerks her head from side to side, a small, vehement motion.

She knows I'm coming.

I narrow my eyes, mouth flat, and continue. A twig snaps under my unsteady feet, setting my teeth on edge. Cait's guards peer into the shadowy woods.

"Hey, assholes!" Her voice is thick but loud. "How long are we going to hang around here? I'm bored. And hungry. And, well, I have to pee, and I'm not going in my pants. Where's the bathroom? Surely you have one?"

"Can it!" one of the sentries growls. The others ignore her, still searching the darkness around them for the source of the crack they must have heard.

Cait doesn't pay the guard any heed. She continues to whine, a long string of noisy complaints, covering the sound of my blundering approach. The guards are suspicious, but they seem reluctant to move away from her.

"If you don't shut up, I'll give you something to complain about." The man who reprimanded her before raises the butt of his pistol.

Before he can drive it down, I'm on his back, shoving the point of Mel's glass shard into his eye. His scream splits the night and he doubles over, fingers clawing at his face. I disarm him easily. By the time the others open fire, I'm already swerving away between the trees.

I zip through the maze of branches, my gait unstable. If I lead them far enough into the woods, maybe I can double back and free Cait before they catch onto me. Then she can slip away and disappear into the forest. She'll be able to evade the guards. No one can become invisible like Cait.

I drop under a fallen log and freeze, waiting. I hold perfectly still, silent even as my lungs scream for air. Two guards blow by me. Their swinging flashlights set my head whirling.

I wait ten more seconds, then sneak back to Cait, stolen pistol cocked and ready. The man with the glass in his eye is still shrieking and clutching at his face. Blood dribbles between his fingers and streaks down his forearms. The remaining guard stands over Cait, his gun fixed on her.

Despite the swimming in my head, I manage a clean shot, straight between his eyes. I put the second, injured guard out of his misery before the first hits the ground. Two quick *pops* and I'm clear. I rush for Cait, pulling apart the knots binding her wrists as quickly as I can.

She's already snarling. "You stupid, idiotic, infuriating—"

"Good to see you too." I pull the rope from her wrists.

She sits up, eyes on the woods over my shoulder, where the guards who chased me through the trees are crashing our way like a pair of angry rhinos. I yank the rope from her ankles as a series of sharp *cracks* reverberate in my skull.

Cait and I dive in opposite directions. Bullets spray around us, throwing leaves and dirt everywhere.

"Don't move!"

A woman steps toward me, her gun trained on my face. I scramble backward over the grass, too dizzy to stand. My shoulders bump into something scratchy.

Bark. A tree trunk.

"Where is she?" The other guard's voice skitters up an octave. "The girl's gone!"

A jolt of excitement hits my stomach.

Yes! Go, Cait! Run!

The woman rolls her eyes. "Then find her! I've got this one covered."

Back pressed against the tree, I lick my dry lips. The world roils around me. I can hear the second guard through the ringing in my ears, kicking up leaves as he hunts for Cait. His wandering steps take him farther and farther away.

After a good minute, he groans. "No sign of her. She's gone, I say."

"I really doubt that." The woman's voice drips with impatience.

A gruesome gurgling noise is the only answer she gets. She glances over her shoulder, her face going pale. "Jenkins?"

The grisly sound continues, sputtering out until it fades completely. The woman shudders and backs away, her gun pointed over my head now. Her wide eyes search the woods behind me.

"Please." The pistol rattles in her white-knuckled hands. "I'll run. I won't tell anyone where you are."

Like a demon, Cait materializes out of the darkness, her dagger tearing through the woman's throat. The guard falls to her knees and her hands scrabble at the bloody gash.

Cait and I don't stay to watch her struggle. Instead, Cait drags me back into the woods in the wrong direction. Away from Mel.

"Wait," I gasp, and she skids to a stop.

"So much blood." She reaches toward me, then drops her hand. Her fingers shake. "How hurt are you?"

"I'm fine. This is mostly Mel's blood." My words warp on their way out. Panic seals my throat around them.

We need to get back to Mel.

I take Cait's hand and pull her to the massive pine, where I crouch down, pushing the thick fringe of branches aside to reveal Mel, curled in the dirt. My heart stutters.

The swollen, violet-and-crimson pattern on Mel's face stands out, stark against her milk-white skin. Blood leaks from her nose, from her mouth, from the worst of the welts, from the slash across her throat. It coats her abdomen and her shin, soaking through the fabric of her clothing. Behind me, Cait gasps.

"Oh, Tommy." She drops to her knees by my side, and I'm shocked to see tears sparkling in her good eye. "Shirt," she snaps.

"What?"

"Shirt! Now!" She clicks her fingers, eyes on Mel.

I yank my tee over my head and pass it to her. Without looking at me, Cait draws her dagger and slices the fabric down the middle. She balls up half and presses it over the wound in Mel's gut. Shifting Mel carefully, she uses the other half to secure the wad tightly in place.

"She's losing too much blood. If we don't stop the bleeding…" Red coats Cait's slender hands. "She won't have long."

My eyes burn. Desperately, I grab Cait's arm. "What can we do? Please, Cait. Please. Save her!"

Cait shoots me a pained glance. "We need to get her to Aaliyah. I only know so much first aid. She won't make it if we're not quick. Where is the Veloster?"

"They cut us off. There's no way we can get to it now."

I drop my head into my hands, fighting the wave of misery that threatens to crush me.

"Okay," Cait says, cool as ever. "Shh, Tommy. Listen. There's a way. It's not ideal, with Mel in this condition, but it might be our best chance."

I raise my tear-stained face. "How?"

Cait casts a wary look over the woods around us. "When I followed you here, I hoped to extract you. That was my only goal. So I had to figure out how. How could I do it by myself, against so many?"

She pauses, frowning. "At first I thought it would be impossible. But then I remembered what Mel did for her team at Levett Tech. It gave me an idea. I would need to distract the Organization, to lure them away from you, wherever you might be. I knew a lone rebel wouldn't be enough of a threat to do that, so I recruited Vik, Hunter, and Sam. We stole grenades and the Telluride and followed you here."

Vik, Sam, and Hunter are here? Dead or alive?

"I climbed a tree and threw my grenades in four different directions, aiming for tents around the edge of the camp. The others did the same. Then, we fired our weapons with the goal of creating as much chaos as possible. We tried to sneak into the camp on the heels of the commotion and find you. We each took a different route to cover as much ground as possible."

"The others?"

"Based on what I heard from those guards, I don't think anyone else was detained. If they escaped, they'll be back at the Telluride."

Back at the Telluride.

Sam's here. Sam can save her.

With a sigh, Cait goes on. "I knew there was a good chance the Veloster would be compromised, and I knew parking on the road would be risky, so I left the SUV at a farmhouse. Parked right in someone's driveway. Hopefully whoever lives there is sleeping and hasn't called the police."

I stare. Cait defied orders to help Mel and me, even after being stripped of her title. She stole weapons, a car, assembled a team. To Cait, there's no higher law, nothing more important, than orders. Nothing.

Until now.

Touched, I take her hand and give it a grateful squeeze. "Thank you."

She squeezes back, then pulls away, running her fingers through her tangled hair. "The thing is, that driveway's far. Five miles or so, through the woods the whole way. We could make a break for it, or we could hope a hole opens in the guards' patrol so we can take the Veloster instead, meet the others that way. I won't lie, traveling five miles through the forest is probably not in Mel's best interest, but Sam can stabilize her better than I can. We need to get to him."

My stomach drops as I examine Mel's bruised, bone-pale face. If we could reach the Veloster, we could get to Sam faster, but we'd need to be both lucky and invisible. My stealth is compromised, and with Mel over my shoulders, I won't be able to fight if I need to.

We won't make it. But if she can hang on until we reach the Telluride, Sam will save her. He'll keep her breathing until we get back to Aaliyah.

We have to take our chances in the woods.

"Let's head for the Telluride. You're incredible, Cait."

She gives me a watery smile. "Let's see whether this works before you say that."

TEN minutes later, Cait's leading me by the hand, helping me navigate as we sprint through the pitch-black forest. Mel hangs across my shoulders, bumping slightly as my steps waver under me. With her keen senses, Cait guides us away from patrolling guards, keeping us hidden. Keeping us safe.

I've never believed in miracles. But I have to admit, I just experienced one.

If one miracle could come to pass, why not two?

Please, Mel. Please. Don't leave me.

Over and over, I beg in my mind, knowing she cannot hear. Pleading with her anyway.

And I run.

Chapter Forty-Three

Mel

Pain is everywhere. It is everything.

It drenches the shadow that weighs thick on my mind, too heavy to move. Too dense to think through.

Sometimes, I catch a flash of something other than pain. Colors. Sounds. They're gone before I can make sense of them.

Please, a beautiful voice filters down through miles and miles of black water. *Please stay.*

The words touch some deep part of me. Slowly, I come to realize how much they hurt. They drip with anguish. I don't like it.

For the first time, I struggle, searching for myself. Where am I?

Mel!

The word draws me, a point of light in a sea of unyielding dark. I fight harder, shoving against the vast, empty veil.

Fiery torture crashes into me, and I shy away, back into the numbing dark.

Mel! The voice is thick. Warped. *No! Stay with me! Fight, damn it!*

A flicker runs through my essence. The voice ... the voice is *suffering*.

I push again, feeling my way toward the haze of pain that hovers, shimmering, at the edge of the emptiness. Once more, torment slams into me.

I arch my back and scream as unimaginable agony rips through my stomach. I'm surrounded by blurred faces, and the pain is too much. Too much. I can't think, I can't *be*…

I float lazily in the dark, seeming to emerge, bit by bit, from a deep, still pool. Every part of me hurts, but the pain is dull now. Unfocused.

My eyelids flutter open.

I'm in my room in the caves, lying in my bed. A fire roars in the grate, gilding the space with a bright, cheery glow. My nightstand and desk lamps are on as well, adding their warm yellow shine.

Tommy's sitting beside me, in a folding chair by the head of the bed. He's wearing a clean hoodie, and the welt on his temple has been tended to. His red-rimmed eyes are shadowed deep purple. He's holding one of my freezing, bandaged hands in both his own.

Sam's curled up on the foot of the bed by my legs with his nose in a Tracie Tanner thriller, my casted shin raised on a stack of pillows beside him. Lisa sits in another chair by my feet, her glasses perched on her head and her face in her hands. Vik and Hunter pore over a stack of papers set between them on the floor, and—

I audibly gasp.

Cait leans against the wall by the door, one tired eye trained on her boots. The other is swollen shut.

"Mel?" Tommy sounds like he just ate a mouthful of gravel. "Are you awake?"

Everyone's attention snaps to me.

"Um. Yeah. We made it out?"

Tommy rolls his eyes, his smile soft. "No, we're still being held hostage."

I snort, then wince as pain radiates through my chest, my abdomen, my jaw, my cheeks. "But … how?"

"Cait. And Sam and Vik and Hunter."

A vague, confused memory of their voices in a dark car flashes across my mind. I can't believe they came after us. Especially Cait and Hunter.

"We did it," I breathe, a tremendous, gleaming sort of pride filling my chest. "We saved all those people."

And we made it out alive. I beam at the others, my joy expanding, overflowing my heart. We're here. We're alive. We're together.

Tommy's green-and-gold eyes are unbearably tender, his answering smile warm. "You did it."

My attention is pulled to the foot of the bed as Sam swings his legs over the edge. Lisa pushes past him before he can stand. "Melanie Louisa O'Hanlon Snow, so help me, if you ever pull something like this again…"

I bite my lip, suddenly nervous. I might've accomplished the impossible, but I also disobeyed a direct order; stole keys, weapons, and a car; and caused five others to follow me into incredible danger. I put the security of the Resistance at risk.

I never imagined making it back to face the consequences of my actions.

Lisa knocks Tommy aside too and pulls me into an enormous hug. My ribs and stomach bark under their stiff bandages.

Shocked, I pat her back.

"I swear," she says. "If you ever … oh my goodness, I never…"

My heart shines brighter, sending warmth all the way down to my numb toes. "I'm sorry, Lisa. I had to try."

She pulls back, a teary smile on her face. "Indeed you did."

Vik and Hunter crowd around her while Sam waits by my feet and Cait hovers several paces behind them. "Thank you," I tell them all. Vik and Hunter both grin.

"You've got guts, Snow." Hunter chuckles and shakes his head. "Sorry I gave you so much shit before."

I purse my lips, still angry with him on Sam's behalf, but he did help save my life tonight. So, I smile tightly. "Forgiven. But maybe try and be less of a dickwad in the future."

Hunter snorts, eyes sparkling with humor. It changes his whole face, makes him ten times more handsome.

"I'm glad you made it out," Vik adds, their smile warm too. "You're a verifiable badass, Mel."

I'm not sure if it's the drugs I must be on, but I never thought I'd feel so cozy here. It reminds me of Christmas Eve at Grandma Snow's, snuggled by the fire in her frosty backyard with Mom and Dad and a thermos of hot chocolate. I didn't know my battered heart was still capable of this feeling.

After five long years adrift, I'm home.

"Thanks," I mumble again.

Vik pats my uninjured knee. "We'll visit later. Must be overwhelming to wake up to a crowd."

I smile and nod as Hunter claps my shoulder, and the two of them exit, leaving Cait standing awkwardly in the middle of the room by herself.

My shining heart hardens.

"Mel…" She glances at Tommy, who's watching us with a carefully neutral expression, before fixing her good eye back on me. "I wanted to say I'm sorry."

Oh, she's definitely been crying. Her voice is rough, her face pink and blotchy.

"For what? Trying to get me executed? Or being horrible ever since I got here?"

"Both."

I glare, my temper rising, blocking out the modicum of pity that struggles to take root in my hardened heart. "Noted."

Cait fidgets, then glances at Tommy again before dipping her chin and following Hunter and Vik into the hall.

When the door clicks shut behind her, Sam finally steps forward. Unlike Vik and Hunter, he isn't smiling. In fact, he's glaring with such fury dread tingles up my spine.

I gulp. Wait for him to speak.

He doesn't.

"Sam…"

"You left me behind." Betrayal flashes in his eyes, and guilt swallows me whole.

"It was a death sentence. I was going there to die."

"I'm supposed to have your back, Mel! We're supposed to have each other's backs."

I bite my lip, keenly aware of the moisture building in his angry, hurt eyes.

"I had to find out from *Cait* what you were up to. Both of you." He glances at Tommy, who winces. "You didn't even say bye."

"I'm sorry." I mean it with every fiber of my being. "I'm so sorry. I should've given you the choice. I just … I never imagined I'd make it out, and I didn't want anyone else to get hurt. Especially you."

"You will never do that to me again. We're a team, right?"

"Right."

I give him a tremulous smile, and he throws his arms around me, burying his face in my hair. "I thought I lost you."

I hug him back as fiercely as my bandaged ribs and aching abdomen will allow. "Thank you for saving me."

"You're *not welcome*." Sam sniffles, then pulls away. "But I'll always save you."

Tommy shakes his head, and I can tell he's biting back a grin as he takes my hand again, his twine bracelet stained with splatters of—

"The bracelet!" My eyes cut to his.

"Yeah. All this time. I can't believe I never realized."

"My mom gave it to you?"

"*My* mom gave it to me. I think maybe your mom gave it to her, though. She asked me to keep it safe."

With an abrupt return to her usual, snappy manner, Lisa asks, "What are you two gabbling about?"

Tommy and I stare at each other.

Lisa shakes her head. "Tommy, Evelyn gave you something before she died? And you never thought to tell me?"

Tommy looks down, cheeks tinged a shade darker. "I didn't know it was important. But yes. She gave me this." He holds up his wrist, showing off the ruined twine, and I shudder. Is that *my* blood?

Lisa goes absolutely still. "Of course. Wait here."

I open my mouth to tell her I won't be going anywhere for a while, but she's already gone, sweeping purposefully from the room.

While we wait, Tommy and Sam fill me in on what happened after I blew up the truck. I don't remember any of it. I gasp, again and again, as the story unfolds.

According to them, we did more than kill the pathogen. Because we uncovered who Mr. Edwards really is—Mara Levett—the Resistance will be able to track her every move. We'll expose who her top Organization associates are, and from there, we'll have access to new information. We might even find something we can use to deal the Organization a fatal blow down the line.

Once their story draws to a close, we speculate about what could be hidden in Tommy's bracelet. A note, perhaps. Or a photo. Coordinates. A map.

My life has turned into a literal spy movie.

Finally, Lisa returns, a serrated blade in hand. A piece of ice slides into my stomach as she cuts the bracelet off Tommy's wrist. I'm about to see Mom's last message to the Resistance. Whatever it is, it was important enough to die for.

Slowly, carefully, Lisa unravels the weave. I watch with bated breath as something small falls out and clatters to the floor. Tommy snatches it up, holding it in his palm for us to see.

It's a miniature computer chip, only about half an inch wide.

I gape.

Lisa takes it with trembling fingers. For a full five seconds, she does nothing but gawk, wide-eyed. Again she says, "Wait here," and practically runs from the room.

Tommy and Sam meet my eyes, their gazes just as shocked as mine.

"No way," Tommy whispers.

I can only stare.

It takes a while, but eventually, Lisa reenters the room, a laptop under her arm. "I've installed the chip," she says, slightly breathless. "It appears to be a video message."

Not the code.

My chest caves in, relief and disappointment thundering through me in equal measure. Those emotions are quickly stifled, though, when Lisa flips open the laptop and I see what's on the screen.

Physical pain splinters through my chest.

Mom.

She looks just like I remember. Shoulder-length, white-blond hair sprinkled with gray frames her beautiful face—pale, like mine. Laugh lines fan from the corners of her ice-blue eyes, which are unusually grave. She's wearing her favorite UNH hoodie, and appears to be in a public bathroom, of all places. No one else is in there with her, unless they're lurking in the corners where the camera can't see.

Grief twists my stomach, stretching up to block my throat and sting my eyes.

Lisa presses a button and the video starts to play.

Mom brushes the hair out of her face, tucking it behind an ear in a familiar gesture. I lean forward, aching to be close to her.

"Lis," Mom says, her voice taut with stress. "I destroyed all copies of the code hidden in Sullivan's house, including several microchips he stashed in the weirdest places. But…"

She wrings her hands. "I did what I could. Frank admitted to the existence of one final microchip he'd hidden elsewhere, just in case. I tried to get the location out of him. I'm horrified to say I used brutal methods, but it didn't matter. The bastard killed himself before I was able to learn where it was. Stole my knife and slit his own throat."

Mom's shaking. Tears fill her eyes. "I never wanted to hurt anyone."

She takes a moment to pull herself together, then says, "So, that's the deal. Sullivan's dead, and there's still a microchip somewhere out there with the code on it. Oh, one more thing. There were a couple guards outside Frank's house. I took one of them out, but the other got away. I have no reason to think he identified me, but I have a bad feeling. I'm scared. Please, if something happens to me and Max, please take care of Mel. Please tell her I love her, and I'm proud of her. And tell her I'm sorry."

Grief burns my heart as Mom blinks back tears. Sniffles. "Love you."

She reaches forward and the screen goes dark.

No one says anything. As the seconds drip by, my anguish slowly melts into a blank sort of numbness that reminds me of the void I almost succumbed to earlier.

Tommy takes my hand again, rubbing circles into my knuckles with his thumb. "Are you okay?"

No. I'm not. But…

"Mara knows."

He frowns. "Mara knows what?"

"She knows this missing chip is out there. Think of how she acted, what she asked us." I push the heels of my palms into my eyes, wishing I could block out the knowledge. "She didn't ask anything about the Resistance. She only asked one question, over and over. Where is the chip?"

Tommy's frown deepens. "She was probably talking about the other chips, you know, the copies of the code your mom destroyed. Even if she wasn't, she doesn't know where the lost one is any more than we do."

Sam's looking between us, a slight crease between his brows, while Lisa cries silently into her hands, her glasses perched on her head. I can't tell whether she's following our conversation or not.

I chew my lip. What should we do with this information now that we have it?

A great weariness drapes over my shoulders. I'm tired. I'm hurting. I want to lie in bed for days, preferably with Tommy holding me close. I want to eat. And eat, and eat. I want to laugh with Sam. I want to read a good book by the fire. I want to write. I want to go outside and run. I want to be safe and happy with the people I love.

But the missing chip is out there, just waiting for the wrong person to find it. The danger the pathogen posed pales in comparison.

I sigh. "We can't risk the chip falling into the wrong hands. Someone has to find and destroy it, and I can think of no one better than me. Mara will hunt me to the ends of the earth after all this. I might as well finish what my mom started before the Organization catches up to me."

Tommy sighs too, his shoulders slumping. He holds my gaze for a long moment, and there's sorrow in his eyes. Acceptance. "You're right."

I give him a small, sad smile.

"Of course she's right." Lisa wipes her eyes on her sleeve, then replaces her glasses. "The Resistance will recover and destroy this lost chip. I will personally command the mission, and as soon as she's back on her feet, Mel will lead the team on the ground. In the meantime, I will start digging around in Levett's records for clues as to where it might be hidden. I knew Sullivan. Maybe I'll uncover something helpful other people have missed."

I nod and turn to my best friend. "Sam? You with me?"

"All the way."

The corner of Lisa's mouth twitches up. "Naturally. Sam, you have far exceeded all our expectations. I am sorry I didn't give you the chance to do so sooner. Having a trained medic in the field will be a significant boon."

Sam's eyes shine, a disbelieving smile lighting his face. Pride blooms in my heart even as weariness soaks through my skin, down past my muscles to settle like a disease in my bones.

Lisa's still talking. "As for the rest of your team—"

I hold up a hand. "I'm sorry to interrupt, but I'm so tired. Do you think this can wait until morning?"

"Oh, it's way past morning." Lisa pulls herself to her feet. "It's late afternoon, actually. You've been out for days."

Days? "How many?"

"Three."

Three. I frown dozily. "Mmkay. Tomorrow morning, then."

"Very well. Tomorrow morning. Sleep tight, Mel."

With a warm smile and a wave, she's gone.

Sam squeezes my shoulder. "I'll see you later, okay? Can't wait to plan our next adventure." He grimaces and I laugh, wincing again at the stabbing in my lungs and stomach. He drops a kiss on top of my head and hugs Tommy briefly. "Good night, you two."

"'Night," I say, at the same time Tommy says, "Thanks, Sam."

The door clicks shut, and Tommy and I are on our own.

"Will you stay with me?" I tighten my hold on his fingers, and his eyes soften.

"If you want me to."

"Yes."

Barely shifting the mattress, Tommy slides under the covers. He wraps his arms gently around my shoulders, pulling me to his chest and resting his chin on my hair. I relax into him, my stress melting away.

The last thing I'm aware of as sleep takes me is his warmth. It sinks deep into my soul, where it glows bright like Grandma's fire, driving out the cold and pain and fear.

CHAPTER FORTY-FOUR

MEL

A FAINT, rhythmic noise drifts down through layers and layers of peaceful oblivion, settling in my mind like softly falling snow. The sound is dim, and yet it builds, pulling me up until I hover, curious, just below the surface.

Scratching. No, rubbing. No... definitely some kind of scratching.

I push aside the last of the fuzzy drowsiness, reaching automatically across the bed toward the sound. My arm knocks into something rectangular, with a hard, metallic spiral at its edge.

Intrigued, I open my eyes.

It's Tommy's sketchbook. He's stretched out beside me, leaning against the headboard, the sketchbook propped against his knee and a pencil in his hand.

"Thank God. I was starting to think you'd gone comatose on me," he teases. "It's been almost a whole day since we saw your mom's video. How are you feeling?"

I stretch. Dull soreness riddles my body. "Not awesome. But better than yesterday."

Concern flashes behind Tommy's eyes. Leaving his sketchbook on my nightstand, he scoots down next to me and brushes a strand of hair back from my face. "Are you hungry?"

Nausea churns in my stomach. Ugh.

"Definitely not."

"Aaliyah said you might feel sick."

He doesn't elaborate, and I don't say anything, either. The silence stretches, lengthening as we gaze into each other's eyes. I love him, more deeply than I ever would've thought possible. And he loves me.

But I have things to do now. I'm not sure where that leaves us.

"I'm sorry," he finally says. His eyes are sad. "You should hate me for what I did, for bailing when you needed me so much. Twice. And yet, you asked me to stay last night." He gives me a tiny, bemused smile, then peers down at our entwined hands.

I see again how Tommy looked as I was interrogated, like he was burning in hell's deepest pit, and I frown. "You think I should hate you? No. I understand why you did what you did. It hurt, and you shouldn't have done it, but I don't blame you for it. I know what you've been through."

He's shaking his head before I'm finished. "That's not an excuse. I was a coward. I let fear cloud my judgment so badly that people died."

He sighs, then goes on. "Taking matters into my own hands instead of figuring out a plan with you will always be one of the worst things I've ever done. But I also did nothing to save our parents, then hid that fact for months. After that, somehow, you still wanted to be with me. And what did I do? I ran out behind your back the second things got hard."

He flips onto his back, folding his hands behind his head and staring at the ceiling. "I just... I wish I were a better man."

A great swell of sorrow fills me. His words, the regret in his tone, the bleak tint to his eyes. Doesn't he see how much I love him, exactly as he is? Mistakes and all.

I reach up to cup his cheek. Leaning his face into my palm, he closes his eyes.

"I mean, yeah, you should've told me sooner how you felt about what happened when our parents died, but I get why you didn't. Even though it was hard, you told me in the end. When you bailed, you came back. You walked through hell itself with me. Can't you see? You are a good man."

Tommy glances my way from the corner of his eye. His mouth lifts a fraction. "You're too nice. That's the problem. You're giving me way too much credit."

I shake my head, pulling him around to face me. "Your mistakes aren't what define you. It's what you choose to do next that matters, and you always work to be better, to make things right. That's what matters. I love you, Thomas Williams. You. Assery and all."

With a tiny, shy smile, he takes my hand and traces little patterns over my palm, my wrist. Keeping his gaze fixed on these, he says, "So you're off to save the world again. What's the plan? Are you and Sam going to look for the chip?"

I huff a sigh. "As soon as I'm fit, yes. I figure we'll have to wait until Lisa uncovers everything she can on Sullivan for official orders, but he lived and worked in Coral City. The chip must be there, somewhere."

Ugh. California. I thought I escaped Coral City forever.

Tommy looks up, heartache and uncertainty all over his face. "Listen. I know I've been unreliable, and I understand why you might not want me to come with you. No pressure. But if you need another teammate, I'm here."

My heart lifts as I trace Tommy's knuckles, a smile playing on my bruised lips. I'm not sure how much control I'll have over who's on my team, but that's a problem I'll deal with later. If Tommy wants to join us, I'll find a way to make it happen.

"Thomas Williams, will you come to California with me?"

Surprise and gratitude shine in those stunning eyes. "You want me to?"

"I always want you." I cradle his face in my hands. "No matter what happens. No matter how long or short the time might be, I want you by my side. As long as you want to be there."

"I'll follow you anywhere, Mel."

His eyes glow, soft and warm and oh-so-beautiful. Skimming his knuckles down my cheek, he gives me a sweet, gentle kiss.

Every fiber of my being glitters with radiant joy. Our future may be grim, but we will face it together. As long as we have each other, no shadow will be too dark.

I'll follow him too. Right to the very end.

Dear Reader,

Thank you so much for taking a chance on this book! I hope you loved the story and characters as much as I do.

Reviews are extremely important, especially for self-published authors. Each review helps this book find new readers who might love it. I'd be so grateful if you considered leaving a written review on Amazon, Goodreads, or social media.

If you'd like to hear about upcoming books in this trilogy first, and be privy to behind-the-scenes information, character art, and sneak peeks, please sign up for my newsletter at medrekwrites.com

ACKNOWLEDGMENTS

THEY say writing a book is a lonely process, and I'm sure it can be, but I was blessed to have enjoyed the support of so many amazing people on the road to making this lifelong dream a reality.

Dad, you were my first reader, my first supporter, and the inspiration who showed me publishing a book was something I could actually do. Thank you for the encouragement and advice, for answering a million and one questions, and for slogging through the earliest draft of ITF chapter by chapter with me as well as for your subsequent read. If I'm able to achieve a quarter of your success in this adventure, I'll be beyond thrilled. (PS: skip chapters 23 and 24 forever and eternity, okay? Love you always!)

Mom, you aren't a reader, and yet you devoured this book cover to cover as soon as I let you see it. Thank you for your unwavering enthusiasm and for lots of fun chats about my imaginary friends and their shenanigans!

Ari and Charlie, you are the lights of my life and my reason for everything I do. Thank you for sharing me with my characters over the last four years. I hope in making this book a reality I have made you proud, and my wish for you is always that you will chase your dreams, whatever it takes. I'm rooting for you in everything you do.

Mike, my loving husband and real-life book boyfriend. You are and have always been in my corner cheering me on—from reading my almost-final draft and giving excellent notes to listening to me gab about this story for years without an ounce of boredom to believing with unflinching certainty I will be a bestseller someday. You are my Rhysand, and I love you.

Laurie. What would I do without you? Thank you for being a wonderful Bubbe, and for many hours of babysitting as I worked to get this book out into the world.

Rosie, the floofiest floof. Thank you for warming my feet at four a.m. as I typed and re-typed and re-typed this book, and for kisses and cuteness and being fluffy and sweet.

Savannah! How does anyone write a novel without a Savannah in their corner? You are without a doubt the best book coach in the whole world, and I'm so so so so grateful we crossed paths. Your enthusiasm for this story and belief in me have meant so much. Thank you for the laughs, brainstorming chats, late-night/early-morning panic texts, book recs, thoughtful advice, many (many) read-throughs, and always-excellent feedback. I've learned tons working with you, and I wouldn't be here right now if it weren't for you. To Luna, Forrest, and Hudson, thank you for the smiles and adorable pics. Rosie is glad there are other floofs proofreading her Mom's work. (Savannah, toss them each a treat from us!)

To my beta readers: Gina, Kelsey, Kara, Robyn, Jennifer, Rebecca, and Sara, and my anonymous Spun Yarn betas. Thank you for taking the time to help make this story the best it could be, and for your thoughtful and thorough feedback. Gina, Kelsey, and Kara, thank you for being there for additional reads, chats, and for answering all my ongoing questions. It means the world to have trusted readers I can rely on.

To Lo at Hey Book Bestie services, and to my anonymous Spun Yarn sensitivity readers, thank you for the thoughtful and comprehensive sensitivity reads. Working with each of you was a joy and a privilege.

Thank you to Two Birds Author Services: to Andrea for an excellent line edit full of helpful suggestions and for your help with my blurb. I'm sorry for the carpal tunnel you likely got from deleting all those em-dashes. And to Michele for making sure Mel's story shines with a thorough proofread.

To Julie at the Spun Yarn for always being there to answer my questions and for coordinating such helpful readers.

To Rena at Covers by Violet, my ever-patient and brilliant designer, for a beautiful cover, gorgeous interior, and eye-catching graphics. Thank you for making this book as pretty as I always dreamed it would be.

To Rachel and the Nerd Fam for your invaluable guidance on my book launch and for helping me get Mel's story into the hands of as many readers as possible.

To my writing group: Gina, Kelsey, Miah, and Casey for always being there with encouragement, commiseration, and endless good ideas. I hope to be by each other's side through many future launches.

To every reader who has or ever will pick up one of my stories. This is all for you.

And to the One from whom all comes. Thank you for everything.

Milton Keynes UK
Ingram Content Group UK Ltd.
UKHW041043181024
449742UK00030B/163/J

9 798990 831605